Monte Walsh

MONTE WALSH

Jack Schaefer

University of Nebraska Press
Lincoln and London

For Archie

Copyright © 1963 by Jack Schaefer
Preface to the Bison Book edition copyright © 1981 by the University of Nebraska Press
Manufactured in the United States of America

First Bison Book printing: 1981
Most recent printing indicated by the first digit below:
1   2   3   4   5   6   7   8   9   10

Library of Congress Cataloging in Publication Data

Schaefer, Jack Warner, 1907–
  Monte Walsh.

  Reprint of the ed. published by Houghton, Mifflin, Boston.
  I. Title.
[PS3537.C223M6 1981]   813'.54   80–25036
ISBN 0–8032–4124–0
ISBN 0–8032–9121–3 (pbk.)

Published by arrangement with Jack Schaefer

Second cloth printing: 1986

Preface to the Bison Book Edition

BACK IN 1963 when *Monte Walsh* first appeared in book form, the dust jacket labeled it a novel. A surprising number of reviewers apparently regarded that as a challenge and wasted a surprising number of words arguing that the book is not so much a novel as a collection of short stories.

As a matter of simple fact, of course, *Monte Walsh* is both. It is a collection of short stories in that its sections or chapters or whatever one wishes to call them (some of which were originally published as short stories) are individual units each reasonably complete in itself. But *Monte Walsh* is definitely also a novel in that all its sections mesh together and the book, taken as a whole, has an organic beginning and ending and meets with fair accuracy the usual dictionary definition: "a fictional prose narrative of considerable length."

Any ambiguity there involved is understandable—at least to me. True enough, *Monte Walsh* did not begin as a novel; equally true, it did not end as just a collection of stories. In the course of the writing, spread out over almost a decade, the book, like Topsy, just growed.

Monte Walsh and Chet Rollins, their eventual character development already foreshadowed and their companionship already well cemented, came into fictional being in the fall of 1954 in a story which I called "In Harmony." At the time I was living in Connecticut and had no locale for my little town of Harmony other than vaguely somewhere in the old cattle-country West.

Nearly four years later, in March of 1958, living now in New Mexico and pondering a piece on the trail-driving days, I remembered those two and their fellow cowhands of that previous piece. Simply by adding a few more characters I had a trail crew for a brief circular round-the-clock story I titled "Trail Herd." A few months later, in June of that year, I used Monte and Chet and some of the Slash Y others in a fictional attempt to impart some of the flavor of a once important aspect of my adopted state. This one I titled "Antelope Junction."

Up to this point, with three Monte-Chet-plus pieces, these spread out in time and written in between many other stories and other writings, I had merely turned out three separate individual tales that appealed to me. Though they had similarity in that Monte and Chet were central figures in all three and each closed with Monte emitting a characteristic yipping, I had no notion that the three would become, respectively, the fifth, ninth, and seventh sections of a future book. All that had emerged in this respect was my obvious tendency, when thinking of a "cowboy story," to think in terms of Monte and Chet and the Slash Y. What would keep them, especially Monte himself, fresh in my mind was the fact that among our nearest New Mexican neighbors was a young man named Archie West who to my mind was (and still is) in many respects, certainly in appearance and temperament and cattle-country capability and simple human decency, precisely my Monte Walsh.

I was right about that tendency—as was shown something over a year later when I wrote "Payment in Full" in October and "Harmonizing" in December of 1959.

It was along about this time that the book notion sprouted in my mind, seed planted there by the suggestion of a friend who had become a Monte fan and encouraged into growth by occasional letters from old-timer westerners who had read some of the stories in magazine publication and asked for more. I was thinking of a book, yes; but only, when I had accumulated enough of them, a collection of "cowboy stories"—most of which, no doubt, would include a character named Monte.

Obviously that notion kept on growing. During the next year, 1960, I managed to tuck in three of them: "Dobe Chavez," "Hellfire," and "Christmas Eve at the Slash Y." And then, as 1960 gave way to 1961, that book notion grew some more, took on its final form.

Not now just a collection of stories, but the addition of enough more of them judiciously plotted to comprise or at least to sketch in the over-all story of the open-range cattle business, its brief beginning and its myth-making heyday and its inevitable swift decline. This summed, symbolized, in the single lifetime career of my Monte Walsh, a man fitted fully to it, faithful to its spirit to his own finish—with counterpoint and comment supplied by his more adaptable, once inseparable companion, Chet Rollins.

On through 1961, while still working on other writings, I managed to start filling in that book notion with four pieces, these four beginning with "A Beginning." And as 1962 came up on calendars, I put everything else aside and with what would be Chet's final comment closing the book already firmly in mind I concentrated on Monte, writing the seven more pieces and eighteen interludes that filled out the full framework.

Now and again through the years since 1963 some well-meaning fool has tried to tell me that the title is wrong and the emphasis in the text is misplaced. This should have been Chet's book, they say; he is the stronger figure, the one who can adapt to change, who achieves the more significant and successful life.

Wrong, say I—as Chet himself would say.

Though I did not see it in just such terms during the writing, I have seen ever more clearly ever since that I was writing a multiple story of two men both of whom, each in his way, lived significant and successful lives. That the book turned out to be primarily Monte's is the result of the fact that I happen to have more respect for the kind of success Monte achieved.

Chet and I, we think that Monte gave a consistently good account of himself in life's sweepstakes—and that this world is now a lonesome lonesome place without him and the way of life and the attitude towards existence he represented.

JACK SCHAEFER
Santa Fe, New Mexico
1980

Contents

A Beginning
1872

A BOY and a horse.

A thin knobby boy, coming sixteen, all long bone and stringy muscle, not yet grown up to knuckly hands and seeming oversize feet, and a big gaunt old draft horse, rough-coated, heavy-fetlocked.

They stood by the rickety fence of a half-acre enclosure, the boy leaning against a big shoulder, looking over the broad back, the horse waiting, at the tag end of a day of waiting, patient, big haltered head sagging against the short lead rope tied to a fence rail. Off near the center of the enclosure the slanted frame shack that served for a schoolhouse quivered on flimsy foundation as the last of some fifteen children of assorted ages and sizes scattered from the doorway, released, racing in dedicated directions away.

The boy leaned against the old horse and watched a stout soft-stomached red-faced man appear in the doorway, shrugging into a jacket, and walk with spraddle-legged rocking gait toward the road past the enclosure gate and take a small bottle from a pocket of the jacket and raise this to his lips as he walked.

Activity died away and the boy watched the stout man dwindling toward the cluster of haphazard ugly one-story false-fronted buildings a quarter mile down the road.

"Shucks," said the boy. "Didn't even close the door." He left the old horse and went to the shack and closed the plank door and pulled at it, testing the latch. He turned and looked out over the distance merging into distance of Colorado plain, muted and brown under afternoon sun of early spring.

"Shucks," he said, moving toward the old horse. "I've had about all I can take of that. He don't know no more'n me

1

which sure ain't much." He untied the lead rope and the old horse raised its head and pushed with graying muzzle at him. He stepped back along the gaunt side, holding the rope, and in one easy up-tilting movement was astride the bare back and at the touch as if energy flowed from the thin knobby body into the big old frame the horse perked, raising its head higher and turning to start toward the gate with heavy old hoofs lifting in clumsy rhythm.

Through the gate and around a corner of the enclosure and the boy and the horse moved into the muted brown of distance. "You ain't much either," said the boy, "but let's see what you can do." The old horse leaned forward into a clumsy trot.

"Trying to wear out my backbone?" said the boy.

The old horse swiveled an ear, feeling the current along the rope, the tingle in the thin legs down its sides, and leaned forward more into a lumbering caricature of a lope. The big old back swayed and bounced and the boy sat flat to it, body moving in unthinking effortless rhythm with it, a part of the horse beneath him.

*   *   *

Another horse.

Solid, compact, power plain in muscles bulging under the sleek hide, pride in lift of the tail and arch of the thick neck, it stood by the end rails of a small corral beside a small half-plank half-dugout barn.

Fifteen feet away the boy leaned against side rails, chin up to rest on the top rail, looking over.

Late afternoon sunlight lingered over the big land, brushing with soft golden brilliance the crest of the slow slope rising behind barn and corral, and the boy leaned against rails and watched the horse and the horse, aware, refusing any indication, stood motionless, head high, looking past him, into the dimness of distance.

"Montelius! You, Monteeeelius!"

The boy turned on too big old work shoes toward the two-room frame house fifty yards away. Flat-roofed, tar-papered, stripped on the outside to close off the worst of the cracks, it thrust its angular ugliness like an affront into the immensity of plain and the last golden sweep of sunlight. The woman in the open doorway had been tall once, well-figured; stooped and beginning to be shapeless now in a dragging overall tiredness. Only faint traces of onetime prettiness remained along the lines of sallow cheeks and in the faded blue of eyes.

"You, Monteeelius! Can't you hear me?"

The boy moved toward the house and stopped by the stone doorstep. She held out to him an earthen crock half full of potato peelings.

The boy took the crock and turned away.

"You finished plowing that garden patch? You know what your father said."

The boy swung back, sudden, sharp. "Yeah. And you know how it is, I'll plant it too and I'll take care of it and he never does a thing around here. Except holler at me."

"He pays for the food you eat," said the woman.

"Yeah," said the boy. "And I earn every snitch doing everything ever gets done around here. What's he do but hang around town and talk big?" The boy turned away again.

"Please, Monte. I saw you. Don't you go near that stud. You know how your father feels about—"

"He ain't my father!" The boy swung back. He stood, scuffing at dust. "My father's dead. Didn't take you long to start giving me other fathers mighty fast." He looked up. "What'd you ever have to go take up with this one for?"

She stared down at him. "We been fed," she said softly. She brushed a hand across her face. "A woman's got to do something."

He saw the warning flush creeping up her cheeks, the mistiness forming in her eyes. "Aw, shucks, quit it, Ma." He turned away again, moving fast toward the little lean-to chicken house by the barn.

He stood by the netted wire chicken yard watching bedraggled hens and one scraggly rooster scratch and peck in frenzied busyness at the peelings, seeing but not seeing, ears attuned to the soft thuddings as the stallion moved in the corral on the other side of the barn. He became aware of the empty crock in his hands and set this, upside down, on top of a post of the chicken yard. Slowly, almost reluctantly, he moved past the front of the barn to the corral and leaned against rails.

The stallion and the boy looked at each other and the stallion raised its head high and swung away, indifferent, looking into the distance of Colorado plain.

"Shucks," said the boy. "It's a horse, ain't it."

Quietly he moved into the barn and came out with a battered flattened pan partly filled with coarse grain. He crouched by the near side of the corral and slid the pan under the bottom rail and shook it to make the grain swish on the metal.

The stallion's ears twitched and it turned its head, watching, waiting. The boy set the pan down and pushed it farther in and withdrew his hand and the horse moved, deliberate, majestic, accepting tribute, and dropped its head to the pan.

The boy picked up a small stick. Carefully he reached in and nudged the pan farther along by the rails. The horse's head followed and the solid compact body turned following until it was roughly parallel to the rails.

Slowly, cautiously, the boy stood up and began to climb the rails. The horse, intent on the grain, ignored him. Slowly, cautiously, he eased one leg over the top rail, then the other, and was sitting there, feet inside on the next rail down. The horse raised and swung its head a bit, rolling an eye, fixing him there. It dropped the head back, ignoring him again.

Suddenly the boy was out from the rails, thin legs straddling the powerful back, hands fastening into the mane. The horse reared, breath whistling through nostrils, body wrenching sideways out into the corral. It plunged and bucked in furious action and the boy clung, eyes alight, hair flying, thin legs locked to the twisting wrenching body. Blind with rage, the horse reared again, pawing the air, tottering on hind legs close to far-side rails, and dropped down crashing into them. The shock shook the boy loose and he pushed out and away and fell scrambling fast to regain his feet and ran for the near side of the corral and threw himself flat and squirmed under the bottom rail as forehoofs pounded into the ground behind him. He lay still for a moment, chest heaving. He stood up and a small wry grin showed on his lips and he looked through at the horse snorting in baffled fury along inside the rails and he saw the smudged bruising on the one shoulder and the tiny drops of blood oozing.

He turned toward the woman running, white-faced, from the house. "I'm all right, Ma," he said. "And that thing's just scraped some is all."

She stared at him, frightened. "What will your—what will he say?"

"Shucks," said the boy. "He maybe won't even notice. He don't need to know."

* * *

In the slow dusk of the plains a sturdy buckboard rested in front of the small barn. The bony half-starved mustang that had drawn it was with the old draft horse in the skimpy pasture beyond the chicken yard. Inside the barn, in the darkening dimness, the boy hung the harness on a high peg, the bridle on another. The long driving reins trailed on the floor and he lifted these to loop them neatly over.

He moved out of the barn and toward the house, shivering a little in the dropping night chill. Lamplight shone in the dusk through the one front window and he stepped into the patch of light to peer in. The woman was busy by the old cookstove. The man relaxed in a chair by the table, legs sprawled out, was big and bulky and florid-faced. He wore dark oiled boots and striped trousers tucked in and a white shirt with black string tie and checkered vest unbuttoned now over plump middle. His soft dark hat and frock coat hung on the wall behind the chair. His voice, hearty and complacent, reached through the flimsy wall of the house.

"Tilman's bringing a mare out here tomorrow. Ten dollars stud fee. He squawked on that but I got the only horse with Morgan blood anywheres around. A gold mine, that's what that horse'll be."

"Morgan blood," muttered the boy. "In a pig's eye." He moved on, up on the doorstep, opened the door and eased in, closing the door behind him. He stepped forward and slid onto another chair well around the table from the man.

"You take care of that pony?" said the man.

"Yeah," said the boy. "Whyn't you let me give him a good meal sometime?"

"He gets enough," said the man. "For what he's worth. You finish that plowing?"

"Yeah," said the boy.

"You feed that stud?"

"Yeah."

"Water in his trough?"

"Yeah."

"Is he all right?"

Over by the stove the woman drew in breath sharply.

"Sure he's all right," said the boy quickly.

The man looked at the woman then back at the boy. A slow tightness spread over his face.

"Aw, shucks," said the boy. "He got jumpy some and scraped himself on the fence but that won't slow him none."

The man stared steadily at the boy. Moving deliberately, without looking away, he pulled in his booted feet and rose from the chair, reached back to take the frock coat from its hook and shrug it on. Moving deliberately, he strode to the door, took a lantern from a nail in the wall beside it, lit this with a match from a vest pocket, opened the door and went out.

Silence in the dingy front room of the flimsy frame house. The woman had turned and was looking at the boy, eyes wide and worried.

"You ain't a-going to tell him," said the boy.

The man came in through the doorway and closed the door behind him. Slowly, deliberately, he blew out the lantern and hung it on its nail, stepped across the room and took off the coat and hung it on its hook.

"Limping," he said softly, facing the wall. He turned to face the boy. "You been monkeying with that horse?"

The boy sat on the edge of his chair. "What would I be doing that for?"

"Because—" Anger broke across the man's face and was caught and controlled again in the cold deliberation that was worse than anger. "Because you are a goddamned sneaking fool about anything on four legs."

The man stared steadily at the boy and the boy stared back, face rigid, body tense. The man turned his head slightly toward the woman. "Has he?"

She stood, back against the wall by the stove, looking from one to the other of them, from one to the other, the boy and the man looking at her. She turned again to the stove, away from them, away from the long strain of the years, and she nodded slightly as she turned.

Silence in the dingy room except for the small sobbing catch of breath in the boy's throat.

Suddenly the man moved, leaping to get around the table,

but the boy was quicker, whirling up and around his chair and heaving it into the man's path, diving headlong for the door. He yanked the door open and was out as the man kicked the chair aside and plunged after him.

He ran toward the outbuildings, the man pounding after. He started along the corral rails and reversed, dodging back, along the front of the barn. The buckboard was in the way, pocketing him in the angle it made out from the barn. He swerved and dashed through the open doorway into the dark interior.

The man stood in the wide doorway, panting, peering into the blackness. He waited while his heavy breathing subsided. "All right," he said, cold, deliberate. "Come on out of there."

"I ain't coming!" The boy's voice snapped out of the blackness. "You ain't a-going to lick me ever again."

"No?" said the man. He turned sideways in the doorway and took hold of the old sliding door and pulled at it to narrow the opening. He staggered, caught off balance, and went down as the lean weight of the boy hurtled into him out of the blackness. Reaching up, he caught one foot in its heavy worn work shoe as the boy jumped over his fallen body in the doorway. He grunted, letting go, as the other heavy shoe stomped down hard on his arm. He pushed to his feet and stood rubbing the bruised arm with the other hand, hearing the clomping footsteps fade away along by the pasture beyond the chicken yard.

He moved slowly toward the house, brushing dust from his clothes. The woman in the doorway backed on in as he approached. "He'll come in and take what's coming," he said. "When he gets hungry enough. And cold enough."

* * *

The house and the barn were dark hunched shapes on the face of the big land in the dim suggestion of light of the new moon dropping down the western sky. Close by the barn, leaning back against a wheel of the buckboard, the boy sat on the ground on several burlap bags folded over, a ragged saddle blanket up around his shoulders over his patched shirt. He sat still, patient, and watched the house, the two patches of light that were the one front and the one side window of the front room.

"He won't wait up too long," he muttered. "There's other things he likes better'n beating me."

Time passed and the moon dropped further down the sky and a new patch of light appeared on the house, the window of the back room.

Time passed and the front room patches of light faded and were gone and there was only the patch of light of the back room.

Time passed and this too faded and was gone and far off a coyote howled and another answered and the boy shifted restlessly and was quiet again.

Time passed and there were small rustlings as chickens shifted on perches in the little lean-to chicken house and there was silence again and the boy rose and laid the blanket on the seat of the buckboard. Shivering in the night chill, he moved toward the house. He stood on the doorstep, listening. Faintly he could hear the slow rhythm of heavy breathing. Gently he turned the doorknob and pushed the door open, holding back, waiting. After a moment he eased in, standing silent by the near wall.

In the dim tracery of the light of the moon through the front window he could see on the table a plate heaped with a congealed mass of beef stew and boiled potatoes and beside this a thick slice of bread. Quietly he moved past the table to the inner doorway. On inside, on the brass bedstead, he could make out dimly the woman asleep under an old quilt and beside her the bulk of the man, lying on his side, one arm laid across her.

Quietly he backed away and moved to the far corner of the front room where a straw mattress lay on the floor with an old blanket over it. He picked up the blanket and took a ragged denim jacket from a hook on the wall above. With these under one arm, he moved to the table, put the slice of bread on top of the congealed mass and picked up the plate. He eased through the outer doorway and set the plate on the doorstep and gently closed the door behind him. He picked up the plate and moved toward the barn.

Fourteen minutes later, the jacket on, the blanket rolled into a neat bundle and tied with a piece of cord and under one arm, leaving the scraped plate on the seat of the buckboard, he moved along the rickety fence of the pasture and in through the gate. The thin mustang shied away as he approached but the old draft horse stood firm, lifting its head to nuzzle against him. He took hold of the halter and led it out through the gate and fastened this again behind him. In the one easy movement, despite the blanket under one arm, he was astride the broad old back. Obedient to the pressure of the thin legs down its sides, the old horse swung away, old hoofs lifting in clumsy rhythm.

Fifty minutes and four miles later they stopped by the wagon ruts of the stage road. The boy slid to the ground. He stood by the big head, scratching with the one free hand around the old ears, rubbing a cheek along the rough coat of the big old neck. He stepped back.

"Get going," he said. "You know the way." He reached and slapped the old horse on the rump.

The horse jerked, startled, and moved a short distance and stopped, looking at him. "Get going!" said the boy, shouting, voice shaking. "You hear me! He ain't a-going to put no stealing charge on me!"

The horse stood, motionless in the thin last of moonlight, and whiffled softly at him.

The boy rubbed a hand across his face, over his eyes. He stooped and picked up a stone and threw it, hard, and it thudded against the gaunt old ribs. The horse jerked around and started back the way it had come.

He watched it go, a shapeless dark blur moving slowly through the scanty sagebrush. He turned and walked into the darkness of the long road away.

*　*　*

The sun was well up, aiming at noontime. The welcome warmth lay over the big land, over the four mules plodding along the stage road, pulling a medium-sized freight wagon loaded with two layers of well-filled grain bags. The man on the driving seat was short-legged, short and round of body, with huge shoulders and thick arms. Under his flat-crowned wide-brimmed hat his face was broad and sun- and wind-tanned. His jacket was off, tucked under the seat, and his thick arms, bared to rolled shirtsleeves above the elbows, showed freckles through their tan. Behind him, sprawled on the grain bags, lay the boy, eyes closed, mouth open, limp body rolling some with the motion of the wagon.

The road dropped to cross a dry arroyo and the wheels jolted on stones and the boy stirred and sat up. He swiveled around on the bags to face forward.

"Come on up here," said the man. "You ain't much company back there."

The boy scrambled forward and sat on the seat beside him. The man turned his head and a slow smile creased his broad face. "A mite better," he said. "Yes. A mite better. When you stumbled into my camp about sun-up, you was plenty beat."

"Shucks," said the boy. "Just tired was all."

The man gave his attention to the mules. "Where'd you come from?" he said.

The boy edged farther away from the man on the seat. He reached back and took his rolled blanket and set this on his knees. "Nowhere much," he said. "Just back down the road a piece."

The man looked straight ahead, watching the mules. "Got any folks?"

The boy edged farther away, against the low side rail of the seat. "No," he said. "Not now."

"Dead?" said the man.

The boy hesitated. "No," he said. His muscles tightened toward the leap out and away and the man's right hand jumped across him and grasped the side rail, the thick freckled arm pinning him to the seat. The man looked straight ahead, holding the reins in his left hand, watching the mules plod on. "Running away," he said.

The boy struggled against the arm, felt the strength in it, sat still. "I ain't a-going back!" he said.

"Of course you ain't," said the man. "And you ain't doing any jumping. I know a man broke a leg that way. Tangled in a wheel."

The mules plodded on. A jackrabbit started up from a clump of brush by the roadside and spurted ahead and swerved off to the left in long effortless leaps and the mules plodded on. "Maybe you've shook that notion," said the man.

"Maybe I have," said the boy.

"Maybe won't do," said the man.

The boy looked at the solid chunk of sun- and wind-tanned face sideways to him watching the road ahead. "All right," he said. "I ain't a-going to."

"Of course not," said the man. He let go of the side rail

and his right hand rested on his right knee. "Running away's the thing sometimes. I did it myself once." He slapped the reins down on the mules' rumps and they paid no attention and plodded on and he sat back more on the seat. "It was a cow. A crazy old milk cow. My folks had a farm and that silly damn cow had to keep breaking into my maw's garden. Fence didn't mean a thing to her. I chased her out and I fixed that fence so many times I got me more'n a mite mad. Took my paw's shotgun and pried the buckshot out of a cartridge with my knife and put some beans in. Figured to pepper her good. Sure enough, next day she was back in and I grabbed that gun and blazed away. Plenty surprised to see her drop like somebody'd poleaxed her with blood showing plenty places. How was I to know when I was off somewhere my paw'd seen a hawk after the chickens and used that gun and maybe cussed like he could when nothing much happened and put a new cartridge in? I grabbed me a few things and took out fast."

The boy looked at the man beside him watching the road ahead and a small grin showed on the boy's lips. "I ain't been back since," said the man.

The mules plodded on, slow, steady, in a loose shambling walk. The wagon was something that followed, apart from them, separated by their plain pretense that it had nothing to do with them.

"Ever drive a four-mule team?" said the man.

"No," said the boy.

"Think you could?"

"Sure," said the boy. "Sure thing."

"Try it," said the man, handing him the reins. The boy took them and pulled them taut, testing the feel of them in his hands. The mules plodded on, separate, indifferent. The man reached under the seat and pulled out a brown paper bag and extracted from this a fat jerked-beef sandwich. He leaned back on the seat, chewing methodically.

The sandwich disappeared. The man reached and took the reins from the boy. "There's bags and there's bags," he said. "Maybe that particular bag ain't empty."

The boy chewed on the second sandwich and the mules plodded on.

"Where you going?" said the man.

"Anywheres," said the boy. "Anywheres there's a job."

"A job's nothing," said the man. "Only something to do. It's the kind of a job that counts."

"A cow outfit," said the boy. "That's what I want. A cow outfit."

"Not milk cows?" said the man.

"No," said the boy. "Not milk cows."

"Of course not," said the man. He raised his head to watch a buzzard high above tilt wings and glide in long slow slant toward the horizon. "Only there ain't many of that kind around here," he said. "Not yet anyways." He sat up straighter on the seat. "Station's not far now. We ought to come in looking good." He slapped with the reins and the mules paid no attention and plodded on. "Forgot my whip," he said, "or I'd make them hop."

The boy funneled the mouth of the brown paper bag and blew into it and clamped the opening tight and smacked the bag with a fist. It burst with a sharp pop. The mules plodded on.

"Noise don't bother 'em any," said the man.

"Let me get on that lead mule," said the boy, "and I'll make 'em move."

The man turned his head to look at the boy. "Think you can?"

"Sure. Sure thing."

"Try it," said the man, beginning to pull in on the reins.

"Shucks," said the boy. "You don't need to stop." He climbed over the front of the wagon and stood on the long swaying tongue. He moved out along it, past the wheelers, to the lead team. He dodged a nip from one of the wheelers and hopped astride the left leader. It grunted indignantly and hunched its back and tried to buck, bumping heels against the front whiffletree. The boy sat tight to it and drummed heels against its sides. It plodded on with the others, accepting him, ignoring him.

He reached forward and took hold of a long ear and twisted, hard. "Yowee!" he yelled. "Get a-moving!" The mule snorted indignation again and as the twist tightened more lunged into a trot, yanking the others into this with it. The wagon moved forward at a fair clip.

Ahead the road swung around jutting rock to the two log buildings and spring-fed water tank of the stage relay station.

The mules, trotting smartly, swung with it and came to a stop by the first building. The agent, limp and lackadaisical, appeared in the doorway of the other building and leaned against a jamb, watching. The boy jumped off the left lead mule, dodging its sidewise kick, and the man climbed down from the wagon.

"Lucky those things know where to go and where to stop," he said. "I couldn't do much, not with you sitting on the reins. Tell you what. You help me unload these bags which the agent here won't do and I'll speak to the driver when the stage comes along. Could be he'll take you on into the first town."

Easily, with the ease of long practice, the man took hold of a grain bag and swung it up on one huge shoulder. The boy took hold of another and struggled with it, getting it to one thin shoulder, staggering under it.

"Name," said the man.

"Monte," said the boy.

"Rest of it," said the man.

The boy hesitated. He looked at the man, at the broad solid face. He straightened some under his load. "Walsh," he said. "Monte Walsh."

"Walsh?" said the man. "I knew a man called that. In the Army with me."

"My father was a reb," said the boy.

"I was Union," said the man. "Ain't that something? But it's a good name." He led into the first building.

They were back by the wagon, last two bags on shoulders. "Tell you what, Monte," said the man. "I got a cousin over in the Indian Nation's got a road ranch. Red Fork Ranch he calls it. North of Darlington on the Chisholm trail, aiming for Wichita. Trail herds stopping there. Cow outfits going through. Red-headed he is. Name's Martin. You manage to get there and hang around maybe he'd feed you and maybe somebody'd take you on. That's a far piece from here. Think you could make it?"

Monte Walsh stood straight under his load. "I'll get there," he said.

"Of course you will," said the man.

* * *

This road came out of sandy distance and dipped to cross where old cottonwoods and scrubby brush lined the sides of a dry watercourse and climbed to lead on into distance again. The several ramshackle buildings by it might someday be a town. Right now they were only a stage stop—two sheds and a longish narrow building fronting the road with CAFE in peeling black paint over the door and a leaning slant-roofed house inhabited by the proprietor and the fat stringy-haired woman who passed for his wife.

Along the road came Monte Walsh, hot, tired, limping in old work shoes whose soles flapped at the toes. His thin body was thinner now in his worn jeans and dirty remnants of shirt. The rolled blanket was gone somewhere and his ragged jacket was off, hanging down his back with sleeves tied loosely around his neck. An ancient hat, picked up somewhere, half the brim gone, holes in the crown, was on his head. He stopped by the narrow building and sniffed the odors of cooking that drifted out the open front door.

A man, tall, stoop-shouldered, full-bearded, with greasy cloth tied around his waist and hanging below his knees, appeared in the doorway. He looked Monte over. His lips pushed out, showing through the beard, and he spat a quantity of dark liquid into the road. "When did you eat last?" he said.

"Yesterday," said Monte.

"How'd you like a good meal?"

"I'd like it fine."

The man shifted the wad of tobacco in his mouth from one cheek to the other. "Afraid of work?"

"No."

"Come on," said the man. He turned back into the building and Monte followed. The fat stringy-haired woman at one end by the stove looked up at him and grunted something unintelligible. The man went right on, out the open back door, and Monte followed.

The man stopped by a big tangled pile of dead cottonwood branches cut into four-foot lengths. Beside the pile stakes were driven into the ground, in pairs in a line, each stake about four feet high, the pairs about eight feet apart. The man picked up a branch length and laid it on the ground inside and against the first pair of stakes. "Pile 'em here like that," he said. "When you finish you get your meal." He went back into the building.

Monte unlooped the sleeves of his jacket and hung it on a stake. He went to work, pulling pieces from the tangled pile and fitting them snugly together between the paired stakes.

Time passed. He had one eight-foot section full, a solid neat section, the branch lengths tightly packed together.

"Good gawd a'mighty!"

Monte jumped around, startled. The man was in the rear doorway. He stepped down and strode over and stood glaring at the piled section. His cheeks and forehead above the beard were turning a dull red. "Tryin' to cheat me?" he shouted. "Packin' 'em in like that! I sell that stuff by the cord! Spread 'em out right an' you could make two outa that one!" He stepped to the piled section and put a foot against it and tried to push it over. It was too well, too solidly packed. Arms flying, he began to heave pieces off the top.

Monte stared at the man. "Whyn't you tell me?" he said.

"Tell you!" The man spun around, a piece of wood in one hand. "Good gawd a'mighty! Ain't you got any brains? G'wan! Beat it!" He stepped forward, stick upraised, and Monte jumped back.

The man stopped. The sound of hoofs and creaking leather came from the road, beyond the building. "G'wan!" he shouted. "Tryin' to cheat me! G'wan, beat it!" He smacked the piece of wood on the ground, snapping it in two, and hurried away, into the building.

Six horses braked hard in front of the building and a big old coach stopped, swaying on its thoroughbraces. The driver jumped down. "Ten minutes!" he shouted. "Pile out!" Five passengers piled out and hurried into the building with the driver where the man and the woman were slapping dishes on the one long table.

Spoons and forks clattered against thick crockery. Jaws worked in hasty rhythm. The man in the greasy apron stepped to the rear doorway and looked out. The jacket was gone from the stake. Monte Walsh was nowhere in sight.

The passengers were again in the coach. The driver, high on his seat, shook out his whip and cracked the tip near the ears of the leaders. The horses leaned into the traces and the coach began to move, to pick up speed downgrade toward the dip in the road.

Inside the building the man was putting coins into a small leather bag hanging from a wall nail near the stove. He whirled about. Monte Walsh, jacket flying out behind, was leaping in through the rear doorway, crossing the room toward the front doorway. He scooped a half-loaf of bread off the table as he went and was on out, stuffing the bread inside his remnants of shirt, bounding on thin knobby legs after the coach.

The man leaped to follow. The greasy apron hampered his leg action and he stumbled through the front doorway and went to his hands and knees in the road. He pushed up and stood staring. He saw Monte overtake the coach and grab and be dragged and pull and climb up on the boot and the coach move on, gathering momentum for the run up and out of the dip. "Good gawd a'mighty," he said. "Cheatin' me again."

* * *

The shadow of the unfinished homestead cabin was long in late afternoon sun as Monte Walsh unloaded stones for the fireplace from a flat makeshift stoneboat. He rolled the last rock off. He unhitched the meager Indian pony and hung the harness on a knob of the cabin wall and ran his hands down the pony's front legs to fasten a rope hobble in place before removing the bridle.

"Well, now," said the gray-mustached man in cap and overalls standing in the doorless cabin doorway, "you sure got more out of that horse in an afternoon'n I ever could. Come on. Food's ready."

Monte sat inside under the unfinished roof on a small keg by the wooden box that served as a table and contemplated the empty plate in front of him that had been filled three times.

"Well, now," said the man. "You sure you can't hold more? Like I told you I ain't got any cash, not right now, but I got plenty to eat."

"Shucks," said Monte. "I'm crammed full."

"Always like to see a young one eat," said the man. "Always wonder where they put it all. Well, now, whyn't you stay around a few days? Like I say I got plenty grub."

"No," said Monte. "Thanks. But I got to get where I'm going."

"Not tonight," said the man. "I got blankets. In the morning I'll fix you up with some breakfast and something to take along." He was looking at Monte's old work shoes, at what remained of them, and the bare toes poking through. They seemed to worry him. He looked at them and away. He looked back. He began to pull off his own hard-worn but still stout cowhide boots.

"Try these," he said. "I got another pair I been saving some."

* * *

This was a real town. Not much exactly yet, but still a town. In the not-quite-dark of early evening the lamplight through doors and windows of the false-fronted straggly buildings was beginning to throw patches of pale yellow out onto the dust of the one street. Monte Walsh sat on a tie rail in front of a blacksmith shop, legs limp and off the ground, resting blistered feet in cowhide boots. Across the way, still faintly distinguishable, was a sign EATS over a door with set-in small pane of glass through which lamplight shone cheerfully. Monte looked at this and away, shrugging thin shoulders. He looked on around, considering possibilities of holing up for the night.

Across and further down the street an Indian, bulky in wrapped-around blanket and carrying a lumpy burlap bag, came out the door of a small general store and swung a leg over a scrawny stunted horse with a rope bridle and rode off into the deepening dusk.

"Shucks," murmured Monte. "He ought to be carrying the horse."

"Hey, bub."

Monte turned on the tie rail. A man had come through the swinging doors of the saloon beside the blacksmith shop behind him. He wore a miner's cap and a jacket stained with coal dust over dirty striped coveralls. "Hey, bub," he said again, weaving a bit on unsteady feet. "Want to make fifty cents?"

"Sure," said Monte. "Sure thing."

The man put a forefinger to his lips and beckoned with the

other hand. He led the way to the corner of the saloon building. He put a hand on Monte's shoulder, leaning on him.
"Going to get 'em this time," he said, low-voiced, confidential. "Get 'em good. Clean me out every week, they do. Let
me win at first to get me going, then clean me out. Get 'em
this time. You got me?"

"Shucks," said Monte. "How'd I know what to be getting?"

"Poker," said the man. "Get out while I'm ahead, see?" He
pointed along the saloon side to an open window near the
back. "You wait by that window. Quiet." He took the stub
end of a cigar out of a pocket. "When I throw this out, you
come around in and on back there and you say, 'Hey, Mister
Felder.' That's me, my name, Felder. You say, 'Hey, Mister
Felder, your wife's took sick over at your house and's calling
for you.' Got that, bub? Got it good?"

"Sure," said Monte. "Sure thing."

"Smart," said the man. "Like me." He moved along the saloon front and in through the swinging doors. Monte moved
back along the building and squatted on the ground by the
patch of light from the window.

Time passed. He heard the chink of glasses, the riffle of
cards, the mutter of men's voices. He waited. The stub of
cigar, lit now, came flipping out. He rose and went around by
the entrance. He pushed the swinging doors open and ran toward the back room.

Two minutes later Monte and the man were in the street a
short way from the saloon. "Worked," said the man. He
tossed a coin and Monte caught it. A quarter.

"Hey," said Monte. "You promised fifty cents."

"Run along," said the man. "That's more'n enough." He
started away along the street.

"Yeah?" said Monte. "It's gone up. It's going to be a dollar
now."

The man stopped, turned back, weaving some. "Want me
to bat your ears off?" he said.

"Want me to go in there and tell about it?" said Monte.

The man stood, swaying, biting at one thumb. He fumbled
in a pocket and took out a silver dollar and tossed it toward
Monte. "Smart," he said. "Like me." He moved away along
the street.

Monte picked the coin out of the dust. "Dollar," he said.

"And a quarter." He moved off, angling toward the door with its cheerful one-paned patch of light and its even more cheerful EATS.

* * *

Rolling country this, rolling into distance everywhere, broken only by far-scattered low thickets of scrub oak. The road, despite a few wheel tracks, was little more than a horse trail. The sun, high overhead, slanting into afternoon, sent down a steady glare. In the meager shade of an oak thicket some thirty feet from the trail Monte Walsh sat on the ground, legs stretched out. He had not eaten for a day and a half. He had not spoken to anyone in that time because there had been no one to speak to, no one anywhere. He had come seventeen slowing miles since morning. The blisters inside the cowhide boots were rubbed raw.

He sat motionless. Nothing seemed to move anywhere. He became aware, by another thicket across the trail a hundred feet away, of a coyote watching him. It had not been there a moment before. It stood still, one forefoot raised, and looked steadily at him.

Its ears lifted and it turned its head to look along the trail to Monte's left. Silently, a shadow sliding, it slipped around the thicket to the right and was gone.

Monte turned his head to look along the trail to the left. Over the last rise rolling down to his shadowed niche came an old Indian, the years long ago lost in the many wrinkles of the stern old face, Cheyenne from the firm set of the features and the shape of the head and the proud carriage of this on the thin old neck, riding bareback on a squat bunch-muscled pinto. He was naked from the waist up, wearing only some kind of faded canvas trousers and moccasins. He was leading on a twenty-foot length of grass rope a heavy-shouldered dark gray mustang.

He came along the trail at a steady dogtrot, seeming oblivious to the jerkings of the mustang on the rope, and he looked to neither side, yet when he was opposite Monte he stopped and the mustang came up and stopped by the pinto's hindquarters and he turned his head to look as steadily as had the coyote at Monte in the shadow of his thicket.

There was no discernible expression in the wrinkles of the

old face. He raised an arm and swung it, pointing on ahead along the trail.

Monte nodded his head vigorously. "Martin's ranch," he said. "Red Fork Ranch."

The old Indian might not have heard. No flicker of expression showed. He raised the arm again and pointed at the mustang.

"You bet!" said Monte, jumping up. He came forward, hobbling on blistered feet, and around the pinto and approached the mustang. It stood motionless, head turned slightly, watching him with one rolled eye. He put a hand on its withers. It stood, motionless. He leaped to throw a leg over and as he leaped it hunched its back, high, and he hit off balance, awkward, and it bucked, head down, hindquarters rising in sudden surge, and he pitched forward and sideways and hit the ground, hard.

Monte flipped over and away fast and sat up. He stared at the old Indian. The old body was rocking on the pinto, shaking in tremendous silent mirth.

"Like that, is it?" said Monte, mad. He stood up. The blisters in the cowhide boots were forgotten. He plunged forward and was astride the mustang before it could hunch, hands fastening into the sparse mane. It reared, angry in turn, and pounded down and forward, bucking, and the rope tautened and was yanked from the old Indian's hand and Monte clung, thin legs gripping the heaving sides.

The old Indian sat still and quiet on the pinto, watching.

The mustang scattered dust like a small whirlwind. Monte leaned forward, upper body tight along the neck, arms around. He caught hold of the dangling rope and whipped a coil around the mustang's nose. He sat up, pulling hard, and the coil tightened and the mustang squealed, fighting for breath, and slowed. It stopped, legs braced, resigned to the day's fate. Monte pulled its head around and kicked it into motion, back toward the pinto.

The old Indian regarded him, impassive, expressionless. The old Indian raised a hand, palm outward, in what could have been a kind of salute. He nudged the pinto into its dogtrot along the trail and beckoned to Monte to follow.

* * *

The scrub thickets cast long shadows over the big land. Two other long shadows moved among them, cast by an old Indian on a squat pinto and a thin knobby boy on a dark gray mustang. They jogged along and the shadows lengthened and they jogged on in a somehow companionable silence.

They came to a sharp fork in the trail. The old Indian stopped and the boy moved up beside him. The old Indian raised an arm and tapped himself on the chest and pointed out along the south prong of the trail. He pointed at the boy and out along the north prong.

"Shucks," said Monte Walsh. "I guess this is where I get off." He slid from the mustang's back. He handed the rope end to the old Indian. He looked up into the stern wrinkled old face looking down and reached to slap the near old leg in its canvas covering. "Thanks," he said. "I hope you know what that means."

The old Indian raised the arm again and pointed at Monte and then at the mustang. He shook again in silent mirth. He raised the hand again, palm outward, in what could have been a kind of salute. He swung the pinto to start along the south prong of the trail and the rope tightened and the mustang followed.

Monte Walsh watched them go, dwindling into distance. They dropped from sight into a hollow and he turned to start along the north prong.

The blisters broke into pain and he hobbled slowly, favoring them as much as possible. Time passed and he hobbled on and there was nothing but the trail leading on, rising some as the land sloped upward. "Shucks," he murmured. "Wonder if that old buck thought it'd be funny to lose me out in the middle of nowhere." He hobbled on.

The shadows were stretching to merge together as he topped out on the rising land and the ground fell away before him in long slow slopes and in the last light of the sun he saw it, several miles away still, out on the level, the long thin ribbon, only a thin ribbon from here, there narrowing and widening and narrowing again and rods wide at the narrowest, the great trail cut deep through brush and sod by thousands of hoofs moving north.

His head turned as his eyes followed it swinging northward. There it crossed the Cimarron, the Red Fork of the Arkansas. There it snaked on through a natural clearing in the black jack forest of stunted oaks that came down to the river and stopped. And there, where the clearing widened in huge sweep, was the big cattle corral, big enough to hold twenty-five hundred head, and some distance away the smaller horse corral and the two stockade-style log buildings.

"What d'you know," murmured Monte. "I guess I've got there "

*   *   *

The one building, the original, built by the first owner when land could first be leased from the Indians, was low with slant sod roof, used now for cookhouse and storehouse. The other was two story, gabled, shingle-roofed, two-roomed, one big room directly over the other, the lower used as bar and store and trading post, the upper, reached only by an outside stairway, for sleeping quarters.

Monte Walsh, blisters healing inside socks inside the cowhide boots, thin body cased now in new-old jeans too big for him and an oversize flannel shirt with sleeves cut down to length, swept the plank floor of the bar–store–trading post with an Indian brush-broom every morning with conscientious regularity. Now and again he carried assorted items from the other building and put them on shelves as needed and as directed by a stout gruffly genial redheaded man. He slapped an ancient cavalry saddle on an always mean-tempered Indian pony and rode out with a coiled rope hanging over one shoulder and rode back dragging firewood for the querulous but competent bent-legged man who ruled the cookhouse. He ate enormous meals to the constant amused amazement of the redheaded man and the never-expressed satisfaction of the querulous man and his thinness tightened toward the rawhide leanness of a young animal.

And whenever a cloud of dust rose to the southward and drifted with the wind over the great trail and came on and was a herd of Texas cattle and these were bedded for the night somewhere in the natural clearings of the black jack forest beyond and men lean and hard and squint-eyed from wind and sun, wearing high-heeled knee-length boots with huge spurs and low-slung cartridge belts with holstered Colt .45's, eight-inch-barreled and wooden-handled, clattered in for supplies and something to rake the dust out of their throats and slow drawling talk of the trail, Monte hung close and listened and looked for the one quieter than the others with responsibility on him and edged closer and asked his question—and was shushed and pushed aside, tight-lipped and disgusted.

And one afternoon when Monte was sweeping and the red-headed man was checking antelope hides left by an old Indian who always pointed at Monte and sketched in the air with his hands an imaginary mustang and shook with silent mirth, hoofs sounded outside and a well-lathered cow pony slid to a stop by the door and a man entered. He was young as most of them always were, not much into his twenties, but big-framed with wide sloping shoulders, and a hard-worn dusty competence came from him.

The redheaded man looked up and promptly set a bottle and a small glass on the counter beside the skins. "Hat!" he said. "Hat Henderson! Wondered if you'd be coming up this year."

"Certain I'm coming," said the man. "And all hell's been coming with me." He poured a drink and downed it. "I get shoved up to trail boss. And what happens? Nothing but trouble. Spookiest bunch of goddamned cows ever rattled horns. Running most every night. Then I lost a man crossing the Washita. Now another one has to go bust a cinch and break a leg."

"Rough," said the redheaded man. "Real rough."

"But we ain't lost any cows," said the man. "You got a bed upstairs for Petey—it was Petey broke that leg—till the stage comes?"

"Of course," said the redheaded man.

"Supposing we put them goddamned cows in that big corral for tonight? Get some rest."

"Go right ahead," said the redheaded man.

The other started for the door. Monte Walsh stepped forward. "Hey," he said. "Hey, mister—"

"Quit it, kid," said the man. "I ain't got time for you." He was out the door and away.

*　*　*

Twenty-two hundred longhorn steers were in the big stock corral, stout, proof against them, made of logs set stockade-style. Seventy-three cow ponies were in the horse corral made of split rails set in post stanchions. In the upper room of the two-story log building a lean whipcord young man, maybe all of twenty, lay on a cot with barrel-stave splints along one leg. In the light of a small kerosene lamp another of about the same age sat by the cot playing euchre with him, with old grimy cards. Sounds of various occasionally boisterous activities came through the floor boards from the room beneath.

There, in the room beneath, apart from the seven men around a big table, the redheaded man leaned on the inside of the short high counter he used for a bar. Hat Henderson leaned on the outer side, cradling a drink in one big hand. Monte Walsh sat on a small box by the end of the counter.

"Hey, kid!" shouted someone at the table. "Bring us another bottle."

The redheaded man handed a bottle to Monte and made another mark on a piece of paper. Monte took the bottle to the table and came back to his box.

"—shift young Jenkins to regular riding," Hat Henderson was saying. "He ain't no Petey. Not yet anyways. But maybe he can make it. Then who in holy hell'll wrangle the cavvy?"

"Damn it," said Monte Walsh. "I'm right here."

The wide sloping shoulders turned some till Hat was leaning on one elbow on the counter, looking down. "So you are," he said. "What there is of you. Think you can handle hosses?"

"Sure," said Monte. "Sure thing."

"Can you ride?"

"Sure. Sure thing."

"I mean ride."

"Damn it," said Monte, sitting up straight on the box. "Anything you've got."

"You don't say?" murmured Hat. He raised his glass to his lips, looking down over it. He swung toward the redheaded man. "Mighty big talk," he said.

The redheaded man chuckled, shrugging his shoulders. He sobered. He nodded his head just a bit.

"All right, kid," said Hat. "We'll try it anyways. Be around in the morning."

And later when they all had left and were rolling into blankets in the clear cool of night out near the horse corral and the redheaded man and Monte had finished wiping the table and counter and putting things in place and sweeping up assorted debris, the redheaded man pointed to the three new unused saddles on their racks by the rear wall. "Maybe you could use one of those," he said.

"Shucks," said Monte. "I can't pay for it."

"Don't I know that?" said the redheaded man, gruff, seeming angry. "I ain't dumb. You trying to do me out of a sale? Pay me when you come back through or send it by somebody."

And in the morning when the chuck wagon had taken on supplies and was moving on and the men were swinging loops in the horse corral and one of them, grinning, led out a rangy dark bay, Hat Henderson said: "Might be fun to see. He sure talked big. But we ain't got time for games. Bring us that little dun."

And when the dun was brought, bridled and ready for him, Monte Walsh slapped his new saddle on it and pulled the cinch tight, fumbling some, conscious of the critical young eyes on him, and he swung up and the horse broke in two mildly, getting the kinks out of its backbone, bucking some in sheer exuberance of release into the morning, and Monte rode out the little storm and Hat said, "All right, kid, likely you'll do. That one and the little black over there and that pinto will be your string. Come on, we'll get the bunch moving. They're pretty well trail broke."

And while the others loped for the big stock corral, Hat and Monte hazed the rest of the cavvy out of the horse corral and started them following the chuck wagon. "Stop when Cookie stops," said Hat, "and keep 'em bunched handy." He struck spurs to his own big gray and left to join the others.

Like a great sprawled snake, weaving and changing shape but always re-forming into the long wide line of crackling hoofs and rattling horns, twenty-two hundred longhorn steers moved north along the trail. Off to the left, drawing ever more in advance, the chuck wagon bumped along and behind it trailed the cavvy and behind this rode Monte Walsh, erect in new saddle, rump flat to it, a part of the horse beneath him.

Another young one was riding north with a trail herd, with the men and the horses that were taking the Texas longhorn to the farthest shores of the American sea of grass, unthinking, uncaring, unknowing that he and his kind, compound of ignorance and gristle and guts and something of the deep hidden decency of the race, would in time ride straight into the folklore of a weary old world.

*   *   *

"Yeah, they'll do that. I had me one somethin' like it in my string last time. Mouse-colored mutt he was. An' mean. Mornin's I was figurin' on usin' 'im he'd know an' he'd get up steam an' take a header right over the rope corral we strung out from the wagon. Someone'd have to run 'im down an' throw 'im. Well sir, we'd took on a kid down at Martin's. Herdin' the hosses an' doin' right fair at it too. He must of been studyin' on that mutt. Know what he did? Snitched a rope—it was Jess's rope an' Jess he didn't think much of that when he found out an' he was aimin' to bust the kid a few but I got in the way an' took that notion away from 'im. He didn't have no real squawk. Rope wasn't hurt none. Well sir, along in the night somehow that kid tied that rope around that mutt's neck an' left it draggin' an' by mornin' that mutt he was so used to it draggin' he'd about forgot it. Well sir, we had 'em in the corral an' that kid slips in there with 'em an' he flips tother end of that rope around the neck of one of the wagon mules with a good knot an' when that mutt he went to sailin' over the corral rope like he did he was one mighty surprised piece of hoss. Rope took 'im right in the air an' flopped 'im back down an' knocked the wind clean out of 'im an' at tother end of that rope that mule was about yanked off 'is feet. Made the mule mad an' that mule he jerked that mutt around some on the ground 'fore he could get up an' finished off kickin' 'im with a thump you could of heard clean to Kansas. Well sir, that mutt he was a mighty careful actin' hoss for quite some time after."

Monte
1872–1877

KNOCK OFF a few years fast. Let a boy emerge as a man, age
in the years unimportant but the seasoning yes, a young one
absorbing the skills of a trade, of a way of life, of an attitude
toward existence. Maybe it will add up to something, if only
to a grasp on one of many like him, separate only in the small
fragments of individuality, who shared that trade, that way of
life, in a time and a place, a short time but a big place, a wisp
of eternity across a third of a continent.

*　*　*

Monte Walsh, coming sixteen, rode up the trail to Newton
wrangling the cavvy with a herd of longhorn steers road-
branded Circle Dot and lost two horses on the way, likely to
a pair of Pawnees who eased them off one night and were
long gone by morning. That bothered him plenty until he
learned there were other wranglers in this and other years
who lost more. When the cattle were loaded on the cars and
the outfit was paid off, Monte took his, less the wholesale
cost of the blanket and tarp and rope that had been supplied
him, in a few silver dollars and a little dun cow pony that always broke in two mildly when he first swung up and then
went about its work with an all-day quiet competence. He
lost most of the dollars at the Bull's Head trying to learn to
take his liquor straight and losing most of that too but he
held on to the horse. None of the men scattering now to find
cold weather work wanted a young green one tagging his
heels. Monte wandered about lonesome and had to take what
he could get. He wore out that winter in and about a small
smelly dugout far back in lonely country helping a lank

27

scrub-bearded wolfer who rarely spoke ten words a day but kept him busy skinning and scraping hides and disposing of the carcasses. There was a bad time the day the wolfer found a forgotten half-finished bottle in among his trapping gear and promptly finished it, becoming surly drunk in the process, and began knocking Monte about, but when Monte came up off the ground with a skinning knife in one hand and an obvious desperate intent to use it in all of him the man sobered fast and backed away and said be black-damned if I don't think you would and thereafter kept hands off. The dugout was forty miles from the nearest settlement and the few trails were clogged with snow so there was nothing to do but stick and Monte stuck. He was worried the wolfer, being a wolfer, might cheat him, but when the snow in the bottoms was melting at midday and they made it the long way to town with a wagonload, the man paid over the promised one quarter of the proceeds before plunging himself into the serious business of blowing the other three quarters on a sustained noisy spree. Monte spent half a day soaking and scrubbing in the back room of a barbershop trying to get rid of the smell and then drifted southward on the dun. He stopped at a road ranch on the Cimarron and paid a red-headed man the price of a saddle and even had a few jingly coins left and he drifted on southward down to Austin looking for the big slope-shouldered man who had paid off at Newton and found him.

"All right, kid," said Hat Henderson. "Looks like you've been growing some. I'll speak to the old man. We start next week."

*　　*　　*

Monte Walsh, coming seventeen, rode up the trail to Wichita wrangling the cavvy with another Circle Dot herd of longhorn steers and never lost a horse along the way though he had troubles enough to keep him from gaining weight and he did lose considerable skin and most of a shirt tearing through brush the night the herd, always spooky, staged a full-scale stampede and the cavvy, maybe out of sympathy as much as anything else, spooked too and led him a five-mile scattering chase. But he had enough changeover mounts waiting by the chuck wagon when the riders straggled in hollering

for them, and he wore down the dun and a stocky gray
finding the others and, by time the riders had the steers gathered plus a few could-be mavericks for good measure, he had
them all. He took his pay this time in Wichita in silver dollars, straight, and found he could take his liquor the same,
straight, standing up, and was not aware of the effect of this
until he suddenly discovered that the drinks-on-me tune he
had been calling to the amusement and cooperation of all
and sundry along Rowdy Joe Lowe's bar had cleaned him
out. He was in a sad state the two days it took his head to
shrink back to size. He was in a sadder state when he learned
that the dun had been found wandering loose in the street
and turned in at a livery stable and a feed bill was waiting
there. He was sad and hungry and wobbly but that did not
stop him from being mad all through when he learned that
the livery man, liking the looks of the dun, figured it had
been eating enough for a herd of elephants and tallied the
bill according. Monte disputed that the best he could in his
condition and wound up, considerably battered, in a corner
of the stable. He tried to come up off the floor again and his
legs failed. But a local man who had a ranch a few miles
out of town and who had enjoyed his performance at the bar
happened by and saw and considered what he saw somewhat disagreeable and wound up knocking the livery man,
equally battered, into another corner of the stable. The livery
man, seeing things now in better perspective, tallied a better
bill and the local man paid this and carted Monte, with the
dun tagging, out to his ranch. Monte wore out that winter
keeping the man's cows untangled from the other stock roaming the immediate range and wondering if the bold looks
the man's daughter gave him meant what they might mean
without ever working up nerve enough to find out. The man
claimed he ate more than he earned, which could have been
true from the way he was stretching up and hanging long
lean muscle on his long knobby bones, but when spring
branding was done the man paid him forty dollars anyway
and he promptly blew most of that on a pair of high-heel
boots and an old much-used cartridge belt and a rusty Colt
he could get cheap because the hammer was bent. The boots
near crippled him the first day but he managed to get them
off without having to cut the leather and he put about a quart
of shucked corn in each and poured in water and let them

sit all night, stretching, and when they dried out on his feet next day he was mighty proud of them. He talked the local blasksmith into straightening the hammer of the Colt so it might function if he had money to buy bullets and he swung up on the dun and drifted southward. He found that the redheaded man on the Cimarron had sold out to a hatchet-faced halfbreed who thought meals should be paid for in cash in advance and he was enough of a trail hand by now to be properly indignant about that. On near Darlington he met an old Indian who remembered him and a certain dark gray mustang and took him to a village of patched buffalo-hide tepees for a surprisingly tasty supper of dog stew. Monte wasted so much time hanging around the village and learning to get along with signs and a few Cheyenne words and round-ing up some scrubby wild horses with several of the old Indian's grandsons that when he drifted on down to Austin there was no Circle Dot herd on hand. That did not bother him long. Other herds were making.

*   *   *

Monte Walsh, coming eighteen, rode up the trail to Cald-well working the drag with a slow-moving Cross Bar herd of longhorn cows and calves, eating dust every mile, helping late cows calve, loading the weaker calves, unable to travel at first, into a wide flat-bottom wagon, sorting them out to their mothers again when the herd stopped for nooning and for night. Their smells would mix in the wagon and sometimes the mothers would not own them and Monte had his trou-bles. The driver of the wagon, a barrel-built man called Sunfish Perkins, was not much help except in offering advice for the first weeks, having sprained an ankle in a bad spill the second day out. But his advice was good and his patience in offering it the same, and Monte learned plenty about the uses of a rope and how to twist a calf's tail so it would bawl the right tune and the necessity of dodging fast when an answer-ing mother went on the prod. He lost a calf that fell when he was heaving it over the low side of the wagon and it broke a leg and had to be shot. He lost an old footsore cow that al-ways hung back and one day dropped out of sight, likely pinched off by one of the Indians usually watching from just over the nearest horizon. He worried about such things, backtracking in the evening to search for the cow, until the trail boss, maybe nudged to it by Sunfish, said quit frettin', kid, it happens, an' you ain't the worst hand I ever had tailin' a herd. When they were paid off in Caldwell he had more money to spend than before and he blew it on a big gray Stetson with a leather band and a younger Colt with working hammer and in finding out he had come of age with the helpful amused cooperation of one of the women at the Red Light Saloon. He stood up to the bars with the rest of the men and they tolerated him in a rough goodnatured way and even included him in their joshing but he knew he was still just a maverick dogie tagging along and a lonesome feeling had him when he watched them drifting away to other pastures in twos and threes, siding each other in the easy comradeship of the range. He wore out that winter hanging around town, doing odd jobs mostly around the stockyards, paying for sleep space for himself and the dun in a livery stable by gentling a few mean-trick horses for the proprietor. He got to be known in town, called on now and again to throw a leg over a stubborn horse and wear it down to easy riding for townspeople too lazy or too soft or too old to do that for themselves. He added some height and he filled out more and, when the grass was beginning to green up that way and the first trail herd swung into sight with its point men riding tall in the saddle, town life and even the Red Light suddenly seemed to lose all attraction and he and the dun headed southward.

* * *

Monte Walsh, coming nineteen, came up the trail riding flank with an Eight Bar Eight herd of longhorn cows and their calves able to travel. He could stand eye to eye with the tallest man in the outfit and give almost as much punishment as he took in a rough-and-tumble. Lean energy burst out of him in antics around the fire at night and one evening the others, figuring he was ripe for it, batted him about with grim good humor and laid him over the chuck wagon tongue and leathered him with their chaps. He sulked a while in his blanket but by morning, though his rump was sore in the saddle, his grin was back in shape. He lost the little dun crossing the Canadian at high water when a jagged branch cottonwood log swept downstream and set the cattle to milling frantic in the river around him. He was knocked from the saddle but he clung to the horn and the dun, fighting hard, kept him up until he could scramble over the backs of several cows to the near shore. He saw the dun go under, pounded down by wild-eyed cows trying to climb on it. He stood by the limp body caught by the current on a sandbar out from the bank downstream and the drops dripping from his lean young face were not all from the Canadian. He stooped and stripped his gear from the body and limped to the cavvy waiting its turn to cross and slapped a loop on a big rangy black in his string and was back in the river with the other men. They dropped three cows and five calves at that crossing but had good luck on the rest moving north. They bypassed Caldwell and drove on to Ellsworth and spent two days camping outside town and spending accumulated pay in town then drove on westering through Kansas and upper Colorado into Wyoming Territory and delivered the herd at Laramie. Monte took his pay this time in gold coins and the big rangy black he knew lacked looks and liked to catch him off guard and try to pile him into brush but he also knew could run when convinced that was wanted like a bullet out of a buffalo gun. After a brief spree the rest of the riders headed back south but Monte, feeling no particular pull to any of them and having caught the come-on smile of a waitress in a hash house, stayed on to sample Laramie some more. He blew the coins in fair style, learning that faro is a tricky game and that poker requires patience and sound judgment and that, for a spur-jingling trail rider with money in his pocket, a cooperative woman, in Wyoming as in Kansas, could be an interesting if not wholly satisfactory companion. When the money was gone and his welcome with it, he swung up on the black, not liking the chill winds beginning to blow out of the north country anyway, and drifted southward. Sometimes he camped alone, chewing on the jerked beef and soda crackers he carried in a little bag, sleeping in his blanket and tarp under the stars, and sometimes he picked up meals by chuck wagon fires and gossip of the trails from and about men he was beginning to know now in the long slow seasonal shuttling of the herds. Dropping down through Colorado he came into once-familiar country and he thought of things he had quit thinking about and a woman's voice calling "Monteeelius" and he rode looking for the old place. He found the two-room shack and the small half-dugout barn, both sagging into ruin, and the fallen rails of the little corral, the whole place deserted, and he rode on, asking questions where he could, and followed the answers and all he found at last was a slow-settling rectangular mound of earth and an unmarked wooden cross. He stood by this, lean and alone, and he looked long at it, head down, worn gray Stetson off and held in his left hand. He reached his right hand into the right pocket of his worn pants and pulled the pocket inside out, empty and frayed. *Nothing and nobody,* he said. *That's what I've got like before. Nothing and nobody.* And something stubborn in him said no, not quite. He raised his head and looked out into the distances merging into distances all around and he felt what he could not have said in words, what he could not even have comprehended in words. He had all that, his because he knew it and was a part of it, the big land, the great emerging cattle country, and he had a horse and the lean hard energy of youth ran strong in him and that was enough for any man; almost, almost enough. He swung up on the black again and moved on, angling always southward, and he stopped in several towns and acquired a little spending money racing the black against local horses whose backers thought his simple statement of fact the boasting of an overeager young one. He drifted steadily southward and he wore out the rest of that winter way down near San Antonio breaking horses for a mustanger who was temporarily on crutches, having let one of the horses pitch him into a fence-post.

* * *

Monte Walsh, coming twenty, six-foot-one in his socks when he had his boots off which was seldom, came up the trail to Caldwell riding swing with a Flying O herd of mixed Mexican longhorns. It was a hell-for-leather outfit, moving fast, maybe because some of the men had good reasons for leaving lower Texas in a hurry, maybe too because part at least of the herd had been slipped across the Rio Grande without what might be called proper purchase papers. Monte did not like it much, not for those reasons which were not exactly his business, but because there was not much com-

radeship around the fire at night and because the trail boss
was a mean-tempered mean-talking man given to shouting
unnecessary orders and shirking his own share of the work.
But Monte had signed on and he gave the job all he had
which was plenty now and he held to it through high water
and forced dry runs and dust storm stampedes and several
near-deadly disputes with other outfits over crossing time
rights. On at Caldwell, when they were holding the herd
while the boss dickered for a quick sale and they tangled with
one of those outfits coming up still nursing a grudge, Monte
did his share, battering all fight out of one of the opposition
and keeping another mighty busy until a third eliminated him
by the not-quite-fair method of whanging him over the head
with a gun barrel. When he was paid off, short-paid too like
the others by the boss who left them little more than drinking
money with the bartender of the Red Light and was long
gone by the time they collected, he blew what he had with a
sort of desperate eagerness to be rid of it and signed on fast
with a Cross Bar herd moving on north. He got all the way
up into Montana this time, to Miles City, and knocked
around there a few weeks and was offered several regular
ranch jobs but the chill winds were blowing and he drifted
southward in company with a rawhide Texan called Powder
Kent who claimed he never felt right too long away from the
Brazos. Monte carried a Winchester in a saddle scabbard
now and occasionally he picked off an antelope and he and
Powder camped together, roasting meat on sticks over a fire,
and they drifted along, stopping at what towns they came to
for a look around and sometimes acquiring extra spending
money by working together in their talk in the right places to
raise interest in Monte's black. Then along down at North
Platte a loser felt aggrieved and insisted on an argument with
Powder who had needled him into a too-big bet and Powder
felt obliged to live up to his name and use a little gunpowder,
since the loser was already making motions toward the same
with the result that, though the loser was in considerably
worse condition, Powder had a bullet hole in one leg. Powder
was a good hand, right comforting to have along in a tight
spot, but not exactly Monte's style, too serious and touchy
about being Texas-born and too sorry for Monte not being
the same, and Monte left him snug in a boardinghouse for-
tified with the recent winnings and the attentions of a solici-

tous landlady and drifted on alone. Early spring found him riding the rough string for one of the new ranches taking over west Texas. The foreman wanted him to stay on but when the first round of branding was done and the work slackened some and far over the horizon the dust of the trail herds hovered over the big land, he asked for his time.

* * *

Monte Walsh, coming twenty-one, lean and hard and squint-eyed from wind and sun, came up the new trail westward from the old Dodge City riding point with a Seven Z herd of wild woolly longhorns combed out of the brush below the Neuces. When the trail boss, who had lost ten dollars two days before betting on a sleek good-looking bay against the black, grinned somewhat devilish and cut to Monte's string five of the meanest trickiest half-wild horses any man might dare to straddle, Monte grinned too. That merely made life more interesting. Of a morning when he would swing up on one of them to top it off before the day's work, he enjoyed the wide-eyed admiration of a sixteen-year-old kid named Sonny Jacobs who was along wrangling the cavvy. Likely he strutted and showed off some for Sonny. There was no strutting when he was at work, a good all-around trail hand earning every dollar of his pay.

* * *

Sum it in a single sentence that would tell it all to any of his own breed: Monte Walsh came to Dodge the way a one-time thin knobby boy had known it could be, tall in the saddle, riding point with as hard-working and hard-playing and competent an outfit as ever came up a trail.

* * *

"Mister Walsh? Who's he? Oh-h-h, you mean Monte. Whyn't you say so? Yep, I know him. Last time I seen him was down at a little old one-trough town in the handle. Behaving about as usual. Which if you don't know what that means you don't rightly know Monte. They had a little old one-room jail in the place. Had a man in it doing three days.

Old Jake Hanlon. He wasn't so old but they just called him that from the way he couldn't hold his liquor and had to blow his stack regular. Interfered with the steady drinkers. The judge—he was only a justice of the peace but he could judge right enough and make it stick—the judge he'd fined every cent Old Jake had out of him already so this time he said three days. He was a three-day judge. Used that so often it could come popping out without him having even to think. This particular day Old Martha Higgs had to go on a rampage. She wasn't so old too but they just called her that from the way she tried to run things all the time. She was a terror, that woman. A terror on temp'rance. Came from Kansas. Always fighting the Demon Rum though I don't recall rum ever being liked much in those parts, only whisky. No kids, no man, no nothing else to keep her occupied. So this particular day she gets herself all cooked up over some pamphlet or other and comes into Mike's place and starts blasting bottles off the shelves with a shotgun. Sheriff runs in and grabs her. Mike makes such a fuss they take her to the judge. He starts saying something about a fine and she bellers she ain't paying not a single cent, even if she had it, for doing the Lord's work and the judge he gets kind of peeved and it pops out. Three days. Sheriff howls he can't do that, there's only one room, Old Jake's in there already. Immoral. Scandalous. Things like that. But the judge has his dander up and he says he's said it and got it writ down already and that's that. Not his problem, he says, carrying out the sentence, only giving it. Sheriff is yanking out his mustache and arguing with the judge and making motions like maybe going after the judge with his own gavel and all us gathered around are near choking and that's when Monte speaks up. Marry 'em, he says. Man and wife, he says, can occupy one room together all legal and proper. That notion takes hold like a fire to dry grass with a wind behind it. We're going to have a wedding right then and there despite all the bellering Old Martha and Old Jake too when he hears and even the judge himself can do. That or use some ropes, we kind of suggests, maybe not really meaning it but meaning it enough to get the notion across. I remember Chalkeye putting it that a woman cantankerous enough to go blasting wild with a shotgun where innocent folks might get killed and a man who couldn't hold his liquor proper and gets hisself where he'd have to be in close

and indecent proximity to an unmarried person of the oppo-
site sex didn't have no call to be standing out against popular
demands. Then that Monte pulls another one. Got to be a
ticket affair, he says. Makes everybody ante up two dollars
apiece to watch the tying. The whole town turns out along
with all us roughnecks passing through and Old Jake's eyes
bug some and Old Martha slows on her bellering when he
dumps close to three hundred fifty in her sunbonnet. I ain't
heard lately but last I knew them two was making out fair
enough. Old Jake keeping sober and Old Martha too busy
keeping him that way to worry the regulars at Mike's."

Two of a Kind
1879

DUSK DROPPED GENTLY over Dodge. Lean and long in the patch
of lamplight, Monte Walsh emerged through the open doorway of a small barbershop into the relative quiet of early
evening along Front Street. Three times he had been here
and each time the town surprised him with its growth. It was
not as wide open as it had been last year or the year before
that but still there was plenty to keep a man occupied while
he got rid of his hard-earned pay. He rubbed a hand down a
smooth-shaven cheek and sniffed himself in slow satisfaction.
"Just like a flower," he murmured. "I reckon she'll like that."
He ambled lazily along the street, considering the possibilities
of temporary time-passing entertainment.

A sudden burst of shouts and guffaws came from one of
the lesser saloons. A man's head appeared over the doors,
looking out. "Hey, Monte," he called. "Come on in here.
This is good."

Monte ambled over and in. A dozen or more men, including the bartender, were standing in a tight circle around a
small table. As Monte approached they opened the circle to
take him in and he saw, sitting beside the table, a big burly
man in a patched jacket. On the table was an empty gallon
clear-glass jug. Not quite empty. Coiled in the bottom, shifting coils angrily, head raised, was a small rattlesnake.

"Tell 'im, Bert. Go ahead, tell 'im."

"Why, sure," said the burly man. "There ain't nothin' to it.
You just put your hand on that bottle and leave it there while
that pet a mine strikes. You leave it there an' I pay you a
dollar. Easiest money you ever made."

"You don't say," murmured Monte.

"Of course," said the burly man, "if you don't, you pay me a dollar."

Monte looked around at the expectant faces. "Any of you made money at it?" They regarded him in silence, expectant, waiting.

"Of course," said the burly man, "if you ain't got nerve enough . . ."

Monte's jaw tightened. He fished in a pocket and took out a silver dollar and laid it on the table. He leaned forward and placed his right hand, fingers outstretched, against the side of the jug. Instantly the snake struck, blunt head smacking against the glass, and Monte's hand leaped back. Fresh shouts and guffaws broke from the others. The burly man reached and took the dollar.

Slowly Monte straightened, staring down at his hand. "What do'you know," he murmured. "Acted like it didn't even belong to me." His jaw tightened again. He pulled out another dollar and laid this on the table. He leaned forward and gripped the table edge with his left hand and placed his right hand against the jug. The snake was still, motionless, with head raised.

"It's got to strike," said the burly man.

Tiny drops of sweat appeared on Monte's forehead. A tremor of effort ran down his right arm. His forefinger moved on the glass and the snake struck and the arm, instinctive, involuntary, leaped back.

Men shouted and pummeled each other around the table. The burly man reached for the dollar. Monte stared down at his hand. "Why, goddamn it," he said. "If I didn't need that thing, I'd cut it off and throw it away."

"There ain't nobody can do it," said the burly man, expansive, grinning. "Got somethin' to do with your arm actin' before your head can stop it. Expect I've got me enough dollars to set 'em up for all you boys."

Time passed, pleasantly warmed with whisky, and two more victims had been enticed in and paid their dollars and a third, bullet-headed, big-nosed, needing no enticement, had stumbled in, needing no additional cargo of whisky to make him mildly belligerent.

"Ain't no stinkin' little ol' snake gonna bluff me," he said.

His dollar was on the table. His hand was on the jug. The snake struck and the hand jumped back a few inches then forward again against the jug and the man glared around at the guffawing others. His hand moved again, away from the jug, and kept on moving and, as he straightened, took the gun from the holster at his side and the men across the table from him leaped aside. The first shot shattered the jug and the snake slithered through broken glass toward the edge of the table. The second shot put a hole through the table top, taking the snake's head with it. The big-nosed man dropped the gun into its holster and looked about, triumphant.

The burly man rose from his chair, took off his patched jacket, laid this over the back of the chair. "I don't like that," he said. "I don't like it at all." He plunged toward the big-nosed man and was met halfway.

The table banged over, catching another man on the shins. He hopped, yipping, and struck out and hit another in the stomach, who promptly replied in what seemed appropriate manner. The contagion spread. The little saloon began to fill with fine tension-easing activity. The bartender retreated behind his bar and watched in routine resignation.

Monte Walsh, eyes alight, picked the likeliest tangle of hammering humanity and started forward. He stopped. He backed away toward the doorway. "Can't go getting mussed up," he murmured. "Not tonight." He slipped out and moved along the street, away from the sounds of carnage behind him. He pushed through figures running toward the sounds and ambled steadily on.

One of the figures stopped, turned, came after him. "Hey, Monte boy. I been lookin' for you."

Monte stopped, turned, recognized the trail boss who had paid him off three days before.

"Yep," said the man. "I sure been lookin' for you. When I hear that ruckus I figured you'd be there."

"Me?" murmured Monte. "Just a decent citizen keeping the peace."

"Somethin' wrong?" said the man. "You sick?" He sniffed. "Smellin' pretty too. Well, anyways, I got a wire from the old man this afternoon. He's got another bunch of cows he wants shoved up here while the grass is still good."

"My oh my," murmured Monte. "Go to working again while I still got money in my pocket?"

"You still got money?" said the man. "You gettin' old? Slowin' down?"

"Shucks, no," said Monte. "Just learning to stretch it out some."

"That's gettin' old," said the man. "Come on. I found some of the others still around. We'll be pullin' out in an hour."

"Not me," said Monte. "I got other ideas."

"Hope they backfire an' blow you somewheres hot," said the man. "You got any other notions might help me?"

"Shorty Austin's in there," said Monte. "Getting an ear chewed off."

"So you was there," said the man. "An' now you're out here. Beats me. Well, anyways, Shorty might do. See you sometime." He moved away, toward the now diminishing sounds of battle.

* * *

Monte Walsh sat by the rim of a round table at the rear of the Long Branch Saloon, a small pile of chips in front of him, paying scant attention to his cards, dropping out of most hands. Elsewhere around the rim sat the impassive black-coated black-mustached houseman, the stout proprietor of a funeral parlor, a young square-built trail-worn cowhand with a short stubby pipe sticking out of round stubbly face, a thin hopeful clerk from the Lone Star general store, a prosperous-looking watch-chained man who could have been a banker, a nondescript narrow-eyed man who could have been anything at all. Monte paid them little more attention than he did his cards. He was waiting out Dodge's recent rule that ladies of the evening should not adorn the evening until it had progressed to midnight.

Monte played along, nursing his chips. He sat somewhat sideways on his chair so he could watch the front end of the bar and the swinging doors beyond. He took a cigarette paper from one shirt pocket, a small tobacco bag from the other. He cradled the paper in one hand and shook the bag over it with the other. A few flakes fell out. He crumpled the bag and tossed it over a shoulder and contemplated the cradled paper in disgust. A small leather pouch landed with a soft thud on the table in front of him. He shook tobacco from the pouch and tossed it back. "Thanks," he said to the stubbly-faced cowhand across the table.

Smoke lifted in two thin streamers from Monte's nose. He won a small pot and even that failed to interest him much. The hopeful clerk left the game, temporarily out of hope, and his place was taken by a railroad section hand.

Business improved along the bar. Two women in attire once gay now like them showing signs of wear came in and were greeted and absorbed into the increasing press by the long brass rail. Monte fidgeted on his chair. Another woman, frowsy in limp-feathered big hat, entered and stood just inside the doorway.

Monte rose from his chair and laid his hat on it. He strode forward. "Beg pardon, ma'am," he said. "Where's Miss Lillie?"

"Who cares?" said the woman.

"She told me she'd be here," said Monte.

"Ain't you heard, honey?" said the woman. "She left on the train this afternoon with that cattle buyer from Kansas City." The woman took hold of Monte's arm. "Come on, honey. Let's you and me have a drink."

"The hell with her," said Monte, pulling away. He strode back to his chair, stopping on the way to push in by the bar and acquire a beer mug full of whisky. He jammed his hat on his head, sat down, set the mug on the table in front of him, shoved a hand into a pants pocket. "Give me another stack," he said to the houseman. "I'm a-going to bust this game wide open."

*　*　*

Monte Walsh woke by degrees, regretting the necessity of waking at all. Something large and lumpy and sharp-cornered inside his head seemed to be trying to break out and a bruise along one temple throbbed in rhythm with the disturbance within. He moved a bit and became aware of assorted aches in other portions of his anatomy. His neck muscles complained but he raised his head anyway.

He lay on a built-in plank cot along the wall of a small solidly constructed room. Beyond his upturned boots he could see a doorway snugly holding a crisscross of stout iron bars. A small patch of sunlight on the floor by it spoke of a small high window behind him with its own bars.

"Nice morning."

Monte turned his head slowly. Six feet away on another plank cot along the opposite wall sat the tobacco-pouch cowhand, more stubbly-faced than before, more worn but not from trail riding, looking about as battered as Monte felt.

Monte groaned and sat up, swinging feet around to the floor. "Jugged," he said. "What in hell for?"

"I been studying on that," said the other. "I figure you got to thinking there was something funny about the game and couldn't make it out so you just started taking the whole place apart." He regarded Monte, round stubbly face solemn, interested. "You were doing right well. Till a batch of deputies came in."

"My oh my," murmured Monte, exploring his head with cautious fingers. "So that was me. How about you?"

"I was kind of thinking the same," said the other. "So somehow I kind of got mixed up in it too."

Monte finished his survey of injuries. A small wry grin showed on his bruised lips. "Must have been a humdinger," he said.

"From what I can remember," said the other.

* * *

"Monte Walsh." The plump man seated behind a wide solid table read the name aloud from a piece of paper in front of him and looked up over his spectacles. "Which one is he?"

"Shucks," said Monte, morose, rubbing his aching head. "You know me. I bought this shirt off you at your store a couple days ago."

"Not before in my official capacity," said the plump man. He swiveled his eyes over the spectacles toward the half dozen onlookers. "What did he have on him?"

"Not much," said a big man, coatless, with a badge pinned to his vest. "Thirteen dollars and thirty-five cents."

"H-m-m-m-m," said the plump man. "We will temper justice to the shorn lamb. Three dollars costs and ten dollars fine and we will return the thirty-five cents." He looked down again at the paper. "Chester Rollins."

"Chet," said the stubbly-faced square-built cowhand standing beside Monte.

"Chet or Chester," said the plump man. "We are not particular." He swiveled eyes again. "And what did he have?"

"Fifty-seven dollars," said the man with the badge.

"Remarkable," said the plump man.

"He ain't been in town long," said the man with the badge.

"Ah, yes," said the plump man. "So we can go the limit. Same costs and twenty-five dollars."

"Hey," said Monte, indignant. "That ain't fair."

"What has fair to do with it?" said the plump man. "The town and me, we can use the money and the law allows it."

"Goddamn it!" said Monte. "I say it ain't fair!"

"Quit it, Monte," said the plump man, forgetting to be official. "Want me to hold you in contempt?"

"Contempt!" yelled Monte. "I got plenty of that!" He plunged forward and took hold of the table and heaved it up and over onto the plump man. He swung to face the onlookers converging now on him and plowed into them, sending one staggering from hunched shoulder, driving a knee into the stomach of another. He plowed on, fists flying.

"Ain't he something," said the big man with the badge, tapping him over the head from behind with a gun barrel.

* * *

Monte Walsh woke again by degrees, regretting again the necessity of waking at all. He lay on the same built-in cot in the same small room. One item was different. The crisscross of bars that was the door was wide open. Monte groaned and rolled his head sideways.

"You didn't do so well this time," said Chet Rollins from his perch on the other cot.

"I didn't see you doing a damn thing," said Monte.

"No," said Chet. "I figured what we had left wouldn't cover more'n one."

Monte sat up, swinging feet to floor, and looked at the open doorway.

"Why, yes," said Chet. "They didn't even wait on the second round. Figured to go ahead while you couldn't talk back. Went the limit on you too. But we can walk out anytime."

Monte conducted another exploration of his anatomy. Suddenly he looked up. "Hey," he said. "That must of about cleaned you out."

"Sure did," said Chet.

"Silly way to go throwing money around," said Monte.

"Ain't it," said Chet. "Come on. I still got a dollar, you got thirty-five cents coming, we can eat good on that."

* * *

Monte Walsh and Chet Rollins sat on the top rail of a small corral fronting on Front Street beside a livery stable. They sat in relaxed full-fed somnolence soaking up afternoon sun. Behind them in the corral lay two two-year-old tame buffalo, pride of the stable proprietor, equally somnolent in the dust except for skin twitchings to dislodge flies.

"I ought to be scratching around for a job," said Monte. "Needing food the way I do. Mighty regular." He took out a pocket-knife and began cleaning dirt from under his blunt fingernails. "I expect tomorrow'll do," he said.

One of the buffalo stood up, shook dust out of its shaggy pelt, lay down again. Chet extracted his stubby pipe from a pocket and began filling it from the small leather pouch. "I could get me a job on the cars," he said. "Punching up cows with a shipment to Chicago. I've done that before."

"Chicago," said Monte. He snapped the knife shut and tucked it away. He took out a cigarette paper and reached a hand for the pouch. "My oh my," he murmured. "So you've been to the big city."

"Born there," said Chet. He lit a match and held it over the pipe and puffed smoke slowly, lazily. "That is, about forty miles out. My folks had a farm." He blew a small smoke ring and tried to flip the burnt-out match through it. "But I don't intend letting anybody know ever again I can handle a plow."

Monte struck his own match. Smoke from pipe and cigarette floated upward in the still air. The buffalo drowsed in the corral dust.

"That fat one with the watch chain," said Monte. "I bet he was the one."

"And that squint-eyed runt alongside you," said Chet. "They must of been working together. Feeding each other cards."

The other buffalo stood up, shook out dust, pawed more

over itself, lay down again. Smoke floated lazily upward over the fence rails.

"Maybe I ought to go find them," said Monte. "I could do with knocking some heads together."

"Ain't you had enough?" said Chet. "Who'd bail you out this time?" He blew another small smoke ring and poked a finger through it. "Your own fault anyways. You ought to know better'n to sit in on a game like that."

"I seem to remember you sitting in," said Monte.

"Well, now, yes," said Chet, amiable, conversational. "Now you mention it, so I was."

Two heavy wagons rumbled by, moving down the street toward the depot. Far off a train tootled. The proprietor of the livery stable came out and strolled down the street after the wagons.

"This town ain't been treating me right," said Monte. He held his cigarette stub out and inspected it carefully. "Not so you'd notice." He took a last drag on the stub and flicked it away as it burned his fingers. He licked the fingers and held them up to cool. "I'd sure like to scramble it some," he said.

Down the street by the depot a crowd was collecting. The train came in and with it a theatrical troupe billed for an evening performance at the opera house. An eight-piece band emerged from the crowd, resplendent in red jackets and bearskin caps, led by a baton-twirling bandmaster with very high bearskin hat, followed by two men carrying a banner on poles. Behind them rumbled the two heavy wagons, gay now with bunting decorations, carrying luggage and the frilled and fur-belowed ladies of the troupe. Behind them, brave in colorful costumes, marched the male performers and a good portion of the depot crowd. The procession moved up the street, bass drum booming, horns blatting. People popped out of buildings along the way to watch, some of them stepping out to join the parade.

Monte Walsh and Chet Rollins swiveled heads slowly as the noise and the splendor passed by. Behind them in the corral the two buffalo heaved to their feet and shifted restlessly, snorting some, pawing the ground. Monte turned his head to look at them. "Those things don't appreciate that racket much," he said.

The procession moved on up the street, more people filling in behind. Monte looked again at the husky young buffalo pawing and throwing dust. He shifted on the rail to turn toward Chet.

"You mean it?" said Chet.

"Double damn right I do," said Monte.

Chet sighed, the glint in his eyes belying the sigh. "All right," he said. "It could be kind of interesting."

Monte swung legs over the top rail and dropped down inside the corral. "Get the gate," he said, "while I shoo 'em out."

Monte circled behind the buffalo, shouting and waving his arms. They moved away from him and saw the gate opening and headed for it and out into the street. Monte was close after them, joined by Chet, and together, yipping and waving hats, they turned the two on up the street. They picked up stones and threw these thumping against rumps and the two buffalo, frightened, confused, broke into a trot, overtaking the tag end of the procession.

Startled squeals and shoutings resounded along Front Street and the parade stragglers scattered, seeking shelter fast, and the two buffalo, frantic now and beginning to feel belligerent about that, broke into a gallop, short tails up stiff, and charged forward, butting and hooking and kicking in stride. The teams of the two wagons plunged and reared, tangling in harness, and the drivers struggled with reins, trying to shout above the female screeches chorusing behind them. The whole parade dissolved into a wild scramble and the two buffalo, detouring around the wagons, plowed on into the rear of the band. Red jackets leaped in various directions, dropping instruments and losing bearskin caps. The bandmaster made the mistake of standing his ground and smacking one of the buffalo on the nose with his baton and immediately thereafter lit out with it hard on his heels.

Monte Walsh and Chet Rollins stood very still in the street watching in solemn satisfaction. They saw people diving through doorways, shinnying up lampposts, climbing on fences and falling back in their hurry and climbing again. They saw horses breaking loose from tie rails and adding to the general confusion in the enthusiasm of frantic action. They saw the bass drum bounce about, impaled on a horn of one buffalo. They saw the bandmaster crash headlong through a store window, followed by the other buffalo.

"My oh my," murmured Monte. "I feel some better."

"Yep," said Chet. "But take a look over there."

Monte looked. In the wake of the confusion people were gathering in small groups, talking angrily, and several were pointing at him and Chet.

"Oh, oh," said Monte. "Where's your horse?"

"Back of the stable there," said Chet.

"So's mine," said Monte. "Let's move."

* * *

Monte Walsh and Chet Rollins, with the dust of Dodge well behind them, drifted southeastward from cow camp to ranch house to cow camp along the grub line and rode into Caldwell one fine sunny morning. In half an hour they had temporary jobs with an outfit that was changing road brands on a herd near the edge of town for delivery on north somewhere and wanted to get off in a hurry. Monte handled a branding iron and he looked up when he could to watch Chet, quiet and steady, swinging a loop on his sturdy short-coupled bay and never missing a cast and throwing stout steers with a simple thoroughness that made hog-tying for the iron relatively easy. When the outfit departed two days later they had a little betting money and they wandered over to the bottoms between Fall and Bluff Creeks where Caldwell horsemen settled their bets and Chet watched Monte swing up on his big rangy black and ride like a bat let loose from hell and lose once and win twice and then they had what could be called spending money.

* * *

Dawn, cool and clean, crept through Caldwell. Behind the stockyards in an ell of outer fence Monte Walsh stirred in his blanket and tarp and stretched like a lazy young animal. He flipped the covering aside and sat up and pressed the heels of both hands to his forehead. As usual on the morning after an expansive evening two small trip-hammers beat in his temples. He looked to the left where Chet Rollins lay in his own rigging, serene in sleep. "My oh my," murmured Monte. "Ain't he peaceful. Old hollow-legs himself."

Monte reached for his boots and pulled them on. He pushed up and walked, somewhat unsteady, following the fence around until he came to an iron-handled pump with a bucket under the spout. He worked the handle vigorously and had a bucketful of water. He lifted this and rinsed his mouth out and drank deep and bent forward and down, raising the bucket higher, and emptied it over his head. He set the bucket down and stretched again, lazy and long, and as usual the beating faded from his temples and he was fully awake and life flowed steady and strong in him. He took a bandanna from a pants pocket and wiped his face, and a broken piece of comb from another pocket and ran this through his hair. He ambled back along the fence and rolled up his bedding. He looked at Chet, still serene in sleep, and a small grin showed on his lips.

He wandered around, searching, and found a dry hard prickly weed. He broke off several small pieces and came back and stood by Chet's boots. "Puts on the left one first," he murmured and dropped the pieces into the right boot and tilted the boot so that these slid forward into the toe.

Not far away on the fence hung a heavy old trace chain. He ambled over and lifted this down. He moved toward Chet dragging the chain behind him. As he approached, swerving to come close past Chet's head, he picked up speed and stomped feet down hard and shook the chain into loud jangly rattling. "Whoa!" he shouted. "Whoa, you bastards! Whoa!"

Chet snapped out of sleep, groggy, confused, and jack-knifed up to sitting position. Frantic in haste he flipped over, scrambling on hands and knees. His feet tangled in blanket and tarp and he went flat, face in the dirt. He rolled over and lay still as silence settled in the ell of outer stockyard fence.

He raised his head and saw Monte, perched now on the top rail of the fence, doubled down in silent laughter.

"You're so goddamned childish," said Chet, "you ain't even born yet." Slowly, reaching for dignity, he untangled his feet, stood up, straightened out his bedding and rolled it. He picked up his left boot, looked again at Monte and back to the boot, turned it upside down and shook it. He wiped the bottom of his left foot on his right pants leg and pulled the left boot on, struggling to get the foot into the tight fit. He stood on his left booted foot and picked up the right boot and wiped the bottom of his right foot on his left pants leg and pulled the right boot on, struggling again to get the foot down in.

The foot went in with a little rush and he jerked back, hopping on his left booted foot, and toppled sideways and down.

"Having trouble?" said Monte from his perch on the rail.

Silent, slow, sitting on the ground, Chet tugged at the right boot. He held it up by the sole, shaking it. The pieces of prickly weed, crushed now, fell out. He picked up one small piece and studied it carefully. He flipped it away and struggled to pull the boot on again. He stood up, round stubbly face serene and untroubled, and moved over to confront Monte on his perch.

"Had yourself some fun, didn't you?" said Chet, amiable, conversational.

"Now you mention it," said Monte. "Why, yes, I sure did."

"It's my turn," said Chet. Suddenly his hands gripped Monte's boots at the ankles and he yanked out and flipped up and Monte went over backwards and down to land inside on neck and shoulders with a squashy sound in a small pile of almost-fresh manure, legacy of a batch of steers shipped out the day before.

* * *

Monte Walsh and Chet Rollins sat limp and relaxed on straight-back chairs by a square table near the one big fly-specked front window of the Red Light Saloon. Sunlight through the window, filtering on through dust motes in the air, lay warm and lazy on the tabletop and on the two worn hats and the two small empty glasses there. Behind the long bar the single day bartender humped on a high stool reading a newspaper. At another table farther back a shirtsleeved man wearing a celluloid collar sat fallen forward, head on folded arms on the table, snoring gently. Near the rear where narrow stairs led to the mysterious upper regions two men sat by another table carrying on a low slow conversation about a lease on a store building.

"Lively, aint it," said Monte. "When I was a kid I thought this town quite a place."

"Always dull this time of day," said Chet. "Kind of between times too. It'll pick up again soon as a few outfits come in."

"That ain't now," said Monte. "Wonder what people do

who live here permanent. Watch the train come in? A dog-fight once in a time? Exciting as all get-out."

"They got jobs," said Chet. "One thing about a job it gives you something to do."

Outside a woman in huge sunbonnet and high choke-neck dress with a bustle under its long voluminous folds behind and with a market basket on her arm passed by the window.

"Not even worthwhile looking at women," said Monte. "Hide themselves inside tents and all kinds of metal contraptions."

A door opened somewhere above. Footsteps sounded on the rear stairway, swish-slap of loose slippers flapping. A woman with straggly dyed red hair up in paper curlers, face haggard and grayish without its usual coating of powder and rouge, body sagging and almost shapeless in a soiled old wrapper, came down and moved along the room and behind the bar. She said something to the bartender who grunted some reply without even bothering to look at her. She took a bottle from a shelf by the long mirror and went back to the stairway and up. The sound of slapping old slippers floated through the big room and died away.

"My oh my," murmured Monte. "That's even worse. And I used to think those things here were really something."

"They were," said Chet. "Once."

"Funny, ain't it," said Monte. "After a month or two on the trail working your fool tail off you come into a town and something like that with its warpaint on looks right good. After a few days somehow they don't seem the same."

"Not so funny," said Chet. "Only natural. You get real hungry, need a meal real bad, even sowbelly tastes good. After a while when you ain't so hungry you start thinking of steak."

Monte reached out a cupped hand, slow, cautious, toward a fly on the table. The hand moved in sudden arc, closing, and he squeezed fingers in along the palm and opened them to let the tiny corpse drop to the floor. "Shucks," he said. "I guess I ain't so hungry. I been thinking . . ."

He stopped. Outside somewhere a snare drum was sounding, a sharp tattoo.

Monte and Chet looked at each other. They rose, taking hats from the table, and moved to the doorway and out.

Down the street, drawn into a vacant lot between two

frame buildings, was a large wagon, a van, high-sided and topped, a huge rectangular box on wheels. It was painted in bright reds and yellows, scrolled and curlicued. On each side, arched around a small glassed and curtained window in wonderfully convoluted letters, appeared the legend: DOCTOR GREGORY'S PATENTED PAIN-KILLER. AN ANCIENT INDIAN REMEDY IMPROVED AND STRENGTHENED BY MODERN SCIENCE. The back of the van, one solid chunk of planking hinged at the bottom, had been let down to rest on stout wooden legs and form a platform. Hinged wings had been unfolded to rest on other wooden legs and widen the platform. A full curtain hung down, masking the interior of the van.

On the right wing an elderly Negro, gray wool of hair topping a seamed black face, lank body encased in old work clothes livened by a short yellow jacket with red fringes, sat on a low stool. A snare drum, suspended from a band around his neck, hung down between his knees. A framework of wire sat on his shoulders and cupped the back of his head and came forward to hold a mouth organ about an inch in front of his mouth. His hands moved with the drumsticks and a superb rhythmic clatter came from the drum.

Men were emerging from various doorways, moving toward the sound. Monte and Chet ambled down the street, joining in the general movement. A small crowd had already assembled by the platform. They eased in for good views.

The drummer jutted chin forward and his lips found the mouth organ. The strains of "Dixie" started toes tapping in the dust. Monte jigged a few steps, slapped Chet on the back. "That ain't bad," he said.

The music stopped. The curtain flapped aside and a man stepped out. Tall, made taller by a gray stovepipe hat. Ends of longish gray hair curled out from under the hat. Heavy eyebrows and a waxed mustache and a pointed beard hid most of the face and what was not hidden had a ruddy overblown look. A red- and yellow-checked vest under a dark brown frock coat worn to smooth sheen in strategic places did its best to cover a plump middle. Gray trousers, stained and sadly wrinkled, led down to frayed endings over old shoes, one of which had a hole cut out to make way for a bunion.

"Ladeees and gentlemen," he said, voice rolling rich and

throaty. He looked over his audience. There were no ladies present. He cleared his throat and dismissed the fact with a dignified wave of hand. "Let me simply say: Friends. I am here in your enterprising community in pursuit of my campaign against the ills and the ailments, the aches and the pains, that beset mankind. A worthy cause. A most worthy cause. But I will not tell you now of the miraculous powers of my secret elixir. No, not if you cry out and beg on bended knee. I will not distribute even a single bottle of it at this time. No, not at any price. But this evening—"

"Quit foggin', Doc," came a voice from the crowd. "Show us what you got behind that curtain."

Dr. Gregory beamed at the speaker. "You anticipate me, my friend. But I can not blame you. No, not at all. I myself am thrilled at the surprise I have in store for you. Fresh from engagements in the glittering palaces of Kansas City. Fresh from triumphant triumphs in—. But no. I will not keep you in suspense. Miss Francine Floriston, the Nightingale of the Prairies!"

Dr. Gregory bowed, swept off his stovepipe hat, stepped onto the left wing of the platform. The curtain flapped aside again and the nightingale emerged. Full figure, plenty of it, ample in curves well-proportioned, not needing yet and not having the discipline of a corset. Neat ankles under a short pleated skirt, swelling hips, trim waist, deep bosom, rounded shoulders rising out of low-cut blouse. Baby-doll face, made so by makeup unable to mask the full knowing maturity of the features beneath.

Miss Francine Floriston stepped forward on the platform; hips swaying slightly, just enough, and stood there, easy, assured, listening to the whistles and shouts of the assembled males.

"What d'you know," murmured Monte Walsh.

"Steak," murmured Chet Rollins.

Miss Francine Floriston assessed her audience, turned her head toward the right wing. "Make it 'Sal,' " she said.

The elderly Negro laid down his drumsticks and took a small whiskbroom from a pocket. Gently he swished this on the drum. His jaw jutted forward and his lips found the mouth organ.

Miss Francine Floriston began to sway with the music.

Her hips moved with it, more and more, more than enough. She put her head back and opened her mouth and began to sing, voice raucous and ringing with vitality.

> "Hare-lipped Sal, she was a beaut,
> She wore a number nine.
> She kicked the hat off a Texas Galoot
> To the tune of Auld Lang Syne."

Abruptly she stopped and the music with her. She turned her head slowly, looking over the assorted townsmen. Her glance stopped on the lean length of Monte Walsh and the square-built solidity of Chet Rollins. Stopped. And lingered. "Howdy, boys," she said and turned and lifted the curtain and disappeared behind it.

Dr. Gregory held the platform. His throaty voice commanded the scene. "A sample, friends. Only a sample. There will be a full performance this evening. Recitations from the finest dramas of the ages. Songs in her inimitable manner by the incomparable Miss Francine. Free booklets of medical wisdom. Yes, free. Absolutely free. Come one, come all. Bring your friends and your families. This evening. At eight of the clock." With a bow and a sweep of stovepipe hat Dr. Gregory too disappeared behind the curtain.

The crowd, buzzing satisfactorily, began to disperse. A man in overalls and dirty flannel shirt jumped up on the platform. "Cock fight!" he shouted. "At Murray's stable! Jim Magee's Calico Killer defending! In half an hour! Fifty cents!" He jumped down and strode away.

The crowd, except for a few hopefuls still watching the curtain, faded away. Monte and Chet, tagging others, ambled on down the street toward Murray's livery stable. "What d'you know," murmured Monte. "Out of nowhere just like that."

They ambled on. "We could flip a coin," said Chet.

"Oh, no you don't," said Monte. "I could lose that way. This is going to be wide open."

They ambled on. "Yep," said Monte. "One good look at that homely face of yours and you'll be out of it."

"Don't be so all-fired sure," said Chet. "I expect she ain't interested only in faces."

"Tell you what," said Monte, bouncing a bit off his toes. "Just for the hell of it, I'll bet you five dollars I beat your time tonight."

* * *

Monte Walsh emerged through the open doorway of a small barbershop into the dimness of evening along the main street of Caldwell. He rubbed a hand down one smooth-shaven cheek and sniffed himself in slow satisfaction. Across the way by the vacant lot between two frame buildings a surprising number of people were crowded together, faces turned toward and lit by the light from lanterns strung on a rope between the two buildings and others on the outer edge of the platform of Dr. Gregory's van. Two small boys squirmed through the crowd distributing pamphlets filled with medical advice on all manner of ailments which invariably ended in recommendations for liberal doses of the patented painkiller. Dr. Gregory himself, on the platform with a once-purple cloak swirling about him and a tin something vaguely resembling a helmet replacing the stovepipe hat on his head, was temporarily the ruler of some far exotic land exhorting unseen warriors in rich sonorous phrases to show themselves like men and fight like bears at bay.

Monte looked up and down the street, at the stragglers moving to join the audience. "Where'd he go and get to?" he murmured. "I ain't seen him since supper."

Monte strolled along and across the street and began pushing in through the crowd. Miss Francine Floriston was on the platform in a sparse spangled gown wailing "Green Grow the Lilacs" with much heaving of bosom and appropriate gestures of grief. Monte, in the front row now, regarded her with complete uncomplicated approval.

Dr. Gregory, in patched long black cape with one end swung gallantly up over a shoulder and a cocked hat with a feather on his head, was a stern aristocratic father upbraiding an invisible profligate son for betraying the innocence of an invisible lovely maiden. Indifferent to such histrionics, Monte stretched tall and stood on boot-toes to peer around through the crowd. "Anything happened to him?" he murmured. "He sure ain't here at all."

Miss Francine Floriston, with a miner's cap atop her piled

curls and a small pick in her hands, prospected about the platform in pantomime, found an invisible nugget, held it up,
archly joyed at her good fortune. She threw back her head
and swung into "Clementine," raucous and rowdy and conta-
gious. Monte's chest swelled and all of him exuded whole-
hearted admiration. He led the applause until his hands hurt
and his throat was raw.

Dr. Gregory, stovepipe hat back in place, was himself
again, full of sympathy for the ills and ailments of mankind,
full of benevolence he would be willing to dispense in the
form of his secret elixir. The elderly Negro was bringing
boxes containing luridly labeled bottles from behind the curtain. Someone pulled on Monte's sleeve. He looked down
into the pinched whiskery face of the meager little man who
was handyman at Murray's stable.

"Beat it," said Monte. "I'm busy."

The little man held to the sleeve, kept tugging. "Hey,
Monte," he said, voice low, excited. "Come outa this a minute. You better hurry." He led to dark shadow back along
the frame building to the right.

"All right, all right," said Monte. "Make it fast. I got
things to do."

"Sh-h-h-h," said the little man. "Keep it down. There's a
couple deputies in town. From Dodge. Maybe out there in
that crowd. They got warrants."

"Goddamn it," said Monte. "How d'you know?"

"I seen 'em," said the little man. "I heard 'em. You an'
Rollins. You was mixed in somethin' in Dodge, wasn't you?
People got hurt."

"Luck and me," moaned Monte. "It ain't ever anything but
bad. Where is he?"

"Rollins?" said the little man. "He was lookin' for you.
Had to scat. They mighty near had him. He got your hosses
an' snuck out. Know that old barn out by the bottoms? He
said you was to keep outa sight an' meet 'im there."

Monte gnawed a knuckle. "A time like this," he said. He
looked around. The little man was gone.

Monte pulled his hat down, low, and moved forward to the
edge of light. Over at an angle he saw Miss Francine, flushed
and moist from her previous exertions, preparing to jump
very prettily from the platform to the ground with a basket
full of bottles on one arm. He forced himself to look away.

A small shock ran through him as he recognized, near the outer edge of the crowd, a big man with a badge pinned to his vest.

Monte gnawed a knuckle again. "Damn oh damn oh damn," he moaned softly. He moved back along the building and struck out, striding fast, into the deeper darkness.

* * *

By the abandoned shell of a barn nearly a mile and a half out of town Monte Walsh stood, quiet, listening into the night. There was no sound anywhere. He went in through the doorless doorway and moved about in the dimness of starlight through the huge holes in the roof. Empty. Nothing there. He stood outside and called, low at first then louder. There was no response. "Funny," he murmured. "Damn funny. He should of beat me here."

Time passed. Monte waited, gnawing on knuckles. "Wonder if they got him," he murmured. "I didn't see the other one. Might of had him somewheres."

Time passed. Monte stood by the abandoned barn, checking the cylinder of his side gun. "Reckon it's up to me," he muttered. "If they got him, I got to get him." He strode purposefully through the night, back toward town. He skirted low buildings and came to the rear of one with bars across a window frame well up out of reach. The window inside, inside the bars, was open. He picked up a pebble and tossed it up and in between the bars. He heard it fall and roll a bit inside. "Funny," he murmured. "They wouldn't be taking him back till morning." He tried another pebble. Silence, unresponsive, held the rear of the building.

He moved around the corner and along the side of the building to the street. This was deserted now. Across and down in the vacant lot the van was dark, platform folded in and up to become the back again. Patches of lamplight along the near side of the street marked the battery of saloons still in active operation.

Monte worked his way along, stopping at each patch to peer in. He was by the front window of the Red Light, peering through the fly-specked glass. His body stiffened. Inside, by the near end of the bar, flanked by three jovial townsmen, a look of serene contentment on his face, stood Chet Rollins.

The swinging doors flapped wide as Monte strode in.

"Hagen," he said. "Ben Hagen. From Dodge. He's in town."

"Was," said one of the men. "He was just passing through. Asking about some hoss thief."

"You know," said Chet Rollins, beaming at Monte, "I didn't know you would go for it. But I sure hoped."

Monte stood very still. "You better spell that out," he said.

"Simple," said Chet, grinning. "You owe me five dollars."

Monte's eyes narrowed in the rock of his lean young face. The three townsmen, seeing, began to edge away. Monte looked down at his gnawed knuckles clenching into fists then at Chet again. "I owe you something all right," he said. "I owe you a bust in the nose."

"Dollars," said Chet. "You set the rules. You said it was wide open."

"So's this," said Monte. He plunged forward, gnawed knuckles smashing into Chet.

Action, fast and furious, raged in the Red Light. The general impression could have been of a dozen men engaged in a frantic free-for-all. The simple fact was merely two men, honed to rawhide hardness by years on the great .trails, engaged in attempts at mutual mayhem. All others in the saloon scattered to safe viewpoints of advantage. The bar shook. Tables went over. Chairs broke into splintered pieces.

"Wow!" yelled someone. "We ain't had one like this in a month a Sundays!"

Chet Rollins, hat gone, shirt ripped, one eye swelling shut, blood trickling from the corner of his mouth, lay in the wreckage of a chair, dazed, coming back to focus on the proceedings. He rolled over onto hands and knees, shaking his head, and pushed to his feet and dove headlong into Monte's middle, carrying him over backwards.

Chet Rollins, one eye swollen shut, nose mashed and bloody, lips split, lay limp with head and shoulders against an upturned table, dazed, coming back to focus on the fact of his position. He heaved around, grabbed at the upturned table, made it to his feet. Head wobbling, feet dragging, he moved toward Monte.

"Goddamn it!" gasped Monte, wiping blood from his own battered lips. "Dont you know when you're beat?" Chet came on.

Chet Rollins, shirt half gone, mottled bruises emerging on the portions of anatomy exposed, both eyes shut, face an unrecognizable mess, lay sprawled over the low rail along the bar. One eye forced itself open into a thin slit. One hand twitched and moved and had hold of the rail. He heaved and his shoulders were rising. The other hand reached and caught the edge of the bar. He heaved again and was on his feet, leaning over the bar. He pushed around, leaning back against it. Split lips moved. "Getting your money's worth?" came through them. He pushed out, wobbling, and moved toward Monte. His knees buckled and he collapsed downward.

Monte Walsh, lean face lumpy and bloody, shirt hanging in ribbons, chest heaving, stood with legs braced apart, swaying some. He took hold of a shred of shirt and wiped his face, wincing as he wiped. He looked around at the scattered audience emerging from its points of vantage. "Goddamn it," he gasped. "He asked for it, didn't he? He kept coming."

Monte fished in the jagged remnant of a pants pocket and pulled out a crumpled five-dollar bill. He leaned down, having to brace himself with one hand on the floor, tucked the bill into one of Chet's limp hands and closed the fingers around it. He straightened, staring down. Twinges of shame and frustration flicked through him, retreating swiftly into the security of renewed hot anger. "Tell him," he said to one of the bartenders coming forward with a damp cloth, "tell that fat-faced bastard if I never see him again that'll be soon enough." Monte turned and limped to the doorway and out into the night.

* * *

Morning, and Monte Walsh, in new shirt and stiff new jeans, stood in the doorway of a blacksmith shop and watched Dr. Gregory's van move out of town toward the west. "I could follow to the next stop," he murmured. "Sure I could. Nothing's holding me." Somehow the prospect failed to please. He turned back into the shop and to limber his stiffened muscles went to work on the bellows for the smith.

Afternoon, and Monte Walsh strolled along the main street of Caldwell. Across the way, on a chair in the sun in front of a small café, he saw a square-built solid figure also in new shirt and stiff new jeans with pieces of sticking-plaster over its nose. Monte scowled and looked away and strolled on, increasing his pace. Somehow irritated, annoyed at existence in general, he headed for the stockyards and saddled the black and rode out, down the trail, and came on the first of several trail herds spaced by their dust clouds on down, and jogged back along with it, swapping gossip with the men of the outfit.

Evening, and Caldwell was well in stride, busy at the business of extracting dollars from newcomers. Three herds were bedded out beyond the limits. A rail crew had arrived for construction of a spur line. Monte Walsh came down the rear stairway of the Red Light, relaxed and temporarily content. He looked at the poker game in progress at the back table and looked away, scowling some, suddenly not quite so content. He wandered forward and bellied up to the bar. He leaned back against it, drink in hand.

A big slope-shouldered man appeared out of somewhere and pushed in and claimed a drink and turned about, leaning back beside him.

"Howdy, Monte," said Hat Henderson. "It's been a while but I'd know you anywheres. A long while."

"Sure has," said Monte. "So here's to you." He tossed off his drink.

"Right back at you," said Hat, tossing off his. "I been hearing about you, Monte, off and on. Hearing plenty. Looks like I'm in luck tonight." He swung around and acquired two more drinks and swung back and handed one to Monte. "Yeah," he said. "Thought I was through for the season. Been up in Nebrasky. Coming back and a wire catches me. Now I got to take a bunch of cows up to Dakota. Late and it could be rough."

Monte held up his little glass and inspected it against the light of a lamp on out overhead.

"Yeah," said Hat. "I got me a few good hands but not enough. An' I ain't so sure how good they are topping broncs. I remember once way back you said you'd ride any hoss I had. Well, I got me some real raw ones for this trip. All I could find in a hurry. I'm needing somebody to teach 'em some sense while we go along."

Monte regarded his drink in silence. He sipped gently at it. He could feel the itch running through him, the tingle down his legs for the sides of a horse with a mind of its own, the

lean energy asserting itself and asking for the action of the
hard work that paid for itself in the doing.

"All right, Monte," said Hat. "I ain't going to talk all
night. How about it?"

"I might," said Monte. He tilted his glass then set it down
behind him. "I just might," he said. He pointed at the poker
table in the rear of the big room. "That is, if you took him
along too."

A slow chuckle came from Hat Henderson. "Which one?"
he said.

"That one," said Monte. "That fat-faced baboon by the
post looks like a mule tromped him."

"Him?" said Hat. "Rollins? I know Chet and his rope.
Matter of fact, I put it to him only a while ago. Know what
he said? He said he'd think about it—if I took you along."

* * *

Monte Walsh and Chet Rollins rode north, point and
swing, all the way past the badlands of Dakota and on around
the Black Hills with a herd of longhorn cows and half-grown
calves that resented the trip and the direction and kept them
and the other riders busy most of the time around the clock.
When they hit an early blizzard and were trying to keep track
of stock moving stubbornly with it in the dark and Chet went
over a high bank on a skittish brainless gray that broke its
neck in the fall and was missing in the murk of morning, it
was Monte, grim and sleepless, who rammed a rawboned sorrel through the storm until it could barely stand on quivering
legs and found Chet staggering along on foot in bad shape
and brought him in. They delivered the herd at Spearfish and
were paid off there and the others headed back south, but
Monte wanted to stay on and see what fun could be dug up
there and Chet shrugged and said why not, and when Monte
found more of his kind of fun than he could handle with
three men climbing all over him it was Chet who sighed,
with the glint in his eyes belying the sigh, and waded in to
make the odds about even. Then the cold weather really took
the land and the two of them wore out the winter bucking
drifts and riding line for one of the new cattle outfits up that
way with Monte complaining about the cold much of the
time. The early spring day they came on a lean winter-worn

grizzly and Monte, maybe for the warming it might give but more likely out of sheer damnfoolishness, slapped a loop and caught a forepaw and the grizzly yanked Monte's black right off its feet and went for Monte bouncing on the ground, it was Chet's rope, flashing out from a short-coupled bay at full gallop, that took the grizzly around the neck and kept it occupied until Monte could get to the Winchester in his saddle scabbard.

"You got about as much sense as a six-year-old," said Chet, amiable, conversational, helping with the skinning.

"Shucks," said Monte. "We got him, didn't we? Maybe this thing on top of my blankets'll keep me warm."

And when the grass was greening above the roots and the spring roundup and branding were done and no one could say they were pulling out of a bad spot for the boss, they asked for their time.

"Shucks," said Monte. "Folks shiver even in summer up here. I like me some real sun. Let's make tracks."

"Anywheres," said Chet. "What the hell. Anywheres at all."

"I've heard there's good cattle country opening down in New Mexico," said Monte. "You ever been there?"

"Looks like I will be," said Chet.

Side by side Monte Walsh and Chet Rollins, content with each other and with the world, at home anywhere in their whole vast part of it, drifted southward together across the big land.

*   *   *

"Monte-and-Chet. You kind of get the habit of saying it that way. Never see one without the other no further'n just around a bush somewhere. And if you get to seeing 'em often like I have, there's a kind of pattern to it. Monte always tangling into something, Chet always pulling him out. Which I won't have you taking as meaning I'm saying Monte can't take care of himself. About as taking-care-of a man in most any kind of scramble you're likely to meet in a month of Sundays. But Chet's kind of likely to be a jump ahead figuring a better way. Like the time only a couple months back Monte done a good job of taking-care-of on some young feller over in Goshen a ways east of here. Kind of changed his

features permanent. Over some woman like it usually is with Monte. This feller was with a big local outfit that stood in high with the town folks and feeling was running mighty strong. They'd salted Monte away in their jail and was figuring on a hearing in the morning. Could of gone rough with him the way they was feeling. But Chet, nothing ever ruffles him, he plays a cool hand. Along in the middle of the night he pops Monte out of the box. Not much to that, not for a man like Chet. A gun in the jailer's ribs at the right time, some rope and a gag, and he and Monte are walking away. But getting him out is one thing. Getting them both away is another. There'll be posses, kind of mean ones, scouring the country before long. That feller's outfit has some salty characters that won't be shook easy. Old Chet, he has that all figured. On the edge of town he has an old wagon stashed, canvas covering rigged over. Their hosses in some kind of old harness. He hopes folks won't know them hosses too well but to be sure he's splashed water over 'em and thrown dust till they're plum dusty and mud-caked. Has a patched fly-rig on one, a silly straw hat with holes punched in it on the ears of the other. Look like a couple old plugs. He sticks a wad of hosshair on Monte's lip something like a mustache and he takes some red paint and slaps little splotches on Monte's face and neck. Gets him to lie down in the wagon on some old bags with a blanket up to his chin. Then Chet rigs hisself in a woman's dress he's got somewhere, a shawl high up, a big flapping sunbonnet on his head pulled down low. Climbs on the seat and tucks his feet up under the skirt and pulls off down the road cool as a cat in a icehouse. Sure enough, sun ain't very high before there's riders sighted here and there. A bunch comes closing in, foreman of that feller's outfit hisself in charge. Chet just sits hunched down like he was female sad and full of mighty powerful female worries. Ma'am, says this foreman, what've you got in that wagon? Chet just hunches down more and tries to look sadder. Ma'am, says this foreman, we ain't aiming to be disrespectful but we got to see. He slides off his hoss and lifts the back end of the canvas. Careful, says Chet suddenlike, keeping his voice high. Smallpox, he says. This foreman jumps at that and he don't look very hard, just a quick peep sighting someone in there with them red splotches. He backs off. Keep away, he says to the others and waves them off. Worst case of small-

pox, he says, *I ever did see. Ma'am, he says, faster you can get away from hereabouts the better. Yes, ma'am, he says, and I hope that man of yours makes out all right."*

Slash Y
1881

CAL BRENNAN put the Slash Y together.

Likely the officers and shareholders of the Consolidated Cattle Company would have said they did. Only the Honorable Robert H. Winslow among them might have had brief passing doubts. They would have been thinking in terms of the investing of money, the acquiring and ownership of range land and lease rights and buildings and corrals and water holes and wells and windmills and dirt-holding tanks and certain shifting numbers of cattle and horses and the natural increase of the same—all of which, to them, was never much more than statistics on the paper of annual reports. In the legal sense they put the outfit together and it was theirs.

But the Slash Y was only incidentally such things. It was really a group of men oddly assorted in size and shape and education and lack of it and disposition and capability, alike only in general cattle-country background and rawhide toughness of muscle and willingness to risk their necks to get a job done, men owned by nobody and by nothing except their own loyalty to each other and to the outfit that paid their wages. Cal Brennan was the man who brought them together.

* * *

Cal came out of Texas like most of the early cattlemen of the west. Whether he was born there or how long he had been there was anybody's guess. He was tight-lipped on his own early years, though he did let slip once that at one time he had been married and had a couple of kids and it was apparent now and again that he had scant use for Indians in

65

general and Comanches in particular and for a while he carried in his war bag a pair of stringy dried scalps and anyone curious enough might have put those facts together for some kind of meaning. He was old enough to have been around for both the Mexican and Civil Wars, but he never joined in talk of them. All that was certain was that when the latter war was over and the trail drives north were starting and Texas longhorns were beginning to seed the ranges of most of the west, Cal Brennan, no young one, already well into the weathered middle years, was riding north with a half-dozen tough young Texans and his own herd of onetime mavericks combed out of the west Texas thickets.

What was certain too and what any of those same young men could have told was that he was a cattleman from way back.

He went up the trails four–five times, ramrodding his own crews, and he was a name wherever the rawhide squint-eyed men rode and sat around fires chewing the cud of the trails and the dust of the long lonely drags. Then his joints began to complain at too long hours in the saddle and he took to staying in Texas, assembling small herds for sale at a fair profit to younger men with the northward itch. What he wanted now was something permanent, his own spread. He knew cattle and he knew horses and he knew men. That should have been a winning combination. But bad luck tagged him. All right, perhaps there is no such thing as bad luck, not in so consistent a sense; it must stem from something in a man himself. Perhaps Cal was too much interested in doing, not enough in having and holding; in some ways he was an old-fashioned hangover living on into an era of increasing big-time operations with money and the manipulations of it becoming more important than the mere sweat of working. Call it bad luck, a jiggle in the cosmic time sequence. Every time he had a fair stake and was establishing his claim to a fair piece of range, that bad luck knocked on his door. When a dry spell killed his best spring and a grass fire ruined his range and he had to sell what stock he had at a loss, he stretched up and looked out westward over the charred land. "New country, new chances," he said. "An' only one direction's ever really made sense to me."

What was west of Texas was New Mexico Territory.

Cal Brennan came into the territory with a younger slow-moving barrel-built cowhand following him like a shadow. Goodnight and Loving and a few others had led the way and more Anglos were coming in, taking over here and there, pushing the Spanish-Americans aside by one means and another, few of those means exactly pretty. Cal knocked around, learning the new land and its ways, he and the barrel-built man, and after a while he had himself a place, acquired by one of those means which he never bothered to mention afterwards. Out where distance slipped into distance in the clean sweep of southwestern spaces and rugged mountains rimmed the horizon. An ancient adobe house with a sagging veranda that had already been many things through a century and more. A rickety pole corral and what had once been a shed. A piece of fair grassland to which his title was as good as any could be in the territory in those days. Best of all in that semi-arid country, not only a good well but a spring-fed year-round water hole not half a mile away. On his land.

Cal set to doing and the barrel-built man was right there with him. In a couple of years Cal was beginning to feel comfortable. He had a small growing herd and when he culled out for cash he could market on the small scale he was operating down at El Paso or up at Santa Fe which for a one-time Texas trail boss was not much of a drive either way. The Indian issue all but faded from his mind. There were no Comanches anywhere around and the Apaches southeastward some on their reservation were, for them, fairly quiet and the Pueblos westward along the Rio Grande even taught him something. When they came to him, quiet and courteous, and asked permission and included his land in a colorful full-scale efficient rabbit drive, he learned that they were people. Not being given to Texas brag, he got along middling well and steadily better with the Spanish-Americans in the general area and when he needed a few extra hands now and again he found that some of them were good horsemen and well acquainted with ropes. Then that bad luck knocked again. All right, maybe he invited it. He had to be doing. There was a huge Spanish land grant adjoining his place that no one seemed to be laying active claim to at the time. It was the same as open range and the grass there looked good to him. He borrowed money and bought cattle and he hocked himself to the limit and bought more and he was set for a killing come spring and a good market.

Come spring and the winter had been a hard one and Cal and the barrel-built man and a couple of young Spanish-Americans were worn and weary and the market was bad.

*   *   *

Cal Brennan came along the wagon trace on a tired dusty bay and stopped by the sagging veranda of the old adobe house and swung down and let the horse stand. He unlooped a small buckskin bag from the saddle horn and counted silver dollars into the hands of two dark-haired swarthy very young men who had appeared apparently out of nowhere and listened to their softspoken *gracias* and watched them go to the small stout corral that had replaced the rickety one and swing up on their own scrawny horses and ride away into distance. He turned toward the barrel-built man sitting on the veranda edge watching him.

"Wel-l-l-l," he said. "That's it. Everythin' gone. Even this place. Man named Winslow's got it. Range deliv'ry of what cows're left end of the week." He moved over and settled slowly on the veranda edge and laid the small buckskin bag beside him.

The barrel-built man pushed up and took the reins of the bay and led it to the corral and in and pulled off the saddle and heaved this on a top rail and rubbed the horse briefly with an old burlap bag. He came out, leaving the bridle hanging on a gatepost, and walked, slow and silent, back to his perch on the veranda.

"But I'm clean," said Cal. "Squared off everythin'. Not owin' nobody a cent. Except you." He reached for the buckskin bag.

"I ain't needing it," said the barrel-built man. He took a remnant of tobacco plug from a pocket of his worn leather vest and bit off a chunk and chewed slowly. "But you do," he said. "For starting again."

Over in the corral the bay rolled, rubbing itchy back, sending up a small cloud of dust.

"I ain't so sure," said Cal. "I ain't so sure I got it in me to start again."

The barrel-built man shifted the quid from one cheek to

the other and spat a quantity of yellowish liquid well out from the veranda. "I am," he said. He thought that over. "Mean I'm sure. About you."

Silence and afternoon sunlight held the sagging old veranda. Off along the wagon trace dust rose and something darker showed in it and seemed to creep through distance and approached and was a light buckboard drawn by a flop-eared mouse-colored mustang at a steady trot. Cal Brennan narrowed eyes into the sunlight to make out the two figures on the seat. His shoulders squared a bit and the weathered skin over his lean face tightened. "Bennie, from the liv'ry," he said. "An' Winslow." He shifted position for a more direct view and leaned back against one of the veranda posts. "Bein' kind of previous," he said.

The buckboard stopped thirty feet away and the two men climbed down. The driver waved cheerfully and led the horse with the buckboard trailing to the water trough by the corral and went to work on the handle of the old pump. The other man, neat in dark business suit with linen duster flapping open over it and a narrow-brim dark hat, shook himself, slapping away dust, and ran a finger around inside his high starched collar and approached the veranda. He nodded at the barrel-built man, acknowledging his presence and dismissing him in the single nod, and faced Cal Brennan. There was an alert brisk efficiency in his movements and in his voice.

"Warm out here," he said. "Even this time of year. Brennan, you are a hard man to follow. I thought you would be around town a while. When I went looking for you, you were gone."

"Certain I was gone," said Cal. The touch of a drawl always in his voice deepened some. "Finished my bus'ness. I ain't exactly fond of that kind of bus'ness. An' maybe of the kind of people mixed up in it."

"Of course," said the man quickly. "You were on the losing end. Squeezed out. But that happens, you know. To all of us one time or another. But sometimes all for the best." He ran a finger again around inside his collar. "Look here, do you mind if I sit down?"

"I might," said Cal. "But I ain't riled enough yet at your bein' here to do anythin' about it."

The man hesitated, studying Cal, then the tiny wrinkles

around his eyes deepened and his mouth twitched in what could have been a small smile. He took off his linen duster and folded it and laid it on the veranda. He eased himself onto the edge leaning back against the next post, turned enough to face Cal across the space between. "Very nicely put," he said. "You mean you are waiting to hear what I have to say before you decide whether to be what you call riled. I have won my first point. I have made you curious. You are wondering why I followed you so fast after what happened in town a few hours ago."

"It took some nerve," said Cal. "I'm givin' you credit on that."

The man's mouth twitched again. "I did think of asking that deputy marshal to come along," he said. He saw the small answering flick of Cal's eye muscles. Encouraged, he hurried on. "But look here. I hope you realize there was nothing personal in what happened. Business. Strictly business. I believe in talking straight and putting things plain." He turned his head, slowly, looking at the old adobe house, the small corral and the pump and the patched-up shed. "I must say this place does not look like much to me. But then very little out in this incredible country does." He looked straight at Cal. "All the same I know that you had something here. Just about everything as a matter of fact. Everything you needed for your little cattle operation. Except one thing. Capital. Money. To carry you through. Am I right?"

Cal raised a hand and rubbed it down a lean cheek and over his chin. "Reckon you are," he said. "But bein' right ain't no odds agin my gettin' riled."

"I think it will be," said the man. "Look here. You were bucking something too big for you. On the money end, that is. You have to have money to make money. Now the money end of things is what I know. Capital is what I have. I am not speaking just for myself in this. I represent the Consolidated Cattle Company. Nothing small scale about it. Backed by a syndicate in New York, though we have our main offices in Chicago. We have been operating in Illinois and Indiana. You know, mostly farm and feedlot business up that way. Some holdings too in Iowa and Nebraska. Now we are pushing into this territory. Sort of jumping the gun, you might say, on other companies that are grabbing everything to the north. We have been keeping quiet, checking the possibilities. Several weeks ago we acquired that Spanish grant just below here, have it tied up tight. That is a big piece of country. And there is plenty of public land adjoining. Open to us as well as to anyone these days. We have the right contacts in Washington. When the government gets around to doing something with it, we can hold plenty of it under tight leases. It will be a big operation. But we had to have this place."

Cal Brennan sat quiet and relaxed against his post, looking steadily at the man. "Water," he said.

"Right," said the man. "Water. Good water for use while other sources are being developed. So now you could say that we have everything. Including what you lacked. But again except one thing. What you had. Experience. Experience in this kind of country. Knowledge. Knowledge of this kind of range cattle business from the grass roots up. That is where you come in."

Cal Brennan straightened a bit against his post. He looked down at the worn toes of his old high-curved-heel boots.

"Yes," said the man. "I already know more about you than you might imagine. Discounting a few things that could give the shakes to my colleagues back east who have not been out here and seen his country, I would say most of it good. For what we need. I have the say-so on this. I want you to take charge of the operation out here. On the ground. I suppose you might call it range manager."

Farther along the veranda the barrel-built man stood up and stretched. His shoulder joints made tiny creakings as he pushed elbows out and back. "Said I was sure," he announced to the world and settled back down on the veranda edge.

Silence and sunlight held the front of the old adobe house. Over by the corral the driver of the buckboard sat on the ground, back to rails, and whittled slowly and methodically on a small piece of wood.

Cal Brennan sat very still on the veranda edge, staring down at his boot toes. He raised his head. "An' how d'you know," he said, "that I wouldn't be stealin' you blind?"

"Two reasons," said the man. "One is that we would cut you in for a few shares of your own so it would be to your advantage to run things straight."

"The other one," said Cal.

"The fact you asked me," said the man.

Silence and sunlight held the front of the old adobe house. Over by the corral the driver of the buckboard held up the piece of wood that was beginning to resemble a whip handle, inspected it carefully, returned to his whittling.

Cal Brennan sat very still, staring down at his old boot toes. He seemed to have forgotten the brisk neat efficient man facing him. "The Montoya grant," he murmured softly, very softly. "That's a lot of good grass. An' backin' to spread out more." He raised his head and looked into the great clean distances of the big land. Beyond the farthest fading horizon he saw in memory long lines of cattle moving north and rawhide-hard squint-eyed men on tough little cow ponies moving with them. "We could headquarter right here," he murmured. Slowly his head turned and he looked steadily at the other man. "Would I be havin' you an' others like you in my hair all the time?"

The man hesitated, looking as steadily back. His lips tightened as decision seeped through him. "No," he said. "I can not always guarantee how the other directors will behave, but I can speak for myself and I can assure you that as long as things seem to be going all right and they receive a reasonable return on their money, they will not interfere much if at all. You would be in charge of the operation here, on the ground. Subject to some instructions on purchases and marketing and of course an annual audit. You know, a thorough check of all records by a good bookkeeper. That ought not to disturb your hair too much." He hesitated again, studying Cal. "We could put something about that in your contract."

"Contract?" said Cal. "Have one of the fool things if you want. But I give my word, I keep it. An' expect others to do the same. When they don't, I do somethin' about it. What you got in mind for a brand?"

"Brand?" said the man. "Of course. I had forgotten that. We will need one registered here in the territory. Do you have any suggestions?"

"I'd kind of like to use mine," said Cal. "Slash Y. Sell it to the comp'ny for a dollar an' a handshake."

The man stood up. Brisk, efficient. "Settled then," he said. "I will see you in town tomorrow to go over the details. And

I will try to have that contract ready. For your protection as well as ours. I doubt we will have any trouble arriving at a figure. And I will be in town as long as necessary to help you get things started." He chuckled, dryly, briefly, reaching for the kind of friendship he did not know how to grasp. "That help for right now I imagine will be chiefly writing checks. You know, drawing on that capital. For the buildings you will need and for stocking the range. Things like that."

"There's somethin' else we'll be needin' more," said Cal.

"Yes?" said the man. "And what is that?"

"Men," said Cal Brennan. "Real men."

*   *   *

New activity fretted the morning serenity of the neighborhood of the old adobe house. Off to the right two swarthy middle-aged men bent low over their forms and their mix, making adobes for what would be a bunkhouse and a smaller cookhouse. Close by the small stout corral where the patched-up shed had been, three men in overalls unloaded planks from a big flatbed wagon for what would be a long low barn. Where the pump still temporarily sprouted its old iron handle the barrel-built man, wrench in hand, bolted together the metal struts of a small windmill tower.

Cal Brennan sat again on the edge of the sagging old veranda. He saw none of the nearby activity. He was looking far in memory into the miles and the years. Every now and then he raised a hand holding a pencil stub to his mouth and licked the end of the pencil and reached to write in his crabbed script a name on a small piece of paper beside him.

A breeze blew the paper and he moved quickly and caught it. He tucked it and the pencil stub into a shirt pocket and rose and went into the old house. In a few minutes he emerged, big wide-brimmed battered old hat on his head, gunbelt buckled around his waist, jacket on over it, a blanket roll tied in its tarpaulin under one arm. Teetering a bit on his absurdly high-curved-heel boots, his one personal vanity, he walked to the corral and in and bridled and saddled the bay and tied the roll on behind. He led the horse out and the barrel-built man was there, by the gate.

"Keep the lid on here," said Cal. "I got some ridin' to do.

Call it two weeks. Tell Winslow when he comes pokin'
aroun' I'll be back when I'm back if not before."

Cal Brennan swung up and rode into the morning sun.

*   *   *

What was east of New Mexico Territory was west Texas.

Cal Brennan and his long-legged bay that was like him in
general contour and disposition drifted through the long leg-
stretching rugged distances. His aging joints complained some
but not too much because he took the going easy and he slept
snug in his blankets and on and under the tarpaulin and
under the open sky and thought of the times when a saddle
was his home and he never would have asked for a better
bed. He stopped briefly at lonely campfires and almost as
lonely ranches and the few far scattered towns and sometimes
in the great clean spaces he met a rider or riders and always
he asked questions. Now and again, after some of the answers,
he grinned and said now who would have thought any woman
would take that one and pulled out the piece of paper and
the pencil stub and scratched off a name—or maybe instead
he closed his eyes for a moment and a grimness gripped his
lean face and he said nothing and scratched off a name and
broke the point of the pencil doing it. And now and again,
not often, meeting some rawhide-hard squint-eyed man, he
would ride or step forward with a sudden warmth lighting his
eyes and exchange outrageous insults and then talk long and
earnestly.

Once, following instructions that had been hard to get, he
rode deep into rocky scrub-timbered country and sighted a
small cabin and moved toward it whistling loud and cheerful
and a rifle barrel poked out the cabin's one window and a
voice gave warning and he put his hands up behind his head
and nudged the bay onward and a man burst out of the cabin
doorway, dropping the rifle, and ran forward and fairly
yanked him out of the saddle and hugged him with rib-crack-
ing vigor and called him all manner of impolite names. And
once again, in a middling town, he talked to a man through
the barred doorway of the brick jail and went away to pay
out dollars from a small buckskin bag and came back with a
gunbelt hanging from one hand and the key to the padlock in
the other and let the man out.

"I got me a leetle bus'ness to attend to south some," said the man, buckling the gunbelt around his waist. "Got to finish that 'fore I do anythin' else. Be seein' you."

"Need any help?" said Cal.

"Thanks," said the man, checking the cylinder of the gun and dropping it back into its holster. "But this is pers'nal."

And again, swinging north and west, near the territorial line, heading back, he came on a district roundup. Representatives of ranches all through the district were gathering, waiting to start, amusing themselves with poker games on spread-out blankets and other more strenuous pastimes. He paid his respects to the roundup boss and picked the neatest and best-stocked of the chuck wagons and absorbed a good meal by its fire and he wandered around watching the fun. He bumped into a few men he knew and passed remarks with them but he kept moving and he felt his age as he saw so many young ones that had come along since his own time. And then he stopped near what seemed a healthy argument.

Four or five men on foot were exchanging vigorous opinions with two men in saddles, one of these a lean young length of rawhide atop a deep-chested leggy dun, the other stocky, square-built, astride a thick-necked black.

"G'wan," said one of the men on foot. "We got ten dollars says you can't."

"Don't do it," said another man a short way off. "That thing's a hell-roaring ringer they brung along looking for easy money."

"Shucks," said the lean man on the dun. "It's a horse, ain't it?"

Cal hunkered down on his heels and rolled a cigarette. The group moved off toward the near edge of the horse herd about fifty yards away. The square-built man on the black shook out a loop and one of the men on foot pointed at a big heavy-muscled gray and the gray, instantly aware, slipped deeper into the herd. The square-built man pushed forward on the black, easing in, and his arm moved, seeming casual and effortless, and the loop leaped over the backs and weaving heads between and had the gray.

Cal pushed his hat higher up his forehead and watched the flurry of activity as men swarmed around the gray and blindfolded it and bridled it and the saddle from the leggy dun was slapped on it and cinched tight. The lean man, on foot now, reached out and slapped a leg of the square-built man sitting easy on the black, coiling in his rope, and moved toward the gray. In one smooth swift motion he was in the saddle, battered old boots slapping into the stirrups, body leaning low as he took the reins. He flipped off the blindfold and the gray, not frantic, frightened, but enraged, knowing, reared high and plunged down, jaws smashing against the bit for head play, and plowed forward pitching.

"Yowee!" yelled the lean man, serene in saddle, raking the gray with his spurs, slapping hard with his hat.

Cal rolled another cigarette and watched the gray high-rolling and windmilling with a skill and a dedicated fury that made his eyes light up some in appreciation.

"Yowee!" yelled the lean man again, gasping now, hat gone, blood dribbling from his nose, but body firm in the saddle.

Cal forgot his cigarette, watching the gray come all unraveled in sheer frustrated rage and unleash a series of deadly tricks unknown even in his own long experience.

The gray leveled and raced, headlong, straight for the cluster of wagons and spread-out blankets and groups of men about them. Pans clattered and fire embers flew under its hoofs and men scrambled and rolled out of the way.

"That ain't polite!" gasped the lean man, trying to yank it around. It reared and toppled sideways, maybe deliberately, into the front wheel of a wagon and went down and the lean man, jolted loose, smacked against the wagon, fell and lay limp, twitching some, fighting for breath. The gray scrambled up, bucking and whirling, and sighted him on the ground and jumped in close, rearing high to slash down with forehoofs.

But a thick-necked black at full run was threading fast through the mix-up and the square-built man in the saddle had a small loop forming and this flicked out and caught the forefeet still in the air and he whipped the rope around his saddle horn, close in, and the black drove on, swinging away, and the gray, yanked off balance, crashed down inches from the lean man on the ground.

Cal dropped the stub of his cigarette with a jerk of his hand and put two burned fingers in his mouth. Licking these, he watched the lean man pull himself up by the spokes of the rear wheel of the wagon and step out, limping, chest heaving.

As the gray struggled to its feet, the now loosened rope dropping, the lean man hobbled in and took hold of the horn and heaved himself into the saddle coming up, leaning again to take the reins. The gray squealed and pitched, once, twice, three times, and stood with legs braced, head hanging.

Cal lengthened up, wiping fingers on his shirt. He pulled his hat down more firmly on his forehead. He rubbed a hand down one weathered cheek and around over his chin. He moved away, looking for the roundup boss, and found him. He nodded toward the lean man and the square-built man standing together now, intent on counting a fistful of old dollar bills.

"Good boys," said the roundup boss. "But footloose. They was ridin' the rough string for the Flying O last fall. Before that with the Double H for maybe a few months. Before that likely a half dozen others. Reppin' right now for the Sombrero over acrost the line that has some drift this way. Likely anywheres next."

"You're gettin' old," said Cal. "Seems I kind of remember you an' me wasn't exactly tied down at about that age."

Teetering a bit on his absurdly high-curved-heel boots, he walked toward the two men.

* * *

Late spring days drifted over the old adobe house and the sagging veranda sagged less on improved foundation and the bunkhouse was up and roofed and the cookhouse the same and the long low barn was about finished and the small windmill pumped with a minimum of squeaking to fill the storage tank on its own stilts nearby and a big corral was sprouting behind the small stout one. Cal Brennan sat often on the veranda in an old rocking chair padded with several ancient tattered saddle blankets and surveyed the proceedings. "Bein' manager has somethin' to it," he said. "Hard on the head, maybe, but easy on the muscles."

And every now and then, by one and by two, rawhide-hard squint-eyed men came riding along the wagon trace and stopped by the veranda to talk to him and he took a little notebook from a shirt pocket and wrote in it and they moved on down to the small corral and turned their horses in and carried what they had tied or strapped behind cantles into the bunkhouse and tested the bunks built along the side walls. Sometimes of an evening and when new ones had arrived the bunkhouse shook with greetings and raw horseplay and shouted remembrances of experiences shared elsewhere in other years out across the great stretches of the big land. With one of the first, a big slope-shouldered man, giving the orders, they dug postholes for the new corral and set the posts in pairs and lashed rail-ends tight between the pairs and sometimes they rode off carrying the Slash Y iron and were gone a while and came back driving a small herd of half-wild horses or a larger herd of longhorn cows with their calves to be fanned out over the big grant rolling southward and always now a few of them were swinging out in long lonely circuit, riding line and stopping drift while the stock learned the limits of their range.

Cal sat in his rocking chair and he wandered around easy and casual, taking care not to get in the way, and sometimes he rode out on his long-legged bay apparently just for the exercise and to keep his aging muscles limber, but there was not much that happened anywhere on the range or closer in by the buildings that he missed. He sat on the veranda and studied his little notebook and once in a while he had to rub out an entry in it. "Ev'ry man's got a right to a mistake or two," he said.

There was the time one of the men who had been around only a few days came to the veranda, long-faced and aggrieved. "Cal," he said. "You disappoint me. I never thought to see the day. Diggin' postholes. That ain't a man's work. You know I ain't goin' to do anythin' you can't do from a hoss."

"Know how you feel," said Cal, "I had leanin's that way oncet myself. But hereabouts an' nowadays things has changed. What needs to be done, gets done."

"Not by me," said the man. "A shovel. You can put your shovel. Makes calluses in the wrong places. I ain't like you yet, ready to climb down out of the saddle."

"In or out," said Cal, frost creeping into his voice, "it's all the same, accordin' to what's needed when. Maybe you better be movin' on."

"Maybe I had," said the man.

There was the time too Cal was ambling past the small corral and saw a lean young length of rawhide inside, who was rubbing down a leggy dun, stop and step over to look at the bloody sides of a tired sorrel and stand very still looking with the muscles of his young face hardening. Cal saw him head for the gate and Cal was there as he came out and words passed.

"It ain't only this once," said the lean young man. "It's every goddamned horse he rides. I'm a-going to scramble him some and mark him with his own spurs."

"You're doin' nothin' of the kind," said Cal. "I got eyes too. An' I'm running this outfit. You hold your fightin' for those new broncs an' don't go goin' off half-cocked."

And a little later Cal caught the right man off from the others and said a few things in a voice that could have withered a cactus ending with: "An' pack your gear an git!" The man stood quivering with anger flushing his face and saw a lean young one and a square-built other young one easing up to flank Cal and he turned on his heel and got.

And again there was the time dispositions took to going sour and the wrong kind of feeling was spreading and Cal was wondering just who was the troublemaker and whether competence at range work could balance a mean temper but before he got around to making a decision it was made for him. A short swift ruckus back of the barn ended with the big slope-shouldered man coming to the veranda with another one on his shoulder, limp and out cold. "I only hit 'im twice," said the big man, dumping the other down. "Next time I'd break his neck. Get rid of 'im." Cal took the precaution of emptying the limp man's gun and cartridge belt before sloshing water over him. Cal gave him a month's pay and watched him ride off, chewing his lower lip, and Cal saddled and rode out, watching, just to make sure he kept on going.

And still again there was the time one of the men came larruping in from the range on a sweaty horse and pulled up short by the veranda. "Sorry, Cal," he said. "I'd admire to stick aroun' an' keep y'all comp'ny. But I hear there's a dep'ty hit town askin' the wrong questions."

Cal rubbed a hand down one cheek and over his chin. "Pick a fresh hoss," he said. "An' Cookie'll pack you some grub. Anyone comes pokin' here, I got plenty of misinformation." He sighed. "Maybe you can get back sometime."

"I sure would admire to," said the man. "Be seein' you."
He swung away toward the small corral and Cal sighed again
and took out his little notebook.

*　*　*

So the days passed and men came and some men went, of
their own accord or sent on their way, and Cal sat on the veranda and studied his little notebook. Late one afternoon he
sat there in the old rocking chair and the Honorable Robert
H. Winslow sat on an old kitchen chair beside him. Over by
the bunkhouse assorted squint-eyed men were scrubbing
away the dust of a day's work with the aid of several tin basins and two roller towels and were passing remarks on the
aromas emanating from the cookhouse.

"My having to be back in Chicago for a while doesn't
seem to have slowed you any," said Winslow. "A great deal
seems to have been happening here. That is a remarkably
rough-looking crew you have there."

"Rough-lookin'?" said Cal. "You disappoint me. They look
downright pretty to me. That thick one on the end, you know
him. Perkins. Sunfish Perkins. Came out here with me an'
been with me ever since. Slow. Yes. An' not too bright. But
he sure can shoe a hoss an' doctor a sick cow an' keep a
windmill runnin'. That big one there's my foreman. Henderson. Hat Henderson. Never knew till I put him down in my
book the right name's Albert. I had to argue plenty to get
him here. Best damn trail boss I ever knew. He could take a
herd straight through hell an' come out the other side. But
touchy. I got to keep out of his way an' not go interferin'
much or he'd pick me up under one arm an' chuck me into
this house an' likely right through the back wall. I saw him
real mad once, some years since, an' I ain't hankerin' to see
that again. But he's got a bump of respons'bility bigger'n a
buffalo bull. The long one next him is Williams. Petey Williams. I don't know as there's anything special you might say
about him except he's a dang good all-around cowman that'd
walk up to a grizzly an' spit in its eye if that come along in
the line of work."

"A grizzly?" said Winslow. "Brennan, you are stringing
me."

"It happens," said Cal. "Petey come on one the other day

lunchin' off a calf. Only he didn't do no spittin'. Only shootin'. Hide's hangin' on the back of the barn. But I was sayin'. Next one there is Austin. Shorty Austin. Called that 'cause he's kind of short-fused on gettin' peeved. One beside him is Joslin, Jumping Joe Joslin. Got that name oncet when he was full of pizen-juice an' accidental-like sat on a stove an' popped up so high he put a hole in the ceilin'. The one fightin' Joe there for a towel is Wyman, Sugar Wyman. I misremember how he got that tag. Like Petey, there's nothin' special you might say about those three except that they rode up the trail with me a couple times when you'd of said they was just about weaned an' they was wildcats then an' they've gone on gettin' maybe wilder an' if there's any kind of devilment a cow-critter can think up they can't handle it ain't been tried yet."

"Well, well, Brennan," said Winslow. "I should say your taste—"

"Next one there," said Cal, "is Kent. Powder Kent. Still don't know the right front name 'cause he won't give it. But Powder's plenty apt. He ain't carryin' that name for fancy. Earned it often enough. I had to bail him out of a tin-can jail over the line an' right away he skipped chasin' somebody or somethin' an' likely earned it again but he made it here like he said he would an' figurin' some of the things that likely'll happen when we start spreadin' out crowdin' the range I find it right comfortin' havin' him here."

"Now listen here, Brennan," said Winslow. "What are you—"

"Just like I do with the next one," said Cal. "Johnson. Dally Johnson. Silly name, maybe, 'cause he's a tie-fast man nowadays, ever since he lost a thumb dallyin'. Had myself a time findin' him. Had to go smoke him out of back country where he was hidin' from a posse. I expect there ain't a trick to maverickin' an' sleeperin' an' changin' a brand he don't know."

"Good heavens, Brennan," said Winslow. "You mean you deliberately—"

"This ain't no boardin' school I'm runnin'," said Cal. "You ever hear of a good man stealin' from his own outfit? An' Dally's a good man. I've rode with him. There ain't nobody'll be playin' games with our stock Dally won't smell it out. Quit frettin'. He's Slash Y now. An' you see that slim one there lookin' like he's splittin' the breeze just standin' still wipin' his face? That's Walsh. Monte Walsh. I got me a sneakin' little suspicion the hoss he can't ride ain't been foaled yet. Nat-ural-born to it. Better'n he knows an' he thinks he knows plenty. An' not just ridin'. I got me a sneakin' little other sus-picion when he's through with a hoss that hoss knows its manners an' its business. Now that thicker one gettin' ready to pour water down Monte's neck if he don't look aroun' fast enough is Rollins. Chet Rollins. Best man with a rope I ever saw. He don't seem to know that himself, maybe 'cause he's too busy taggin' Monte an' pullin' him out of troubles. That Monte's a bear-cat at tanglin' into things. Damnfool things. They been mixed into some mighty fine brawls in town three–four times already."

"Very interesting," said Winslow. "And just what kind of reputation do you think—"

"The right kind," said Cal. "An' there's one more inside the cookhouse there. Eagens. Skimpy Eagens. He's been a lot of things, some good, some not so as you'd mention, but he's hobbled by age an' a game leg now an' he's cookin'. Good grub too as you'll find out. Only he wasn't what you might call partic'lar about bein' clean. Smelled kind of high. So one day the boys, likely it was Monte's notion, stripped him down naked as a plucked chicken an' doused him in that water trough an' used hoss brushes till he didn't have much skin left. He took that surprisin' quiet. But next mornin' he put somethin' in the griddle cakes an' the boys spent most of the day lightin' out for likely spots an' gettin' their pants down fast. Worked out about even. They ain't botherin' Skimpy again an' he's keepin' reasonable clean."

Cal rubbed one hand down one cheek and over his chin. "I've been yappin' about the men 'cause I'm sure goin' to be needin' 'em, what with you gallivantin' aroun' doin' silly things. What's this I been hearin' about you buyin' a mixed herd, deliv'ry down by the border?"

"I have not mentioned that yet," said Winslow. "How did you—"

"I got ways," said Cal. "Call it jackrabbit telegraph. Why'd you do it?"

"A bargain," said Winslow. "A real bargain. I would have waited to consult you, but the man claimed he couldn't wait. I couldn't let it slip."

"If you'd inquired some," said Cal, "you'd have found I let it slip. If you was dry ahind the ears you'd know better'n to go fussin' with one of them border herds. Mixed is right. Likely seventeen diff'rent brands an' no straight papers on a one an' plenty cows still wet from bein' sneaked across the river. Now with you gettin' in my hair like you said you wouldn't, I got to go down there an' get 'em. Still short-handed too for that kind of doin'. Have to slap our brand on 'em right there an' fast before too many squawks an' claimers gather an' things get nasty. Have to bring 'em up here through mighty dry country an' past the Apache reservation which ain't always healthy."

Cal looked at Winslow as if he pitied him some. "Me an' some of the boys'll be leavin' in the mornin'," he said. "You remarked they was rough-lookin'. What kind d'you think you need to make good on a fool stunt like you just pulled?"

*　*　*

Barren and sun-scorched, the land rose northward from the ribbon of green that marked the Rio Grande to a long flat-topped ridge. Over and beyond in a wide hollow of sparse grassland three dark-skinned young ones, little more than boys, on three thin ponies held the main herd of cows and half-grown calves and a few old bulls. Several hundred yards away two more held the cut, the cattle already branded and ear-marked. Off to the side an even younger one rode lazily in a circle around some fifteen grazing horses. And in between, moving through dust and heat, the men of the Slash Y worked, silent mostly, grim-faced, shirts drenched with sweat, working against time.

Cal Brennan tended the fire, keeping the irons hot. Petey Williams and Chet Rollins roped the big ones, stretching them out on the ground for Hat Henderson and Monte Walsh with iron and knife. Nearby Powder Kent dragged calves squirming at the end of his rope for the expert atten-tions of Dally Johnson.

"Jeeeeesus, Cal!" said Hat Henderson, wiping a sleeve across his face. "When you scared up those kids, why didn't you find us a man or two?"

"There ain't many down this way," said Cal. "Not as I'd look at twice."

Time passed and the herd dwindled, slowly, slowly, and the cut increased the same and over the ridge top came a tired horse, a solid little bay, caked mud drying on its legs, sweat streaks drying along neck and flanks, and the man in the saddle showed slim and compact through the dust on him and the face under the big sombrero was lean and swarthy and black-mustached. A rifle stock poked out of its scabbard opposite his coiled rope and that inevitable addition, a worn Colt .45, snugged into its holster along his right thigh like a part of the man himself. He held back a moment, hand firm on reins, studying the scene before him, then with a small shrug of shoulders came on.

Cal Brennan dropped the wood in his hands and picked up the rifle lying near and moved out some. The man came on, following the trace of a trail that snaked on past, and stopped, aware that every man seeming hard at work was aware of him and that Cal Brennan stood not thirty feet away with a rifle in his hands. He placed his own hands in plain sight on his saddle horn and looked out over the work in progress and a tiny shock of recognition ran through Cal Brennan and his mind leaped back two years and he was in El Paso selling a few steers and crossing the river in the slow dusk to Juarez for some Mexican chili and finding it in a little café and finding it so hot he was stepping into a little cantina for something cooling. There was a game of some kind at a back table and a pretty girl was serving drinks and rolling her eyes at the men playing. And suddenly a shot was sounding and Cal was hunting cover fast behind the bar and peering over and at the table a slim compact black-mustached man was rising to his feet with a gun in his right hand and across from him a man was going down, dropping his own gun as he went, and the black-mustached man's gun was speaking again, three times, and the three lamps were shattering out and the man himself was a shadow slipping through the rear door and Cal was muttering to himself: "Neat an' thorough."

Cal stood still, rifle in hands ready to come up, remembering in almost the same flash various tales he had heard since, and the man, looking now at him and the rifle, shrugged shoulders again and lifted reins to ride on. He was passing Cal, quiet, careful to keep his hands in plain sight, when the trouble started.

By the fire Dally Johnson had a calf pigged tight and
Powder Kent was heading back to the herd. The calf bawled
and its mother, big and mean and circling unnoticed near
from the cut, came charging in. Dally saw her and dodged,
shouting, and she was right after him, big horns hooking
close.

Cal turned and saw the cow hard after Dally and other
men swinging their horses but too far away and he was bringing the rifle up when he heard the thud of spurs and the
grunt of a horse and the solid little bay from the trail scud-
ded past him. It drove in and turned the cow and dodged
away with fancy stepping as the cow twisted hooking at it and
drove in again, blocking, and the cow ducked on around
after Dally again. But the man in the saddle had his rope
loose now and he nipped the flying hindfeet and stretched her
out with a thump that knocked all the fight out of her.

"Neat an' thorough," muttered Cal Brennan. He walked
over, rifle barrel dropping low, to the man coiling in his rope.
"You're mighty handy with that hemp," he said.

"*Gracias, Señor*," said the man. "Een your words, I thank
you."

"It's me doin' the thankin'," said Cal. He rubbed his free
hand down one cheek and over his chin. He drew in a deep
breath. "An' in my words I'm sayin' maybe if you ain't tied
to anythin' else right now, it could be we could use you an'
that rope. That is, till we finish brandin' here and move these
critters up the trail a piece. We got hosses enough if we use
'em careful."

The man looked down at him, eyes narrowed some.
"But the name," he said slowly. "The name, eet ees Dobe
Chavez."

Cal drew in another deep breath. "I know that," he said.
"An' I'm feelin' some better already, hearin' you speak it
straight."

"There ees a reward," said the man. "Across the reevair."

"That ain't here," said Cal. "Not that it means a damn
thing to me, but how is it on this side?"

"*Nada*," said the man. Then with a sudden grin: "Not at
thees leetle moment."

"We'll work your tail off," said Cal cheerfully, slapping
him on a leg. Cal turned away. "Hey, Petey," he yelled.
"Climb down an' help over here by the fire. We got us anoth-

er rope. Monte, get him a fresh hoss. Don't think you need worry about pickin' it gentle."

Time passed and the work moved, faster, but quiet, very quiet, with a slow tension mounting and Cal Brennan alert and watchful. And later, in the soft dusk of evening, they sat around the fire, quiet still and not just from being tired, eating slowly which was unusual, the others watching Dobe Chavez without looking directly at him. Something was there, in the air, something out of the past and the place and the long stretches of the Rio Grande southeastward to the Gulf. It was Powder Kent, edgy perhaps that he had let Dally down not noticing that cow, who spoke. "Damned if I ever thought," he said, not to anyone in particular, not mean, just testing the situation, letting the words out flat to lie there in the firelight. "Damned if I ever thought I'd be sittin' aroun' a good cow camp campfire along with a goddamned greaser outlaw."

Silence around the fire. And into the silence came the voice of Dobe Chavez, the same way, not pushing, simply putting out the words to fall any way they might be taken. "Ees right," he said. "Ees vary fonny. Nevair did I theenk to be like thees weeth, what you say, goddamned gringos."

Silence around the fire, tightening, moving with the almost imperceptible shiftings of position of Dobe Chavez and Powder Kent toward the possible explosive instant.

"The hell with it," said Dally Johnson. "He knows what to do with a rope, don't he?"

And another long day passed with Dobe's rope keeping pace with Chet's and the last of the herd was branded and the dark-skinned young ones were paid off and the men of the Slash Y moved north through the dry lonely spaces, pushing the herd into the nights, and Dobe rode swing like a man used to moving cattle fast for whatever might be the reasons, and it was Dobe's gun that spoke its piece, neat and thorough, alongside Powder Kent's the early morning they flushed out three renegade Apaches hoping to start a stampede and cut off the stragglers. Then they were back at the old adobe house and Cal Brennan counted out silver dollars from a buckskin bag into Dobe's hand and Dobe stood quiet, staring down at the money, making no move to head for the solid little bay out by the small corral.

"Anythin' wrong?" said Cal. "Ain't that enough? It's the goin' rate."

"Thees money," said Dobe. "What ees eet to me?"

"How in hell would I know?" said Cal, somewhat sharp. "What you gettin' at?"

"I leeve by the gun," said Dobe. "I leeve good. Some of the time. But there by the reevair, what you call it, the taste eet ees bad in the mouth. *Una semana,* one of the weeks, two of the days more, I leeve now by the work. Weeth the Slash Y. The taste, eet ees good."

"All right, Dobe," said Cal. "Over in the bunkhouse there the third bunk on the right, eet ees empty."

* * *

So the days passed and again Cal Brennan sat on the veranda in the old rocking chair and again the Honorable Robert H. Winslow sat beside him. Off to the west the late afternoon sun, tipping the far mountains, sent color streaming out across the great bowl of sky.

"You know," said Winslow, "I really regret having to go back east tomorrow. This country does sort of take hold of you."

"You'll be forgettin' that part of it," said Cal, "soon as you're back there countin' all the money you been spendin' out here. That's what I don't take to much back there. Too much countin' of money." Cal shifted a bit in the old chair. "But I reckon I been kind of hard on you now an' again. Hard to take maybe. An' you been patient an' ain't been in my hair lately. Which reminds me I ain't been full paid yet for my brand. I got the dollar. Haven't quite felt like claimin' the handshake 'fore now." He leaned forward, reaching to take the hand extended quickly to him.

"A fine time for it," said Winslow. "I certainly feel easier about this whole proposition than I did a while back. The range is stocked, the ranch operating. I even begin to understand your feeling about the men. I think you said we might be able to make a shipment this fall and start getting back some of that money. It seems to me you have your problems licked."

"There you go," said Cal. "Disappointin' me again. Showin' you don't know as much as a knee-high youngster raised out here. Problems licked? Why, we ain't even really started on 'em. We got about half a dozen water holes to develop so the damn cows won't walk off that money you're worried about gettin' to drink. We got about ten mile of drift fence to put up to the east there that'll be our soft spot come winter. The grant's been regarded as open range for quite a spell an' we'll be busy separatin' a lot of people from that notion. Expect some won't separate easy. There's nesters an' two-by-four ranchers aroun' the edges that'll be seeing what they can get away with an' thinkin' up ways of tryin' to keep our calf crop low. We'll have to do some more separatin' on them. You ever see one of them sudden rains come whoopin' down arroyos like Noah's flood, an' making bog holes from here to Christmas? You ever been caught in one of them blizzards this country can throw out of them mountains when it gets to feelin' mean? I could keep talkin' till your ears dropped off but that'll give you some idea. The real work's just startin'."

Cal Brennan looked out by the other buildings and on over the big land. In the small stout corral Monte Walsh, serene and secure in the hurricane seat, was taking the kinks and wild-eyed notions out of a seeming whirlwind that was a thick-rumped little sorrel that had never felt a cinch before. In the bigger corral beyond, Chet Rollins, rope in hand, was looking over a dozen or more equally wild-eyed horses for the next likely candidate. A half mile beyond two men raced forward, rocking in saddles and yipping, Powder Kent and Dally Johnson betting as usual their quarters of Skimpy Eagen's evening pie which would get in first. Off to the east a dust cloud floated upward that would be Hat Henderson standing in a bouncing wagon that had carried posts and wire to the line, yelling to the team to get a move on in the direction of food, likely exchanging insults with Petey Williams cavorting in saddle alongside. Off to the west by the mountains a thin spiral of smoke drifted above the first showings of timber that would be the campfire of Shorty Austin and Jumping Joe Joslin and Sugar Wyman who were building a line cabin for later winter use. And down from the long low ridge fronting the mountains jogged two others, that seeming incongruous pair, the slim deadly compactness of Dobe Chavez and the barrel bulk of Sunfish Perkins.

Cal rubbed a hand down one cheek and over his chin. "I reckon you're right after all," he said. "We're in good shape. We got the makin's."

* * *

"Absolutely the most astonishing performance I ever saw anywhere. You won't believe me—I can tell from your manner you don't believe half of what I've been telling you about that western trip. But it happened. It most certainly did. The train had been crawling, just crawling, all day. Dull. You have no idea how dull. And monotonous. The country out there takes your breath away at first—and then it puts you to sleep. Always more and then more and then more of the same. Too much of it. You can't take it all in so finally you stop trying. I was in the last car—it was a tremendous train, three whole cars. I was sitting on the back platform—observation platform they called the dinky thing—and there was another man there too. I think we both had retired there to escape another man, an insufferable bore, in the car. Then the train stopped. They are always stopping out there on a siding to let one from the other direction go past. But this time we were on the edge of a small town. I suppose you'd have to call it a town although it was only a hit-or-miss collection of what looked like mud huts and a few wooden buildings that seemed about ready to fall down. And quite a few big pens along the tracks full of cattle. Except for one pen that had several dozen horses in it. And another that was empty—of animals I mean because there were a dozen or so men in it. They seemed to be in two groups. Arguing. Amazing how people out there are always arguing—and usually ending up making some kind of wager and putting everything they own on it. These must have been arguing about those horses because they lassoed one and brought it into the pen with them and put a saddle on it and while two men held it one from one group mounted and when they let go the horse went positively mad, jumping all over the pen. That man sat there in the saddle as if he were in an easy chair and with the horse cavorting all over the pen he took out a paper and some tobacco and rolled a cigarette. And took out a match and cupped his hands and—

"No, no. That isn't what I mean. That was just a begin-

ning. A curtain-raiser, so to speak. That man lit the cigarette all right. But when he jumped down those in the other group didn't appear to think much of what he had done at all. They lassoed another horse out of the other pen and it took four men to hold this one while they put a saddle on it. Then one of the second group mounted. He was tall and lean and when he moved he looked like he'd been made out of a piece of spring steel. He did it so fast I didn't see him moving. One second he was standing by the horse and the next second he was in the saddle and the four men who had been holding were jumping away. If that first horse was mad, this one was simply insane. It was all over the place and up in the air most of the time. And this man sat there just as easy as had the other man—and then he started doing it. What I mean. He took off his hat and threw it away and a shorter solid-looking man ran and grabbed it. He took off his cartridge belt with its gun and tossed that and the shorter man grabbed it too. Then off came one boot. Then the other boot. With the horse cavorting around like a skyrocket all the time. Then he un-buttoned his shirt and tossed that away too. Now don't ask me how he did it, but his pants came off too. His pants. He was sitting in the saddle in his long underwear. And socks. Then the socks came off too. About this time the other man on the platform with me had had enough. Disgusting, he said, and went inside the car. But I noticed later he was right by a window on that side . . .

"Did that man finish the job? Right down to the skin? I don't know. Right about then the train started to move on. But the last I saw he had one arm out of that underwear and was working on the other arm. Knowing the way people are out there in that country, I rather think he did."

In Harmony
1882

THE HORSE ROSE in the air, spine arched, and switched ends and came down stiff-legged. Monte Walsh, easy in the saddle, took the jolt with a grunt and raked the wet flanks with his spurs. The horse doubled its forelegs under and rocked down on its side and Monte stepped out of the saddle going down. "That won't get you nowheres," he said. The horse bent its head backwards and rolled the white of an eye at him. It lunged to its feet and Monte stepped into the saddle coming up. The horse stood, head hanging, legs braced.

"Watch 'im," said Chet Rollins from his perch on the inside gate of the small corral. "He ain't done yet."

"Who's riding this thing?" said Monte. "Think I was weaned just—"

The horse exploded, coming off the ground with legs spread-eagled, and hit again running and streaked straight for the corral fence. Monte wrapped reins around his hands and yanked its head to the left till the nose almost hit the straining shoulder and it swung in an arc, stumbling, fighting its own forward weight for footing. It lined out again straight for the opposite side of the corral. "Go ahead break your fool neck," said Monte. He loosened toes in the stirrups, ready to leave the hurricane deck. The horse saw the rails ahead and faltered and swung this time on its own and raced around the inside of the corral. Monte took off his hat and slapped it in hearty rhythm against the heaving withers. "Yowee!" he yelled. "Run, you bat-brain! Catch your own tail and eat it!"

The horse stopped. Its head drooped. It was a statue of disgust and dejection, motionless except for heaving ribs and a slight quivering of legs. Monte swung down and walked around by the drooping head. "Well, now," he said. "You be-

91

haved medium to good considering—" He leaped backward. The horse's head was up and a forehoof slashed the air half an inch in front of his shirt. He leaped in close and grabbed an ear in each hand and hung his weight on the horse's head, pulling it down.

"Playful, ain't he?" said Chet Rollins from the corral gate. He jumped down and ambled forward through the settling dust and loosened the double rigging and pulled the breaking saddle off the horse. He ambled back and set the saddle on a top rail and opened the gate into the big main corral. Monte let go of the ears and took hold of the headband of the hackamore and in one sweeping motion stripped the hackamore down and off the horse's head and jumped aside. In a swirl of dust the horse sliced through the open gateway.

Monte Walsh and Chet Rollins sat on a top rail, backs to the small corral. In amiable silence they watched the half-broken horses in the big corral move with restless twitchings and roll off the sweaty itch of the day's working. Monte inspected his blunt battered fingers. He pulled a jackknife out of a pants pocket and opened it and began cleaning dust from under his fingernails. "Action," he murmured. "That's what I need. A little action." Chet turned his head slow and looked at him. Monte closed the knife and slipped it back in the pocket. He pushed his hat up his forehead. "Shucks," he said "That's just a job."

Chet fished a stubby pipe out of one shirt pocket and a small leather tobacco pouch out of the other. He took a long time filling the bowl to final satisfaction. He sighed. "It's only been two weeks since—"

"That long?" said Monte. "That's a mighty long time." He reached an arm and lifted the pouch from Chet's pocket and took a paper from one of his own shirt pockets and rolled a cigarette. He leaned over and tucked the pouch where it belonged and lit his cigarette from Chet's match over the pipe. He settled back on the rail and watched the two streamers of smoke that emerged from his nose. "At my age anyway," he said.

Chet sighed again. He drew in a lungful of smoke and took the pipe from his mouth and blew a series of lazy drifting rings and reached to poke a finger through the last one. Beside him Monte shifted rump on rail and turned a bit toward him.

"No," said Chet. "I ain't got a cent."

The hot glaze of midafternoon shimmered over the two corrals and on out over the plain. Off to the right Skimpy Eagens came out of the cookhouse carrying an empty bucket and disappeared into the supply shed and emerged with the bucket full of potatoes and disappeared again into the cookhouse. Monte flipped his cigarette butt into the dust and pushed out from the rail and landed light with one boot covering the butt. He strode to the side fence and vaulted it and angled to the bunkhouse. Inside he began a thorough search, unhurried, competent, pulling out the pockets of the clothes hanging on wooden pegs along the end walls, peeling back blankets and feeling under the lumpy straw mattresses in the bunks along the side walls. Several dollar bills and some change began to accumulate in his left pants pockets.

"There'll be a little ruckus," said Chet from the doorway, "when the boys get in."

"Shucks," said Monte. "They always ante in an emergency." A quarter hit the floor and rolled. He bent to retrieve it. "This is an emergency," he said. He pushed past Chet in the doorway and strolled toward a fenced enclosure behind the barn, collecting his saddle and bridle and a rope from the barn on the way. The experienced cow ponies in the enclosure eyed him with wary suspicion and drifted to the far side. He dropped his gear by the fence and slipped through. He carried the rope coiled in his left hand and shook out a loop with the right. He looked the horses over and picked a short-coupled pinto and with sure instinct the pinto knew and drifted further away among the others. He strolled forward with the loop trailing on the ground beside him and the horses shifted toward the left and he angled that way and they bunched in the corner, the pinto far back among them. He strolled closer and they broke, scattering to left and right to race past him, and the pinto feinted fast to one side and wheeled to plunge to the other and around, snorting, head high, hoofs pounding, and his right hand flipped forward and the rope snaked out and the loop opened and dropped over the pinto's head. It reared back, testing the rope and his hold. Its forefeet dropped to the ground and it stood, patient and resigned, watching him approach.

Ten minutes later, jogging along at a steady pace along the wagon trace toward town, he heard hoofbeats behind him.

Chet Rollins on a chunky gray came alongside and pulled to the same pace. They jogged along in a companionable silence.

"Poorest outfit I ever was with," said Monte Walsh. "Only seven dollars and seventeen cents."

* * *

The unorganized town of Harmony slept in the afternoon glaze. Curtains were pulled or flour bags hung at the windows of the few adobe houses to shut out the sun. The doors of the livery stable and the blacksmith shop and the stage station were closed for the same sensible reason. The wide porch of the combination hotel and office building served the same purpose. A blanket hung down over the one wide window of the barber shop. An innovation, an awning, shaded the front of the general store. Even three of the four saloons had the solid doors behind the swinging doors closed. Down the brief length of the main, the only recognizable, street not a twitch of movement disturbed the silence. Two freight wagons stood motionless in the street dust, their ox teams lying down under the yokes. Across the way an old farm wagon sagged over its axles, its team still and wooden, too dulled even to flick tails at flies. Harmony reigned in Harmony. And over the last rise of the rolling plain that stretched its long lonely miles all around and on down to the main street jogged a short-coupled pinto and a chunky gray.

"Well, lookathere," said Monte Walsh. "One new shack and a frill on the store."

The two knowing cow ponies swung together to the tie rail in front of the one open saloon. Monte and Chet Rollins dismounted and eased cinches and stepped up across the plank sidewalk and went inside. The bartender, perched on a stool behind the bar and hunched forward on his elbows reading a newspaper, looked up and saw them coming. He reached under the bar and set out two small glasses and a plain labelless bottle, half filled with a dark deadly liquid, and returned to his paper.

"Not that stuff," said Monte. "We can pay."

The bartender turned his head to look up sideways. He waited. Monte fished in his left pants pocket and pulled out one of the dollar bills and laid this on the bar. The bartender swiveled on the stool and reached with both hands, one to take the dollar, the other to take a bottle with a bright label off a shelf behind him. He set the bottle by the two glasses and in the same motion restored the first bottle to its place beneath the bar. He settled again on his elbows over the paper. "That'll cover four," he said.

Monte Walsh and Chet Rollins drained their first pair and leaned with backs against the bar surveying the interior of the saloon. An old man in too-large clothes that looked even older sat slouched on a chair near the front staring dull-eyed out the one side window at the blank wall of the next building. Farther back the two freighters from the two wagons outside slept with long puffing snores by a streak-topped table. One was upright, head back, mouth open. The other was slumped forward on the table, head cradled in his arms by an empty bottle.

"Mighty lively," murmured Monte.

The bartender slapped his hands down on his newspaper and pushed up straighter. "What d'you expect?" he said. "A brass band an' dancing girls? Won't be payday for any outfit around for a week or more." He settled again to his paper.

Monte Walsh and Chet Rollins drained the second pair. Monte stooped down and peered toward the back of the saloon. At this level he could see, behind a round table in a corner, stretched out on three chairs in a line, the long thin form of a man lying asleep with a hat over his face. Monte strolled back and fingered the top chips in a box on the round table. He picked up the deck of cards beside the box and riffled them with little snapping sounds. The figure on the chairs stirred and a voice issued from under the hat. "What've you got?"

Monte tried to sound joyful. "Six dollars," he said.

"That ain't even drinking money," said the voice.

Monte strolled toward the front. Chet Rollins was inspecting what looked like a framed picture on the wall but there was no picture in the frame. Between the board back and the glass many nails in zigzag patterns stuck out from the wood, their tips almost touching the glass. Along the top were slits in the frame. Along the bottom, behind the glass, was a row of little compartments. The one in the middle offered, in gilt letters, the golden legend: $10. Two others, spaced out on each side, proclaimed $5. The others were blank. Pasted to the back boards in an upper corner, plain through the glass, was a diagram showing a coin being inserted in one of the slits and tracing with a dotted line its course bouncing from nail to nail and dropping into the $10 compartment.

"Ain't that cute?" said Chet. "Those blamed nails're so close together over the winners nothing could get through if it tried."

The bartender slapped hands down on his newspaper. His voice was aggrieved. "Man so stupid he can't figure that out," he said, "deserves to lose his money." He settled to his paper again.

Footsteps sounded on the plank sidewalk outside. Two pairs of polished boots showed beneath the swinging doors and two top hats above them passing by. Monte Walsh and Chet Rollins stood by the bar and looked at each other. Monte reached for the bottle but the bartender's hand was there first. The bartender went on reading, his hand holding the bottle. Monte fished in his pocket and extracted another dollar bill. The bartender's hand left the bottle and took the bill.

"Wonder who's dead?" murmured Monte. The bartender turned his head and looked up. "Funeral ain't it?" said Monte.

"No," said the bartender and returned to his reading.

Monte Walsh and Chet Rollins drained the third pair. Monte strolled over to the old man by the window. He was beginning to bounce a bit off his toes as he walked. "Hello, Johnny," he said. The old man's head lifted and swung toward him. Monte leaned closer. "Buffalo," he said.

The old man straightened on the chair. His eyes brightened. "Where?" He jumped up and looked around and his eyes focused on Monte. "Aw-w-w, you," he said. "Cows. That's all you know. You ain't never seen 'em. Thick as flies they was, right around here." He waved an arm in a wild gesture and his voice began to climb. "Skinnin' was what I did. Any jack kin shoot a gun. You gotta know to skin." He moved out into the open and began to flourish an imaginary knife. "Cut it around the neck. Up by the horns. Slice it down the belly. Clear to the tail. Slit it down the legs. Peg it through the nose. Hook on the team and start—"

"Not now, Johnny," said Monte. He was headed for the door and the sound of hoofs and creaking of wheels outside.

The old man subsided, shaking his head, and returned to his chair.

Outside on the sidewalk Monte Walsh and Chet Rollins watched the stagecoach swing in by the hotel down the street. They saw two men climb out and recognized these despite their dressed-up appearance as the proprietor of the general store and one of Harmony's two land-claim lawyers. They saw these two stand aside, very respectful, while a third man climbed out, very neat and respectable in a matching suit and tall hat. They saw the three be greeted on the hotel porch by the two who had passed the saloon and all of them disappear inside. They looked at each other and returned to the bar in a companionable silence.

Monte filled the two glasses again. The old man was off his chair and coming close. "Lemme tell you," said the old man. "Sixty-seven in one day. That's what I did. It was out—"

"Some other time, Johnny," said Monte. He leaned over the bar and reached under and found another small glass and filled it from the bottle and handed it to the old man. "Make it last," he said and the old man retired to his chair hugging the glass to his outsize old shirt front.

The bartender took the bottle and set it on the shelf behind him. "Ought to count that," he said and returned to his reading.

Monte Walsh and Chet Rollins raised their fourth pair and looked at each other over the glasses. "Preacher?" suggested Chet.

"No," said Monte. "Wrong kind of collar. Railroad man maybe."

The bartender groaned. He folded his paper and set it aside. He picked a cloth from under the bar and began to wipe already dry glasses with mechanical gestures. "It's a judge," he said. "Kind of a judge. Justice of the peace. Sent out by the county to civilize you heathen."

Monte studied his glass, shifting it to catch the light from the doorway through the whisky. "Anything interesting for him to judge today?"

"No," said the bartender. "Ain't been a payday lately."

Monte studied the glass some more. "You mean," he said, "you get a judge here today and there ain't a thing for him to judge about?"

The bartender shrugged shoulders and eyebrows at the

same time. He made a point of turning about and retiring with his cloth to the other end of the bar.

"My oh my," murmured Monte. "What'll he think of the place?"

Chet Rollins sighed. He drained his drink and picked up the paper and edged away from Monte and unfolded the paper and inspected the front page.

"What kind of a judge d'you think he is?" said Monte. "Five-dollar kind?"

Chet folded the newspaper slow and careful and put it down. He pointed at the nail-studded contraption on the wall and held out a hand, palm flat. Monte fished in his left pants pocket and pulled out a nickel and laid it on the palm. Chet ambled over and dropped it through one of the slits. It joggled from nail to nail and bounced into a blank compartment. Chet ambled back. "See?" he said.

Monte paid no attention. He was cradling his drink in his right hand and rocking slow and soft on his boot soles and staring upward dreamy-eyed. "Looked like a five-dollar judge to me," he said.

Chet sighed again. "I ain't listening," he said. "I ain't even here." He ambled to the opposite side of the saloon and set a chair by the wall and sat on it, tilting it against the wall and settling his feet on one of the rungs.

Monte reached his left hand into his left pants pocket and took it out and counted what was in it. He put the hand back in the pocket and took it out empty. He drained his drink and set the glass down with a little flourish. He strolled out into the middle of the floor and reached up and pushed his hat off his forehead. "Yow-eee!" he yelled. "I'm a-howling!"

The old man turned on his chair and regarded Monte with a vacant stare and turned back to his glass and the window. Chet Rollins sat still and studied his boot toes with a pained expression on his face. The two freighters stirred a little and went on snoring. The man lying on the three chairs at the rear jackknifed up to sitting position and surveyed the room and retrieved his hat and lay down again. The bartender groaned and tossed his cloth aside and leaned on his arms on the bar to watch developments.

Monte pushed his hat farther back and scratched by one ear. He strolled over by the freighters, bouncing off his toes with each step, and fingered the high crown of the hat of the one slumped over the table. With gentle touch he tested the space between the top of the crown and the head beneath. He strolled back to the middle of the open space and pulled his gun and fired and the hat lifted off the freighter's head and flapped to the floor with a neat hole through the crown. The two freighters jerked on their chairs, struggling out of sleep, and their eyes focused on Monte. They saw him dropping his gun into its holster. They saw him stand, rocking on boot soles, grinning at them. "Yow-eee!" he yelled. "I'm really a-howling!"

They looked at each other. One fumbled a coin out of a shirt pocket. "Tails," he said and flipped it spinning and caught it and slapped it on his other wrist. A slow smile spread over his face. He tucked the coin back into the pocket and started to rise. "Shucks," said Monte, rocking forward. "I mean both of you." He took hold of their table and tipped it onto them and they went sprawling and came up off the floor in a roaring rush.

The bartender reached under the bar and took hold of a heavy bung-starter and walked down the length of the bar and around the front end. "That ain't polite," said Chet. He was quiet on his tilted chair but his gun was out of its holster and held in his right hand on his lap. "All right," said the bartender, "but it's a lot quicker." He laid the bung-starter on the bar. He threw back his shoulders and drew in a deep breath and plunged into the whirling melee in the middle of the floor.

"Yow-eee!" yelled Monte Walsh, slammed into the bar to the tune of rattling glass and bouncing off and using the momentum to drive a shoulder into the bartender's midriff. "Three's more like it!"

* * *

Justice Coleman rocked with slight little testing sways in the swivel chair that adorned the office that had been his for almost an hour. He liked the chair. It fitted his rear proportions and did not squeak with the rockings. Encouraged, he leaned back in it until it rested against the edge of the rolltop desk behind him. He folded his hands in his lap and looked straight ahead to inspect the battered lean figure of Monte Walsh. "Disturbing the peace, eh," he said in a careful judi-

cial tone. He turned his head a bit to the right to inspect the
battered figures of the two freighters and the bartender.
"There would appear to be ample evidence," he said and
turned his head to the left toward the row of townsmen along
the wall for appreciation of his remark and obtained it. He
looked straight forward again at Monte Walsh. "Well, young
man, I expect you are expert at explanations."

"Shucks, no," said Monte. "Things were so damned peaceful, seemed to make sense disturbing them."

Justice Coleman unfolded his hands and folded them again
with fingers reversed. "So you proceeded to disturb them," he
said. "Logical. From your point of view. But, alas, not legal.
So it becomes my duty to disturb you."

"Go right ahead, Judge," said Monte and shoved his left
hand into left pants pocket.

"I intend to," said Justice Coleman. "That will be ten dollars—" He stopped. He straightened in the swivel chair and
pushed it with his feet against the floor as far back as possible butting against the rolltop desk. Monte Walsh was halfway to him, hands out to grab, before intercepted by one of
the freighters in a flying dive, followed close by the bartender
and the other freighter. Justice Coleman tucked his feet out
of the way under the swivel chair and watched a repetition of
the original disturbance. He began to be worried. Reinforce-
ments sprang from along the wall. He sighed in relief. He
pushed his feet out again and settled into a more comfortable
position and looked down at Monte Walsh flat on the floor
with a man sitting on each leg and arm. "—or ten days," he
said.

*   *   *

The last light of the sun low to the horizon shone through
the one high window in the rear wall of Harmony's new
shack. The bright patch it cast on the front wall was marred
by four perpendicular shadow lines made by four iron bars
set into the window frame. There was no glass in the window. An outside shutter had been swung back and hooked to
the outside wall. The door to the shack stood open. A grillwork of iron bars filled the doorway, hung on heavy outside
hinges at one side and fastened with a heavy padlock on the
other. A plump graying pear-shaped man in old dungarees

and plaid shirt stood by the grillwork peering through at Monte Walsh inside on the edge of the cot along one wall.

Monte lay back on the cot and put his hands up behind his head and regarded the ceiling. "Shucks," he said. "How was I to know they'd got a jail too."

"Don't go getting snooty," said the pear-shaped man. "It ain't just for you."

Monte continued to regard the ceiling. "Now me," he murmured. "I'd be plumb ashamed to be running a jail."

"It's a job," said the pear-shaped man. He turned away and disappeared from view. Monte waited a moment. He came to his feet in one motion and made a quick circuit of the shack. It was firm and solid. He stopped by the grillwork door. Near the bottom, between two cross-strips, a segment of bar had been removed leaving an opening about ten inches square. "Have to be a circus freak," he said, "to wiggle through that." He put the one chair in the room under the one window and stood on it and looked out. A hundred yards away Chet Rollins sat easy and casual on the chunky gray holding a lead rope fastened to the bridle of the short-coupled pinto. He saw Monte's face between the bars and waved his free hand in cheery salute and took hold of his reins and swung the horses away. Monte watched him jogging into distance. "Why that low-bellied snake," he said. "Leaving me here." He returned to the cot and lay back again and regarded the ceiling.

The bright patch on the front wall faded and the diffused light of dusk crept through the shack leaving darkening shadows in the corners. Monte heard slight sounds by the doorway and turned his head. A plate heaped with beef stew was coming through the small square opening near the bottom and being set on the floor just inside. "Wondered what that was for," he murmured. A large tin cup of coffee followed the plate. He sat upright on the cot. The hand holding the cup was small and feminine. He came to his feet, light and quick, and was over by the doorway. Outside a neat figure, plump and pleasing, was rising upright from a stooping position. It filled out an old gingham dress with satisfying completeness and the head above the dress was young and healthy with a broad glowing good-natured face and a quantity of darkish hair pulled back and tied behind with a small ribbon.

"My oh my," said Monte. "Where'd you come from?"

She stepped back a pace and looked him over. "You don't seem so much," she said. "I thought you'd be horrible. Beating up three men . . . Oh. From that house next door. That's where we live. We've been here three weeks already."

"No," said Monte. "All that time and I've missed you?"

"You wouldn't see me," she said. "Not the places you'd go. Just put those dishes outside when you're through." She started away.

"Hey," said Monte. "You married to him?"

She stopped and swung at the waist to turn her head back toward him. "I don't see as that's any of your affair. But it's no. He's my father."

"Lovely," said Monte. "Just plain lovely."

She turned around to face him, hands on hips. "Listen, mister cowboy. This is business. See? You mean a dollar a day to us on the feeding and that's fifty cents profit if you don't eat too much."

"Shucks," said Monte. "I'll just nibble a little." He was talking to her back as she departed. He squatted on the floor and sniffed the stew. He cleaned the plate and finished the coffee. He set the dishes outside through the square opening and retired to the cot and the ceiling. The dusk deepened into darkness and a thin sliver moon emerged in the sky. He heard soft sounds at the window and rolled his head to look. In the faint light of the moon he made out fingers tying a rope to one of the bars. He came to his feet, light and quick, and stepped up on the chair by the window. The round stubbled face of Chet Rollins beamed at him through the bars. "Nice evening," said Chet. He was standing on his saddle on the back of the chunky gray. The short-coupled pinto, ground-reined, waited patiently thirty feet away. Chet's face sank from sight as he dropped down into the saddle.

"Hey," whispered Monte. "Don't—"

"Nothing to it," came Chet's voice from below the window. The gray moved out from the rear wall and the rope stretched taut between the bar and the saddle horn. Chet tickled the gray with his spurs and it plowed forward, head low and straining, and the window frame, complete with its bars, ripped out of the wall and bounced to the ground.

"Why that double-crossing jackass," murmured Monte. He

watched Chet dismount and amble over to the fallen window frame and start unfastening the rope. He heard running footsteps coming from the house next door. He jumped off the chair and stepped over by the grillwork door. The pear-shaped man appeared in a nightshirt, a shotgun in his hands, eyes wide and popping as he tried to see into the dark interior. "What's going on in there?" he said.

"Nothing much," said Monte. "I tripped over the damn bucket."

"Well, quit it," said the pear-shaped man. "I need my sleep." He bent down and took the plate and cup and departed toward the house. Monte retired to the cot and lay back and closed his eyes.

"What're you doing in there?" said Chet Rollins from the window opening. "Packing a trunk?"

"Go fly a kite," suggested Monte.

Chet shifted his feet to firmer position on the saddle and leaned on the edge of the window opening. "That judge can't boss outside of town," he said. He waited. There was no response. He sighed. "Who's the girl this time? How'd you meet her stuck in there?" He waited again. He sighed again and pushed out from the window edge and dropped down into the saddle.

Monte opened his eyes and raised his head, listening. He heard soft hoofbeats, muffled in the dust, fade away. He settled his head back down and wriggled into a more comfortable position on the cot. "Three times a day for ten days," he murmured and was asleep.

The thin sliver moon arched downward and dipped below the horizon and the first faint glimmers of the light before dawn crept into the shack. There were small scraping noises in the neighborhood of the window opening. Monte Walsh stirred and wriggled on the cot and suddenly was still, eyes wide open. He had company. He rolled his head and saw Chet Rollins a few feet away, flanked on one side by Dally Johnson and on the other by Shorty Austin.

"I could yell," said Monte.

"We could ram a gag down your throat," said Chet.

"Coming peaceable?" said Dally. "Or do we have to truss you like a dressed chicken?"

"Better had," said Shorty. "One of those dollars was mine."

"Did you think," said Chet, leading the way to the window, "I was going to finish topping those broncs all by my lonesome?"

* * *

The unorganized town of Harmony was wide awake in the afternoon glaze. Curtains were pulled at some of the houses to shut out more than the sun. The street doors of the livery stable and the blacksmith shop were wide open. New signs offering new bargains were tacked on the front of the general store under the awning. Cow ponies in rows stood patiently twitching tails along the tie rails. Down the brief length of the main street floated the sound of voices and chinking glass emanating from all four saloons. The temporary harmony of the beginnings of serious drinking reigned in Harmony. And out beyond the last close rise of the rolling plain, skirting around it and staying below the skyline, jogged a deep-chested leggy dun.

"Got to be cagey about this," murmured Monte Walsh. He circled and came in behind the livery stable and swung down and rapped on the rear door. He rapped again and it opened and disclosed a short hunchbacked man holding a pitchfork. The man stepped aside as Monte led the dun in. "Keep this thing for me and my gear," said Monte. "Likely some days before I'll be needing 'em."

"Sure thing, Monte," said the man. "Grain 'im any?"

"Shucks, no," said Monte. "Don't go giving that thing fancy notions." He started back out the door and stopped. "You ain't seen me," he said. "I ain't in town."

"Sure thing," said the man, staring at him. "If you say so."

Monte moved out the door and along the rear of the stable. Part of a month's pay burdened his left pants pocket. He ducked across the alley between the stable and the barber shop and rapped on the rear door of the shop. It opened partway and the upper portion of a thin little man in old checkered trousers and a once-white shirt peered around it.

"Any one in there?" said Monte.

"Not right now," said the barber. "Only me."

"That's plenty," said Monte. He pushed in past the little man and settled himself in the one barber chair. Twenty-five minutes later, shaved, hair cut and shampooed, he strolled out the way he had come and back across the alley and on past the livery stable to the rear kitchen door of the combination hotel and office building. He went in and tossed a greeting at the combination cook and waiter who was pounding chunks of beef with a hammer and strolled on through and around and along a hallway to an open doorway with a board nailed above it marked Sheriff. He leaned against the doorframe and regarded the broad back of a big curly-headed man sitting at a desk by a window busy shuffling papers and tucking them away in pigeonholes.

"Howdy, Mac," said Monte. "Heard they gave you a badge."

The big man turned his head and saw Monte. "I ain't proud," he said. "Somebody had to take it." He returned to his papers.

"Well," said Monte. "I'm here."

The big man did not look up. "So you are," he said. "Looks like you anyway."

"Mighty quiet," said Monte. "Ain't you after me?"

The big man shifted his chair around and put a hand on each knee and looked up. "What is it you've been doing now?"

"Nothing much," said Monte. "Finished a batch of horses and got straight with the boys. But I got ten days to do."

The crinkles around the big man's eyes deepened and he leaned back in the chair and put both hands up behind his head, elbows wide. "Ain't anybody told you?" he said. "Judge inquired around the next day. Figured why you did it and killed the charge. He ain't through laughing at it yet." The big man hitched his chair back around and returned to his papers.

"Shucks," murmured Monte. "That ain't fair. I was counting on those days." He studied his blunt fingers and pulled a match out of a pocket and began cleaning dirt from under a fingernail. He flipped the match at the big man's broad back and strolled out along the hallway and out the front door of the building and along the street to the small house beside the jail. He took off his hat and held it in his left hand and rapped with his right on the front door. He waited and rapped again. The door opened and he saw a neat figure, plump and pleasing, which filled out an old brown skirt and a faded frilled shirtwaist with satisfying completeness.

"It's you," she said and started to close the door and caught it and held it open a little way and peered around it. "Why aren't you over at one of those saloons?"

"Shucks, ma'am," said Monte. "They're all right when there ain't anything better to do. There's a nice little buggy over at the livery stable. I thought you and me'd take a ride."

"After what you did?" she said and started to close the door again. Monte's left boot was in the way. "Well, now, ma'am," he said. "I know I did kind of run out on you back there a bit."

She pushed on the door. The boot was still in the way. "On me?" she said. "Well I never! It took Father half a day to fix that window!"

Monte transferred the hat to his right hand and fished in his left pants pocket and pulled out a five-dollar bill. "Kind of like to make that right," he said. "Fifty cents profit for ten days. That's what you'd have made on me. Here it is."

"Why—why—you—" With quick movement she pulled the door further open and slammed it back against the boot and Monte tottered hopping on his right foot and she closed the door with a vigorous snap. It opened again a few inches, almost on the rebound, and her voice came through. "And don't you ever try to come near me again!" The door closed with a definite click.

"Now ain't that a girl," murmured Monte. He tried to feel his left toes through the boot leather. They seemed to be intact. He put his hat on and pulled it down and limped across the street and sat on the edge of the plank sidewalk and studied the house across the way. "Can't let any of the boys beat me to her," he murmured. He looked up the street. Something had been added. Two freight wagons now stood at one side, their ox teams chewing cuds in placid endurance. A slow grin spread over Monte's face. He uncoiled onto his feet and limped up the street. A small jingle sounded from his left pants pocket. He slapped his left hand over it. "Got to unload that," he murmured. "Might get in the way."

He limped into the saloon opposite the freight wagons. Lined along the bar were Chet Rollins and Dally Johnson and Shorty Austin and the rest of the Slash Y crew. At a table by the wall sat two freighters with a half-empty bottle between them. There was a neat hole through the crown of one of their hats.

Monte limped to the bar. He pushed in between Chet Rollins and Powder Kent. He looked sideways at Chet and Chet looked at him and grinned a sheepish little grin.

"Have trouble shaking the sheriff?" said Shorty Austin.

"Check your hardware," said Dally Johnson down the line. "There's a jailbird loose in here."

"Shucks," said Monte. "Some of you might have told me." He beckoned to the bartender. He fished in his left pants pocket and laid a fistful of crumpled bills and change on the bar. "Keep your damn count," he said. "But they're all on me long as that lasts."

"Well, whatta you know," said Dally Johnson, reaching quick for a bottle. "He's celebratin'."

"Addled," said Powder Kent. "But in a mighty encouraging way."

Chet Rollins said nothing. He sighed. He picked up his glass and added another drink to those already behind his belt. His eyes began to brighten. Color was climbing up his cheeks. "Finished that bunch," he said. "Nothing really pressing for a while." He started to turn toward Monte.

"No," said Monte. "You ain't even here. Remember?" He pulled a bottle toward him and leaned over the bar and reached under and found a small glass. He drained one, two, three, four. He set the glass down with a little flourish and stood rocking on his boot soles, letting the whisky settle some. "Feel about right," he murmured and strolled out into the middle of the floor. He took off his hat and sent it skimming and it smacked into the bottle on the table between the two freighters and the bottle fell gurgling into the lap of one of them.

"Yow-eeee!" yelled Monte Walsh. "I'm a-howling!"

*   *   *

"Good Lord, Brennan, what's happening over in the bunk-house? Sounds as if someone was being murdered!"

"That? That's just Shorty blattin' 'cause he's lost a hand. Probably tried to run a bluff."

"Poker?"

"In a way. Somethin' Monte thought up this winter. They got some beans in there. Pinto beans. They divvy 'em around, fifty each. A right cutthroat game. First man out's got to help

Skimpy next day with wood, dishes, slops an' such. Without skippin' his reg'lar work any. No playin' a waitin' game. They got a stiff ante. Five beans. Second man out's got to rub everyone's boots. Winner gets a whole pie. Skimpy antes that 'cause without playin' he wins anyway."

X Y Z
1883

THIS WAS a bad year at the Slash Y. Oh, the days rocked along about as usual most of the time, strenuous and full of the hard rough work that stiffened the spines of the men and made them proud they could do it with the swift seeming careless ease of old hands at the game, and nothing much really drastic happened except in one brief burst of bitter activity. Even the weather cooperated, kicking up a fuss only often enough to keep life interesting. The shareholders of the Consolidated Cattle Company had no complaints when they saw the annual audit and when the dividend checks came from the Chicago office. From their point of view it averaged out a good year.

It was a bad year at the Slash Y nonetheless, leaving a bad taste in the mouth of memory.

* * *

Likely it was a bit of foolishness on the part of Jumping Joe Joslin that started things off wrong. Along in early spring, when winter had left the levels and was retreating for last holdouts in the hills, Jumping Joe noticed that his saddle cinch was worn thin and he meant to replace it and then he was fool enough for a few days to forget about it. Long enough to ride into a little trouble.

He was out riding line where the long low ridge fronted the mountains and an occasional silly cow, remembering the patches of early new-green grass summoned by melting snow in the badlands just beyond, sometimes went wandering and foundered in a snow-filled hollow. Joe had roped one such by one horn and yanked her out and coiled in his rope and was shooing her down to the wind-swept level when she showed stubborn and doubled back again. He slapped spurs to his horse and raced alongside and when he swung to head her that cinch let loose. Not all the way with a clean break which would have meant only a sudden spill with him and saddle sailing free, but partway through, just enough to slacken the grip and let the saddle start to slide around the horse's barrel. Down he went, right shoulder and back thumping hard, off foot still caught in twisted stirrup, and the horse, startled and frightened, raced on, dragging him over the rough ground. He sloshed through wet snow and puddles and he bounced from bump to bump and he was too busy to do much more than grunt. By the time he had heaved himself up some grabbing at his own leg and managed to free the foot, he was bunged plenty and had a strained ankle and an assortment of nasty nicks from flying hoofs. Worse than that, he was afoot, having been too busy to hang on to the reins. Wet with sweat and the dragging through snow and mud. And afoot. Out in the middle of apparent nowhere. Already shivering from shock and the chill air.

Jumping Joe Joslin stood with weight mostly on one foot and watched the horse hightailing into distance northeastward. He cursed it competently with all the epithets and obscene references he could cull out of long and various experience in many places. He thought better of that and cursed the cow. He thought better of that and cursed himself. That done, he shrugged battered shoulders. Such things happened. It could have been worse; in a rocky area his brains might have been scattered from here to there and everywhere in between. He hobbled to pick up his hat. He pulled his gun and wiped mud from it and raised it and fired twice into the air. Shorty Austin might not be too many miles away, on down by the lower end of the ridge. No response. He fired again, twice. Still no response. Shorty must have reached the lower end and swung eastward through the broken land down that way. Jumping Joe shrugged shoulders again, wincing at the twinges beginning in them. He started hobbling in the same general direction as the horse northeastward.

Back at the ranch headquarters Monte Walsh on a leggy dun was in the big corral checking the first batch of winter range saddle stock brought in a while before by Chet Rollins now gone for another batch, sorting out those that would need his personal attention before the real start of spring work, hazing these on into the smaller corral. He saw a riderless horse approaching at a steady trot, head at a left sideways angle to hold trailing reins from under forefeet, empty saddle tipped at a grotesque angle to the right. Three minutes later he had opened the corral gate and gone through and closed it without leaving his own saddle, unleashed his rope, flipped a loop over the head of the riderless horse, and dismounted to tie it by a rein to a corral rail and inspect the damage.

"Joe's," he said and was astride the leggy dun again streaking into distance southwestward.

* * *

Jumping Joe Joslin, as required by his calling, was made mostly of gristle and bone and guts with the constitution of a mountain mule. Any other time the banging he had received would have kept him in his bunk one day, maybe two, on a chair in the sun maybe one or two more, then he would have been limping around doing close-in chores and in a week would have been riding out again with nothing much more bothering him than the joshing of the others for being so damned careless and the half dozen new scars now added to the collection adorning his anatomy. But this time he must have been off his feed. After a day in bunk he was still there and after another day in bunk he was still there and the next morning when the others were up and gone he was still there and he was coughing till his throat was raw and his eyes were watering and his nose running and by evening he was still there, eyes and nose dry now, too dry, and he was running a fever.

Range manager Cal Brennan fussed over him all day like a hen with a sick chick and flipped through the pages of a home remedy book he had. "You lame-brain empty-headed coyote, you," said Cal. "If you was a cow, I might know what to do. Bein' as you're only a man an' a poor specimen at that, I just don't know."

Midnight and Cal had not gone over to his bed in the old adobe ranch house. He sat by Jumping Joe in the bunkhouse and in the light from a lone lamp on the table pulled close he laid damp cloths on Joe's forehead. There was not much sleep being enjoyed in the other bunks along the walls. Then

Joe took to talking in a hoarse strained voice and what he said made no sense at all.

"That ties it," said Cal. "Hat. You better hop into town for Doc Frantz."

"Right," said foreman Hat Henderson, sitting up and reaching for his pants.

"The hell with him," said Monte Walsh, already pulling on a boot. "That overgrown ape'll lumber along and take a couple hours getting there. I'll make it in one."

In the dark of night on a big rawboned bay that fought the bridling and the saddling and tried to paw the stars out of the sky before leveling into full gallop Monte Walsh streaked eastward toward town.

* * *

Windblown, bleary-eyed, with a layer of irritation laid over his customary resignation at the vagaries of life in such a land, Doc Frantz stepped up on the stone doorstep and appeared in the bunkhouse doorway. A lean jacketed arm reached out of the night past the doorjamb by his legs and set a small brown leather bag on the floor and disappeared outside again. The sound of two horses being led away drifted in through the open doorway.

Doc Frantz picked up the small bag and stepped forward into the room. "You better have something here worth my coming," he said. "Pulled out of bed. Pushed all the way. Your Walsh behind me whipping my horse about every jump. Now what is it? It better be good."

While Cal Brennan held the lamp close, Doc Frantz sat on the edge of Jumping Joe's bunk, placed a hand on the flushed forehead, frowned, took an old-fashioned stethoscope out of the small bag, put the earplugs in his ears, opened Joe's old underwear to expose an expanse of hard hairy chest, and bent low, tapping with one forefinger and listening. He buttoned the underwear, pulled the blanket up over the chest, tucked the stethoscope in the small bag, and looked around. "Maybe you two-legged jackasses know cattle," he said. "Maybe you even know a few other things, though I doubt it. You sure don't know pneumonia when you see it."

"He ain't a-gonna die, is he, Doc?" said Sugar Wyman.

"Die?" said Doc Frantz. "I haven't found the sickness yet

that can kill you range wolves. It takes bullets and knives to turn that little trick. But I'll have to have him in town where I can keep an eye on him. Leave him out here and you'll manage to kill him out of sheer stupidity."

* * *

Jumping Joe Joslin lay on a hard plank bed with a feather mattress over it in a small adobe house in the sparse small town of Harmony tended by a short fat ageless Spanish-American woman who continually chased innumerable small children of unknown paternity out of the room and slapped Joe down whenever he tried to climb out of the bed and made him take everything Doc Frantz said he should. His fever climbed and burned like a bonfire in him and he lay there alternately talking nonsense and cursing his own general foolishness and then that tough constitution began to assert itself and fought the fever and sent it flying. Four days and the crisis had come and passed and he lay there grinning kind of pale at the remarks of Dobe Chavez and Powder Kent in town for the mail. Four more and he was thinking of trying to inveigle the woman into the bed with him. Then he was sitting in a chair taking the sun in front of the house and telling long tall tales to the innumerable small children.

That was that, just one of those things that came along in the course of living, a minor incident, a ripple in the routine of the Slash Y that no one, not Jumping Joe himself, would think much about afterwards. But it had one important result as seen later in retrospect.

"No," said Doc Frantz. "Maybe you don't realize it, but you're still wobbly. You're not going back out and join your pack till at least a full month is up. Maybe two. I'm not having my good work undone. Maybe you don't know it, but it was touch and go there for a while with your lungs."

So Jumping Joe was still trapped in town while out on the range the Slash Y was sweating into the spring roundup short one man. Which again was not much of a problem. With the trail drives out of Texas slackening now, there were always a few fair cowhands out of work or congenitally footloose wandering through the territory, stopping for meals and talk, usually drifting west into Arizona where ranching was beginning to take hold. Cal Brennan looked them over and picked a temporary replacement.

"Why, sure," said the man. "I'll stick around an' help you over your hump."

He gave his name as Jim Kiens and likely that was right because several of the men remembered him by it from having bumped into him now and again in years past. He was of the right rawhide breed or certainly seemed to be. He sat a horse with easy assurance and never complained at any cut to his string and he handled a rope with the same assurance and he knew what to do and how to do it any time without being told more than once. He fitted into the outfit without any fuss beyond the inevitable horseplay and testing of temper and after the first few days he got along well with everybody. He did have a sometimes habit of talking in big ideas, that only a man with cotton in his head for brains would keep on working forever at forty and found playing nursemaid to other people's cattle, that a smart man would make his pile some easier way. But that was no original tune, being the usual growsing complaint of a ranch crew, only a little off-key at the Slash Y, and after a while this Kiens quit it anyway. He was a good worker, no doubt of that. By the time spring branding was done and Jumping Joe was back a bit soft and fat around the middle and raring to activate himself down to lean hardness again, Cal was thinking he might ask this Kiens to stay on permanent. Cal could juggle that into his working budget without too much finagling of figures. But Kiens took the notion away from him by asking for his time.

"Enough's enough," Kiens said. "I've seen you through your gather. Your man's here. Expect I'll be movin' west. Got friends over Tombstone way."

Cal even felt a bit sorry to see him go.

* * *

That was that again, nothing unusual in any way. But a little tag end of worry not tied to anyone or anything in particular kept nagging far back in Cal Brennan's mind and one evening, alone in the old ranch house, he took his little tally book out of his shirt pocket and looked at it and pulled open a squeaky drawer of his old desk and took out last year's little book and looked at it too. That tag end of worry in his mind clicked into clear focus. Somehow the calf count this year was not quite what he thought it should be. Maybe, just maybe. Not by much, not on the scale the Slash Y operated, and winter losses showing up in the spring were always unpredictable anyway. And Shorty Austin and Petey Williams had brought in a pair of wolf pelts about six weeks back. That could account for some early losses. But again, if so, why had no one mentioned coming across a cow or two with swollen teats? Well, then, maybe the men had been careless working the back country and had missed some stock.

Cal chewed a pencil stub in thought. He shook himself and tossed last year's little book into the drawer and tucked this year's into his shirt pocket. He was expecting too much, that was all, hoping to ring up a record every year, an oldtimer like him who knew only too well what the chances were in what was a gamble always, a gamble against luck and weather and nature's fanged competition and the natural perversity of cloven-hoofed cow-critters that sometimes seemed bent on suicide with only the muscle and know-how and sheer stubborn persistence of a few men riding long lonely miles in solitary trust to bring up the betting odds. Men like his, even if he set them to combing cattle out of the brakes of hell, would not miss many. And no more one year than another. The calf crop was down a notch. Such things happened.

Cal shut his mouth on his thoughts. He felt ashamed of having let even a flicker of a possibility his men had slipped up some slide through his mind. After a few days of trying he forgot about that curious little discrepancy in his tally book. He did not even think of it again until along in midsummer.

* * *

Monte Walsh ambled along seeming half-asleep aboard a rat-tailed roan, easing a half dozen plump grass-bellied horses toward the open gate of the big corral. Close in, facing the gap, remembering its meaning, two of them broke to the right, heads high sniffing for the freedom of the open range. Monte and the roan, in instant explosive partnership, swept to head them and turn them. Reluctant but resigned, they trotted in with the others.

Monte leaned down from saddle to close the gate. He straightened, wiping sweat from under his hat brim. Out on the plain that stretched to the long low ridge he saw a rider approaching, followed by a strange humped shape. Monte squinted into the summer sun. As usual he recognized the horse before the man. A scrawny cat-hipped pinto with one flop-ear. That would be José Gonzales from his tiny valley behind the ridge, leading his one burro piled high with dry piñon branches under rope which he would unload in town and cut into cookstove lengths and peddle from door to door.

"Wonder what's doing," murmured Monte. "He don't have to come past here." Monte nudged the roan into movement. Roan and pinto stopped, nose to nose.

"*Buenos días,* Señor Montee," said José. "There ees *un poco* something you must know."

"Why, sure, José," said Monte. "Likely there is. I don't claim to know too damn much."

"The *cañon* back of *el ojo,* the spring, what you call Black Caballo. You know eet?"

"Why, sure," said Monte. "You ain't lost me yet."

"I cut the wood," said José. "I see two of the calfs. Fat, they are. Big. Fat. But nothing of the brand. Nothing of the knife on the ears."

"What d'you know," said Monte. "A couple of mavericks. Must be your lucky day, José. You slap your brand on 'em?"

"You make of the joke, no?" said José. "The cows, I see also. They are Slash Y."

Back at the ranch buildings Cal Brennan sat in an old rocking chair on the veranda of the old adobe house reading the stock news in a two-week-old newspaper. He lowered the paper and looked over when a rat-tailed roan jounced to a stop a few feet away. He twitched a bit on the chair when Monte Walsh mentioned a couple of slick-ear calves. Suddenly, without any warning at all, that curious little discrepancy in his tally book was in his mind again.

"That José," said Monte. "So honest it hurts his pocketbook. Next time we slaughter a beef, maybe I better drop over his way with a quarter."

Cal Brennan said nothing. He was remembering too what he had heard recently, that a man named Kiens had not drifted on into Arizona but had been seen loafing around one of the small settlements beyond the ridge, on the other side of the mountains, along the river. He let the paper fall in his lap and looked off into distance.

"Shucks," said Monte. "Two calves. Me and Chet'll take an iron and ride out there in the morning."

"You do that," said Cal. "An' you do more'n that. You take Dally too. Find those two calves. Then I want you boys to work through that whole area out there an' see what else you find."

So early next morning when the light before dawn was creeping over the big land Monte Walsh and Chet Rollins and Dally Johnson rode out on three tough cow ponies picked for all-day endurance with the makings of several quick meals in their saddlebags and a running-iron behind Dally's cantle and they were gone all day and into the night and they came back worn and brush-torn to leave gaunted horses in the corral with good feed in the trough and went to the ranch house where Cal Brennan and Hat Henderson waited in the starlight on the veranda.

"Took you a while," said Cal.

"Damn right it did," said Monte. "Two calves my eye. We found nine more up the canyon. Seven on by the edge of timber. Five in that hollow back of the humps."

The big dark shape of Hat Henderson stirred on its chair and a kind of grunting sigh came from him.

"Twenty-three," said Cal gently. "An' all the same?"

"Damn right," said Monte. "There was more a course. But these I'm talking about—slicks, all of 'em."

The silence of the night, dark and somehow waiting, seemed to close in and hold the neighborhood of the old veranda.

"So you boys were careless," said Cal. "Lettin' 'em slip through you like—"

"Quit it, Cal," said Chet Rollins, voice flat, hard. "You know better'n that."

"Yes," said Cal gently, very gently. "I know better'n that. Maybe I'm wishin' I didn't. Dally. What do you make of it?"

"I don't like makin' a single goddamned thing of it," said Dally Johnson.

"Spell it out," said Chet. "We ain't a bunch of kids."

"Somebody . . ." said Dally slowly. "Somebody . . . when we was gatherin' . . . must of been pushin' 'em back . . . leavin' 'em where they wasn't likely to be noticed till fall . . . figurin' to nip off some unbranded stuff along about weanin' time."

Cal Brennan sighed, long and slow. "Somebody," he said. "That somebody's got to have a name. Hat. When you was workin' that part of the range, when you fanned men out, who'd you put in there?"

"Jeeeesus!" said Hat. "You know what you're asking me to say, Cal? Just where anyways? That's a lot of country."

"Certain it is," said Cal. "But maybe we can narrow it down some. From the humps on up past the spring. Think hard, man. Get it straight."

Hat Henderson twisted big hands together and stared down at them in the dimness. "Well, now, we held the gather on those flats below the ridge. We swung out an' I started dropping off where the Diamond Six's run that fence. There'd be nothing of ours other side of it. Dobe was first. That's for sure. Monte next, where that brush grows so thick in them dry arroyos. I remember that from figuring he's the only one crack-headed enough to go brush-popping like a damn fool an' snaking cows out of that stuff. Others here an' there on up. You say from the humps past the spring. Well, when we got up that way there wasn't many men left. We was saving north of the spring for the next day. Yeah, I got it now for that stretch. There was Chet here—"

"Goddamn it!" came the voice of Monte Walsh, thin, knife-edged. "You mean anything by that and I'll—"

"Quit it, Monte," said Chet Rollins. "He's right. I was there."

"Chet here," said Hat. "An' Shorty an'—an' Powder. An' to show you I ain't meaning a thing, Monte, I'm saying I was there too. End man on the swing. Right down from that timber where you say you found some."

Cal Brennan had been stiffening some in his chair. "Kiens?" he said.

"Him?" said Hat. "I left him with the wagon an' to get the fires going. Seeing as he didn't know the country much yet."

Cal sighed again, long and slow. He seemed to have shrunk back into shadow in his chair. "Chet an' Shorty an' Powder. An' you, Hat. I'd as soon say it was me." And Cal kept on talking, trying to convince himself as well as the others, aware he was failing and talking anyway, talking just to have the words said and to have some basis for confronting the days ahead. "To be fair it could be anybody, bein' that nobody can be sure how much those cows've shifted since. To be fair too it could be there's a pocket in there somewheres they was hidin' in an' they was plain missed. Like you say, Hat, that's a lot of country. I expect this is something we just got to live with. For now anyways."

* * *

No, Cal had not convinced anyone, least of all himself. It was too plain a possibility, with Kiens ruled out, that one of his regular men was or had been infected with rustling fever. He could cross off Jumping Joe, who had been recovering from his own fever of another kind. And himself. And Skimpy Eagens, the cook. In any fair facing of facts, it could be any of the others.

While the impact of that situation was spreading through the Slash Y, slow because there was scant open talk of it, Cal tried another move. He pulled Dally from regular work and put him to riding long hours and many miles. Dally carried an iron and he paid particular attention to calves and three times he roped and hog-tied husky young ones and looked long at their ears and built small fires and heated the iron and used it.

"Three," he told Cal. "Just a samplin' that likely means more an' we'll have to look sharp in the fall gather. Our somebody didn't just leave some slicks back in the rough country. He must of been plenty busy even before the brandin'. Sleeperin'. Earmarkin' so we'd think they was already burned an' pass 'em in the shuffle."

"Somebody," said Cal. "I'm gettin' to hate that word. It still means anybody. Even you, Dally."

"Yes," said Dally, eyes narrowing in his weathered scramble of features. "I reckon from where you're standin', Cal, even me."

* * *

So the days moved along, seeming about as usual. But there was a slow increasing drag to them. An uneasy suspicion hung over the Slash Y. Oh, work was being done and well done, but it was done with the hard indifferent competence of men doing merely what they were paid to do. The zest was gone, the strong subtle undercurrent of pride in the work, of simple unthinking confidence and loyalty in each other. Tempers were growing short. Tension was creeping into the bunkhouse. Men were becoming guarded in their talk. They tended to withdraw into themselves, singly or by twos, forming tight increasingly defensive little groups according to the personal trusts between them.

"Godamighty, Chet," said Monte Walsh. "I'm about ready to blow. Can't look straight at anyone. Always wondering is he the one. It ain't those silly calves. Shucks, there's hardly a one of us ain't snitched a calf one time or another when we was hungry. Or maybe done a little mavericking. You know well as I do there's cowmen mighty respected now got their start that way. But things ain't as free and easy as they used to be. And this bastard's letting the rest of us down. Hitting his own outfit. He's kicking us where it hurts. Shucks, I always liked old Cal. Best damn boss we ever found. But every time I see him looking at you, I get to thinking he's thinking how Hat gave your name. I feel like busting him one. Maybe we ought to pull out."

"Shut up," said Chet Rollins. "You're just blowing. I didn't know you're not one to pull out when things get rough, I'd of shook you long ago."

So the days moved along, seeming, only seeming, about as usual. A company shareholder came West and spent a week's vacation sleeping in the ranch house and loafing around on a quiet old horse and he thought everything was fine, rather stern and hard but fine, and he never knew the fact he had a quiet horse and the lack of any delighted attention to his tenderfoot antics meant anything at all. But Cal Brennan knew. He knew in every fiber of his lean aging carcass. The feeling of an outfit functioning, grim or rollicking as occasion called and always together, was slipping away. Oh, the cattle were fat and healthy and unless something drastic happened the balance sheet would satisfy the company. But the Slash Y, his Slash Y, was coming apart. The split-up would come, certain as the seasons. He moped on the old veranda, rocking slow in the old chair, and beat his brains as he would, there seemed to be nothing he could do. Not until the big rain.

*   *   *

There had been the few normal midsummer thunderstorms, better than normal because the rain came down relatively slow, soaking into the ground, good for the thirsty grasses. This one, late and unseasonal, swept down from the mountains, torrential, sheeting the ground in rapid runoff, and flashfloods roared along the arroyos and rushed in walls of sand and silt-clogged water to dwindle at last in little rivulets and shallow pools along the far courses.

Back along the ways fresh built sand and mud bars waited for the unwary. The storm passed and the sun shone and the surface of the bars dried quickly, but below moisture remained, lingering in treacherous ooze.

Men rode in pairs, tailing up and coaxing or lashing into activity cows that had blundered hock-deep and more into trouble and struggled a while then in the resignation of their kind had lain down to accept the inevitable whatever that might be. They had their ropes and one of each pair carried a small short miner's shovel for use with those in too deep or too exhausted to help themselves being helped.

Monte Walsh and Chet Rollins, mud-caked to the knees, mud-spattered above, pulled reins to look at a big crinkle-horned cow belly-deep in the damp clingy clayey sand and her six-months brindle calf the same about ten feet from her.

"Shucks," said Monte, disgusted. "I thought those old Mexs knew more'n that. Silly as those shorthorns Cal's been trying. Mighty fine mother, leading her young one astray. I ain't wading in that stuff, it could be up to my neck. How about that log we passed back there a ways?"

Ropes taut to a good-sized cottonwood limb washed from somewhere far up the wide arroyo, they stopped again by the bogged cow and calf. Dismounting, they heaved the limb, teetering on one end, and let it fall splatting out on the bar beside the terrified calf. Shovel in hand, Monte crawled out, low on the log, and began to dig. The gummy sand fought the shovel and slow curses came from him as he wrenched to free each shovelful. Sweat dripped from him as he scooped under the belly, around the legs. He had them clear, well down. He laid the shovel across two branch stubs and raised a hand high. Chet's rope, small-looped, sailed out and dropped over the hand and arm. Monte widened the loop and flipped it over the calf and drew it snug, under the tail and forward around the chest. "Take it away," he said.

Chet swung into saddle and tickled his horse with spurs. Wise, knowing, top-hand too, the horse eased forward and the rope tightened from the saddle horn and the horse dug hoofs in, belly low, straining in slow steady pressure. With a soft plop the six-months calf, bawling in sudden access of new terror, came free and slithered to solid ground.

"You'd think we was killing him," said Monte, " 'stead of saving his fool life. Now mama won't be so easy."

She was not. They both had sessions out on the log, sweating and cursing, sliding off into the gummy stuff and scrambling back, digging around her, dodging her wicked crinkle horns when she summoned energy out of exhaustion to throw her head in panic, and both ropes were needed drawing taut to saddle horns and straining horses before she came loose with a positive loud pop. She lay limp, wild-eyed, while Monte dismounted to throw off the ropes. She staggered to her feet and hooked viciously at him. "Grateful, ain't she," he said, dodging and leaping for his saddle. "At least she ain't broke a leg."

Monte Walsh and Chet Rollins, mud-caked just about all over now, jogged along down the arroyo. Suddenly Monte pulled reins and Chet, ambling on, had to swing in a small circle to stop beside him.

"That calf," said Monte. "Slipped my mind fussing with the cow. It ain't branded."

"Crazy," said Chet. "You. Earmarked plain as day."

"Earmarked," said Monte. "But no brand. Must be another of those goddamned sleepers Dally found. We're shy an iron but we can use a cinch ring."

Monte Walsh and Chet Rollins jogged back up the arroyo. Suddenly Chet pulled reins and it was Monte had to swing to a stop.

"That calf," said Chet. "You certain?"

"Certain I'm certain," said Monte. "I was climbing all over him."

"It don't make sense," said Chet. "That calf was branded. I know damn well it was. I remember that cow. Only one with horns like that. I had my rope on her calf. I dragged him to the fire."

* * *

Long shadows lay over the big land. Where a side cut led
out of the arroyo four horses waited, patient, ground-reined,
indifferent to the low rumbling complaint of a weary crinkle-
horned cow roped to a small tough juniper and a brindle calf
lying hog-tied forty feet from her and four men standing
around it looking down.

"Find a brand on him," said Monte Walsh, "and you make
me a monkey's uncle."

"That's the one," said Chet Rollins. "I had my rope on
him."

"All right," said Cal Brennan. "We got that straight. Dally.
See what you think."

Dally Johnson knelt by the calf. His fingers moved over its
flank. They paused where tiny hairs were shorter, stiffer. He
stood up. "Yes-s-s-s," he said. "I could of guessed. Our somebody wasn't missin' a trick. Hair-brandin'. Burned off the
hair without singeing the hide so it'd grow back again."

Cal Brennan sighed, long and slow. "All right," he said.
"Somethin' like this is what I been waitin' for. Chet. It's up
to you. We're puttin' all our cards in your hand. When you
slapped your rope on this one, who was handlin' the iron?"

Chet Rollins stood still, very still, head down, staring at
the coiled rope in his hands. "It was kind of mixed up," he
said slowly. "We was moving 'em along mighty fast. Two
fires going. I was roping for one, Dobe the other. My fire,
Powder was pigging and using a knife. The iron—"

Chet raised his head and looked away into distance.
"Shorty," he said. "Shorty Austin."

* * *

In the early dusk of evening a patch of light and the
sounds of Skimpy Eagens busy by his old cookstove came
through the open doorway of the cookhouse. On the bench
along the front of the dim empty bunkhouse sat nine dark
shapes, hunched and silent. Over in the small corral another
shape, a lean length of rawhide, moved quietly, saddling a
horse and lashing a blanket roll behind the saddle.

In the old adobe ranch house, in the light of a kerosene
lamp hanging from the ceiling, Cal Brennan stood by his old
desk, weathered face stern in shadow. Ten feet away, back to
the closed door, stood Shorty Austin, hard angular body still,

upright, the flat planes of his broad rugged face full in the lamplight, rigid, expressionless. His hat was in his hands, held by the brim, and he turned it slowly, around and around.

"Shorty," said Cal. "Shorty boy. Why did you do it?"

"I still ain't talkin'," said Shorty. "I still don't know what in hell you're blattin' about."

"You been named twice," said Cal. "That's enough."

"An' who named me?" said Shorty, eyes narrowing and color beginning to seep up under the sun- and wind-tan along his jaw. "You been blattin' so damn much, maybe you'll tell me that."

"It don't matter," said Cal. "Facts named you an' they don't lie. Was there anybody in it with you?"

"In what?" said Shorty. "I'm gettin' goddamned tired of you blattin' around. You got anythin' you got to say, get it over with."

"All right, Shorty," said Cal. "I'll say it. You rode up the trail with me years back. You was a good man. A mighty good man. I picked you for my Slash Y an' you was still a good man. An' now you've let me down. Me an' the others." Cal paused. From outside he could hear the sound of hoofs approaching and stopping, then of footsteps moving away. "All right, Shorty. You tried an' you didn't get away with it. Lucky you didn't or you know what we'd have to do. You didn't an' we'll just leave it at that. Your hoss is outside. An' your gear. You're ridin' away. If I was you I'd ride a long ways. A mighty long ways. An' I wouldn't come back this way again."

Shorty's hat stopped turning in his hands. Color was high up his face now, under the tan. "My pay," he said. "Since June."

"Pay?" said Cal. "You got the gall to mention that? You ain't earned it."

Abruptly Shorty turned, reaching for the door handle, opening the door. Something in the manner of turning, in the glint of his eyes swinging away, caught at Cal.

"Shorty!" Cal's voice held him for an instant of hesitation in the doorway. "I wouldn't try it again, was I you. Not ever again."

Cal listened to hoofbeats fading away eastward. He reached up to the lamp and turned the wick down. He stood in the dimness a moment and a long sigh came from him. He moved out and down toward the dim shapes along the bunk-house. "All right, boys," he said. "That's that."

"I got it," came the voice of Monte Walsh. "Counting you, Cal, and Skimpy, there was thirteen of us. Unlucky."

* * *

So that too was that and the days rocked along again, bet-ter, some better. But a bitterness remained, a kind of canker in the minds of the men, and with it a feeling that nothing was really finished. Shorty Austin was gone, Shorty who had been with them from the beginning, and he left a hole in the comradeship in the bunkhouse of an evening and the secret something that had been there with him the last months seemed to remain after him, hiding in the shadows of let-down after a day's work, hovering over the Slash Y like the faint felt threat of a thunderstorm just beyond the horizon.

That feeling was strongest in old Cal Brennan, not at-tached at first to any single nudging in his mind except per-haps the memory of a glimmer of a glint in a man's eyes. He sat on the veranda all one day, rocking slow, and his thoughts moved, slow too, but sure and to their goal. Brands. Marks burned into the hides of cow-critters to assert owner-ship. Once there, claims hard to disprove, at least to town-bred judges and juries. And a damn nuisance, any such dis-proving. And never certain in a land with little law and that far off and tangled in the racial politics of a raw territory. Yes, brands. Always around again to brands. Or the lack of them. But what use would unbranded stock be to a man un-less he had a brand of his own to put on them?

Or of a partner working with him?

In the morning Cal saddled his long-legged bay and he rode north all day through rugged country, skirting the west-ward mountains. He slept that night in an adobe shack in a little settlement called Blanca and in the morning he paid in thanks his swarthy host who would have been insulted at an offer of money and he rode westering some through more rugged country that climbed steadily and he was out on the upper level rolling toward Santa Fe and the great green mon-archs of mountains beyond. In the ancient capital he found the right man and held the territorial brand book in his hands. He flipped the still few pages to the latest additions and ran a finger down these. There it was.

The name: James M. Kiens. The brand: X Y Z.

"Shorty . . . Shorty boy," Cal muttered to himself. "So I was right. He got to you." Cal looked long at the brand. X Y Z. He closed the book with a soft snap. "Not missin' a trick," he muttered. "Lose out on one, try another. Just cross the Slash and add a Z."

Cal rode back the way he had come and as he jogged through the lonely miles he had plenty of time to think. He arrived at the ranch in the first dark of night and after one of Skimpy Eagens's quick catch-up meals he called Dobe Chavez and Powder Kent from the bunkhouse and talked to them in the light of the ceiling lamp in the main room of the ranch house. "Now remember," he said. "This is Slash Y trouble an' the Slash Y is handlin' it. But I don't want no grandstand stunts, no goin' it alone by either of you buckaroos. Anythin' happens, you bring word here."

In the morning Dobe and Powder rode out, leading two spare saddle horses and a packhorse with a light pack, southwestward across the plain and over the long ridge to the winter line camp in the first tier of foothills climbing to the mountains. They settled in and each day thereafter Dobe rode north and Powder rode south, quiet, keeping to cover, looping in long circuit through the foothills and returning by early evening. They carried rifles in their saddle scabbards and each of them, now and again as he rode, instinctive, out of old habit, pulled his side gun and spun the cylinder, checking the load.

* * *

It was Powder brought the word. He came larruping in on a lathered horse along the middle of the afternoon of a clean sweet late September day and swung down talking fast and to the point. "Durin' the night," he said, "they cleaned that flat below the humps an' headed 'em up them arroyos into the hills. I found the tracks an' followed some to see where they was goin'. Looks like they're aimin' for that notch up by old turtletop. Five men, I'd say, though I ain't certain. I left somethin' at the cabin for Dobe which I hope he can make out an' come in like you said, Cal. An' now, by God, Cal, no matter what you say, I'm takin' a fresh hoss an' I'm ridin'."

"We're all ridin'," said Cal, a grim little smile that had no humor in it showing at his mouth corners. " 'Cept for Sunfish an' Joe an' Skimpy who'll stay here. We're finishin' this thing if we got to keep going from here to Christmas."

In the dark of night before moonrise they were at the line cabin, eight men, silent mostly, dropping into blankets for a few hours uneasy rest. Cal sat hunched on a log in no mind even to try to sleep. "Where's Dobe?" he muttered to himself. "If that fool's gone an'—" He started with a little jerk. The sound of hoofs, muffled, directionless, came to him. Stopped. He noted that Powder Kent, dim shape in blanket fifteen feet away, was sitting up, gun in hand. He peered into the silence of the night. "Ees you," said a soft familiar voice and the slim deadly compactness of Dobe Chavez seemed to materialize out of nowhere. Cal could see the glint of teeth showing in a grin. "Always," said Dobe, "to know how the ground goes, eet ees good. I see what Powdair he scratch on the door. I go find José who cut the wood and Manuel who take the sheep into thees ground. They tell me of thees mountain."

*   *   *

Only a hint of glow to the east spoke of dawn when they moved out, nine men jacketed against the night-cool on nine deep-bottomed range-bred horses, jogging steadily into distance, Cal Brennan and Dobe Chavez in the lead, working upward, always upward, into the high rock regions. The sun rose, warm on their backs, warming the air, and they shed jackets and rode on, working upward. Three times they stopped to breathe the horses and once by a trickle of springfed stream to water them briefly.

"Where you takin' us, Cal?" said Sugar Wyman. "You ain't aimin' for the notch."

"Maybe they kept on that way," said Cal. "It's the shortest way over, yes. They can't be movin' fast, not with the stock they took to worry along up these grades. An' they don't know we know yet. I'm wrong, we can still catch 'em before they get down the other side. But I'm playin' a hunch. I figure they'll want to change brands soon as they can an' maybe

hide 'em out for a while. Dobe's found out about a place that
ain't been used since Marino an' his gang of hoss thieves was
cleaned out years back. Hard to track into if anyone was
tryin' that. We're goin' direct."

The sun was high overhead, arched past noon, and they
moved steadily on, winding up high slopes forested in
patches, and the hours in saddle of this kind of riding began
to tell on Cal and he felt old and tired and dull anger burned
in him that certain men and circumstances should lay this
kind of dirty business on him far out past the reach of the
scant law of the territory in this great clean wilderness of
mountain land. Then he thought of the eight men riding with
him, of each in turn, testing them in his mind like coins between his teeth and striking the true metal, eight men riding
quiet and uncomplaining wherever and into whatever he
might lead them, and he felt better and he shifted weight to
ease his aging bones and rode on and they came out on an all
but bare reach of rock where the ground seemed to drop
away into nothingness before rising again, abrupt and sheer,
to the final peaks beyond.

"Ees right," said Dobe. "Manuel he tell me right."

"Leave the hosses here," said Cal. "We'll just take a look
over."

Crouching low, they moved on foot to the edge of rock.
Hundreds of feet below, a narrow canyon, not much more
than a stony now dry stream bed, ran between sharp rock
ledges. On ahead it widened into a pine-clumped little valley
that stretched three quarters of a mile between steep side
slopes and dwindled again in narrowness to be lost in the
clefts of the climbing rock.

"Watch it," said Hat Henderson, suddenly grim. "Don't go
showing against the sky."

A third of the way up the valley, near the edge of trees
around a central clearing, was a small slant-roofed cabin,
chimney fallen, doorway and windows blank, chinking long
since gone from between the logs. Thirty feet in front of it a
once-stout log shed leaned crookedly, roofless, walls partly
ripped down. Out from the shed ran the remnants of railed
fence of a good sized corral now obviously patched into temporary reuse. Along the left side of the corral, outside, stood
four saddled horses rein-tied to the fence. Inside forty-odd
footsore cows and half-grown calves and yearling steers

milled restlessly in the far right corner. In the opposite corner
where a small fire sent a thin streamer of smoke upward four
men worked over a hog-tied steer on the ground. And between them and the frightened cattle another man, hard
angular body upright in saddle, paced slowly on a chunky
roan, coiled rope in hand.

"Goddamn it," said Monte Walsh, bitter, low-voiced.
"That's Shorty. I'd know that horse anywheres."

"No," said Cal, voice the same. "Not the Shorty we used
to know."

"Kiens," said Pete Williams. "That's the son of a bitch
there with the iron. Who're the others?"

"It don't matter," said Hat Henderson. "Picked up from
them hangouts along the river. Two-bit crooks. It don't matter a damn. They're done for too."

"Yes," said Cal. "It's certain now an' it's come to that."
He sighed, long and slow. "All right. We're finishin' this complete. I don't want no tag ends left to bother us afterwards.
We're showin' this time so maybe it'll stick nobody plays
smart with the Slash Y. Hat. You an' Petey an' Dally drop
back an' work around to the head of this pocket which is the
way they'll make a break if they get the chance. Then you
start comin' down to the buildings. We'll give you forty minutes before the rest of us bust in this lower end."

*   *   *

Deep in the narrow stream bed canyon Cal Brennan
picked his way carefully along the bottom, leading his horse,
and five of his boys followed. A mile and more away, at the
head of the valley, screened by a stand of young pines, three
more led horses cautiously down along the edge of an ancient
rockslide.

Cal led his horse out of the stream bed to the soft springy
needle-carpeted ground where the canyon began to widen.
He swung into saddle and took his rifle from its scabbard.
Behind him five men did the same.

Cal lifted his old silver watch from a pocket of his worn
vest and looked at it. "All right," he said softly. "Spread out.
Take it slow. Closer we can get before they know, the better.
Anythin' breaks, ram on in."

Cal nudged his horse forward, weaving through the trees,

and the others moved out, spreading as the valley widened. All but one, close beside Cal like a shadow.

"Damn you, Dobe," said Cal in low hoarse whisper. "I know I'm old an' tuckered plenty but I can still hold up my end. Swing out."

"No," said Dobe Chavez. "Hat he tell me—"

A shot slammed out of bushes fifty feet ahead and Cal jerked in saddle as his horse reared and his rifle dropped to the ground and he followed down in plunging fall.

"Peegs!" shouted Dobe. "They hide one!" Dobe's spurs sank in and his horse leaped, pounding forward, and crashed into the bushes and the hidden gun slammed again and Dobe's rifle matched it, speaking its own piece, neat and thorough, once, twice, and a man's voice rose in a gurgling cry that stopped abruptly. Blood dripped from a slice along the neck of Dobe's horse as he swung back to Cal.

"Only . . . nicked," gasped Cal, up on one elbow. "Get on . . . in there." He was speaking to the rump of Dobe's horse as it pawed high, wheeling on hind legs, and raced away. From on ahead, out the sides, he could hear the pounding of hoofs as the others, all caution gone, drove on into the valley.

Old Cal Brennan heaved to his feet and pulled a bandanna from a hip pocket with a savage little jerk and stuffed it under his shirt low by his belt on the left side where a small spreading stain showed. Limping, stumbling, holding his side, he hurried to the near slope and dragged himself up some ten feet. He leaned against a big rock and looked up the valley. A grim smile that had no humor in it tightened the corners of his mouth as he watched, in snatches through the trees, his boys in their brief bitter burst of activity.

* * *

The men in the corral had wasted time jumping to stomp out the fire and to open the gate and drive the cattle out. The man on the chunky roan was scattering them on up the valley. The other four ran now angling across the corral toward the side fence and their horses just beyond it. But Monte Walsh, on a big rawboned bay that was hammering its heart out for him in furious rush, was streaking in toward their horses, jamming his rifle back in its scabbard, fumbling in a pocket. They slowed, pulling their guns, firing, and Monte

and the bay drove straight on and the bay screamed once and
its forelegs crumpled and it went down, somersaulting, and
Monte was thrown rolling over to crash into the corral fence.
He was up, moving swift, steady, behind the partial protection of the rails, pocketknife open in hand, slashing at the
tied reins as the four horses reared back jerking. Freed, they
scattered fast and Monte flung himself down, belly flat by the
lowest rail, and reached for his side gun as Sugar Wyman
raced on past, heading for position at the far end of the
corral.

From the opposite side came the coughing blast of Powder
Kent's rifle and one of the men in the corral went down. The
other three turned and ran, weaving and ducking through the
cross fire, toward the front end and the possible protection of
the cabin beyond it. But Chet Rollins was sliding to a stop
there in a flurry of dust. He leaped from saddle and jumped
through the empty doorway of the cabin and the barrel of his
rifle appeared in the blank front window and steadied on the
frame and another man went down. The remaining two, desperate, snapping a few shots at the cabin, dashed for the
ruined shed and flung themselves over the remnants of walls
and ducked down inside.

Silence, sudden and strange after the sharp crackling of
sound through the little valley, then a scattering of shots
from the men in position around, answered from the still
solid lower bulwark of the shed.

Monte Walsh appeared around the left front corner of the
corral, easing along close to the rails, gun in hand. Shots
snapped from the shed and dust flew by his feet and splinters
from a rail and he jumped back.

Silence again except for the faint drumming of hoofs as
the man on the chunky roan raced away up the valley and
into the cover of trees.

From his post by his big rock Cal could see the rear of the
cabin. Out of brush to the left came Dobe Chavez to stop
and look up at the lower edge of the roof a few feet above his
head. Out of brush to the right came Powder Kent. Both
dropped rifles and Powder cupped his hands and Dobe put a
foot in them and jumped as Powder heaved and Dobe was on
the roof. He lay flat, reaching down to take the rifles from
Powder. He grasped Powder's right wrist and pulled as
Powder braced feet against the rear wall and scrambled up.

Together they crawled forward and lay flat by the front edge, rifle barrels poking over.

Rifles roared from the roof and shots answered from the shed and Dobe's rifle jammed and he flung it aside and rose to his knees, taking his side gun as he rose, and it bucked blasting in his hand and he jerked back, dropping it, falling, and the rifles of Chet Rollins below and Powder above roared together.

On up the valley from somewhere in the cloaking of brush and tree clumps more shots sounded like echoes. Silence followed, everywhere, seeming complete and unending. At his post by the rock Cal took out his old silver watch. "Eleven minutes," he said. "Eleven little minutes since I gave the word."

* * *

In the serene light of afternoon sun slanting down the valley Cal Brennan, stripped to the waist, sat on one end of a rickety split-log bench brought from the cabin while Hat Henderson, big hands surprisingly gentle, placed a pad made of a piece of his shirt over the gash along Cal's side and wound a strip of blanket around, tight. On the other end of the bench sat Dobe Chavez, also naked to the waist, gnawing on his black mustache in silent endurance as Petey Williams bandaged his right shoulder with some of the same materials. Out through the valley ranged the others, rounding up horses and cattle and driving them toward the corral.

"Shorty," said Cal.

"He tried to bull through," said Hat. "Shooting every jump soon as he saw us. I think I winged him, then Dally got him."

"Which made it complete," said Cal. "An' I didn't do a damn thing." That grim little smile tightened his mouth corners. "Not that I was needed any," he said. He sighed, long and slow. "All right. I better talk now 'cause I ain't apt to be able to say much soon, just hang on to a hoss. Have Monte take his pick an' head back right away. He can change to a fresh hoss at the line camp. He moves along the way he can maybe he'll have the doc out there by time me an' Dobe get there. Doc'll have to dig that bullet out of Dobe an' I expect I'll need patchin'. Chet an' Powder can go with us to see we make it." Cal sighed again, wincing as Hat wound more blanket around him. "Which leaves the real chores for you, Hat, an' the others. It's only decent you bury 'em. They set some new posts so there must be a shovel or two around. Chuck their gear in the cabin so if they got any friends ever come lookin' they can have it. Then you'll have to work them cows back down to the range. We'll leave what grub we got in the bags."

"Sure, Cal, sure," said Hat. "Quit fretting yourself."

"I'll try," said Cal. "An' one thing more. You get back down I want you to knock over one of them steers. Save the meat for Skimpy an' bring me the hide. That brand-changin'll show plain on the underside. In case anybody ever gets to askin' questions."

*　*　*

So that too was that. Monte Walsh rode a horse fast steep miles to a shuddering stop barely able to stand at the line cabin and another faster miles across the lower levels into town and borrowed another there to ride back out with Doc Frantz by way of the ranch buildings. He and Doc and Sunfish were at the cabin with a supply of candles and a good fire going along in the small hours of the night toward morning when Chet Rollins and Powder Kent brought Cal and Dobe to the door tied to their own saddles. Doc worked over Dobe, muttering something about range wolves, and he worked over Cal, muttering something about an old he-goat, and he said with sleep and food they could be moved down to the ranch by late afternoon.

The Slash Y had lost no stock, except one steer whose hide, scraped clean, hung in the barn with the old scar of the Slash Y brand and the fresher cross on the slash and the added Z showing plain. It hung there undisturbed, though rumors about it did spread here and there through the back country. But no direct questions were asked, not in the neighborhood of the Slash Y. Down at Socorro and up at Santa Fe certain officials did hear at last that certain men of troublesome reputation seemed to have disappeared from their hangouts along the river, but they regarded this as a kind of

backhanded blessing no sensible person would look into too
closely.

Yes, that too was that. The days were rocking along again,
seeming about as usual. But a bitterness still remained. A
nasty unpleasant job that had to be done had been done, but
no one took much pride in it or thought of it without tasting
the bitter. Likely more than one of the men lay awake at
times thinking of Shorty Austin lying under dirt and piled
rocks up in the lonely dark of the mountains. Tempers were
still edgy and there was not much free and easy talk in the
evenings.

And one of those evenings they were loafing around the
bunkhouse, fidgety and sullen, with a slow casino game going
at the table in the light of the one lamp lit and others were
doing this and that with no particular interest, and Jumping
Joe spoke up. "Dally," he said and there was a sharp edge on
his voice. "Why did you have to plug him? Whyn't you run
him down, grab him, anythin' but that?"

"Save him for a rope, that what you mean?" said Dally,
short, irritated. "You know goddamned well that's what it'd
of had to be."

"I hadn't—I hadn't thought of it like that," said Joe.
"Maybe I was thinkin' wrong."

Dally turned away to sit on the edge of his bunk, head
down, staring at the floor. He pulled a broken bridle from
under the bunk and started taking it apart. "Grab him," he
said to no one in particular. "Christ a'mighty, he was shootin' too, wasn't he?" Dally let the bridle drop from his fingers
and they clenched into fists as he stood up. "You think wrong
too damn much, Joe," he said. "I'll bet back there a ways you
was even thinkin' it was me."

"Maybe I did," said Joe, rising to his own feet. "Yes, by
God, maybe I did." He braced himself for the shock, fists
coming up, as Dally exploded into action toward him.

"Quit it, you two!" shouted Hat Henderson, jumping between them, sending them reeling apart. Instantly, on the rebound, they both piled into Hat and he staggered into Sugar
Wyman on a chair by the casino table. "I ain't takin' that
from anybody," said Sugar, heaving Hat away and following
with fists flying and tangling with Dally on the way.

Fast action, mixed-up, indiscriminate, held the center of
the room.

"My oh my," said Monte Walsh, grabbing the lamp off the table as it tottered and jumping to hand it to Dobe Chavez sitting upright on his bunk. "Hold this," said Monte, "so I can see who I'm hitting," and plunged headlong into the slugging scramble.

"What the hell," said Chet Rollins, following Monte in.

"Reckon it's free," said Powder Kent, rising from another chair by the table as it banged over on his shins. "May I have this dance?" he said, bowing low to Petey Williams by the wall. He straightened, belting Petey with nice precision alongside the jaw. He staggered back as Petey bounced off the wall and rushed into him, hammering, and the two of them were part of the general mix-up.

"It does seem to make some sense," said Sunfish Perkins, on the edge of his bunk, pulling on his boots. He stood up, took a deep breath, and his barrel body plowed into the whirling melee.

Anyone against everyone, lovely, lovely, hitting out against all the hoarded tensions of the days and the secret thinkings of the nights and the regrets for doing what had to be done. Bitterness ran down arms and out in the thuddings on flesh. There was tart sweetness in the bruising of bodies careening against walls and crashing into bunks. And Dobe Chavez, shoulder bandage showing from under his old underwear, sat on his bunk and held the lamp and shouted himself hoarse in impartial encouragement to them all.

One by one temporary exhaustion claimed them. They sat on the floor leaning against walls or drooped on the edges of bunks, bodies limp, chests heaving, silly lopsided grins on battered faces.

"What d'you know," murmured Monte Walsh. "I ain't felt so good in months."

The door opened and Cal Brennan stepped in, body at a slight angle because of the stiffness down his left side, followed by the lean youngish length of Sonny Jacobs from the Diamond Six to the south.

"What in holy hell," said Cal, surveying the wreckage, "has been goin' on in here?"

"Nothing much," gasped Hat Henderson. "We was . . . only having . . . a little argument."

"What about?" said Cal.

"Damned . . . if I know," said Hat. "What was it, Dally?"

"Search me," said Dally Johnson, cheerfully spitting out blood from a split lip. "I've plumb forgot."

"Well, you sure are a sick-lookin' bunch right now," said Cal. "But Sonny here's got somethin' to tell you."

"Yessiree," said Sonny, grinning wide. "But maybe I oughtn't tell it to a beat-up batch of castoffs like you all. Anyway, the old man's at the ranch with his whole family even the kids and some eastern dudes too. He wants to put on a little doings for the folks. Told me to ask you boys down to sort of add to the local color. Show what kind of mangy half-human critters inhabit these parts. We're barbecuing a beef and tapping a keg of beer and it just might be there'll be a bottle or two of something stronger."

"Right neighborly," said Cal. "You boys need something like that. Skimpy an' me'll stay here an' the day's yours."

"Which ain't all," said Sonny, grinning wider. "We got us a little stud down there we ain't been able to do a thing with. Me and the others've got together a little purse that says there ain't a one of you can ride him. By the which and wherefore and whatever and of course, meaning that slack-jawed piece of nothing much you tolerate around here under the name of Monte Walsh."

*　*　*

In the morning Cal and Skimpy sat on the old veranda and watched them, slicked and reasonably presentable, jog away southward with Sonny, all of them, even Dobe erect and grinning despite his shoulder, and Cal felt right good. He knew. He knew by the way they sat their saddles and the way the horses feeling the tingle along reins jounced with springy strides, that this bad time was over and his boys would be ready for the rough tough fall roundup and shipping with the old grim rollicking zest in the work.

And the men themselves, jogging along, knew too. They knew, certain as sunrise, that Monte Walsh would ride that stud to a fare-you-well and likely there would be calf-roping and steer-busting just to show those eastern dudes how things were done out here in the big land and they would come jog-ging back to Cal with money in their pockets and good barbecue in their bellies, ten men separate and individual, and somehow something more, single and indivisible, the crew of the Slash Y.

* * *

"They had a Englishman out at the Slash Y last fall. Had put money in the comp'ny an' Brennan's had word he's to be treated gentle. No ragging of this one regardless how tempting he is. Which could make sense in a way. He was having a hard time. Man he'd brought across the water to do his dirty work was took sick in Saint Louie an' wasn't with him. Why, the poor feller had to do all kind of heavy work for hisself. Had to unpack his own doodads. Had to dress hisself of a morning an' the three–four other times he might do that in a day. But what I started with was he made a mistake first thing. It was Monte come in to pick him off the stage. Englishman's fed up with traveling an' brushing his own clothes an' maybe even shaving hisself an' he's in a hurry to get where he's going. Look here, my man, he says to Monte, meanwhile looking down a nose that'd do credit to a mule. Take those bags, he says, an' be quick about it. Well, now, Monte was about ready to do just that, it being the nat'ral decent thing to do. But that 'my man' an' the way it's said stops him cold. I was watching an' I says to myself, oh oh, here's a Englishman going to be bouncing around in pieces right quick. But no, Monte's been primed by old Cal an' he just chews a knuckle an' lets it go. I reckon he did a lot of letting things go by time they was out to the ranch.

"Well, now, this Englishman was after some hunting. Had his own guns, five of them too, an' enough other gear to set up for a store. Let it be known, offhand-like, he'd bagged birds an' knocked over critters all the way up to a he-elephant in places where hunting was hunting. Didn't need anybody to tell him anything about that, but he could use a native to guide him some. New country. Wouldn't object to the man that'd met him in town. So Monte was the one had to take him out an' keep him out of serious trouble.

"That was days. Evenings Monte was hatching something else. Gave Cal five dollars for an old plug they had around that might've been worth ten if you was feeling real generous an' was blind too. Hoss too stupid to learn much but Monte *manages to teach it the one wrinkle he has in mind. Tickle it with a spur just right an' pull its head around an' it'll freeze solid with head up pointing where you've aimed it. Along comes the last time he'll be taking this Englishman out an' he saddles this hoss. They're in the hills somewhere. Monte spots a couple antelope way off, tickles the hoss. It stops, froze solid, head where he's aimed it. Your hoss, says this Englishman, what's it doing? Sh-h-h, says Monte, it's pointing some game. Englishman looks, finally makes out the antelope. My word, he says. He's always my-wording when things take his interest. My word, he says, does that hoss do that often? Too damn much, says Monte, which is why I don't use him much. They ride on an' Monte spots a deer way ahead that slips into some brush to let them slide by. Tickles the hoss. My word, says this Englishman, he's doing it again. Looks hard. Nothing there, he says. Could make a mistake, says Monte an' pulls his side gun an' pops into the brush. Out jumps the deer hightailing away. My word, says this Englishman, staring at the hoss. Just a nuisance, says Monte, 'cause he can't tell me what it is. No good for ranch work, says Monte, though I did break him of pointing cows. Always pointing something, might be just a jack rabbit. Birds? says this Englishman. No, says Monte, guess they don't have no smell for him. Got to have hide or fur. They ride on. My word, would you sell that hoss? Gosh, no, says Monte, too dangerous. Like once I thought it was a deer an' it was a grizzly that near scalped me.*

"Well, now, there must of been plenty my-wording before they got back with the elk head this Englishman wanted. 'Cause next day when he left that hoss was being shipped with him an' the whole crew, Cal included, was in town with three hundred dollars to spend forgetting all the things they'd been letting go."

Antelope Junction
1884

FIVE MEN on five stout cow ponies, tagged by a packhorse on a lead rope, stopped on the last rise rolling out of sun-washed heat-shimmered distance to look down on the cluster of squat false-fronted board and adobe buildings known, where known at all, as Antelope Junction.

Out of distance on beyond, thin trace in the big lonesome land, snaked a single narrow-gauge rail line, final stretch straight as taut string to the cluster of buildings, ending in a short strip of double switch-rails alongside a sagging adobe station and three poled corrals in a row. Out of distance to the left, emerging from arroyo-broken badlands, trailed the thinner fainter trace of wheel tracks that could, under stress of necessity, be called a road.

"There she is," said foreman Hat Henderson, easing rump to new position in saddle.

"Pretty, ain't it," said Monte Walsh, dry, disgusted. "Oh my yes."

"Off your feed, Monte," said Sunfish Perkins, raising a hand to his shirt collar and slipping it inside under his dusty neckerchief to lift sweat-soaked cloth from skin and let a little air circulate. "Thought you were hell on hitting towns."

"That ain't a town," said Monte. "Two bars and a beanery. Anyways you know damn well what's itching. And Cal sends five of us. To pick up fifteen measly cows."

"Bulls," said Chet Rollins, busy applying match to stubby pipe poking out from round stubbly face. "High-priced yearling bull calves. The company's mighty particular about 'em."

"Bulls are cows," said Monte, nudging his leggy dun closer to Chet's thick-necked black, reaching with one hand to take a small pouch from Chet's shirt pocket, extracting with the

139

other a small paper from his own pocket. "Steers too," he said, making a tiny trough of the paper between fingers and sprinkling tobacco along it. One hand rolled the cigarette while the other tucked the pouch in Chet's pocket. "It could make a man mad," he said. "Cal's sure chasing us around. One bunch up to Nebraska chewing dust all the way. Just about through spitting and another bunch up to Raton. And right away off again on this fool jaunt."

"Ees bad," said Dobe Chavez, grinning under dusty dark mustache. "We come of the miles thees time, seventy. Now two–three days driving of thees leetle bulls to the ranch. Ees vary bad: Ees enough to keel a man."

"That ain't what I mean," said Monte, aggrieved, fishing in pocket again, extracting a match, lighting it on blunt fingernail. "It's the timing. Another week and it'd of been payday."

"If you'd taken it easy up at Raton," said Chet, amiable, conversational, "maybe you'd have something to jingle in your pants right now."

Monte drew on the cigarette and sent the match flipping. "I didn't see you easing off any," he said.

"No," said Chet. "That's why I ain't complaining now."

"Shucks," said Monte. "I ain't complaining. Just talking. I bet there ain't two dollars on the whole bunch of us."

"Lucky if that," said Hat, lifting reins to lead on down. "Come along while I check on those cows of the male variety. Then we'll strip pockets. We might have enough for a bottle."

* * *

Antelope Junction drowsed in late morning sun, devoid of all signs of active life. A dog lay limp, motionless, in the slim shade of a water trough beside a rock-rimmed well topped by an umbrella-like wooden hood in the center of what would have been the plaza if Antelope Junction could have enclosed a plaza. Two cow ponies drooped, sunk in wise lethargy, by the tie rail of a longish low building that proclaimed in faded paint on weathered plank over a double doorway ROOMS & EATS and beneath this the legend in faint scriptish eloquence, *Biggest Beefsteaks West of Boston*. A lone mule lay, legs tangled in harness, apparently lost in sleep between the shafts of a decrepit wagon that leaned sideways against its wheels in front of a solid structure with adjoining barn that was café and livery stable and stage stop. On the sagging roofed platform of the one store, general merchandise no longer very general, an old man was stretched on a bench, flat on back, battered old hat over face, holes showing in soles of toe-upturned boots. Against the front wall of a low otherwise blank building simply and sufficiently labeled SALOON sat two figures, rumps on ground, knees hunched up, well hidden from sun and scrutiny by tattered blankets up around shoulders and faded cone-crowned wide-brimmed hats tilted far forward.

Across what would have been the plaza, where the lone track led in out of distance and became two, the plank door of the station hung open on loose hinges. In the small square dim interior insulated against outside glare by the thick adobe walls and strips of jagged cardboard tacked at close intervals across the windows, a long thin bald-topped man leaned back limp and loose-jointed in an ancient wired-together Morris chair beside a warped old desk littered with yellowed papers and magazines, gazing intently up at the fly-specked ceiling. Fastened to one corner of the desk top was a telegraph key. Beside it lay a flyswatter made of a small piece of leather tacked to a thin board.

Stealthily the bald-topped man reached to take the swatter. Stealthily he rose from the chair to long thin height and swung the swatter with soft smack against the ceiling. He collapsed back into the chair and laid the swatter on the desk and took a pencil stub and made a tiny mark on a well-marked piece of brown paper. He leaned back and resumed his study of the ceiling.

The dim interior dimmed a bit more. The bald-topped man rolled his head slightly to look at the big slope-shouldered figure almost filling the doorway.

"You in charge here?" said Hat Henderson.

The bald-topped man straightened in the old chair. He looked carefully around the small room. "I do not see anyone else here," he said, "so I suppose I am." He rubbed one hand over his bald top. "I will let you in on a little secret. I never see anyone else here."

"Bulls," said Hat. "A little matter of fifteen pedigreed bull calves. Due in here today. What train they likely to be on?"

"What train?" said the bald-topped man. "I am full of se-

crets today. Very free with them too. I will let you in on another. There is one train." He rubbed again over his bald top.
"That is, if you care to call it a train."

"When's it come in?" said Hat.

The bald-topped man pointed to a piece of cardboard
tacked to the wall. "According to that schedule," he said, "at
11:07. In the A.M. Very precise and scientific, that schedule.
It is figured out in terms of miles and weights and steam
pressures and wheel sizes and revolutions per minute and
such. Very precise. Not 11:06. No. Not 11:08. No. At
11:07." He rubbed again, this time down over his long thin
face. "The trouble is, that schedule does not mean a thing."

"Jeeeeesus!" said Hat. "I ain't trying to pull your teeth! All
I want to know is when the damn train comes in!"

The bald-topped man looked at Hat, friendly, sad, sharing
the grief. "That is the one secret I do not know," he said.
"Two years, three months, seventeen days, I have been here.
I have kept charts and I study them. And I have not figured
that secret yet. All I can say is that train favors the afternoon. The late afternoon. It is a trifle closer to five o'clockish
than anything else. Then again it fools me and sneaks in
somewhere around three. Once last year at 2:13. I try to regard all that as joyful, something new and refreshing each
day. It is not. It is depressing." He rubbed a hand again down
over his face and the face emerged a bit brightened. "Would
you care to see my charts?"

"No," said Hat. He rubbed a hand down over his own
face. "All I want to know is about today." He pointed at the
telegraph key. "Can't you find out on that thing?"

"That thing?" said the bald-topped man. "Did you notice
any wires out along the tracks? No, of course not. No sane
man can notice what is not there. They sent me that thing
two years ago but they never got around to stringing any
wires. But it is there. I tell myself it should be used. So I tap
myself out messages now and again. I sent myself one this
morning. Would you care to know what it was?"

"No," said Hat, gnawing on a knuckle.

"I will tell you anyway," said the bald-topped man. "Just
three words but conveying vast and formidable information.
It was: 'Hot again today.' "

"So we wait," said Hat, regarding chewed knuckle in disgust, turning away. "Maybe the whole goddamned day." He

turned back. "Mind if we put our horses in one of those corrals?"

"Delighted," said the bald-topped man. "Always delighted to extend hospitality to horses. To nice horses." He saw he was speaking to a disappearing back and sighed and sagged in the old chair to study the ceiling.

Outside Hat Henderson stepped down from the low platform bordering the rails and regarded his travel-worn crew with grim grin. "I been pulling teeth," he said. "All I can make out is the damn train'll be here when it gets here. Likely not till late afternoon. So we wait. We'll unsaddle an' shoo the hosses in here." He took his reins and led toward the first gate.

"Gentlemen. Please."

Five heads turned. The bald-topped man stood in the station doorway, flyswatter in hand. "Not in there," he said. "That one is occupied. It is not safe at all. Not in the least."

Five heads turned again, this time toward the first corral baking quietly in the sun, apparently as empty as the other two.

"Jeeeesus!" said Hat. "Is that yapping coyote trying to pull our legs?"

"In the corner there," said Chet Rollins, pointing.

Four more heads concentrated on the corner. Through the rails showed sections of a raw-boned mottle-hided horse, weight settled on three legs, big hammerhead drooping almost to the ground.

"That is a very dangerous animal," said the bald-topped man. "And that, gentlemen, is not a secret."

"I get it," said Monte Walsh. "It must of been losing his hair made him like that."

"Something sure did," said Hat, shrugging wide shoulders, leading toward the second corral. "But he's in charge here an' we might as well play along."

Saddles and pack were off and perched on the top rail of the second corral, bridles hanging from horns. Horses were turned inside. The trimmed-down trail crew of the Slash Y started in unspoken unanimity across the tracks. The bald-topped man watched them go. His voice reached after them. "Gentlemen. You might care to know that I have killed seventy-three thus far today. This is four more than yesterday at this time."

The trail crew of the Slash Y stopped, turned, stared at him.

"Shucks," said Monte. "I ain't got nothing to lose but my pride. I'll bite, mister. Seventy-three what?"

"Flies," said the bald-topped man.

"My oh my oh my," said Monte, striding with the others on across straight for the blank building labeled SALOON. "I'd sure be scared was it me cooped up in there all alone, fighting the things."

*   *   *

Antelope Junction drowsed in midday sun. The dog, limp and motionless again, had moved a few feet to stay in the slim shade of the water trough. The two cow ponies still drooped by the tie rail, betraying life at long intervals with futile tail-switchings. The lone mule, rousing once, had tangled further in harness and subsided again into apparent stupor. The old man had left his bench and shuffled slowly into somewhere. The two figures hunched against the saloon building had become three, had followed the shade and were around by the left side wall. A shapelessly fat woman had padded on bare feet out of one of the scattered adobe houses or huts in various stages of disrepair that could or could not have been inhabited, had hung a few gaudy garments on a line and had disappeared inside again. And close by the front corner of the little station on opposite side from the corrals, where a scraggly cottonwood helped the little building create a patch of shade, the trail crew of the Slash Y lounged on the ground, relaxed in assorted collapsings. Four of them could have been asleep. Not Monte Walsh.

"We had one measly pint," murmured Monte, contemplating a small empty bottle by his right boot. "Split five ways. Just about enough to make a man know he's thirsty."

He studied the bottle for a moment. "Ought to be a way," he murmured, "to get something more out of it." His face brightened. He pushed up, took the bottle, counted off fifty paces, set the bottle upright on the ground, came back to the others. His boot toe nudged Dobe Chavez.

"Hey, Dobe," he said. "See that bottle over there. Bet you can't hit it."

Dobe sat up, stared at the bottle, then at Monte. "Ees *loco,*" he said. "For that you break the *siesta?*"

"Shucks," said Monte. "I mean shooting through your legs."

"The legs?" said Dobe, interested. "How ees that?"

"Like this," said Monte, spraddling legs, bending down double to peer back between them.

"Eees still *loco,*" said Dobe, but grinning, pushing up. He took a stand, back to the bottle, legs apart. In one graceful motion his right hand swept gun from holster and his body bent double, hand pushing between legs. Gun roared and bottle shattered.

"What the hell?" said Hat Henderson, starting up.

"I'll be blowed," said Monte. "You must of practiced that."

"No," said Dobe, grinning wide, slipping gun back in holster, patting it. "Thees gun and me, we know each of the other."

"Hey," said Sunfish Perkins, climbing to his feet. "Looks like we're having company."

Across the way figures had suddenly materialized, three in front of SALOON, four in front of ROOMS & EATS. One of the latter was striding purposefully forward, a solid square-faced man, hatless, in spurred boots and matching pants and vest and checkered shirt. He was heading straight for the scraggly cottonwood. He hitched suggestively at his gunbelt as he strode. He called out, purposefully loud: "You there! Don't you try getting away!" He came close and stopped, solid on boots, hands on hips. "All right! Who fired that shot?"

"Who ruffled your feathers?" said Hat Henderson, mild, deceptively mild.

"There's a law here," said the man, still loud, purposefully loud, "against using firearms within the limits! Tell me now! Who did it?"

"It might be I did," said Hat.

"Why you double-distilled liar," said Monte Walsh. "I did."

"There you go," said Chet Rollins, moving in. "Both of you. Trying to hog the glory. It's mine."

"The hell it is," said Sunfish Perkins. "That was me."

A slow smile spread over the square-faced man's features. "I'm smart," he said, friendly, low-voiced, confidential. "I've rode a bit too. I know just from hearing you boys blat it was that black-mustached buckaroo there who ain't said a thing. I know too just from looking at him he's good with that gun. Better'n me by a longsight. Might be I even could dig up his name, having heard tell of it once or twice. You boys are Slash Y. I saw the brand when you rode in a while back. I kind of keep an eye out a window over there."

"My oh my," said Monte. "Peeping at us. And I thought everybody around here but that bartender was dead waiting to be buried."

"Now frizzle your hell-popping souls," said the man, cheerful, low-voiced. "Can't you at least help me by trying to look impressed? Maybe even a mite scared? Expect you don't know it but right now this minute I'm giving you a tongue-lashing that's taking the hide right off you. Pieces of it lying all over the ground. I didn't make that fool law. Wouldn't be bothering you except I'm sheriff and election's near and I need the pay and those yokels back yonder are voters and I got to put on a show times like this. Like I say, I'm smart. Suppose I try to take Chavez in, why I know I got to handle all of you. Suppose I got away with it. Couldn't collect a fine. You ain't in Johnny's place which means you're plumb broke. So I'm just telling you off mean like this and letting you go because you didn't know about that law.'"

"Not so smart," said Monte, bright, hopeful. "I knew about it."

"Didn't hear you," said the man. "I got well-trained ears. But don't go getting me wrong. Any of you really start something I'll have to do what I can. I'm middling good myself when pushed into it. But what'd that mean? Maybe grief for one or two of you and certain grief for my missus. So what I say is you plain got to use some gunpowder making noise, do it on the way out. Then I chase you to the limits and it'll look good to the voters and no harm done. That sound fair?"

"Fair enough," said Hat.

"Good," said the man, slow smile spreading again. "I take that right kindly. Now I see from your faces you're all a-quivering, all broke to bits, by this tongue-lashing I been giving." He chuckled. "At least that's the way I'll tell it where the votes are." He started to turn away.

"Hey, wait," said Monte. "Is this place always half dead?"

"Well, now," said the man. "We liven up some along toward evening. A few riders always coming in. Poker game at Johnny's most every night. Jake Morrel deals faro for anyone likes that."

"Any girls?" said Monte.

"Not that kind," said the man. He strode away. About by the wooden-umbrellaed well he hitched suggestively at his gunbelt, half turned, called out: "Remember now! Any more of that and I'll have your guns!"

Hat Henderson stared after him, scratching one ear. "I could almost stand living in this place," he said, "just to vote for that man."

"I bet," said Sunfish Perkins, "he plays a mean poker hand. Wonder who he is."

"Morrison," came a voice from the side. The bald-topped man was in the station doorway. "Cliff Morrison. You gentlemen might care to know it is one year, ten months, fourteen days he has been in office. In that time there have been six—beg pardon, now seven—shootings. Four of these—beg pardon, again, now five—were not serious. Two were. But not fatal. I regard that as a remarkable record. Of course, fights of various kinds are something else again. Would you care to know the figures?"

"Damned if we would," said Hat, collapsing to the ground, stretching out, closing eyes.

"Dobe," said Monte. "What do you think? You been mighty quiet."

"Ees a good man," said Dobe, subsiding in easy motion to siesta position. "Ees right he win the leetle game. The gun ees for the use, not the play."

"Shucks," said Monte. "Well, anyways, I knocked off some waiting time."

* * *

Antelope Junction drowsed in early afternoon sun. Four men slept or seemed to sleep under the scraggly cottonwood. Not Monte Walsh.

He sat, knees hunched up, arms wrapped around them, chin resting on them, surveying under pulled-down hat brim the sun-baked stretch across the way. A speck of movement caught attention. From behind one of the haphazard adobe huts appeared a small parcel of humanity, a knee-high boy, black-haired, brown-skinned, naked as a plucked jaybird. Serious, intent, the small parcel began to explore the intricacies of an old smashed egg crate.

"My oh my," murmured Monte. "Ain't that scandalous."

From behind the hut, hurrying, came another parcel, a waist-high girl in flour-sack dress. Expertly she hoisted the boy onto one small hip, rump foremost, and staggered away out of sight, smacking the bare rump in process.

"That's the way things go," murmured Monte. "Something male steps out for a little fun, something female clobbers him."

Attention was caught again. Out the door of the one store came the old man, stumbling under the weight of a box filled with assorted items. He made it down from the roofed platform and along to the decrepit wagon. He hoisted the box to the top of the tailgate and with a heave sent it over. At the clatter the mule raised its head, looked around, dropped the head again. The old man walked up by the mule and surveyed the tangled harness. He bent down and went to work on it.

Monte raised head a bit. Without shifting gaze he stretched one leg to nudge Chet Rollins. Chet sat up, stared at Monte, noted direction, looked, saw, settled to watching position.

The old man was satisfied with his untangling. He kicked the mule in the side. No reponse. He moved back a bit and kicked in a tenderer portion of anatomy. The mule grunted, struggled to feet, stood with legs apart, head drooping. The old man climbed stiffly to the wagon seat and took the reins. He slapped them down on the mule's back, clucked hopefully. The mule stood, motionless. The old man reached into the wagon, picked up an ancient limp whip, applied this with mounting indignation. The mule stood, motionless.

The old man climbed stiffly down, went back to the store, in. He came out carrying what looked like a hoe handle.

"Beating won't work," said Monte.

The old man climbed stiffly on the seat again. He reached into the wagon, lifted out an ancient big-roweled spur and a length of cord. Carefully he lashed the spur to one end of the hoe handle. He reached with this and jabbed the mule close by the rope-tail. The rule raised its head, grunted its own indignation. The old man jabbed again, hard, raking with the spur. Slowly, regretfully, the mule leaned into harness and the wagon moved. It swung in a slow arc, wheels creaking, and moved toward the road out of town.

"My oh my," said Monte. "Keep your eyes open, learn something every day."

"Man over beast," said Chet, relaxing down on back again, closing eyes.

Monte regarded him in disgust. He reached and plucked the small pouch from Chet's shirt pocket, explored its interior with blunt forefinger. He tucked it back in the pocket. He looked around at the others, all flat on ground. "Remind me of hawgs," he murmured. "Sleeping and growing fat." Faintly from the station came the sound of a sharp smack. He turned head in that direction. "Hey! Killer!" he shouted. "What's the score now?"

The bald-topped man's voice floated out, mildly triumphant. "One hundred and seven. Six ahead of yesterday."

In solemn satisfaction Monte regarded the others sitting up around him. "Hey!" he shouted again. "You got another swatter?"

"No," came the voice. "And I refuse all offers of assistance. This is a private feud."

"Jeeeesus, Monte," said Hat. "You're worse'n a goddamned horsefly." He stood up, stretched, stared out along the lost lonesome track, folded down again to the ground and lay back. "Hell of a way to run a railroad," he said. "Taking so damn long I'd say if we only had something on us we'd lay over here tonight and see what Morrison means about livening up."

* * *

Antelope Junction drowsed in midafternoon sun. Hat Henderson and Chet Rollins sat on the station platform, backs against the building, legs out, flipping pages of old yellowed magazines. Sunfish Perkins and Dobe Chavez hunkered on heels between the platform and the rails playing mumblety-peg, wearily, uninterested, with a long-bladed wicked-looking jackknife. Monte Walsh sat on the platform edge, long legs dangling, morosely surveying the structures across the way.

"I see how he got that way," said Monte. "You take to counting things. That makes four who've gone into the saloon since I squatted here. One fat, two thin, one about middling. Wonder what they're drinking."

Chet Rollins looked up. "There's a well out there," he said.

"Little sunshine, spreading cheer," said Monte without turning around. "Three times I been out to that damn thing since you stuck your nose in those pages. You know what's in there? Water. Ain't there something we could swap?"

"Peeg!" said Dobe Chavez, jumping up, taking hold of his hat with both hands, yanking it down on ears in disgust. "Stupid peeg!"

"Who?" said Monte, interested.

"Ees me," said Dobe. "Of a certainty. I forget." He strode off toward the second corral. He came back, carrying his bridle. On each side where headband and cheek strap met in a metal ring was soldered a silver dollar. He picked up the jackknife and began to pry them loose.

"Shucks," said Monte. "That ain't enough for tonight. Worth only another pint for now. Just a teaser. Make us thirstier'n ever."

"Peaches," said Chet Rollins.

"Now that," said Hat Henderson, pushing to his feet, "is the smartest remark I've heard this whole damned day. Come along."

Purposefully the trimmed-down trail crew of the Slash Y strode across what would have been the plaza and into the one store. Purposefully they strode back to the platform, each carrying a luridly labeled tin can, top removed, a small flat piece of wood sticking up. They sat in a row on the platform edge, eating peaches, lifting cans to gulp the syrup.

"Well, well, well," said Chet Rollins. "Here comes some of the livening."

Along the trace of a road, swinging in from the badlands, a four-horse stage swayed at a fair trot toward town. It pulled past the other buildings and stopped by the combination café and livery stable. The near door opened and an impressive figure backed out, a tall man, wide and softish of body, in an immaculate obviously expensive light gray suit whose pants were tucked into gleaming dustless high black boots with high curved heels, the whole of him topped by a huge high-crowned wide-brimmed white hat.

"My oh my," said Monte. "Ain't that pretty? Ain't that a hat?"

"Wonder how he'd look," said Sunfish, "after a couple days tailing cows out of mudholes."

There was activity on the other side of the coach. Three figures had descended through the other door and moved now into sight, headed toward ROOMS & EATS, a plumpish middle-aged man in sober attire escorting two women.

"Remarkable," said the bald-topped man from the station doorway. "Four people. I must mark that down. Three has been the record to date."

Monte Walsh pushed out from the platform and landed light on dusty worn boots. Bouncing a bit off his toes, he started away.

"Hey, Monte," said Hat. "Where you going?"

"It's a free country," said Monte, bouncing on. "A man has a right to a closer look."

He angled in by ROOMS & EATS to take an apparently casual look through a wide low window. The three travelers were well inside, backs to him, the two women surveying the three bare-topped tables and rickety chairs and poster-plastered walls, the man listening to the stringy proprietor in greasy apron explain the situation. The voice carried plainly out through the still-open half of the double doorway. "Train'll be in any time now. But was I you I'd wait over here. The agent over there is, well, now, he's a mite peculiar. Talk an arm off you without half trying."

Monte bounced toward the doorway, thinking up a possible excusing inquiry. He stopped. One of the women was speaking. "Did you see them? Over by the tracks. Cowboys. How picturesque."

"Yes," said the other. "At a distance like that. But you know how they are when you get close."

"Goodness, yes," said the first with a small giggle. "All sweaty. They smell. Just like cows."

Monte Walsh turned away, striding back the way he had come, no longer bouncing. Back in his place in the row on the platform edge, he scowled down at his dusty worn boots.

"All right, Monte," said Hat at last. "What happened? We didn't see anybody bite you."

"If those things wore pants," said Monte, "I'd of scrambled them and this whole damn town. They said we smell. Like cows."

Silence lay over platform and station.

"Likely we do," said Chet Rollins, amiable, conversational. "That is, between scrubbings. Allover scrubbings I mean."

Silence lay again over platform and station. The bald-topped man disappeared inside. After a while a soft smack drifted out.

"Remember, boys," said Hat. "No popping at these cans."

"Shucks," said Monte. "They ain't no young heifers themselves. Just a couple baggy old cows."

* * *

Antelope Junction livened a bit in late afternoon sun. A buckboard with a patient flop-eared bay between shafts stood in front of ROOMS & EATS. Three cow ponies ignored each other's presences by SALOON's tie rail. A team of gaunt draft horses waited at the side door of the café and livery stable for someone to remember to unload the sacks of grain on the heavy wagon behind them.

Five men sat on the station platform watching the passings and repassings across the way.

"That makes seven going in to Johnny's," said Hat. "Add your four, Monte, and it's eleven. Throw in the bartender, twelve."

"No," said Monte. "Ten. Two came out."

"Gentlemen." The bald-topped man was in the station doorway but no longer bald-topped. He wore a round visored cap with small brass plate in front proclaiming AGENT. "You might care to know that it is getting along toward five o'clockish. I think you can begin to hope."

A stout red-faced red-haired man distinguished by open leather vest over polka-dotted shirt stepped out the door of SALOON. He was followed by others in bunches, not hurrying but plainly intent on going somewhere. They strung out behind the red-haired man who was angling past the well. Three of them stopped by the cow ponies, unlooped reins, swung up, followed.

"Fifteen," said Hat. "We were way off."

"Shucks," said Monte. "They must use back doors in this place."

Other men mysteriously appeared, tagging along, some from the haphazard houses, several from the store, three from ROOMS & EATS.

"Well, well," said Monte. "Pretty Hat too. Must be a convention."

On came the growing crowd, moving past not far away to line along the front rails of the first corral. The three on the cow ponies swung down and one of them, rangy and very young, towheaded, slipped a lead rope around his horse's neck, handed the end to a companion, started to unsaddle.

"Morrison too," said Hat, returning a cheery wave from that square-faced individual. "We might as well see what's doing."

In compact bunch the trail crew of the Slash Y elbowed way to positions along the rails. The red-haired man stood by the gate, thumbs hooked in vest armholes. "Morrison," he said. "You have the stakes. You heard the proposition. No help from anyone. He has to do it alone."

The towheaded young one came forward, face serious, tight-lipped, saddle and bridle dragging from one hand, a coiled rope in the other. He heaved the saddle up on the gate. "Open it," he said.

The red-haired man slipped the holding bar, swung the gate just enough for the other to slip through, quickly closed it again.

In the rear left corner of the corral the raw-boned mottle-hided horse stood motionless, weight settled on three legs, big hammerhead hung low. The towheaded man began to shake out a loop. Slowly the horse raised head, looked across the corral at him. Almost imperceptibly its weight shifted and it was balanced on all four feet, muscles tensed, waiting.

"Walleyed," murmured Monte Walsh. "And smart. Some bat-brained bastard's sure done a job spoiling that thing."

Warily the towheaded man advanced, jiggling loop to keep it open. The horse stood motionless, watching him. The man's arm flashed and the loop snapped out and the horse leaped sideways out of the corner and dropped big head and the loop slid off its shoulder and in the same rush of movement, a sudden silent fury unleashed, the horse wheeled and drove toward the man and reared to strike with slashing forehoofs. The man dodged, desperate, and ran toward rails, hauling in rope as he ran. The horse stopped, motionless again, watching him. Back against rails, he sorted out coils and began another loop. The tan of his young face had faded to a grayish tone and his hands shook.

"Too damned smart," murmured Chet Rollins. "Watches the rope."

Cautiously, reluctantly, the towheaded man stepped out again. He feinted with the loop and pulled back and as the horse leaped sideways threw to anticipate the leap and the loop leaving the faltering hand flattened in the air and fell useless and the horse, disregarding it, drove at him and he ran, frantic, and dropped to the ground and rolled under the bottom rail.

"All right, Morrison," said the red-haired man. "I'll thank you for the money."

Sullen, silent, the towheaded man, dragging rope, came around to the gate, took his saddle and bridle, went toward his horse.

"Yessiree," said the red-haired man, hooking thumbs again. "That there horse is my meal ticket. I live right well off him. And why? Because there ain't nobody can handle him. I got forty dollars here that says there ain't a man can ride him. I got twenty more that says there ain't a man can even put a saddle on him."

Along by the front rails Monte Walsh shifted weight from one worn old boot to the other and turned a bit toward Chet Rollins.

"No," said Chet.

"Shucks," said Monte. "We need some."

Chet sighed. "Not that bad," he said.

The red-haired man was talking again. "I'm disappointed," he said. "Might say plain shocked. I come down this way because I've heard tell that hereabouts there're men that fancy themselves in the saddle and ain't afraid of anything with four legs and hoofs. And what do I find? One boy with nothing but peach fuzz on his chin who flips his tail the moment that horse gets playful. Why, where I come from—"

"Quit yapping, mister," said Monte Walsh. "I ain't got any cash. But in the next pen there I got a nice little dun. It ain't the company's. It's mine. There ain't a better cutting horse this side the Cimarron. I'll just put him up against that money of yours."

"The dun, eh," said the red-haired man, rising on toe tips to look toward the second corral. "How'm I supposed to know it's worth a damn?"

"It's Slash Y," said the square-faced man. "That means

something in the country south of here. If he says it's good, it's good."

"What the hell," said the red-haired man. "It's a sure thing anyway."

Monte turned away, striding to get his gear.

"Mister," said Hat Henderson. "I can hoof it too if I have to. I got a little bay over there. He's pretty fair too. I'll just set him against forty more of your money that Monte rides that thing."

"Ain't it hell," said Sunfish Perkins. "The rest of us ain't got nothing."

Monte was back, heaving saddle and bridle on the gate, rope in hand.

"Ees *loco*, Monte," said Dobe Chavez. "But no worry. We take of you good care. We take you back to the ranch. We dig the hole there."

"Shucks," said Monte, sliding through briefly opened gate. "It's a horse, ain't it?"

Across the corral the horse stood motionless, watching him. Its nostrils were flaring a bit, showing red-socketed. He stood motionless, studying it. He heard the gate behind him open.

"Give me that," said Chet Rollins. "You got glue in the seat of your pants. But you ain't so good with a rope."

Monte turned a little and looked at Chet. His lips shaped in a small wry smile. He held out the rope. "I knew you would," he said. "So did you."

"Yes," said Chet, low-voiced, unsmiling. "Likely I did."

"Hey," said the red-haired man. "No help allowed. That's the proposition."

"Lookahere, mister," said Chet, raising voice. "You said a man couldn't do this, couldn't do that. You didn't say the same man had to do the roping and the riding."

"Right," said the square-faced man. "That you didn't."

"What the hell," said the red-haired man. "Can't say I like it but I'll take it. But only one man in there at a time."

"Shucks," said Monte, coming back through the gate. "One'll do."

Inside the corral Chet advanced, loop forming under stubby fingers, chunky body suddenly light on old worn boot soles, round stubbly face a serene moon of sun and windburnt rock. He feinted with the rope and the horse leaped sideways and the loop flashed out, low, skimming, reaching for the weaving forefeet, and the horse, seeing, reared and the loop dropped useless and the horse drove forward, lips drawing back from big yellowed teeth, and Chet waited and dodged ducking under the flailing forehoofs and ran to new position by the opposite rails, hauling in rope.

The horse stood again, watching him, watching the rope. He feinted and the horse leaped and he feinted again, low, and the horse reared and he threw and the rope rose, loop opening free and over the big hammerhead. Quickly he hauled in to tighten it and the horse, feeling it grip on neck, not pulling back, not straining against it, drove forward along it at him. He crouched, waiting, hauling in rope, and as the horse reared with forelegs arching up to slash down he sent swirls flicking up the rope to wrap around them and dove from under and rolled over in the dust and came to feet running, rope held firm dragging around left hip. As it pulled taut, he heaved against it and the horse, forelegs pulled together, staggered and toppled on its side. Scrambling fast, he jumped in close and whipped the rope end between the caught forelegs above the twists and jumped back before snapping teeth in the big head lunging could reach and pulled the rope tight. "Hell of a place," he said. "No snubbing post." He dropped the rope end. Eyes intent on the horse struggling up with forelegs clamped together, he backed toward the front rails putting out a hand behind him.

"Playful's the word, ain't it," said Monte, reaching between rails to put another coiled rope in the back-stretched hand.

Out in the corral the horse raged, concentrating on the first rope, crow-hopping, loosening the twists, striving to shake them. Quick and light on old worn boot soles, Chet circled, second rope alive in stubby fingers. It flashed out, low, and he yanked up and it had the hindfeet. He ran again, heaving against left hip, and the horse went down again and he ran on, paying out rope, and stopped against side rails and passed the rope end around a post, pulled it tight, and flipped a fast knot. He turned, sweat beginning to streak dust on face, and approached the snorting squirming horse. Suddenly he dove in and dust rose and dust settled and the horse lay still, quivering, and he sat, wiping sweat from serene moon-rock face, on the big hammerhead.

A bridle trailed through air and landed close. He reached

with one foot and pulled it in. Methodically he unbuttoned his old flannel shirt and pulled it off, disclosing chest and back surprisingly white in contrast with tanned forearms and neck and face. Methodically he began to fold the shirt.

"Twenty dollars coming up," said Monte Walsh.

*   *   *

Antelope Junction buzzed considerably in the immediate vicinity of the first corral. The horse stood, silent, quivering, one rope clamping hindlegs and fastened to a side post, the other stretching the big head toward an opposite post. It was bridled, saddled. A folded old flannel shirt was tied around the head, over the bridle, over the eyes.

"Plumb outlaw," said white-and-tan and generally dust-colored Chet, coming out through the gate. "It ain't going to be licked."

"Shucks," said Monte, going in. "It's still a horse, ain't it?"

He untied the rope holding the hindlegs, shook slack down, saw the loop loosen and fall around hoofs. The legs spread a bit, bracing, and the horse stood, quivering. He circled to opposite side and untied the other rope. The horse stood, listening, waiting. Holding this rope, he circled warily in. He dropped the rope and leaped forward and in one smooth swift motion vaulted into saddle, legs swinging forward, boots smacking into stirrups, upper body arching over saddle horn to take the reins. And still the horse stood, knowing, waiting.

He reached and loosened the loop around the neck, slipped reins through under it, flipped it off over the head. He worked at the folded shirt and with a sudden jerk flipped it away.

The horse shook, shuddered, pent fury flooding through raw-boned sweat-streaked body. It plunged forward, head striking down, smashing against bit for headplay, and drove ahead, bucking, in partial circuit of the corral. It stopped, shuddering, seeming to shrink and bunch together within itself.

"That ain't much," said Monte, serene in saddle.

The horse exploded, rearing up, up, and driving down with a sideways wrenching motion, and Monte swayed with the harsh movement, head jerking at the wrench, hat flying off, but body firm in saddle, long legs locked against the heaving sides, and as the horse paused, gathering itself again, he raked from shoulders to flanks with his spurs. The horse squealed and leaped, coming down stiff-legged with jarring jolt, and on the instant reared, up, up, and drove down with the same sideways wrenching. Again and again it pounded, reared, pounded, reared, and Monte swayed and swung, head jerking, color draining out of face, blood beginning to dribble from nose.

The horse stood, shuddering, bloody froth flecking its muzzle, eyes red-rimmed and bulging. Again it reared up, up, tottering on hindlegs, and deliberately toppled backwards and Monte, dropping reins, hands on its shoulders, swung feet out of stirrups and pushed out and away from under, rolling over and coming up fast, and as the horse struggled to its feet was in saddle again.

"Ain't he a daisy," said Sunfish Perkins, smacking hand on top rail.

The horse reared again, up, up, tottering, and Monte, panting hard now, had gun out. He struck the barrel down between the big ears and it thudded dully on bone and the horse dropped to four feet again, dazed, shaking big head.

"I can play rough too," gasped Monte, slipping gun back in holster.

The horse plunged ahead, bucking, and flung itself in reckless lunge sideways against rails to crush him against them, but Monte had right foot out of stirrup, swinging back and up and over, and took the jolt standing in left stirrup and as the horse staggered out, catching balance, he was back in saddle, raking deep with spurs.

The horse plowed out into the center, smashing head against bit, and stopped and swung head up and around, jaws open, striking for Monte's left leg. Instantly old boot in heavy stirrup swung and crashed full into the reaching jaws and the horse screamed and jerked head around straight, high, and drove, blind with rage, unseeing, unheeding, forward in brute furious rush into the side corral fence. Its chest struck a post and this cracked and split and rails bent and broke and Monte, pushing out and back from the saddle, landed sprawling and the horse sank quivering then still over the wreckage of the fence.

Dust settled over the corral, over the splintered fence, over the body of the horse, over Monte Walsh standing with hands holding to a top rail of unbroken fence, head dropped between them, breath coming in gasps, watching small drops of blood drip from his nose down by his feet.

"God a'mighty!" said the red-haired man. "The son of a bitch killed my horse. All bets off!"

"Mister," said Hat Henderson, stepping close, mild, deceptively mild. "I say he rode him."

"You're damn right he did," said Chet Rollins, opening gate and going through.

Sunfish Perkins and Dobe Chavez moved up, flanking Hat.

"Well, well," said the square-faced man, slow smile spreading. He looked at them then at the red-haired man. "There's no votes in this. I say the same."

Out in the corral Chet placed Monte's hat on Monte's head, shook dust out of his own shirt, began to pull it on.

"Shucks," said Monte, turning to lean back against rails, looking at Chet. His lips shaped in a small wry grin. "We're lucky. A couple more of those goddamned twists and he'd of shook me sure."

"Maybe," said Chet, picking up a rope and beginning to coil it. Monte moved out, took the other.

"Hey, you two," said Hat Henderson, stuffing money in a pocket. "We're through playing games. Till later anyway. We got work coming up. We got to get that last pen ready. The train just tootled down the line."

*　*　*

Antelope Junction, deceptive in deepening dusk, had an almost cheerful appearance. Patches of yellow light from windows seemed to beckon, welcome, in the darkening immensity of the big land under the unbelievably deep sky. The trail crew of the Slash Y sat on rickety chairs around one of the tables in the front room of ROOMS & EATS intent on second rounds of Biggest Beefsteaks West of Boston. At another table across the room sat the man in the big white hat, staring at emptied plate and coffee mug. The hat was pushed back at a jaunty angle. He wore a very neat clean silk scarf neatly knotted around his throat. A diamond stickpin glittered in this. Prosperity exuded from him. He drummed gently with fingers on the table, looked across at the steadily eating crew, drummed again.

"This stuff," said Monte, "tastes like they run it to death then stomped it."

"Better'n our own jerky and biscuits," said Chet, solemnly chewing.

The greasy-aproned proprietor came through an inner doorway and laid a pie already cut into five approximately equal pieces on the table. "You want any more," he said, "you pay again." He disappeared back through the doorway.

"Those cows now," said Monte.

"Bulls," said Chet.

"Cows," said Monte.

Jaws chewed in slowing beginning-to-be-satisfied rhythm.

"What about 'em?" said Sunfish.

"Why, shucks," said Monte. "They don't look like much to me. Built more like hawgs 'n cows. They come out of that car like tame puppydogs."

"Barnyard stuff," said Hat. "They been used to being handled and pushed around. Ain't even feeling the itch yet. Wait'll they get some growth and been out on the range a while. They're good stuff. Not all horns 'n bone. They put on plenty meat. It won't be long before they'll be getting us mighty fat sassy calves."

Jaws chewed in even slower rhythm as plates emptied.

Across the room the man in the white hat stood up. "I'm a man of decision," he said to the universe in general about him. He came across the room, dragging his chair. "Mind if I join you?" he said.

"We ain't particular," said Hat.

"Fine," said the man. "And dandy." He pushed the chair in between Monte and Chet, its back to the table, and spraddled it, folding hands atop its back. "The name," he said, "is Johnson. Oscar J. Johnson."

Hat waved a fork in circuit of the table. "Slash Y," he said, taking the pie tin and scooping one of the pieces onto his plate.

"A fine brand," said the man. "I've heard it mentioned back in Kansas City." He turned his head a bit to look at Monte. "I hope you will permit me, sir, to state that I like your style. I repeat it. I like your style."

"Shucks," said Monte, reaching for the pie. "You can jabber that way all you want."

"Fine," said the man. "And jim dandy. Permit me to explain. What do the folks back east think of when they think of a cowboy? You, my boy. You. Youngish but not a kid. Tall. Lean. Nice shoulders. Thin hips. Devil-may-care bring-on-your-grizzlies look on your face. Sit a horse like you were born there and have never been off. That's what they think of. Precisely."

"My oh my," murmured Monte around mouthful of pie. "And I don't even carry a mirror. What're you selling?"

"Selling?" said the man, offended. He chuckled, overlooking the offense. "Well, yes, in a way you might say I'm selling. Only what I'm selling won't cost you a cent. The other way around. I'm offering you something, free gratis. Opportunity. A job."

"I got one," said Monte, reaching for crumbs in the pie tin. "Forty a month and all I can eat and plenty chances to break my neck."

"Not like this one," said the man. "This is something special." He hitched his chair more toward Monte. "Look. I'll lay it on the line. I'm partner in a show. One of these wild west things. They're mighty popular back east. We're not up to Bill Cody's of course but we do all right. Booked solid in a few weeks up through Illinois, Indianny, all through the corn country. Probably go into Chicago. You know how it is. Some riding, some roping, hold up a stagecoach, bang away at some Indians, give the town folks some shivers. Bronco-busting goes big. That's for you. Nothing like that brute out there today of course. Just good broncs that'll buck enough to make it look good. It's worth fifty a week."

"We'll just slide out of this game," said Hat, pushing back his chair, rising, three others with him. "It's your hand, Monte. See you at Johnny's." He disappeared out the front door, the others following.

"Fifty a week," murmured Monte, licking crumbs off fingers. "Just to loaf a little in a saddle."

"And expenses," said the man. "Here, have a cigar." Deftly he produced a match, scratched it on the underside of the table, held it out. "The way to live," he said. "Travel. See all the good towns. Money in your pocket. People cheering, shouting at you doing what you can do better'n a one of them without even working up a sweat. Come back hereabouts to treat old friends between seasons."

"M-m-m-m," murmured Monte, watching smoke trail in two thin streamers from his nose.

"Of course," said the man, "we'll dress you up some. You know, all the trimmings."

Monte looked steadily at him.

"All right, all right," said the man. "Not too fancy. You got the look anyway." He produced another cigar, lit it, studied Monte through smoke. He looked away. "And women," he said. "Yes, sir, one thing I've noticed is women back through those towns sure do go for a man in boots and spurs and big hat. Specially when they've seen him up there cool and easy aboard a bucking horse."

"You don't say," murmured Monte, inspecting a blunt fingernail.

"I do say," said the man. "It'd bug your eyes to see them flocking around our boys after a show." He stood up. "You just think it over. Opportunity. A chance like this doesn't come walking along every day. I'll leave it like this: I'm suffering on something that passes for a bed here tonight because I'm meeting a man tomorrow. Then I'll be taking the train out. If I see you around in the morning, I'll know you're going with me. At my expense of course. There'll be plenty time for us to get acquainted waiting for that train." He smiled, disclosing expensive gold fillings, waved his cigar and disappeared through an inner doorway.

"My oh my," murmured Monte. "Things do kind of happen around this place." He rose and went out the front doorway and strolled toward SALOON, rolling the cigar between fingers and flicking ash from it. He stepped through the swinging doors, surveyed the livening in progress down the left and at the rear of the long room, located the four standing by the front end of the bar along the right. He moved to join them.

"We been waiting, Monte," said Hat, pushing a small filled glass along the bar. "Anything we should drink to?"

"Shucks," said Monte, taking the glass. "I could give it a whirl."

Five men stood by the bar end, fingering glasses, looking everywhere but at each other.

"Goddamn it!" said Monte Walsh. "I ain't thinking of stealing horses! Just make me a little real money for a change!"

"Sure," said Hat. "Sure. Sure, Monte. A man'd be a fool to pass up a thing like that."

"You're goddamned right," said Monte. "I been chousing other people's cows, peeling other people's broncs, sweating my goddamned skin off for peanuts ever since I got big enough to hit out for myself. And what've I got? The clothes I'm standing in and one scrawny little old horse."

"I ain't even got that," said Sunfish.

"Ees right," said Dobe. "Ees one beeg hell of a life."

"So that's it," said Chet, short, matter of fact. "We got something to drink to." He raised his glass.

Five men drank, stood fingering glasses, looking everywhere but at each other. Silence held the front end of the bar.

"Hey, look," said Sunfish, pointing at Monte's left hand. "A seegar. He's living high already."

"Shucks," said Monte, flipping the cigar out over the swinging doors. "Those things can wait. This is tonight."

"Damned if it ain't," said Hat, beginning to count out money into five small piles on the bar.

* * *

Antelope Junction slept in clear star-pointed dark of night over the big land. Not yet the five figures, unsteady on feet, uncertain in movement, fumbling with blankets under the scraggly cottonwood by the station corner.

"If any of you was to ask me," said Hat, "which you won't being too pie-eyed to think straight like me, I'd say we did mighty good. Five of us. Only one hundred piddling little dollars. And we made it last the whole goddamned evening."

"We'd of made it last longer," said Sunfish, "if you'd of had the sense of a flop-eared jackass to remember how that Morrison runs a bluff."

"Me?" said Hat. "Hows about Dobe bucking the tiger like he had dollars coming out his ears?"

"Ah-h-h," said Dobe. "The poker." He spat in disgust. "The faro now. That ees the game."

"You can lose faster at it anyways," said Hat.

"And ween faster," said Dobe. "I ween too. For a time."

Silence settled, broken only by soft grunts and rustlings.

"I ain't running out on you, Hat," said Monte, sitting up.

"You don't need me. Not with those tame things. Act like maybe they're even housebroke."

"Sure," said Hat. "Sure. Sure, Monte. They won't be no trouble at all."

Silence settled again.

"Hey, Chet," whispered Monte. "Maybe I could get that Johnson to take you on. Roping."

"No," said Chet, short, matter of fact. "I don't look like a cowboy. So I'll just go on being one."

* * *

Antelope Junction drowsed in morning sun. The limp dog, after a night of foraging activity, already lay, motionless, in the shadow of the water trough in what would have been the plaza. On top back rail of the third corral sat Monte Walsh, boot toes hooked behind the second rail.

Moving over the first rise rolling into distance southward fifteen young fat lazy shorthorn bulls padded along under a rising dust cloud, shooed ahead by four men on four stout little cow ponies, tagged by a lean packhorse on a lead rope. The little cavalcade pushed on and dropped out of sight.

"Shucks," murmured Monte. "They might of waved. I ain't gone and died."

He pushed out from the fence, landing springy-kneed, and strolled around the corral and across the way. In the doorway of ROOMS & EATS stood the man in the white hat, neat, spruce, polished, prosperity and good cheer exuding from him.

"Fine," he said. "And dandy. Absolutely jim dandy. I knew you would see opportunity beckoning in the bright light of morning. Our host is stirring up some breakfast. Come along and join me." He stepped out and threw a brotherly arm around Monte's shoulders.

Monte winced under the arm. He straightened shoulders and came along.

"Yes, sir," said the man, leading toward the table. "You string along with Oscar J. and you'll go places." He folded into one chair, waved at another. "Now how about money? You need some? You know, sort of an advance."

Monte winced a bit again. "No," he said. "Not till I start earning it."

The man leaned back, admiration plain under the big hat. "That's what I like to see," he said. "Spirit. Stand on your own two feet. We'll go far together, my boy. I can see it now. Top billing. That's what you'll get before long. By earning it too. Riders? They're everywhere these days. Dime a dozen. Stay on a horse. Do good work on a horse. But awkward. Bags of potatoes. Now a natural rider. Rare, my boy, rare. The moment I saw you out there I knew. Knowledge. Science. Know what the horse'll do before the horse does. Master of every—"

"Shucks," said Monte, stirring on his chair. "I just throw a leg over and ride."

"Of course," said the man, beaming at him. "A natural. That's you. But Oscar J. knows. Wait'll you see how I play you up on the posters. I couldn't sleep on that bed. Spent the time thinking up good ones. Like this . . ."

"What's the matter?" said the man. "You aren't eating."

"I ate some with the boys," said Monte, rising. "See you later, I got a few things to do." He strolled out the doorway and breathed in deeply and moved along to the left. He stopped and sat on the store platform, pulled off one boot, turned it up, shook it. A silver dollar fell out. "Kind of mean," he murmured. "But I had to hold it out." He picked up the dollar, put on the boot, strolled on. He stopped by an adobe hut. "I guess this is it," he murmured and opened the door. He stepped into the small front room and settled into a slant-backed old chair fastened atop a small platform. A small brown-skinned big-mustached man bustled in from the back room.

"Shave," said Monte.

"*Sí, señor,*" said the small man, bustling around a small stand with various items on its top . . .

Monte rose from the slant-backed chair, stepped to the wall, surveyed himself in a small cracked mirror. "So that's what folks back east think of," he murmured. He turned to the small man. "Bath?" he said. "Scrubbing? All over?"

"*Sí, señor,*" said the small man, pointing to the back room. Monte looked through the doorway. In one corner, suspended from the ceiling, small stepladder standing near, was a fair-sized washtub. A rope hung from one handle. Just beneath its outer edge hung a bucket with holes punched in the bottom. Monte reached to the small stand, took a small cake of soap from its top, a towel from its undershelf. He reached again and took a half-filled bottle of toilet water.

"My oh my," murmured Monte, stepping out the front door of the adobe hut, sniffing himself. "Just like a lily." He strolled toward ROOMS & EATS, slowed, stopped to look in SALOON.

"Howdy," said a man behind the bar, wiping glasses. "Monte, ain't that what they called you? Come in. Have one on the house."

"You was singing a different tune yesterday," said Monte, stepping in.

"There was five of you then," said the man, pushing a drink forward. He leaned on the bar. "You know, Monte. It ain't the money you boys spent here last night. I was plain tickled to see you take that blowhard. He was sure strutting in here before."

"Thanks," said Monte, tossing off drink, strolling out. He started again toward ROOMS & EATS, slowed, shifted to amble vaguely over toward the tracks. "Those colts at the place," he said. "That new bunch of three-year-olds. There ain't a mean one in the bunch. Chet can top 'em off all right." He ambled on.

Out of somewhere among the haphazard houses appeared the bald-top man, aiming for the station, carrying several small pots.

"Hey, Killer," said Monte. "How'd you finish yesterday?"

"One hundred and eighty-nine," said the bald-topped man. "That is not a record. No. But I will let you in on a little secret. I am trying something new today. I intend to make me some flypaper." He moved on.

A breeze stirred and a dust devil whirled out from behind the station. Monte watched it pass and disintegrate over by the livery table. "No more of that," he murmured. "Not for me. Dust in your nose, your mouth. In the coffee. In the biscuits. Cooking yourself in the sun. Sleeping in wet blankets. Tailing up dumb cows. Smelling of 'em. No more. It's high living for me."

He strolled on, angling toward the first corral. "Women," he murmured. "Flocking around. Money in my pocket. Regular." He leaned against front rails, staring over, unseeing.

Gradually his eyes focused on a patch of pressed dust where a rawboned mottle-hided horse had hit grunting on its side.

"Yes," he said, suddenly, loud. "Yes. That fat-faced cow-smelling baboon sure threw him."

He fidgeted some, not liking his thoughts. He strolled on, was passing the second corral. Inside, by a small water trough where some hay lay on the ground, stood a deep-chested leggy dun, chewing in slow rhythm. "Almost forgot," murmured Monte. "Got to get rid of that thing. Can't take him on the cars." He stared at the horse. "Who'm I kidding?" he said.

* * *

Far out in sun-washed heat-shimmered distance fifteen fat lazy yearling bulls plodded in compact bunch, Dobe Chavez and Sunfish Perkins riding point, Hat Henderson and Chet Rollins and the packhorse bringing up the drag. They worked down to a wide steep-sided arroyo, along it to a crumbled low stretch, and pushed across.

"Can't hurry these things," said Hat, looking at Chet, "or they'll start dripping lard." There was no response. He tried again. "It'll be something different," he said, "when they've been out on the range a while and sniff a few cows." He sighed and quit.

The little herd plodded on. The riders slouched in saddles, enduring dust and heat and time.

Chet's black pricked up ears and turned head to look back. Chet and Hat swung in saddles. Far down the back trail beyond the arroyo crossing, dust floated upward. A rider, tiny, indistinguishable in distance, came into view around a shoulder of land, driving forward along the hoof tracks. Straight to the arroyo he raced, disdaining to swing aside to the low crossing. The horse reared, pawing sky, then plunged downward, plowing down the high bank and out of sight. Hat and Chet pulled reins, staring back. The horse reappeared, head and shoulders heaving up over the near bank, scrambling up, lining out, belly low, straining legs a blur across the distance.

"Jeeeeesus!" said Hat. "There ain't but one crack-headed son of a wild jackass rides like that."

"Yes," said Chet Rollins, straightening in saddle, ten years sliding from his shoulders as he straightened. "There's only one."

* * *

Dust flew from under pounding hoofs. The leggy dun stretched out like an oversize frantic frightened jackrabbit.

"Yow-eee!" yelled Monte Walsh, standing in stirrup. "Hold up, boys! I'm a-coming!"

* * *

A friend of this newspaper who recently returned from travels through the Territory reports the following incident:

On Saturday evening last a small boy was struck and injured by a wagon on the main street of the town of Harmony. The accident occurred when the small boy, Arturo Montoya by name, was playing with a dog and suddenly ran out from behind a building. The driver of the wagon, one William Hotchkiss, stated that he was unable to stop or turn the horses in time. The boy suffered a badly crushed leg.

The local doctor took care of the boy but expressed it as his opinion that his patient would have to be taken to Denver for expert surgery or he would never walk again. Needless to say, neither Mr. Hotchkiss nor the boy's parents and relatives were in a position to meet any such expense.

At this juncture the men of one of the local ranches rode into town, their pockets heavy with pay for a month's hard work, their minds made up to get rid of it to the tune of a weekend of revelry. They inquired what was the trouble. They fidgeted about and talked among themselves. Then they promptly emptied their pockets and gave it all to the doctor for "that poor little cuss." There being nothing further for them to do in their penniless condition, they turned about and rode back to the ranch.

We understand that at the time of this writing young Master Montoya is in a hospital in Denver.

Christmas Eve at the Slash Y
1884

THE DAY dawned still and clear, windless with the winter night chill of the high country lingering in the air. Stringy clouds clung gray and heavy to the tops of the mountains to the west but that was nothing unusual in late December. The sun, below the horizon to the east, sent edgings of color along the far high-hanging clouds and the first faint pink flush of a fine morning touched the roof of the cookhouse in which the men of the Slash Y were finishing a late and particularly hearty breakfast.

Range manager Cal Brennan set his coffee cup down and pulled a doubled-over paper bag from a side jacket pocket, unfolded this, shook it gently. A soft rattling sound came from it. "I ain't takin' the trouble," he said, "of decidin' who's goin' an' who's stayin'. I'm makin' it an even chance for everybody, includin' Skimpy here an' myself too. There's twelve of us an' there's twelve beans in here. Nine white an' three brown. White ones go. Brown ones stay."

He held the bag by his left hand up above eye level and reached into it with his right hand. The hand emerged holding a white bean between thumb and forefinger. "Well, well," he said. "Bein' nice about this's paid off nice too." He passed the bag to foreman Hat Henderson.

Hat held it up, reached into it. A white bean. "Reckon I live right," he said and passed the bag to Monte Walsh.

Monte held it up. "Gambling's a sin," he said. "That's what my mother used to say. Must be true 'cause I never have any luck at it." He reached in. A brown bean. "See what I mean?" he said, aggrieved. "And I got new boots too."

"No bellyaching," said Powder Kent, taking the bag. A

white bean. He flipped it up and caught it coming down. "Don't fret, Monte. Miss Annie won't even miss you. Not with me there."

The bag passed on down and around the long table. White beans. Sunfish Perkins held it up. A brown bean. "Aw, hell," he said. "I ain't much on dancing and such anyways."

The bag passed on. Chet Rollins held it up. Two beans left in it, a white and a brown. Chet's glance flicked across the table at Monte slumped on the bench staring down in disgust at the bean in his hand and flicked back to the bag. He reached in. It could have been a white bean emerging between thumb and forefinger but before anyone could be quite certain it slipped from his fingers and back into the bag. "Damn," murmured Chet, softly, cheerfully, and reached in again. A brown bean. He tossed the bag to Skimpy Eagens standing at the end of the table. "It's all yours," he said.

* * *

The sun was an hour up, warming the air, driving the night chill back into the mountains under the hanging clouds. Monte Walsh and Chet Rollins and Sunfish Perkins sat on a top corral rail, facing in, watching the nine white-bean winners saddle up and strap behind saddles blanket rolls containing whatever extra adornments each cared to or could carry along. The nine had a forty-five mile ride ahead of them but what was a mere forty-five miles to the prospect of Christmas Eve festivities at the headquarters of the Triple Seven for which folks were gathering from an even wider radius around—festivities that in one form or another would likely continue all the next day and perhaps the next or until energies and the food and liquor supply gave out.

"You know," said Monte, morose. "I been thinking. That bag game wasn't exactly fair. First pickers had best chances what with more white beans still in there. I'll bet Cal had that figured."

"Sure," said Chet. "But you can't squawk much. You were one of the first."

Monte gnawed on a knuckle. "That just goes to show," he said. "Luck and me we ain't even acquainted. Someday I'm a-going to—" He stopped. Skimpy Eagens had left his horse and was calling to him. "Come along, Monte," said Skimpy, bending to slide between corral rails. "Something to show you." He led toward the cookhouse.

Inside. on the wide plank shelf near the big old wood stove, limp well-washed flour sacks were tucked down over two humped objects. Skimpy removed the covering of the first with a flourish, disclosing the plump plucked carcass of a wild turkey in a battered roasting pan. "Cal brought that in two days ago," he said. "It's stuffed. All you got to do is get a good fire going and put it in. About two hours. A little basting'd help."

"Basting?" said Monte, somewhat brightened.

"Just scoop up hot juice and dribble it over," said Skimpy. He lifted the second covering, disclosing a squat dark ball of pudding in another pan. "Course those plums ain't fresh, only canned. But there's a snitch of brandy in it. Just warm it up some."

"What d'you know," said Monte, brightened more.

"Not till tomorrow," said Skimpy. "That's what they're for. And maybe I'll show you something else. Cal figured to let you just find it when you started rooting for food but maybe he's hoping you'd just miss it." Skimpy pulled open a bulging potato bag under the shelf and took out a full un-opened bottle of whisky.

"That," said Monte beaming, "is the best yet. I'll just take charge of that right now."

"You can read, can't you?" said Skimpy, holding the bottle up. A small piece of paper was flattened around it with a tag end of string. On the paper was written in Cal Brennan's crabbed scrawl: "Not to be opened till Christmas."

"All right," said Monte. "But put that thing back quick."

"Too late," said Sunfish Perkins from the doorway. "I got a good look."

*　*　*

The sun was an hour and a half up, warming the air, reaching for the rim of frost left around the inside top of the corral water trough by the night chill. Monte Walsh and Chet Rollins and Sunfish Perkins sat on the same top rail, previous positions reversed, watching the dust of the nine white-bean winners fade off northward into the nothingness of distance across the big land.

"Hope that horse of Powder's stumbles and breaks a leg," said Monte. "The leg being Powder's."

Silence along the rail.

"Know what I'm a-going to do?" said Monte. "Soon as it warms up more I'm a-going over to the house and bring that leather chair of Cal's out on the porch and sit in the sun. No sense wasting sun this time of year. I'm a-going to catch up some on the sitting I ain't done in a long time. I'm a-going to sit there thinking of how Hat's been working us these last weeks. I'm a-going to sit there thinking up ways of talking you two into bringing me food so I don't even have to move none. Then I'm a-going to sit there and sit there some more trying to make up my mind should I slip into town tonight and see what's doing which likely won't be much or just take over that bed of Cal's and catch up on all that sleep I missed last month riding line extra for Petey 'cause of that bad knee of his."

Silence along the rail.

"Yep," said Monte. "That's it. And tomorrow if I feel up to it maybe I'll show you two how easy I can beat you at horseshoes but that seems kind of strenuous right about now but maybe I'll do it just to work up the right kind of appetite for that turkey and pudding and the other fixings you two'll fix."

"Sounds turrible exciting," said Sunfish. "Then what'll you do?"

"Why, shucks," said Monte. "Then I'll just sit some more and see how much mileage I can get out of my third of that bottle."

Silence along the rail.

"Well, now," said Chet, staring down solemnly at his hands on his knees. "Hat mentioned something about rehanging those crooked barn doors. Also something about working over the harness gear.

Monte shifted sideways to stare at Chet.

"And also again and likewise," said Chet, "something about putting a new gate on that other corral."

Monte stared at Chet, horrified. "You mean," he said, "you mean you're a-thinking of us killing ourselves working while the rest of 'em are off having fun? Why, it's only those silly damn beans stuck us here, that and Cal being so worrying womanish about some of us being around if something happens."

Silence along the rail.

"Dog—gone!" said Monte. "There ain't nothing happening or a-going to happen. You ever see anything so peaceful as this place right about now?"

Silence along the rail.

"Aw shucks," said Monte. "You ain't really thinking that?"

"Why, no," said Chet. "Did I say I was? Hat mentioned those things so I figured I ought at least do the same."

"Right," said Monte. "You've mentioned 'em. Now what's it really you're a-thinking of doing?"

"Sitting on that porch in the sun," said Chet. "Maybe playing a little euchre with you two so's to settle who cooks when. But mostly just sitting. That is, when I ain't sleeping."

"Me too," said Sunfish Perkins.

*   *   *

The sun was well past noon, the sunlight warm and reassuring. Monte Walsh sat on the ranch house veranda relaxed limp and lazy into the depths of the mouse-chewed remnants of a once imposing leather-covered armchair. A few feet away Chet Rollins leaned back equally limp and lazy in a spindle-sprung rocker padded with the remains of old saddle blankets. Both chairs were placed at precise angles for maximum sunlight benefit. A few more feet away Sunfish Perkins sat across-legged on the porch floor leaning forward to play solitaire with an old deck of cards.

"My oh my," murmured Monte. "It tires me just to hear him. Where's he get the energy to slap those cards so loud? How's he doing it with all that fat around his middle?"

"No fat," said Sunfish without looking up. "Muscle."

"Oh my yes," murmured Monte. "Certain and no doubt whatsomever. The kind of muscle they pack into lard pails."

Silence on the veranda, a lazy companionable silence broken only by the soft plop of old cards on old cards.

Over in the first corral a horse whinnied. On the veranda three heads lifted and looked into the distances of the big land. A small darkish speck moved against the seemingly endless reaches of plain to the southeast.

"He got a late start," said Monte. "That is if he's aiming at the partying up north."

"What's he doing heading over here then?" said Chet.

Silence on the porch. Sunfish gathered up the cards, set them in a neat pile on the floor, stretched out his legs and leaned back against a porch post. The speck became larger and was a man on a horse.

"Simple," said Monte. "The horse's lame."

"G'wan," said Sunfish. "You can't tell this far."

"Want to bet?" said Monte. "It's favoring the off forefoot."

Silence on the porch. The man and the horse came closer and were Sonny Jacobs of the Diamond Six and a smallish neat sorrel definitely favoring its off forefoot. They came closer and stopped by the porch. Sonny crossed his arms and leaned on these on the saddle horn surveying the veranda and its occupants. A wide smile creased his broad young face. "I never thought to see the day," he said. "Blamed if you don't look like three old ladies sitting around at a sewing circle."

"That's better'n you look," said Monte. "Which is plain foolish, expecting to get anywheres on one of those bat-brained horses you raise down your way. What'd it do, step in a badger hole?"

"Hell, no," said Sonny. "Shied at a rabbit and into some goddamned cactus. I worked on that fetlock maybe half an hour but must be some spines still in it. You got anything particular to say about which one of yours I take?"

"Shucks no," said Monte. "Be a relief to see you on a decent horse. Any one you want in the corral there long as it's the gray."

Three heads turned slightly to watch Sonny ride to the corral, dismount, open the gate, lead the sorrel in. His saddle rose into view from inside, heaved up to rest on a rail. Dust rose in the air over the corral and a rope flashed briefly through it. The saddle disappeared down inside. The gate opened and Sonny came out leading a biggish flop-eared mean-looking gray. He closed the gate, swung up, and rocked in the saddle as the horse plunged forward, bucking. Four lively minutes later he sat serene in saddle by the porch as the horse stood quivering under him. "You sure can pick 'em, Monte boy," he said. "He'll be right interesting."

"And go the distance," said Monte. "And in good time

without you kicking him into it. And he ain't afraid of no rabbits. You sure you ain't afraid of him?"

"Plumb scared to death," said Sonny, smiling wide. He reared the gray spinning on hind legs and started away fast and swung in a short circle back. "Almost forgot to tell you. I came up your east range. Following the drift fence. There's a stretch of it down." He swung again and was gone.

Silence on the porch. Three men sat still, very stilll, looking at one another and away.

"Damn," said Sunfish.

"No, sir," said Monte. "I ain't a-going to move. Let it stay down a while. When the others get back'll be time enough."

Chet sighed. "Yes-s-s-s," he said. "Yes, I guess maybe it will."

* * *

The sun was well into the afternoon, the sunlight full on the porch. Monte Walsh reclined in the remnants of armchair, limp and lazy, eyes closed. A few feet away Chet Rollins reclined in the old rocker, head dropped sideways onto one hunched shoulder, breath coming in soft sighs not quite strong enough to be called snores. A few feet more away Sunfish Perkins lay full-length on a doubled-over old quilt with a corner of it bunched up under his head, definitely snoring in long slow rhythm.

Monte wriggled a bit in the armchair. He opened his eyes, blinking into the sunlight. "Funny," he murmured. "Sun's right up there right on the job but I feel kind of chilly around the edges." He closed his eyes and let laziness relax him deeper into the armchair remnants.

Slowly, then with increasing swiftness, the sunlight faded. Over by the other buildings a loose piece of roofing tin rattled. A gust of wind, whirling, picking up dust, swept past the veranda. Monte opened his eyes and raised his head some. He sat up straighter. His eyes focused into distance to the west. Laziness left him in a silent rush. "Chet," he said, voice low, urgent. "Chet. Take a look."

Chet snapped out of sleep and straightened in the old rocker, looking. Off to the west the mountains were gone, erased in a great drab grayness that filled the horizon and obscured the sun. Another gust swept past and in the following stillness, suddenly heavy and ominous, Sunfish Perkins grunted and pushed up from the porch floor and stood, looking too.

High overhead wind sighed, long and seeming sorrowful, and died away into distance eastward.

"Coming this way," said Sunfish, shivering. "And colder by the minute. Must be snow in it."

"That ain't good," said Monte. "It ain't any damn good at all."

"Sure not," said Chet. "If this turns into something and any cows get through that fence, they'll drift with it clean over into Texas."

"Aw, hell," said Sunfish. "And I was dreaming so nice."

"Finish it later," said Chet. "What've we got in the corral?"

"Two apiece," said Monte. "That is, we did have before Sonny stole one. Come along." He led fast toward the bunkhouse.

Ten minutes later the three of them, in heavy jackets, gloved, hats pulled well down, led three horses, saddled, out of the corral. Over the saddle horn of Monte's rat-tailed roan hung a coil of light baling wire. The wind came in long sweeps now, leaning against them, and the sky steadily darkened.

"Sunfish," said Chet. "This gets bad like it looks it could, we'll be needing plenty of relays the next day or two. You swing out and bring in some more of the saddle stock. Six or eight anyway. Then you can get a fire going in the house where likely we'll hole up and something hot cooking. Monte and me, we'll get that fence."

"Got you," said Sunfish. He swung up and left at a lope around the corner of the corral.

"Shucks," said Monte. "Looks like his bean wasn't as brown as mine. Yours too. Bring in a few horses. Cook a meal. And we got six-seven miles just to get there, then there's ten miles of fence."

"Sonny rode it," said Chet. "Mentioned one stretch down. One. Could be in the first mile." He swung up, started off.

"With my luck," said Monte, mounting and moving up alongside, "it'll be the last mile. Damn Cal and his silly goddamned beans. Why does it have to be us?"

"If I knew I'd tell you," said Chet. "But it is."

"Yeah," said Monte. "It sure is. Well, let's move." He slapped spurs to the roan.

*   *   *

Under the darkening sky wind moved over the big land, swirling dust, whipping the short winter-cured grasses. The first flurries of snow skittered with it, big-flaked, hardening as the temperature dropped. Like a long blurred pencil-marking across the bigness, the drift fence came out of distance and went into distance, not so much a discernible fence as a dark gray line of tumbleweed banked against the poles and wires. Where some violent freak of wind, likely an oversize dust devil, had smashed sometime recently against massed tumbleweed and used this as a battering ram to rip wires loose from posts, a rat-tailed roan and a chunky bay stood, patient and enduring, heads drooping, rumps hunched into the wind. Not far away, moving away, two men worked steadily and rapidly, alternating at posts, wire cutters in hands, tugging to lift the ground-sagging barbed wire strands and snipping short lengths of baling wire with which to lash each strand back into place on the posts.

"Should of done this when the fence went up," shouted Monte Walsh against the wind. "You and Hat and your goddamned staples. They ain't worth a hoot in this country. Soon as the posts dry out they rip loose."

"Live and learn," shouted Chet Rollins. "They work fine back where I was raised."

The wind rose in intensity and the snow increased, small-flaked now and hard and stinging, and two tough little cow ponies waited, patient and enduring, and two men, fingers numbing, worked steadily and rapidly on down the line.

And across the darkening miles, back by the ranch buildings, another man, big barrel body swinging in saddle, raced on a sweat-streaked mottled roan to pocket a batch of skittery horses in an angle of fence and push them through a gate into the big holding corral and follow them in and close the gate and open another at the other end and work them on into the smaller regular horse corral.

*   *   *

Swirling snow, wind-driven, filled the darkness of early night, making a grayness over the big land in which vision died at fifteen feet and all directions seemed the same. A rat-tailed roan and a chunky bay, sleet-crusted, pushed through the grayness, angling into the wind at a steady jog. The men in the saddles were hunched low, jacket collars up, hats pulled down with short lengths of baling wire over the crowns and holding the brims down over their ears and ends twisted together under their chins.

The roan raised its head higher and looked to the right, snorting snow out of its nostrils and whinnying.

"Christ a'mighty," said Monte Walsh, drawing rein. "What now?"

"What say?" shouted Chet Rollins, stopping beside him.

Off to the right, lost in the swirling grayness, a horse whinnied.

They swerved right. Moving abreast, wind at their backs, they advanced slowly, peering ahead. They stopped. Directly in front of them stood a small scrawny horse, showing pinto through the patches of snow gathering on it.

"Ain't that one of Gonzales's?" said Monte.

"Saddled," said Chet. "What's holding him?"

The horse sidled around to face more toward them and raised its head. One rein hung limp. The other drew taut, fastened to some object on the ground rapidly becoming indistinguishable under a mantle of snow.

In one swift motion Monte was down and striding forward. In one swift matching motion Chet had swung in saddle and scooped up the reins of Monte's horse. He watched as Monte bent low, following the taut rein of the other horse down, fumbling to untie it from around a man's wrist. He watched as Monte brushed snow aside and heaved, rolling the object over so that the whiteness of a face under an old cap looked up into the swirling snow.

"José?" said Chet.

"Who else," said Monte, dropping to his knees, bending lower.

"Alive?" said Chet.

"Yeah," said Monte. "And drunk. Smells like a god-damned saloon."

"Not too drunk not to hang on to the horse," said Chet.

"Maybe the cold caught him too. That ain't much of a coat he's got."

"Yeah," said Monte. "He's sure out cold now. Be stiffer'n a poker in another hour like this." Moving swiftly, Monte stepped to the roan and with fumbling gloved fingers began to unfasten the cinch. "What d'you figure he's been doing out here?"

"Been into town," said Chet. "Stayed too long. Too many *primos* and too much *vino*. Likely he was getting some things for the kids. Tomorrow's Christmas or have you forgot?"

"I been trying to forget," said Monte, pulling the saddle blanket from under his saddle, fastening the cinch again. "Ain't this a hell of a way to be spending Christmas Eve." He stepped back by the pinto and spread the blanket on the snow-covered ground and rolled the limp body of José Gonzales onto it. He wrapped the blanket around, tight. "That'll help some around the middle anyways," he said and, stooping, picked up the wrapped body and laid it, belly down, over the saddle on the pinto. A half-full burlap bag hanging from the saddle horn was in the way. He unlooped this and handed it to Chet. With his rope from the roan he lashed the body down reasonably fast. He took the pinto's reins and led it around and swung up on the roan. "Give me those leathers," he said. "And let's move. I'm almighty hungry."

* * *

The central room of the old adobe ranch house that had been many things in its time was warm and cheerful in the light of two kerosene lamps and a big fire in the huge stone fireplace. Cal Brennan's old desk was pushed into a back corner by the well-filled gun rack. Three straw mattresses and a pile of blankets from the bunkhouse were ranged beside it on the floor along the wall. A fair-sized iron kettle and a wide flat pan and a big coffee pot sat on the raised hearth, keeping their contents hot in the flickering glow from the fire. One whole front corner of the room was filled with fragrant piñon firewood.

Monte Walsh sat in the mouse-chewed remnants of arm-chair at safe range from the fire on one side of the fireplace, working on his seventh biscuit, his third cup of coffee, his second bowl of the Sunfish specialty, stewed beef swimming in a sauce of mashed beans. Sunfish Perkins himself sat in the old rocker on the other side of the fireplace, watching with considerable interest the activity near the closed front door. There, well away from the fire, the somewhat stiffened meager body of José Gonzales, stripped naked, lay on the floor. His worn clothing, patched long underwear and ragged jeans and shirt and thin coat and cap and old boots, were draped over and about a stout ladder-back chair before the fire. His half-full burlap bag sagged against the front wall by the door. Beside him on the floor knelt Chet Rollins, rubbing Gonzales's bare arms and legs with melting snow from a nearby pail.

"Gosh," said Sunfish. "There ain't much of him, is there?"

"Not exactly in your overweight class," said Monte. "But there's enough of him to have more'n any of us's got. A wife and two kids."

"And a sister," said Sunfish. "Dobe'd never let you forget that."

Over by the door José moaned softly and kicked feebly with one foot. "Go ahead, kick," said Chet. "I know it hurts like hell thawing out."

"And he eats prodigious," said Monte. "Looks like we got another boarder till this thing lets up."

"I ain't hauling in no other mattress," said Sunfish. "He can have yours. We'll just take you up on that talk about Cal's bed. You'll freeze your gizzard in that little room with no fire but you'll freeze fancy."

Over by the door José's head raised a bit and thumped back on the floor and he began to thrash about in aimless feeble motion. "Well, well," said Chet. "So you're wiggling all of them now." He picked up a piece of toweling and began rubbing with this.

"Shucks, Chet," said Monte, rising and ambling over. "You got to eat too. I'll wrassle with him some."

Sunfish heaved to his feet and began to serve up stew and biscuits and coffee. "What's he got in that bag?" he said.

"A litte food," said Chet, settling into the armchair to start on his first bowl of the Sunfish special. "A few things for the kids."

"It ain't much," said Monte, suddenly, sharply, looking up from his rubbing. The other two stared at him. "Aw, shucks," he said, returning to work. "Tomorrow's Christmas, ain't it?"

Silence in the big old room.

"It's sure doing things outside," said Sunfish, squatting on the raised hearth out of range of direct heat from the fire. "Must of been four inches already when you came in. Maybe it'll be like that one two years ago."

"Colder," said Chet. "That ought to mean less snow."

Over by the door José opened eyes and stared unaware at the ceiling. He turned away on his side, doubling up, muttering bitterly in Spanish.

"No cussing," said Monte. "That ain't polite. Reckon you're about ready to try navigating some." He slipped an arm under the thin shoulders and rose to his feet, bringing José up with him. José wobbled on unsteady bare feet and reached out instinctively to brace himself against the front wall.

"Exercise," said Monte, looking down at him from head-taller height. "That's what you need. Walking'll do it." He laid an arm along one thin shoulder and across the back and under the opposite armpit and began propelling him across the floor, back and forth.

"Easy," said Chet around a mouthful of stew. "Slow down. He ain't made of cast iron like you."

"Shucks," said Monte. "He's doing fine. Ain't you, José?"

Moving his feet mechanically, unaware of the motion, José turned his head to look up vacantly at Monte.

"Aw, come on," said Monte, cheerful. "You're doing fine. Stepping out like a trooper." He propelled José over by the ladder-back chair and released the arm holding him, ready to grab again.

José stood steady enough, staring down at the clothes on the chair as if unaware of what they were.

"Quit it now," said Monte, stern. "Don't you go being stupid on me. It's plumb indecent the way you're parading around here. Put those things on."

Mechanically, moving out of old habit, José began dressing.

"Well, lookathere," said Sunfish. "Monte, you get too old to straddle a hoss, you can hire out as a nursemaid."

José had on the patched underwear, the ragged pants and shirt. He stooped to pick up one of the boots and sat down on the chair as if to put it on and simply sat there, holding the boot, staring into the fire.

"Still being stupid, eh?" said Monte. "I ought to bat you one. Want to roast yourself?" He took hold of the chair and pulled it and José in it back to a safe distance and José simply sat there, holding the boot, staring into the fire.

"All I got to say," said Sunfish, "is he's going to be mighty exciting company if he stays that way."

"He'll snap out of it," said Chet. "Shock, I guess. He's been through a little something."

"Wish we had a guitar around," said Monte, dropping into the old rocker. "He sure can tickle one of those things."

Silence in the big old room.

"Dog—gone," said Monte, aggrieved. "I just realized. Chet, you've got my chair."

"And keeping it," said Chet.

On the ladder-back chair José stirred and the boot fell to the floor. His head rose higher *"Gracias,"* he said. *"Muchas gracias."* The other three turned heads to look at him and he was José Gonzales again, the quiet little man whose ancestors had come into the big land with the early conquistadores and who clung now in this Yankee invasion time to his one remaining piece of small sparse valley on the western edge of the Slash Y range, the nearest neighbor and an honest neighbor and that seven miles away, and there scratched out a living somehow for himself and family with a few chickens and a small garden and a few goats and a rare willingness to haul firewood the long way into town on his one old burro. "I theenk there was snow," he said. "I theenk I fall from the horse." He looked around at the three and smiled a small apologetic smile and shrugged his thin shoulders. "I be dead, no?"

"Not no," said Monte. "Yes. Oh my yes, yes. Deader'n a last year's tumbleweed. Sunfish, I reckon he's ready to eat. That is, if Chet left him anything."

Silence in the big old room, warm and cheerful, as three men watched a fourth finish the last of the stew, the last biscuit, and start on his third cup of coffee.

"Wonder when the others'll get back," said Sunfish.

"Three–four days, more'n likely," said Chet. "They wasn't figuring on leaving till day after tomorrow anyways.

And you know how the snow piles into those hills up that way."

Moving quietly on the ladder-back chair, José leaned down to set his cup on the floor and pick up one of the boots. *"Muchas gracias,"* he said. "I theenk I go now."

"Whoa there, José," said Monte. "You ain't going no-wheres. It's colder'n an icehouse outside. Snowing to beat hell."

José stopped moving, bent over some, boot in hand, and looked at Monte.

"Goddamn it!" said Monte, sharp. "We ain't a-going to cart you in a second time."

José let the boot drop and sat very still, looking into the fire.

"Aw, hell," said Monte. "You're beat up and that horse of yours ain't got much. Tell you what. When this thing lets up, I'll ride over with you."

Silence in the big old room. Sunfish rose and went to the corner of the room and picked up several pieces of piñon and returned, put them on the fire. He sat again on the hearth, shifting weight uneasily.

"Los niños," said José. "I theenk I go." He picked up one boot and began to pull it on.

"Two women," said Chet softly. "And a couple of kids. José, have they got food and firewood?"

"Un poco," said José. He picked up the other boot.

"The hell with him," said Monte, rising and striding to the one front window to look out into the swirling grayness.

"Can't let him go like that," said Sunfish. "Hey, Chet, ain't Cal's bearskin somewhere around?"

"Must be," said Chet, pushing up from the armchair and heading for the closed door to the left side room. "And he sure could use some socks."

"Give the goddamn fool one of our horses," said Monte savagely without turning from the window. "But I ain't hav-ing a thing to do with it."

Five minutes later José stood in the center of the room, a shapeless small bulk in a long old bearskin coat, minus the fur in patches, that came down to his ankles, an old pair of Cal Brennan's gloves on his hands, cap on head with the piece of toweling down over it and his ears and tied under his chin.

"Ain't he something," said Sunfish. "Looks like a mangy he-bear with the mumps."

"I nevair forget," said José. He started toward his burlap bag by the door and Monte Walsh, leaving the window in long strides, was in the way.

"You goddamned little gamecock," said Monte, bitter. "You really set on it?"

"*Sí*," said José simply. "*Los niños*." He shrugged shoulders inside the old coat. "Ees Chreestmas." He started around Monte. He was stopped by a lean hard-muscled arm that clamped over his shoulders and held him firm, immovable.

Monte drew a deep breath and looked across the room at Chet Rollins.

"All right, Monte," said Chet. He sighed. "Looks like it's us again."

"And me," said Sunfish Perkins. "Maybe you two can take care of José here. But somebody's got to take care of you."

* * *

In the dim driven darkness of storm over the big land, out through the gate from the partial protection of the high-railed small corral, into the open of swirling snow and wrenching wind, four men, bundled thick against the cold, led four saddled horses.

"Shucks," said Monte Walsh, hefting a half-full burlap bag hanging from his gloved right hand. "This thing's mighty puny. Rest of you wait a minute." He strode off, carrying the bag with him, pushing through the knee-deep snow on the ground, to the door of the bunkhouse, opened it. Inside, he flipped off a glove, fumbled for a match, lit the lantern on the old kitchen table in the middle of the long room.

"What d'you think you're doing?" said Chet Rollins from the doorway.

"I got two pair of socks I ain't ever wore," said Monte, heading for his bunk and squatting to reach under. "And a deck of cards that's almost new."

"Whatever for?" said Chet.

"For this goddamn bag," said Monte. He turned, crouching, to look at Chet. "Ees Chreestmas," he said and turned back.

"Damned if it ain't," said Chet, watching Monte move on and pull a box of checker men from under Dally Johnson's bunk and a mouth organ from under Powder Kent's pillow. "I got a pair of spurs I ain't used yet," he said, heading for his own bunk. "And some tobacco I been hiding from you."

Two minutes of swift movement later the bag was two-thirds full. "What they really need is food," said Chet. He picked up the lantern and led out and over to the cookhouse. Inside, he set the lantern on the big old stove, picked another and empty burlap bag off a chopping block in a corner, and with Monte helping began to stuff it with cans from the wide cupboard nearly filling one end of the room. He stopped. He was looking at two humped objects under limp well-washed flour sacks on the wide shelf by the stove.

"Now wait a minute," said Monte. "Don't go getting foolish complete."

"Ees Chreestmas," said Chet, stepping over and taking the larger of the two objects out of its pan and wrapping its flour sack around under it.

"Aw, hell," said Monte. "You going to be so damned smart, do it right." He moved over and picked up the other object.

*   *   *

Far out in the directionless storm-clogged darkness of night, four men on four tough little cow ponies, sleet-crusted beyond recognition, slugged through two feet and more of snow into the teeth of the wind up the side slope of a long ridge. Monte Walsh in the lead on a deep-chested leggy dun peered from under the brim of his pulled-down hat, wiping a gloved hand often across his face, picking the way. Behind him Chet Rollins on a thick-necked black rode close, very close, beside José Gonzales shrunken down almost out of sight inside the old bearskin coat on a short sturdy roan. And behind them came Sunfish Perkins, big solid shape firm in saddle on a rough rangy bay.

The snow underfoot thinned as they climbed and they came out on the flattened bare-swept crest and the wind here wrenched and beat at them and they dropped down the other side, slow, the horses fighting for footing on the slope as the snow underfoot thickened again, and the wind was less brutal here, rushing past overhead, and Monte stopped and the others pulled up bunched with him to breathe the horses.

"How's he making it?" said Monte.

"He's doing it on nerve alone," said Chet. "But he's doing it."

"He's a goddamned fool," said Monte. "But he's got that all right."

They pushed on, angling down the slope, and José sank slowly forward in the saddle and the reins fell from his hands and he took hold of the saddle horn with them both and clung to it, leaning forward over it, head down, and Chet leaned far over and grabbed the trailing reins and straightened, leading the roan in close beside him, and Sunfish Perkins moved up, close in on the other side, and they pushed steadily on, the three behind almost abreast, following Monte's lead.

Time passed and they might have been moving into anywhere in the whole of the vast storm-ridden land or perhaps not have moved at all in the blank featureless directionless dark of the storm and still Monte led steadily and the other three followed.

The swirling snow in the air slackened some and vision lengthened and clumped junipers, snow-sided, could be seen and out of banked snow ahead rose the top rails of a rickety corral with an open-end shed at one side and a burro and a thin horse dim shapes in it and beyond that another shed with a pen attached and a small chicken house and beyond again a low three-room adobe house.

They stopped by the corral and three of them dismounted and looped reins around a rail and Chet pulled José out of the saddle and set him on his feet, unsteady and exhausted past speech, and took one arm and Sunfish took the other and they moved toward the house and Monte unlooped two burlap bags from saddle horns and cradled one in each arm and followed.

"Hello in there!" shouted Chet. He began stomping and shaking to get rid of crusted snow and Sunfish and Monte took the example. They waited. "Hello in there!" shouted Chet again and the door opened and in the doorway stood a woman with a blanket wrapped around her and up over her head, eyes peering out bright and frightened at them. Behind her they could see in the faint light from a small fire another woman, standing by the fireplace wrapped in a heavy shawl, an old single-shot rifle in her hands.

The first woman backed away, one hand at her mouth, as they pushed forward. *"Madre de Dios!"* she said. "José!"

"He's all right, ma'am," said Chet quickly. "Just wore out *mucho* from trying to get home. We put him in bed with plenty of cover he'll do fine. Some rest is all he needs. That your bedroom over there?" With the woman leading he and Sunfish took José through the inner door to the right.

The other woman had set the rifle somewhere. She had looked at each of them in turn and now looked past Monte out the open front door. "Dobe?" she said.

"Shucks, no, ma'am," said Monte, reaching back with one foot to close the door behind him. "But if he'd known about this storm, he'd of sure been here. Now where'll I put these things?"

She pointed to the left inner doorway.

Bags cradled in his arms, Monte strode over to the doorway, into it, stopped. Dimly he could make out a mattress covering most of the floor of the small room, snuggled close to a woodstove in which the remains of a fire still glowed. On the mattress from under the top edge of a ragged heavy quilt two small heads, stocking-capped, peered up at him. *"San Nicolás,"* said one in an awed whisper and both of them disappeared, ducked down under the quilt.

Monte looked down at the old quilt and the tiny quiverings that marked two small shapes beneath it. Carefully he stepped over a corner of the mattress and set the two bags on the floor against a wall. Carefully he stepped back, still looking down. Slowly he began to back out through the doorway and whirled, startled. The other woman had been close behind him.

In the faint light from the fireplace he saw her face, tired and sagging some in the relief of long waiting over, smiling gently at him. *"San Nicolás,"* she said softly.

"Aw, shucks, ma'am," said Monte, embarrassed. "Kids say the silliest things." He fidgeted. "I got to go unsaddle that horse José rode," he said quickly. "We'll just leave him here 'cause likely you'll be needing him. José can swap him back for that pinto first good chance he gets." Monte fled to the door and out.

The snow had stopped now and the silent valley stretched away gray-white and cold to the horizon all around and high overhead in the moving cloud masses wind sighed, long and seeming mournful. Monte strode to the corral, sending snow ahead of his boots in spurts, and led the roan around to the rickety gate and in and to the shelter of the open-end shed and the low nickering welcomes of the old burro and the thin horse. He removed the saddle and leaned over a waist-high railing that shut off one corner of the shed and set it beside a packsaddle on a small sawbuck there. He looked around in the near darkness. "Where in hell's the hay?" he said. "Ain't he got any?"

Something tickled his nose and he looked up. A few wisps showed sticking through the cracks between the poles of the roof. He strode outside and stood on tiptoe to reach up and pull from the conical pile covering the roof poles a plentiful supply and a cascade of snow. He scooped up a double armful and took it in. He stood, quiet and still, watching the horses and the burro start on the hay, feeling the edge of weariness seep along his muscles in the absence of motion. "My oh my," he murmured. "Kids sure are crazy sometimes."

From back by the house came new sounds. He strode to the corral gate and out and moved toward them. In the lee of the end wall where the snow was thin Sunfish Perkins had scraped a fairly bare spot and pulled there a batch of dead piñon trunks from a pile nearby and was working on them steadily and competently with an old rusty ax. "They ain't got much in there," he said. "Grab yourself a load." Monte bent down, picking up stove lengths, and moved toward the house and met Chet coming out for more of the same.

Ten double-trips later they stood in the central room surveying a shoulder-high stack ranked along the wall between the fireplace and the near corner. "That ought to hold 'em for a spell," said Sunfish, coming in behind and leaning the ax against the stack.

Shuffling sounds came from the room to the right. José Gonzales, thin and meager and indomitable in patched long underwear and a pair of Cal Brennan's wool socks, struggled into the doorway with two women trying to hold him back. He pulled free and braced one hand against the doorjamb and stood straight and his head rose, erect and somehow dignified. "Señores," he said. "Thees ees your house."

"That's mighty kindly of you, José," said Chet quickly. "Some time maybe. But we got a ranch to think of. We got a break in this storm too."

"Get back in that bed," said Monte. "Ain't you been fool enough for one night?" He turned toward the outer door. "Come on, let's scat."

Out by the corral three men swung up on three tough little cow ponies and headed for the horizon of ridge. And back at the house a woman with a blanket wrapped around her and up over her head stood in the partially open doorway and watched them go. *"Vayan con Dios,"* she said softly.

*   *   *

Far out beyond the ridge where the gray-white land rolled seeming endless and distance died away into distance under the massed clouds of midnight, wind whistled in long fierce sweeps, blowing the brittle snow into long drifts belly deep on the three horses slugging patiently through them, needing no guidance, driving straight for the home corral. The bay led and the black followed and the leggy dun moved in sturdy stride behind. No more snow fell but the cold had deepened and was steadily deepening.

Monte Walsh caught himself toppling slowly forward in saddle. He straightened and shook himself vigorously. "Watch it," he muttered. "That's bad." He tried to wriggle his toes inside his worn boots. There seemed to be no feeling in them.

He looked ahead and saw Chet Rollins swaying some, catching balance in jerky movement. He slapped spurs to the dun and it plowed forward through the snow and he came alongside Chet. "Wake up!" he shouted. "Get down and walk!" He looked ahead. The big body of Sunfish Perkins, hunched down, was rocking slowly forward, jerking back, rocking forward again.

"You too," muttered Monte. He slapped spurs again and the dun plowed forward again and he was alongside Sunfish. "Snap out of it!" he shouted.

Sunfish's head turned slowly to look at him. "What's eating you?" said Sunfish drowsily.

"Goddamn it!" said Monte, reining in the dun with one stiffened hand, forcing his reluctant body to swoop down so he could take the reins of the bay close by the bit and yank the horse to a stop. He straightened in saddle. "Tired and cold," he said. "Hell of a combination. We'll freeze solid sitting these saddles. Get down and walk."

"Yeah," said Sunfish, shaking himself. "Reckon you're right." Moving stiffly, he climbed down and started to shuffle forward, leading the bay.

Monte turned back. The black had stopped behind them. Chet sagged in the saddle, blinking at him. "What you stopping for?" he said drowsily.

Christ a'mighty!" said Monte. He dismounted and in one furious heave yanked Chet out of the saddle and into the snow. "Give out on me now," he said, grim, "and I'll bust you one you'll remember." He yanked Chet to his feet and Chet stood swaying, blinking drowsily at him.

"Ain't you got ears?" said Monte. "I said get walking!" He took the reins of the black and put them in one of Chet's hands and closed the hand over them. He turned Chet forward and gave him a push that sent him stumbling ten feet through the snow, the black jerking on the reins and stepping out to follow.

"Keep moving," said Monte. He took the reins of the dun and moved up by Chet and reached out to push him again. He moved up and pushed once more.

"Quit that," said Chet, standing straighter and moving under his own power. "Keep it up and I'll try kicking your teeth in."

"That's the talk," said Monte. "But just keep moving."

Silent in the great white cold of distance, three men leading three horses in single file pushed steadily forward, moving stiffly, intent on the effort of driving one foot ahead of the other through the resistant snow.

Monte Walsh felt the blood moving in his legs, feeling returning to his feet, energy building again in hard muscles of his body. He looked ahead and saw that the same was happening to the others. He saw the big barrel body of Sunfish Perkins smashing steadily through the long edged drifts, breaking trail. "My oh my," he murmured. "I'd never tell him but that sure ain't lard he's packing on that carcass of his."

* * *

Cold had crept into the main room of the old adobe ranch house. The fire in the fireplace dwindled to ashes and a few faint embers. Sunfish Perkins, still bundled, knelt in front of it, whittling shavings over the embers from a piece of piñon with clumsy stiffened fingers on the knife. Monte Walsh was lighting one of the lamps. Chet Rollins, finishing shedding his jacket and hat and the bandanna that had been tied over head and ears under it, was starting to unfold blankets and lay them on the mattresses.

Chet stopped, straightened. Slowly he turned and picked up his jacket and started to put it on.

"Hey," said Monte. "You locoed?"

"We ain't fed the horses," said Chet.

"Think I'd forget that?" said Monte. "Why'd you think I ain't stripped down? Just thawing out a little first. You get busy with those beds."

Monte pulled up his jacket collar, pulled down his hat, slipped on his gloves, went out the door. Down by the first corral he looked through rails at the dark shapes crowding close, expectant, and began counting. "Six and Sonny took one and left one," he murmured, "which keeps it the same and Sunfish brought in seven and José swapped even." He nodded and went to the barn and pushed open one of the protesting doors. "That thing ain't a-going to be fixed soon," he said and went on in, reaching in the dark to pull down a bale of hay. He carried it out by the rails, slipped off the twin cords, and heaved it over, a half at a time.

He leaned on rails, looking through at the horses jostling one another to get at the hay. Suddenly he pushed out and returned to the barn and with experienced hands took two battered pails from nails on a beam and lifted the lid of a big tin-lined wooden bin and dipped the pails in. One weighing heavy in each hand he went out to the corral and in through the gate and to a trough along one side and emptied the pails into it, scattering the contents along the full length. "Come and get it," he said. "You're too damned stupid to know but it's a Christmas present." He watched the horses catch the meaning, the rattle of the pails, and drift over, crowding each other. He saw the pinto, coming late and wary, ease in between two others. He saw the smallish neat sorrel approach cautiously and slide in too. "When I wake up," he said, "if I ever do, maybe there'll be some more." He left the corral, walking slowly, aware of the weariness dragging his legs, and moved up to the house.

Inside, Sunfish Perkins sat on the hearth out of range of a new healthy fire, slumped back against the side stones of the fireplace, head dropped sideways, snoring in steady rhythm. Chet Rollins sat in the remnants of armchair, head nodding but still awake.

"I thought maybe you'd bring that bottle," said Chet.

"Shucks," said Monte. "I'm too damn tired even to drink. Likely it's froze solid anyways. Come on, let's tuck him away. Take the head. There ain't much in that part of him."

Together they lifted Sunfish and carried him to one of the mattresses and laid him down and spread a blanket over him. "If he dies in his sleep," said Monte, "at least he'll have his boots on."

Silence in the big old room except for slight rustlings as two men pulled off each other's boots and one blew out the lamp and both lay down on mattresses and reached to draw blankets up over them.

Silence in the big old room except for the outside sound of wind hunting along the eaves and finding no entrance.

Monte lay flat, looking up at the old beamed ceiling. "Know what we'll be doing when we get up?" he said. "We'll be eating beef and beans and riding out to thaw windmills and if that crust that's starting already on the snow out there gets bad we'll be hauling feed to a lot of hungry cows."

"Yeah," said Chet drowsily. "That's about it."

Monte raised on one elbow to look over at Chet stretched out flat. "You think I don't know," he said, "you fixed it some way for that brown bean just 'cause I already had one? Well, it's kind of got you a bellyful."

"It ain't so bad," said Chet drowsily. "Somehow wherever you are things are always happening."

"Shucks," said Monte. "That just goes to show. That's what I keep telling you. Luck and me, we—" He stopped. Chet was asleep.

Monte lay back down and stared up at the shadows from the firelight flickering between beams. A small wry smile flicked on his lips. *"San Nicolás,"* he murmured. "That's me. To a couple silly kids and some horses." He stretched long and lazy under his blanket and in the act of stretching was asleep.

*   *   *

Christmas day dawned cold and clear over the frozen white wonder of the big land. The first light of morning sun touched the capped peaks of the mountains to the west and moved down them, pink flushed, and moved over the badlands at their base and a small valley where a three-room house sent smoke drifting up from chimney and stovepipe and moved on over the long ridge that screened this and other valleys and on across the wide white miles where the blurred tracks of three men and three horses showed in the snow and moved on to glow softly on the drifted flat roof of an old ranch house where three men slept the deep dreamless sleep of tired muscles and the simple uncomplicated assurance that they had done and would do whatever needed to be done.

*   *   *

"So you think it's funny I wouldn't sell that man a drink just because he wanted to pay in pennies? Nothing funny about it. I'm fed up to my eyeteeth with him and his pennies. I've got a whole bag of 'em already and I'm not taking any more. Let him carry the wad to some town that's got a bank. He had no call to take after Rollins—that's Chet Rollins— like he did anyway. Chet didn't mean to bust up his wagon. It was just that Chet's hoss spooked when that snake come crawling out a drainpipe unexpected and when it come down, that's the hoss, it was spang on top the wagon and the blamed wagon's so rickety it falls apart. All the same this Martin claims . . . Oh, Martin? He's the man with the pennies. He claims the wagon's worth at least a hundred dollars. Maybe it was, new. But it's old as he is by then. Demands damages. A hundred dollars. Chet offers him fourteen which is all he and Monte—that's Monte Walsh—has on them at the time but Martin says no, a hundred, and after they bat it

around a bit with Martin getting nasty Chet tosses him on top what's left of the wagon which shuts him up for the time being. Next thing they know a week or so later Martin's been to the county seat and got a judgment. Against Chet. For a hundred dollars. Chet's been sent some kind of notice to appear but hasn't paid any attention. He knows the blamed wagon wasn't worth anything like that. Mac—that's our sheriff—doesn't like the job but he has to do it and he takes the papers out to the ranch and lucky it's him and not Martin or there'd have been fur flying. Mac cools 'em down some by pointing out that lynching Martin or putting him through a meat grinder won't wipe out the judgment and it'll still have to be paid. Of course, Chet can appeal it but that'll be a real nuisance and likely cost more'n the hundred by the time he's through even if he wins. So they pay. He and Monte. But do you know how they pay? They draw a hundred ahead from old Brennan—that's their boss—and they take a pack hoss and two full day's riding to every town within reach that's got a bank and they make up the tally and when they come in to pay they've got a flour sack full of pennies. Ten thousand of them. They find Martin and they pull their guns and they say: There's your money and now you're going to get busy while we watch and you're going to count each and every goddamned penny in there and you're going to write us out a receipt for each and every one hundred of them you count."

Trail Herd
1885

THE TRAIL HERD was bedded on a wide flat finger of plain stretching between long low hills. To the east, out of the hills, the plain spread vast and open into limitless distance. To the west, between the hills, it dropped imperceptibly across the miles to the lower level of an ancient long-dry lake bed.

Large and luminous in the clean depth of sky an incredible number of stars looked down on the wide land and on the dark speckling blotch of the bedded herd and on Monte Walsh riding slowly around the rim serene in saddle atop a deep-chested leggy dun.

"Keep a-moving," murmured Monte. "Want me to fall asleep astraddle your knobby backbone?"

The dun swiveled an ear back toward him and ambled on. It felt him slumping lower into the saddle and slowed to a stop, head drooping. Monte pulled himself awake. "Keep agitating those legs," he said, "or I'll give you a leathering. Personal." The dun sighed and raised its head and ambled on.

Monte stretched erect in saddle and looked around. Off to the left he could see the compact blotch of the cavvy in its rope corral and the dirty gray blob of the chuck wagon canvas and the small individual blobs on the ground that were others of the trail crew sweetly sleeping. Faintly he could make out the glimmer of the remains of the cook fire.

Off to the right, across the big speckling blotch of the herd, he could see the slow-moving small blur that was Chet Rollins atop a chunky gray. A soft breeze stirred and Chet's voice drifted to him, a melancholy tuneless monotone.

"Now, all you young maidens, where'er you reside,
Beware of the cowboy who swings the rawhide.

195

He'll court you and pet you and leave you and go
In the spring up the trail on his bucking bronco . . ."

"I've heard frawgs could croak better," murmured Monte. His attention was caught by movement nearby in the herd. The old barren cow, point leader of each day's drive, was heaving to her feet. He stopped the dun with a touch on reins and watched. Head high and swinging, slow, the old cow tested the air. Slowly she turned until she was facing back over the herd, back down the long finger of plain between the hills.

"Got the worries, old girl?" said Monte. He turned his head to look in the same direction. Clean and cloudless with its myriad stars the sky arched into distance to meet the far horizon. "Nothing back there but sky and a thousand miles of grass," he said. He tilted his head to look up. "My oh my," he murmured. "Time has been footprinting along." He swung the dun and started back around the rim of the herd.

Toward him out of the dimness of dark, easy and comfortable atop gently jogging gray, came Chet Rollins, round stubby pipe poking out of round stubbly face. The two cow ponies stopped, nose to nose.

"Quite a man," said Monte. "That braying of yours gave old Gertrude the itch."

Chet extracted a match from a pocket of his open jacket, scratched it on blunt fingernail, applied it to the pipe. Monte nudged the dun forward, reached and pushed Chet's jacket further open, plucked a small leather pouch from Chet's shirt pocket. Out of a pocket of his own shirt came a small paper. Defty he hollowed this between fingers and poured a portion of tobacco along the tiny trough. In the one easy moving one hand tucked the pouch back in Chet's shirt pocket and the other rolled the cigarette. He raised this to his lips and licked along the paper edge.

"One of these days," said Chet, "I'll quit buying tobacco."

"No," said Monte, aggrieved. "I ain't ready to quit smoking." Out of one of his own jacket pockets came a match which flared briefly. "Shucks," he said. "Always carry my own papers and matches, don't I?"

The cow ponies drowsed, heads drooping. Monte dragged deep on the cigarette and watched smoke float from his nose in two tiny streams. "Wonder what's keeping the boys," he said. "The dipper up there's been dipping." He drew again on the cigarette, inspected its shortened length, stubbed it out on stirrup leather. "Im a growing boy," he said. "Need my sleep."

"Don't be so damned previous," said Chet, amiable, conversational. "They're coming now."

Monte swung the dun to face the night camp. Two dim blurs had left it and were moving toward them. These came closer and were Dally Johnson astride a squat bay and Powder Kent astride a short-coupled roan.

"Anything doing?" said Powder.

"My oh my, yes," said Monte. "Busy every minute. We had to fight off two jackrabbits and a horned toad."

"Old Gertrude's uneasy," said Chet. "Better keep an eye on her."

In companionable silence Monte and Chet jogged to camp, dismounted, eased cinches and picketed their horses by the others kept ready, saddled, for night duty. Together they pulled blankets from the bed wagon beside the bigger chuck wagon and unrolled these on soft spots earlier picked and claimed. Monte straightened and looked toward the remains of the cook fire. On the tripod over it hung a battered coffee-pot.

"Monte," said Chet, low-toned, casual. "Why not forget the coffee tonight. You'll sleep better."

"Shucks," said Monte, starting away. "Gabriel tooting wouldn't keep me from sleeping."

Chet sighed and collapsed down on his blanket. He raised on one elbow, watching.

Over by the chuck wagon Monte pushed a hand under the canvas and pulled it out holding a tin cup. "Good old Skimpy," he murmured, moving toward the embered fire. "Always leaves me some in the pot." Leaning down, he tipped the battered pot until a dark liquid gurgled into the cup. Squatting back on his heels, he poked a finger into the liquid and yanked it out fast and shook it vigorously. He bent his head and blew into the cup and sloshed the liquid around in it. He tried the finger again. "Just right," he murmured and raised the cup and tilted back his head for a long drink.

"Ow-w-w-w-w!" yelled Monte Walsh, uncoiling upward like a tight spring suddenly released, spluttering, spitting. Frantic in haste he plunged toward the chuck wagon and tripped

over the wagon tongue and went sprawling. Still frantic in
haste he scrabbled to the water pail hanging by the wide
tailgate and grabbed the dipper. Water dribbled down his
shirt as he gulped and spat, gulped and spat.

He stood by the chuck wagon, dipper in hand, and looked
around. Not far away, up on one elbow, Chet Rollins regarded him with solemn interest. Elsewhere about lay five other
figures, under blankets, quiet, apparently lost in sleep. He
reached and let the dipper drop with a clatter into the pail.
He waited. No sound, no movement marred the quiet. "Some
bat-brained baboon—" he said and stopped. There was a
quivering under one pulled-over blanket, a strange small
moaning sound. The blanket flipped back disclosing the lean
whipcord length of Petey Williams, shaking, knees doubling
up.

"Lordy!" gasped Petey. "Oh Lordy Lordy Lordy Lordy
Lordy! Maybe that'll learn you not to come thumpin' in
every night clitterin' an' clatterin' an' wakin' me up."

"Why you—" said Monte, starting forward.

"Easy, Monte," came the voice of trail boss Hat Henderson. "Or we'll all take a hand."

"Not me, Monte boy," came a voice from the chuck
wagon. "Anybody likes my coffee an' says so like you do kin
have all he wants anytime."

Monte looked around, calculating the odds. The slender
shape of fourteen-year-old Juan Rodriguez, brought along to
wrangle the cavvy, did not count. But the wide sloping
shoulders of Hat Henderson, sitting up on his blanket, were
enormous in the dim starlight. The black-mustached face of
Dobe Chavez, sitting up too a few feet away, could have
been wearing a hopeful grin. The big barrel body of Sunfish
Perkins bulged huge under his blanket.

"Shucks," said Monte. "If that damned pepper hadn't
made me feel right puny, I'd scramble the whole bat-brained
bunch of you." Injured dignity emanating from him, he
stalked to his blanket, took off his hat, lay down, set the hat
over his face and pulled the blanket over him.

Silence settled on the camp.

"Holy hell!" said Monte Walsh, lifting the hat off his face
and setting it aside. "How'm I going to get my sleep without
my coffee?"

"Quit it," came a voice. "Or we'll put you to sleep permanent."

Silence settled again. Monte lay still looking at the myriad stars overhead. He raised a bit and spit to one side. He lay still again. A small quivering began to shake his midriff. "My oh my oh my," he murmured. "Bet I looked like a new-branded calf diving for that water." He began counting stars. At seven he was asleep.

* * *

The boot toe against his ribs was hurried, not gentle. Monte Walsh plunged awake in the dark, grabbing. The thick-muscled leg of Hat Henderson pulled away from him.

"Snap it, Monte," said Hat. "Everybody out. There's a storm coming."

Monte pushed to his feet. High overhead the stars shone, large and luminous in clean depth of cloudless sky. The air was still, soft and still.

"Shucks," said Monte to the retreating back of Hat Henderson. "What's the fuss? Regular spooning weather."

"Not for long," said Chet Rollins, gathering up his and Monte's blankets and stepping to toss them in the bed wagon. "Take a look yonder."

Monte turned to look down the long finger of plain between the hills. Dark and ominous, piling in heavy layers, a great bank of clouds blotted the horizon. As he looked, lightning played high over them and laced through them and the low mutter of thunder rolled in dim blankness of distance.

"What d'you know," murmured Monte. "Old Gertrude sure has a nose." In the one swoop of moving he picked up his hat, jammed it on his head, and was running toward the leggy dun.

He heaved on the cinch, tightening, and behind him heard Chet Rollins gently cursing at the same chore. Other voices floated on the still air, cheerfully complaining, wryly joshing. Over them rose the voice of Hat Henderson, responsibility spurring him, he who was a cold bolt of concentrated action in the midst of an emergency, now as always worrying and wailing in the anticipation of it. "Jeeeesus, boys! We gotta hold 'em! Those fool cows get a-running out into that open it'll take a week to gather 'em again! Those we can find!"

The cinch slipped in Monte's hands. He grabbed a fresh hold and heaved. The dun, disliking the prospect, sidled away and blew out its sides, eating air. "Go ahead, be smart," said Monte, making it grunt with a knee hard in its distended ribs. "I'll twist a couple of your ears off. Personal."

"Frettin' again, Monte," said a voice above him close by the dun's rump. Petey Williams grinned down from the back of a hammerheaded sorrel. "Mebbe you oughta stay an' help Skimpy lash down the wagons. Feelin' puny the way you do." The sorrel responded to spurs and took off fast.

"I'll puny him," muttered Monte. "Maybe biscuits. Petey's a hawg on biscuits." He stepped into stirrup and swung up to join Chet out to the herd.

*   *   *

The night air hung motionless, still, too still, clinging and oppressive. Silent now, waiting, wearing slickers now untied from behind saddles, the trail crew of the Slash Y, eight men on eight homely tough little cow ponies, rode circle around fifteen hundred four- and five-year-old longhorn steers and an old barren cow. And out of the southwest, the long back trail they had traveled hundreds of miles from the wide vegas of New Mexico territory, the great bank of clouds, huge, indifferent, funneled forward between the hills.

Whisperings of wind ran through the bunch grass. The cattle were up, shifting restlessly with rattlings of horns as they pushed against each other. Arching high above, the topmost layers of clouds, driven from behind, rolled forward, blotting out the stars. The first drops of rain, large and irregular, fell with tiny splattings on the dry ground. Suddenly, as if scenting the herd, wind leaped in rushing gusts and a wall of rain, swirling, torrential, swept over.

The wind beat in rushing gusts and the rain poured in heavy sheets and the cattle shifted and swayed in frightened mass, trying to work downwind before the storm, individuals and small bunches making frantic dashes to break away. Around them, battered, drenched, sighting by sound and instinct and intermittent flashes of lightning, swinging superb with every twist and wrench of saddles, rode the trail crew of the Slash Y, yielding ground downwind but holding the circle, tough little cow ponies as alert, as dedicated, as desperate as the men, squat hard-muscled rumps quivering as they leaped, dashed, pounded to head the runaways, push them, shoulder them, bully them back into the herd.

Abruptly the cloudburst passed. The rain dropped to a steady downpour and this slowly thinned and the air was alive, crackling with electricity. Fireballs hung on tossing horns and little lightnings streaked along the ground. The rain died away and the mutter of thunder dwindled.

"Looks like we make it!" The voice of Hat Henderson lifted out of the dark. "Close up an' quiet 'em down!"

From elsewhere out of the dark rose the voice of Chet Rollins in hoarse tuneless somehow soothing monotone.

"I love not Colorado where the faro table grows,
 And down the desperado the rippling bourbon flows.
  Oh-h-h-h-h,
 I love not Colorado where the card sharp fleeces fools,
 And a girlie-girl won't give a man . . ."

Lightning in one great flare of flame ripped the dark and a steer reared bellowing, outlined in fire, and thunder broke like a cannon shot. Out of the void of darkness following the flash came the heavy rising roar of the herd in motion, a dark tide of panic-stricken animals, pouring downwind in relentless onrush.

Above the muffling roar, the cracking of hoofs, the rattling of horns, climbed the shrill yell of Hat Henderson: "Jeeeeesus! Ride, you mavericks! Ride!" And Hat and seven other men rode.

Out in front Dobe Chavez and Powder Kent, caught in the onrush, engulfed by it, surrounded by frenzied running steers, jostled, hit, battered, their horses fighting to hold their feet, ears flat, heads slugging in desperate effort, plunging forward, kicking in stride, taking advantage of every break to work out toward the side. On the left flank Petey Williams and Monte Walsh and Dally Johnson and Hat Henderson, strung out, racing headlong into the dark, ripping off slickers at full gallop, striving toward the head of the herd. On the right flank Sunfish Perkins and Chet Rollins, dropping back to dash around the rear of the stragglers and drive forward after the others.

"Puny is it?" yelled Monte Walsh, yanking the dun past the tail of Petey Williams's sorrel to join him in smashing in toward the lead steers, flailing at them with his slicker. A horn tip raked across his thigh, ripping through cloth, drawing blood, and he did not know it. The slicker flapped in shreds. Pounding alongside a big steer, he flung the remnants in its face. He pulled his gun and began firing into the ground in front of the foremost steers.

Other guns were out and sounding, flaring in the dark, a barrage angled out across the rushing forefront of the strung-out stampede. The leaders swerved, swinging to the right, the others blindly following. They hit the first slopings toward the hills and slowed some on the climb and, under pressure, swung still more. More, and the herd was running in an arc, a wide u-shaped course. Still more, and the leaders were swinging back into their own tracks, catching up with the stragglers, and the rough flattened circle was closed. The cattle milled around it, gradually slowing in weariness, letting themselves be crowded inward, slowing more to a shuffling walk, slowing at last to a stop, sides heaving, tongues hanging.

* * *

Gray and forlorn under overhanging clouds, dawn crept over the great open plain that was miles closer now and slipped down the wide finger between the hills. In the dim half-light the chuck wagon with trailing bed wagon, lurching behind their four-mule span from where the camp had been, stopped a quarter of a mile away. In a few moments the first flickering of a fire showed, fed on wood carried and kept dry under the canvas. From back down the finger of plain a weaving blotch of dark shapes approached, the cavvy coming up.

In the gray growing light the trail crew of the Slash Y left positions around the herd and gathered together, men with eyes bleared and bloodshot, clothes torn and mud-spattered, horses bloody and sweat-streaked, legs quivering, worn close to exhaustion and still standing to whatever more might be asked of them.

"Those bonehead cows ain't going anywheres," said Hat Henderson. "Not now for a while anyways. I reckon we can go in and get us something hot."

"Hey, look," said Sunfish Perkins. "There's the horses coming. The kid musta held them."

"Of a certainty, señor," said Dobe Chavez, grinning. "He is of my people. A boy in the years. A man with the horses."

"Damn lucky for us," said Hat. "We got us a day ahead. I saw a couple bunches break into the draws over there. Must be strays all through those hills."

Silent again, the trail crew of the Slash Y started toward the chuck wagon, horses wearily plodding.

"Coffee," said Monte Walsh. "Ain't that a lovely smell? If Petey tries messing with—"

"Petey," said Chet Rollins. "I ain't seeing him around."

"Jeeeesus!" said Hat Henderson, rising in stirrups to look about. "Has that fool gone an'—" He stopped speaking and sank down into saddle, shoulders sagging. He spoke again, voice heavy. "All right, boys. Spread out an' look sharp."

Quiet, separated each in his own searching silence, seven men rode back over the wide trampled ground reaching toward the hills beyond. There was daylight now, veiled with stringy gray mists under the overhanging clouds. It was the voice of Powder Kent that called. The others gathered with him on the flat bench a short way up the sloping where a colony of prairie dogs had riddled the sandy soil. They looked down at the sprawled shape, the lean twisted whipcord length of Petey Williams, rain-washed face upturned, strangely white and empty, head awry at grotesque angle. Thirty feet away the sorrel, crumpled on the ground, both forelegs broken, raised its head and whinnied softly at them.

Hat Henderson shifted weight in saddle, turning to see who was closest to the sorrel. His voice was small, tired. "All right, Monte. Shoot the horse."

Monte Walsh stared at the still, twisted shape. He forced his head to turn a bit and stared at the sorrel. The muscles along his jaw ridged and the tendons in his neck stood out taut. "Goddamn it!" he said. "I broke that horse. Taught him his manners."

Fury flared in Hat Henderson, shaking him, shaking his voice. "You soft-brained bitching bastard! I said shoot that horse!"

Monte swung to face the other man, tense in saddle, body muscles tightening toward the blessed relief of motion, action. A shot sounded and, caught by it, he turned and saw the sorrel's head dropping, the whole body going limp, and he turned more and saw Chet Rollins slipping gun back into holster. The muscles along Monte's jaw twitched. A small humorless smile showed on his lips. His head moved in a slight nod, saying what he could not say in words, what he could not even comprehend in words. *Thanks, Chet. That's how it is. You've rode with Petey too. You helped me break that horse. I blow a lot and I strut a-plenty and maybe I can ride a horse or two you can't and take on two to your one in any kind of brawl. But dig down to bedrock you're the better man.*

Slowly, wearily, Hat Henderson dismounted. He moved close by Monte and reached and slapped Monte's leg. He did not look up. "Petey an' me run together a long while," he said. "Kind of like you an' Chet." He strode forward and scooped up the already stiffening body and came back to his horse and heaved it over his saddle. He took the reins and started leading the horse toward the new camp.

Silent, staring at the ground, the others followed. It was Monte Walsh who carried Petey's saddle in front of him over the tired shoulders of the dun. It was Dobe Chavez who turned back and leaned down in weary but still graceful sweep from the back of his tired bay to pick from the ground the muddied felt that had been Petey Williams's hat.

*   *   *

The fire was little more than a smoking smoulder, fighting the heavy moist air. The trail crew of the Slash Y hunkered on heels close by it, scooping food from tin plates. Hat Henderson laid his, emptied, on the ground beside him. "Got to bring in those strays," he said. "That rubs out today. Three days on to the Spring an' that's only a stage stop. I reckon we got to do it right here." He straightened. "Dobe. Sunfish. Get a couple fresh hosses and out to those cows. We'll holler when we're ready." He strode to the bed wagon and pulled out two shovels.

The mists had lifted some and rain fell in a thin drizzle. Chet Rollins and Monte Walsh worked on the deepening grave. Skimpy Eagens, limping on old game leg, rigged a canvas shelter for his fire. Young Juan watched in mournful useless silence. Hat Henderson and Dally Johnson and Powder Kent leaned over the stiffened body of Petey Williams. They wrapped it carefully in a blanket. Around this they rolled a trimmed-down tarpaulin. Around this they stretched two bridle reins and tied them.

"Jeeeeesus!" said Hat, stretching up from the task. "Ain't there anything we can use for a cross?"

The fire burned better under its canvas shelter. Coffee was hot in tin cups. Hat Henderson looked up from his. Out of the drizzle young Juan was approaching, riding bareback on his little bay. He was dragging something on a rope after him, the weathered broken cast-off endgate of an emigrant wagon.

"You're all right, kid," said Hat Henderson. "Dally. Get an iron and stick it in the fire. We'll rig a marker outa that."

The two best boards were fastened together with horseshoe nails to form a crude cross. Dally Johnson knelt on another board, running iron in hand, burning letters into wood. The others watched, silent, intent.

Dally looked up. "Maybe," he said, "maybe this ought to say Peter."

"Petey," said Hat Henderson, quick, sharp. "That's what he was all the time I knew him. That's what he'd a wanted to be."

Dally reached and laid the end of the iron in the fire. "When was he born?" he said.

Silence. "Damned if I know," said Hat. "About my age but I never did know exact. We got to leave that go."

Dally took the iron and bent over the cross. "What's today?" he said.

Silence again. "It's April anyways," said Chet Rollins. "That's close enough."

Dally finished and rose to his feet. They all stared down at the crude cross. Near the top of what would be the upright, the Slash Y brand. Under this, on the wider crosspiece, the simple legend:

PETEY WILLIAMS
died on trail
April, 1885

"All right, Dally," said Hat Henderson. "I reckon we're ready. Kid, slip on out and fetch Dobe and Sunfish."

"Goddamn it!" said Monte Walsh, kicking viciously at a clod from the freshly dug grave. "That's a hell of a measly marker for a man like Petey!"

Small and alone in the big land they stood around the grave, seven riders and an old man and a boy. Using ropes slipped under, they lowered the rolled tarpaulin into the grave. They stood in an uneasy silence.

"Jeeesus!" said Hat Henderson. "Ain't there anybody knows any of the words?" The silence held again. "Maybe just as well," he said. "Petey never was much on churches."

"He was a damn good man with a rope," said Powder Kent. "Maybe that'll count some."

"Petey never cussed much," said Sunfish Perkins. "Only when he was mad and that don't mean nothing."

"He was almighty good company," said Chet Rollins. "Always keeping things lively."

"The long-legged loon was one up on me," said Monte Walsh. "That coffee sure fixed me plenty."

The silence held again. Hat Henderson broke it. "Petey wouldn't want us moping around like a bunch of mangy coyotes," he said. "We got work to do. Skimpy. An' you kid. You can fill this hole. All right, boys. Fresh hosses all around. We got to comb those hills."

* * *

The herd had grazed part of the day and watered at pools collected in old buffalo wallows. It was bedded again close to where the last night's run had ended. In the deepening dusk clouds still hung overhead, blotting out most of the stars emerging in the high clean depth of sky above. The three dark shapes close by the bedded herd were Monte Walsh on a rat-tailed skittish roan and Chet Rollins on a thick-necked black and Hat Henderson on a big rangy bay.

"Hate to stick you two with it," said Hat. "You're bushed as the rest of us. But it's your watch. Looks nasty but maybe it won't do more'n rain a bit. I'll try an' keep an eye open. Anything happens we'll all come a-fanning."

Monte Walsh and Chet Rollins watched him jog away toward camp. "Creeping catfish," said Monte, wriggling inside shirt and jacket. "Feels like I'll never get dry again. Been raining off and on all day."

Chet fumbled in a jacket pocket and found his pipe in shirt pocket and extracted the small pouch. He began to shake tobacco into the pipe.

"A hell of a life," said Monte. "Wearing out your backside in a saddle all day, all night, chousing cows that belong to somebody else. If you ain't cooking in the sun you're feeling like a cold sponge. A hell of a life."

"Yeah," said Chet. "Ain't it." He found a match, scratched it on blunt fingernail, applied it to the pipe.

"Forty and found and break your fool neck," said Monte. He forced the roan to sidle closer to the black and reached and extracted the pouch from Chet's shirt pocket. He fished in his own and extracted a wad of wet gummy small papers. He stared down at these in his hand and in disgust threw them on the ground.

"You'll get to a pipe yet," said Chet, taking the pouch.

"What in hell did we ever come on this junket for anyway?" said Monte. "We could of stayed at the ranch. There's that new bunch of three-year-olds to be broke."

"Hat was shorthanded," said Chet. He found another match, scratched, tried again on the pipe. "Shorter now," he said.

"Petey," said Monte. "You ever think he didn't even know who he was working for? Who we're working for. Not even a man. Just a goddamned syn-di-cate. A bunch of soft-bellied money grubbers back east somewheres."

"Yeah," said Chet. "That's right, ain't it. But Petey wasn't thinking of that. Petey was just doing what he signed on to do." Chet swung the black and started off around the herd.

"A hell of a life," murmured Monte, starting in the opposite direction. "Seems like I ain't slept in a week. Maybe two." The roan shied at a low bush, swinging its rattail and skittering sideways. "Quit that," said Monte, clamping down on the reins. "I ain't in no mind for games. Just to sit here trying to forget I got wet pants on."

* * *

The clouds gathered overhead, moving silently, closing all gaps. Monte Walsh pulled out of a doze in the saddle. Sudden wind rushed in violent gusts down the finger of plain toward the open. He looked around. The cattle were up, beginning to push against each other. Back a bit around the curve of the herd a dark blur was Chet Rollins on the black sweeping to head a batch of runaways. Another batch broke loose. Monte wheeled the roan, spinning on hunched hind legs, and lit out after them. He had them back. He snatched a quick look toward the camp. All he could make out was the flicker of the low fire, licking up under the lash of the wind. It was blotted for an instant as a figure ran past it.

The wind increased in violence and whipped rain with it. The herd shifted and swayed with rattling of horns. Two men on a rat-tailed roan and a thick-necked black dashed back and forth, holding the frightened steers against the hills rising beyond. Over by the camp a sharp crack sounded, and another, and others following. The canvas top of the chuck wagon had ripped loose on one side and flapped up in the gusts like a huge whip snapping.

"Good God a'mighty!" said Monte, hearing the heavy rising roar of the herd in motion. "Here we go again!" A dark shape rushed past him, Chet Rollins bent low on the black, scudding fast for the head of the rushing herd.

Monte Walsh dug spurs in. The roan leaped into full gallop. "Yoweee!" yelled Monte, leaning forward to shout in one of its ears. "You let that fat-faced baboon beat me to the point I'll rip your hide off! Personal!"

Out from the camp in ragged sequence pounded other dark shapes, angling to join them. The trail crew of the Slash Y, seven men on seven tough little cow ponies, raced headlong into the rain-drenched dark.

* * *

"*Yep, that's our Monte. I see you been talkin' to Sugar. That's the one he always tells. Scratch any of us Slash Y an' we'll come up with one about him. About Monte. Me, now, my favorite's the one about when we was up at Cheyenne. Took a bunch of cows up there. Kind of like the old days. We'd delivered an' we was seein' the town. Fed our faces at a fancy hotel for a starter. Good food but only little dabs an' we had to go the limit twice around to fill up. Then Sunfish got to talkin' how he'd never been to a real theayter an' when he's laid away he'd like to have that in his tally book. So Hat herded us down the street an' into this place. Fair enough but I seen better in Kansas City. Show was all about a pretty young gal whose father's rottin' away in prison for somethin' he didn't do. She's out to clear his name. Mix-up of some kind about a gold mine an' a killin' her father's thought to of done. Only one that knows the straight of it's an old prospector that's lost, hidin' away somewheres scared to show. She's got a job cut out for her—find that old boy an' coax 'im to speak up. There's a good-looking young one hangin' around, in an' out, an' why he don't take on the job for her beats me. Reckon he was just on hand for to have someone to marry her at the finish like they usually do. There's another gent around too, mean an' with wax on his mustache that he favors plenty, an' why that gal don't know that kind is no good beats me too. He's after the gold an' to keep her old man behind bars an' to grab her off too. Plain as a wart on a wasp's hind end that likely he's the one really did the killin'. But she's that silly she falls for his greasy palaver an' is always tellin' him her plans.*

"*Mighty attractive, that little gal, when she's rigged out in a buckskin outfit huntin' for that old boy. Has a cute little popgun she carries in a holster too. Finds him up a draw somewhere an' talks to him good. He's a shaky one not goin' to last long an' she makes him see that before he cashes in he ought to get up enough dander to set things straight. But it's gettin' night an' they got to make camp till mornin'. Old boy's asleep by the fire. They got a red light under some sticks up there on the stage that's right pretty. Young gal's some modest an' she sleeps behind a bush. Along comes this Indian crawlin' mighty creepy with a knife in his hand. Yep, that no good one's hired him to knock off the old boy. He's crawlin' along, makin' quite a thing of it with that knife, an'*

*the gal wakes up, sees him, goes all to shiverin', pulls herself
together, takes out that little popgun. Indian has the knife up,
ready to start slicin', an' she pulls the trigger. An' the thing
misfires. Blank in there's a dud. She tries again. Another dud.
Indian's gettin' tired holdin' that knife up an' trying to stay
lookin' fierce an' she tries again. Same thing. An' that's when
our Monte takes a hand. He stands up an' he has his old hog-
leg in his hand an' he levels it at that Indian an' he says,
ma'am, he says, if you'll kindly step a bit out of the way I'll
take care of that painted-up polecat for you.*

"Yep, that's what he did. You didn't know him, you'd
think he was plumb serious too. Gal up there looked around
wild an' let out a squawk an' went flat. Man they had bein'
that Indian took one look an' dove right through some canvas
they had painted to look like rocks. Manager of the place an'
a couple others came runnin' to grab Monte. Some more in
the seats around that didn't like havin' the show shook up
started in to help. We wasn't going to let Monte be manhan-
dled that way for a little thing like that so the rest of us took
a hand too. A right lively little scramble in there for a while.
Kind of like old times on the trail. Turned out to be kind of
expensive when we forked over fines next day. But Monte
come out of it all right. That little old gal herself showed up
an' argued pretty with the judge he had no call to be hard on
a man for being gentleman enough to want to help her out of
a spot of trouble. Yep, Monte had his picture in the paper
standin' alongside her."

Payment in Full
1886

SUNLIGHT AND SILENCE lay soft and limp over the range headquarters of the Consolidated Cattle Company. In the big corral a dozen or more cow ponies drooped in drowsy dejection,
no longer even trying to push for places in the meager patch
of shade from the water tank on its squat tower just beyond
the side rails. The only indication of life near the long barn
was a lone gamecock that stood propped on stiff spurred legs
by one corner and occasionally rocked down to peck morosely at the dusty ground and relapsed into stillness again. Only
a thin wisp of smoke from the tin chimney of the small cookhouse beside the weathered adobe bunkhouse betrayed any
suggestion that there might be something able to move and
moving in some activity inside.

Over by the straggling adobe ranch house a light buckboard rested in full sun close by the shallow veranda. Between the shafts was a bony flea-bitten bay horse, apparently
motionless, but pulling quietly, furtively, at the reins whose
ends were looped around one of the scarred poles supporting
the veranda roof. The rein ends fell with a soft plop to the
ground and a tiny lizard that had been lying in sun on the
veranda floor scuttled down a crack between two boards.
Quietly, furtively, the bony bay began to move, obviously
worried about squeaks from the buckboard behind. It eased
forward a few feet, ten feet, fifteen feet, and was in the
sparse shade of the one scraggly cottonwood by the veranda
and immediately relaxed all over, drooping into a replica of
the cow ponies in the corral. The lizard poked its head up between the boards and crawled out and lay again in the sun.

Inside the house, in the dim interior of the big main room
opening off the veranda, two men occupied two chairs look-

ing at each other. One, near the door, relaxed back in the mouse-chewed remnants of what had once been an over-stuffed leather-covered armchair, was long and lean within old worn range clothes set off by a wide belt with huge silver buckle and absurdly high-curved-heel boots. He was ageless, any age at all past the half century mark, with the deep tan of his lined face and its wide untrimmed mustache and the many wrinkles radiating out from the eyes defying any con-ceivable exact calculation. A bottle half-filled with an amber liquid was on the floor at the left of the armchair within easy reach. A small glass filled with the amber liquid was in his right hand. The other man, further into the room, sat on a straight ladder-back chair behind what had been a rolltop desk but now was a flattop with the marks of the forcible re-moval of the upper structure plain on the showing surface. He was medium in every way, in size, in shape, in apparent age. A tinge of soft plumpness bulged the cloth of his neat pinstriped suit. He wore, beneath the coat and vest, a white shirt surmounted by a celluloid collar from which protruded a small snap bow tie and both, the shirt and the collar, offered signs of recent sweat and dust. His round face with features small and somewhat pinched in proportion to the bone and flesh behind them was a mottled pink from recent unusual ex-posure to wind and sun. On the desk top in front of him lay a derby hat.

The armchair man swirled the amber liquid in his glass. His voice was mild, carrying a bare suggestion of a drawl. "Sure you won't join me?"

The desk man frowned slightly. "You know I don't drink. It interferes with my figuring." He spoke with a slight uncon-scious sharpness of accent, a hint of habitual regard for his own words as valuable commodities that should be shaped with precision. He leaned back in his chair. "I'm not being intentionally rude. It's business, that's all." He sighed and ran a finger around inside the celluloid collar. "An aggravating business too, I must say. For me. The directors send me out here every year thinking they are giving me a kind of vaca-tion. Nonsense. I have a sensitive nose. There's nothing out here but heat and dust and flies and smells and—" He stopped. He seemed to be a bit worried. There was move-ment in the armchair.

Not much movement. The body of the armchair man remained still, relaxed, but his right hand raised to tilt the contents of the little glass into his mouth and his left hand reached to take the bottle from the floor to replenish the glass. "An' rattlesnakes," he said gently. "An' hosses that don't handle easy. An' men that ain't always full civilized."

The desk man tried a small smile. "Well, yes. But I don't mean anything by that. You are used to it. Maybe you even like it. But me, I'm a city man." He pushed the derby to one side of the desk and sat up straighter. "I figure if we get right at this annual accounting I can clean it up this afternoon. Maybe in time to be back in town before the night stage. That way I can get in a few days at Kansas City before I have to be back east." He put both hands on the desk top and leaned forward on them. "Business first. Pleasure later. Now—where are the books?"

There was movement again in the armchair, a repetition of the previous maneuver. The amber liquid slid down the lean man's throat with no noticeable action of his neck muscles and no noticeable effect. "Where they always are," he said. "In the second drawer on the left."

The desk man pulled open the second drawer on the left and took out several limp dog-eared notebooks and laid them on the desk top. "I do wish you would use regular account books," he said. "I'd be happy to supply them."

"No," said the armchair man. "I'd get lost in the things. But I can make trail fair enough in those."

The desk man sighed and took a small pad of paper and a pencil from a side suit pocket and laid these too on the desk. He opened the first notebook and settled to his work. Outside sunlight and silence held undisputed sway over the surface showing of the range headquarters of the Consolidated Cattle Company. In the big main room of the ranch house were silence and relative dimness, broken only by the occasional tiny scritch of pencil on paper and the brief flare of a match lighting a cigar by the desk and occasional soft repetitious movement in the armchair.

* * *

The desk man looked up. "I make it an eighty-two percent calf crop this year," he said. "Isn't that a little low? It was eighty-six last year."

The armchair man swirled amber liquid in the little glass and regarded it with affection. He did not look up. "A rough winter," he said gently. "A mighty mean spring. I'd say eighty-two's a right encouragin' figure." His voice rose a notch and the drawl became a bit more definite. "As a matter of straight fact, if you can find another outfit in the whole territory that's done better'n seventy-five, I'll eat that silly hat lyin' there beggin' somebody to put a bullet through it." He raised the glass and amber liquid slid silently down his throat. His voice dropped back and the drawl faded. "Plain too. No sauce to help it down."

The desk man looked at the derby lying to the left on the desk top and reached to flick dust from it. He sighed and returned to his work.

*   *   *

The desk man held a finger in place on the page in front of him and looked up. "What's this? Eighty dollars for wolf poison! Good Lord! Eighty dollars! I don't recall anything about wolves in your reports."

The armchair man raised his head from contemplation of the little glass. Traces of what could have been a smile leaked out around the fringes of his mustache. "Just between you an' me," he said, "that wasn't wolf poison. The boys talked me into lettin' 'em have some doin's here for some of the other outfits along about Christmas time. That was for liquid reefreshment." He studied the expression on the desk man's face and something resembling a soft chuckle came from him. "They didn't have to talk much," he said.

The pink flush on the desk man's face had become a shade deeper. He sat up straighter on his chair. "A bit thick, I must say. Do you realize that it takes four good steers at the going price to make eighty dollars?"

"Certain I realize it," the armchair man said gently, very gently. "A rough winter. The boys were doggin' it hard. Pullin' plenty more'n four cows through."

The desk man chewed slowly on the eraser end of his pencil. Small frown furrows marked his pink forehead. Gradually the furrows smoothed away. He sighed and returned to his work.

*   *   *

The sun was lower in the west, opposite the open ranch house door, sending a patch of clean golden light into the big room. The armchair man raised his head, listening. Outside in the big corral a horse nickered and the sound of hoofs floated faintly in the stillness from beyond the corral. It came closer and the complaining creak of the corral gate drifted through the space between the buildings. Faintly, seeming to hang outside in the soft air, a voice followed. "Hey, look at the town rig. Bet you Plug-Hat Platt's here."

The desk man heard nothing. He was intent on his work. He closed the last notebook and consulted his paper pad, making a few more notations. He leaned back and looked up. "That's done. Everything seems to be in order. Of course, I found three errors in your addition. But an improvement, I must say. There were five last year." He permitted himself a smile. "And it looks moderately good. Moderately. Not up to last year. No. As you say, it was a hard winter. But I will be able to assure the directors they can expect another fair return on their investment when the fall shipments are made. Barring accidents, that is." He stopped, smile disappearing. He reached into an inside coat pocket and took out a small sheaf of folded papers. "Good Lord, I've been so busy I almost forgot these." He held them up, waggling them in his hand, and permitted himself another smile. "These were shoved into my hand the moment I got off the train to take the stage. Obviously a joke. I know about you people out here. Go to any lengths for a joke. I thought the man acted sheepish. He wouldn't even stay around so I could question him. It was smart of him, though, to get hold of some Santa Fe Railroad paper to use."

Amber liquid slid down the armchair man's throat. "I was wonderin'," he said, "when you'd get around to mentionin' them."

The desk man's hand stopped waggling the papers. The smile left his face. "So you know about them too?"

"Certain I know about 'em," the armchair man said. "They're real enough."

The desk man leaned forward, staring. He leaned back again. The smile returned to his face, this time with effort behind it. "Come now, man. Obviously you're in on the joke too. But it won't work. Not with me." His voice acquired a slightly triumphant tone. "Why, if there was anything to these things, they would have had to be entered in your books here. For the record, I mean. Not that I would ever endorse them for payment. Good Lord, no."

"Shucks," the armchair man said gently. "That Santy Fee man knew better'n to try an' present 'em to me. He saved 'em special for you."

The desk man sat still, very still. Shock showed on his face. Slowly he laid the papers down and unfolded them one by one. His voice came, hushed, almost a whisper. "Good Lord. Claims against the company. More than eighteen hundred dollars. Eight . . . teen . . . hundred . . . dollars. Doctor's bills. Salaries for trainmen laid up with injuries. Repairs to a locomotive." He stared down at the unfolded papers.

"Shucks," said the armchair man. "It wasn't too bad. Some of the boys had a little run-in with a Santy Fee freight train."

The desk man jerked on his chair. His chest swelled under the pin-striped vest and coat. His voice climbed. "A little run-in! Eighteen hundred dollars worth! Good Lord, man, what happened?"

"Shucks," said the armchair man. "I missed the fun. But my foreman was in on it. You wait a minute. I think the boys have been gatherin' outside here." Without moving in the armchair he raised his voice, a sudden surprisingly resonant roar rocking through the room and out the door. "Hey! You! Hat!"

Footsteps resounded on the veranda accompanied by the soft jingle of rusty spurs. The doorway darkened, almost filled by the big bulk, the wide sloping shoulders of Hat Henderson. The dust of the day's work lay thick on him. He stepped in and the smell of sweat and worn leather and horses and cattle and the far spaces of a big land came with him.

The armchair man bobbed his head a bit toward the desk man. "Platt here," he said, "has been combin' through my pen scratches as per usual. I think you met him last year."

"Sure," said Hat. "Sure. I remember him." He favored the desk man with a barely perceptible nod. He reached up and pushed his battered wide-brimmed hat back on his head. He looked down at the armchair man. "Now you lookahere, Cal.

You plain got to do something about that windmill over on the west flats. We put in near half a day shoving cows all the way over by the creek because the damn thing ain't pumping hardly at all. It's all wore out. It ain't worth trying to patch any. I'm telling you we need—"

"Shut up, Hat," the armchair man said gently, affectionately. "You make a mighty poor liar. I checked that mill myself last week. An' I ain't needin' no help on ways of gettin' money out of the company right now. You know well as I do there's things that got to be played straight. Anyways, Platt here knows what it'd be for."

The desk man stiffened on his chair, swelling within vest and coat, afflicted with a need to offset the vast looming presence of Hat Henderson, to assert some command over the situation. "I know all right," he said. "Maybe I'm beginning to know too much how things are handled out here. Eighteen . . . hundred . . . dollars. Why, that's an outrage. I can tell you that as soon as I'm back East, I'll have the company lawyers onto this. Those responsible will have to pay. And I demand an explanation."

"What he means," the armchair man said, "is he wants to know what happened. You tell him, Hat."

"What for?" said Hat quietly and over on the ladder-back chair the desk man felt a small shiver run down his spine, a recognition of something intangible suddenly in the room, beyond his grasp, something between two men suddenly indifferent to his presence, intent on each other, a big dusty cowboy standing relaxed yet watchful, looking down, and a lean ageless man sitting easy and limp in an old armchair, looking up.

"What for?" said Hat Henderson quietly. "The little dude has made up his mind already."

"Maybe he has," the armchair man said gently. "But don't you go makin' the same mistake. I'm manager of this spread. I ain't ever let you an' the boys down yet. Now you just tell him. From the beginnin'."

"Well-l-l-l, now," said Hat. He sank down, knees bending, until he was hunkered on his heels, balanced on his toes, rump dangerously close to his spurs, and as he sank, clearing more of the way, more of the late afternoon sunlight flowed into the room, golden and warm and reassuring. "I'd say it began with that goddamn order some company jackass sent through last month. Clean out all hosses not being used or likely to be used. That meant—" He stopped. His eyes had focused on the bottle to the left of the armchair. "Why, you lying cheating old polecat, Cal. Holding out. I thought there wasn't none of that rat poison left."

"Wolf," said the armchair man.

"All the same," said Hat. He rocked forward, stretching out full length, supporting his weight with his left hand on the floor, reaching with his right to take the bottle. He rocked back, hunkered on heels again. He held the bottle and regarded the small amount remaining in the bottom with disgust. He tilted the bottle and the last of the amber liquid slid down his throat. He flipped the empty bottle in an arc back and out the doorway. "I'm plumb ashamed of you, Cal," he said sadly. He hitched himself around a bit to face the desk man more directly.

"Well-l-l, as I was saying, that fool order meant rounding up that bunch of half-wild-stuff, mostly batty old mares and maverick geldings, too mean to do much of anything with, that'd been roaming the canyon country south of here. I reckon maybe they was chewing up grass that might carry a few more cows but they wasn't doing nobody any harm. Just hiding out there an' enjoying life and Cal here had to be so goddamned honest an' put 'em in that stock tally you called for last year. So, natural to some folks, some peeculiar kind of folks, that gives somebody a notion. Clean 'em out. Sell 'em off. Squeeze out a shade more profit for folks that don't really need—"

"Certainly," said the desk man, feeling better, asserting himself by interrupting. "That makes sense. Get rid of poor stock to make way for better. At the same time realize what you can on assets otherwise useless. That's good business."

"Well-l-l-l, now," said Hat. "You can call it good business if your mind runs that way. I call it a hell of a tough job I go to do. Rough country over that way. All broke up and full of thorn thickets. An' them hosses was worse'n wild ones. Knew too blamed much about men an' ropes an' such. When Cal sprung that little notion on me, I thought he was kidding. Shooting's the way to get rid of them things, I says. If they got to be got rid of. No, he says, this order says shipped and sold. Well-l-l, when a job's got to be done, it's got to be done.

I took four of the boys, all I could spare at the time, and went after them things. Jeeeesus! We had us a time! They wasn't hosses. They was crosses atween anteelopes an' mountain goats. An' mean. Spooky as she-bears with cubs. Took us all one day an' half the next combing 'em out of them thickets. Not much sleep 'cause we had to hold what we had already and they was ready to take off any time. We wore down two good saddle hosses apiece gathering them things. An' holding 'em. Took us all the rest that second day to get 'em to that little old broke-down corral out on the flats that ain't been used in years. Only about five mile but they didn't have no herd sense. Too mean, I reckon. When they broke and they broke often, it'd be in all directions at the oncet. I'm telling you, mister, me an' the boys did some riding. But we got 'em there, every last one of the fool things, forty-three it was, an' we hazed 'em into that corral. Patched it up some where it was broke an' just flopped on the ground for some shut-eye."

Hat Henderson sighed. His voice became plaintive. "Maybe you got another bottle stashed away somewheres, Cal? I ain't talked this much since the last time."

"Too bad," said the armchair man. "Wolves are all dead."

"Sure," said Hat. "Sure, Cal. But that's what you was saying before." He shifted attention again to the desk man. "Well-l-l-l, come morning we fixed to shove 'em along some more. You can believe it or not, mister, but them things was so ornery they wouldn't come out. Couple of us had to go into that little old corral an' haze 'em out and the moment they was out they was breaking in all directions. But we bunched 'em an' we started 'em moving right. We was heading for that corral an' shipping pens over on that spur line of the Santy Fee. We get 'em there an' we'd have 'em. An' they was getting some better. They was learning some. Sure, they wasn't traveling too good. They'd run like rabbits for a stretch an' we'd be scuttering to hold 'em together. Then they'd stop an' balk an' mill around and we'd have to shove 'em even into a walk an' sudden they'd be running again an' the same stunt over an' over. But they was staying bunched more. We could breathe a mite easier. An' then . . ."

* * *

They came over the last rise sloping down a half mile to the thin tracery of tracks, sharp against the clean cloudless blue of the big sky of the big land, forty-three batty dry mares and maverick geldings and five tired men on five tough little worn weary cow ponies. Almost directly below them was the splotch of posts and rails and plank chutes that were corral and shipping pens. Off to the right the tracks led into distances merging into distances, fading at last into far horizon. Off to the left the tracks led into and were lost in a range of low humped hills. Well back into the hills a thin fraying streamer of gray smoke floated upward.

The horses, trotting over the rise, slowed on the down slope, stopped, staring ahead at the pens. The dust of their movement, drifting forward, caught up with them, swirling slowly and rising to blot out some of the blue of the sky. The voice of Hat Henderson lifted out of the dust from behind the bunched herd. "Easy now. Easy does it. Sunfish, you slip on ahead there an' open the gate."

A shape emerged from the left of the dust cloud, the thick barrel body of Sunfish Perkins sweat-sodden in saddle on a ratty flop-eared gray, swinging out and forward, loping down toward the corral. From out of the cloud where he had been broke three riderless horses, heads high, sniffing at open distance. From thirty feet away, lost in the cloud, came the grunt of a horse hit hard with spurs. Into the open streaked another shape, the slender compactness of Dobe Chavez erect in saddle on a scrubby stout-rumped roan already in full gallop, swooping in swift headlong rush to intercept the three and drive them back.

From the right of the herd, drifting through the dust, came the cheerful voice of Monte Walsh. "Ain't that a pretty sight down there? Almost time to be celebrating. We ain't lost a one and the corral's right ahead. Makes a man feel good almost like when a woman says yes."

"They ain't in there yet," came the voice of Chet Rollins from somewhere near.

"Quit yapping," came the voice of Hat Henderson. "An' move 'em along. Easy. Easy."

Slowly the herd in its slowly swirling dust cloud began to move down the slope, the horses stepping gingerly, reluctant, knowing. Sunfish Perkins was back in position on the left. The herd began to pick up speed, the leaders trotting, beginning to push out beyond the dust cloud. Faster, into a lope, and the mass of moving animals was plunging into a gallop, fanning out, pushing out to the sides, seeking to split to right and left of the cluster of pens and corral. Five men on five tough even more knowing cow ponies raced with the herd, sweeping, swerving without a break in rushing headlong stride, closing it in, aiming for the angled pocket made by the pens along the tracks and the much bigger corral jutting out. The herd thudded into the pocket, brought up short against the pen rails, a milling mass of squealing, kicking horses, hemmed in by five men in an arc out around them.

"Jeeeesus!" rose the voice of Hat Henderson as he slid his chunky bay to a stop on its rump. Two scrawny rawboned geldings had made it past the outer corner of the corral and were hightailing for faraway places. "Maybe we better let them two go!"

"Let 'em go, hell!" yelled Monte Walsh. The words seemed to be floating in empty air. Long lean-hipped body forward in saddle atop his leggy dun, he was already jumps away, spinning around the corral corner, lining out after the two. The leggy dun sretched out like an oversize jackrabbit, as dedicated as the man in the saddle. It soared over a wide clump of upthrust cactus, disdaining to swerve aside. It drove in angling across the course of the two geldings and they braked on sliding hoofs and shifted across its rump to strike dodging in another direction. It reared in stride, pawing at sky, and pivoted on taut hindlegs and lit streaking after the two. It drove in on them again.

"Yow-ee!" yelled Monte Walsh, slapping across the nose of the nearer with coiled rope in hand. "That won't get you nowheres!" The two swung, slowing, disgusted, and trotted back toward the others with Monte and the dun triumphant behind.

Chet Rollins shifted a bit in saddle atop his thick-necked black and looked at Monte. "You'll break a leg someday doing that," he said, amiable, conversational.

"Shucks," said Monte. "What's a leg? I got two, ain't I?"

The herd, hemmed in the wide angle, was quieting now, beginning to accept the inevitable. The gate along the near side of the corral stood wide open, swung all the way back, but no horse showed any interest in the opening.

"All right," said Hat Henderson. "Close in. They ain't got a chance now an' they know it."

Careful, alert, five men on five tough little cow ponies began to move in, crowding the herd closer into the pocket, closer to the gateway. Two old mares were jostled almost into the opening. They looked in, deliberate, reluctant. They took a few steps forward, resigned, ready, and were inside and the others were shifting to follow.

Off to the left where the tracks snaked out of the low range of hills a streamer of dark gray smoke drifted upward and a whitish vapor floated over the last hill. Into view, along the track, chugging steadily into the strain, came a small locomotive followed by the wood-piled tender, nine freight cars, and a caboose. In the locomotive cab the engineer sat relaxed on his stool, elbow on right window edge, head out of the window. A slow smile spread on his ruddy rough-featured face. "Hey," he said for the benefit of the fireman in the rear door of the cab. "Let's have a little fun." He reached up and took hold of the whistle cord.

SCREEEEEEEEEE!

Ahead, at the cluster of pens and corral, forty-three batty dry mares and maverick geldings exploded into sudden simultaneous action.

"Wow!" said the engineer, staring ahead in fascination. The fireman crowded behind him to push his own head out the window for his own view. Several horses were leaping across the tracks ahead. Instinctive, unthinking, the engineer pulled again on the whistle cord.

Ahead, at the cluster of pens and corrals, five men, two still rocking in saddles on pitching cow ponies, three stretched at odd angles on the ground with heads lifted, watched forty-three batty dry mares and maverick geldings heading for the horizon in forty-three different directions.

"We better move along fast," said the fireman softly. "Get past there quick as we can."

The engineer said nothing. He was busy with the throttle.

Ahead, moving now in instant silent simultaneous decision away from the pens and corral, five men advanced purposefully toward the approaching train, Monte Walsh in the lead on his leggy dun, Chet Rollins a few jumps back on his thick-necked black, Sunfish Perkins laboring behind on his own short thick legs, Hat Henderson limping, stumbling, hobbling, hopping, Dobe Chavez pushing up from the ground and taking a step and collapsing down and grimacing under his trim dark mustache and crawling on hands and knees.

Monte Walsh reached the oncoming train and the dun reared, pivoting on hindlegs, and raced beside it. Monte loosened feet in stirrups and took hold of the saddlehorn and hopped up, crouching with feet on saddle, and dove through the side door of the locomotive cab and the dun swerved aside, slowing. Monte reappeared almost at once, heaved out on the rebound by the fireman, but one hand was clenched on the fireman's belt and the fireman came with him. They lit hard, rolling over and over, hammering at each other as they rolled.

Chet Rollins had swung and was racing beside the locomotive. His coiled rope was in his left hand, a loop forming in his right hand. His right arm flashed and the loop dropped over the locomotive smokestack. The thick-necked black lowered its head and swung away, shoulders slugging into the sudden strain coming. The rope tautened with a jerk and the locomotive shuddered and rocked a bit on the tracks and the black flew off its feet and Chet pushed out and away and the black hit the ground, squirming and kicking and dragged, and the smokestack ripped loose and fell clattering down the side of the locomotive to the trackside. A shower of sparks rose and descended over the cab and the high hissing of escaping steam sounded and inside the cab the engineer threw back the throttle and jammed on the brakes. The train slid smoking and steaming to a stop.

Back at the rear end and in rapid order five trainmen hopped down the steps of the caboose. They stood in a group staring forward. Up at the locomotive the engineer peered out the side door and jumped to the ground. He waved at the five and started to shout. His voice was cut short in his throat. The hatless battered chunky shape of Chet Rollins had hurtled into him from behind.

Back by the caboose one of the trainmen leaned in over the steps reaching for something. The other four started forward. Monte Walsh, bruised and scratched and cinderstained, rose from the trackside, leaving the fireman limp and finished, and moved purposefully to meet them. They converged on him in a rush.

"I'm coming, Monte," bellowed Sunfish Perkins, pounding in. He lowered his head and plunged forward and at the last instant turned sideways at the waist so that one thick shoulder jutted out and the full weight of his barrel body crashed into the melee. One of the trainmen, three ribs cracked, staggered away and sank down moaning and hitched himself further away.

"Save some for me," boomed Hat Henderson, hobbling, hopping, diving in.

The fifth trainman was there now, a monkey wrench in his right hand. He skipped about looking for a chance. He saw one and swung. The wrench thudded in a glancing blow on bone. Sunfish Perkins sagged and collapsed out of the melee, dazed, head wobbling.

A gun roared and the man with the monkey wrench dropped it and spun halfway around and clutched with his left hand at his right shoulder and sat down suddenly, all fight out of him.

"Ees a nasty man," said Dobe Chavez from forty feet away on the ground, slipping his gun back into its holster. He started crawling forward again. He was close to the whirling melee. He heaved forward and his arms swept around a pair of legs.

Dust and cinders flew and the cinders fell and the dust floated gently in the air and the sun of early afternoon lay soft and golden over the big land and over the remnants of fast furious action along the side of a stopped crippled train. Silence settled over the scene. By the trackside, a few cars from the caboose, five trainmen reclined in varied positions on the ground showing no inclination to rise. A short distance away, down the slight embankment, the fireman raised his head and sat up and seemed to regard that as sufficient exertion for the moment.

Close by the five trainmen Dobe Chavez sat on the ground, leaning forward, investigating his right ankle. A few feet away Sunfish Perkins also sat on the ground, exploring with cautious fingers one side of his head. Monte Walsh leaned against a freight car, chest slowly heaving, combing with blunt curved fingers multitudinous cinders out of his hair. Hat Henderson stood on the slight embankment with weight balanced chiefly on one leg, looking down at the bloody knuckles of one hand.

He raised his head. "There must of been another one," he said. "That goddamned engineer. Where'd he go?"

"Coming," said Monte. "Chet took care of him."

Down the trackside, along the train, came the engineer, face splotched, one leg dragging a bit, sullen, disgusted, coming in little spurts as shoved from behind by Chet Rollins. He stopped, was permitted to stop, about ten feet away facing Hat.

"You didn't keep it fair," he said. "I heard shooting."

Dobe Chavez looked up, tight-lipped, eyes ominous. Monte Walsh took two steps and kicked at a monkey wrench on the ground. "One of your boys had that thing," said Hat Henderson.

The engineer stared down at the monkey wrench. "I see," he said. He sighed. "I hope you understand I got my own notion of him now."

"How was I to know?" said one of the trainmen from the ground, left hand tight on right shoulder. "I thought maybe it was a holdup."

"They'd of had their guns out, stupid," said the engineer. He sighed again. "An' what in holy hell am I going to do now? Stuck out here with this train. Can't get any decent draft with no stack. Leaking steam too. I couldn't budge the thing."

"Unhook," said Chet Rollins. "Leave the cars here."

"Yeah," said the engineer. "Maybe I could creep along. But you know what that means? It's twenty miles to the mainline, ten more to the yard. Supposing I get another engine. There's no place to turn around out here. I got to back the whole damn distance. Whyn't one of you ride to the operator at the mainline so he can wire for a repair crew?"

Hat Henderson stiffened. "There ain't a one of my men doing any riding for any railroad," he said. "I don't give a hoot in hell what you got to do. We got our own troubles."

"Yeah," said the engineer. A wry grin of remembrance flicked on his face. "I reckon you do." He sighed again and waved savagely at his men to come along and started away toward the front of the train.

Five dirty dusty disheveled battered cowboys watched six equally dirty dusty disheveled and even more battered trainmen move away, two of them leaning on others, stopping briefly to collect the fireman. They saw them stop by the tender and fuss, cursing, with the coupling, and climb or be helped one by one into the cab. The wisps of smoke floating above the locomotive began to increase and faintly they could hear the rising hiss of steam. Slowly, groaning and grunting in short puffs, the locomotive and tender crept into motion, moving slowly away.

Hat Henderson raised his head higher and looked around. Not far from where the locomotive had been a leggy dun and a thick-necked black with trailing rope cropped patiently at the few tufts of bunch grass along the edge of the slight embankment. On near the pens and corral a chunky bay and a ratty flop-eared gray and a stout-rumped roan were engaged in the same occupation. Hat Henderson looked down. "Sunfish," he said. "How's that head?"

"I sure know I got one," said Sunfish. "But that won't bother my riding."

"Dobe," said Hat. "What's with that leg?"

"Thees ankle," said Dobe Chavez, "he won't work. But ees nothing on the horse."

Hat Henderson drew in a long breath and let it out slowly. "Chet," he said. "And you, Monte. Bring the hosses over here. We got forty-three fool critters to find."

* * *

The sun was low in the western sky, ready to drop behind the ragged edging of mountains in the distance, sending its soft golden light through the open doorway all the way to the flat top of the onetime rolltop desk.

"Well-l-l, now," said Hat Henderson. He rose slowly to full height, blotting out some of the sunlight, making shadow and the looming feel of his presence reach across the desk. "It wasn't too bad. Course Dobe's hoss had a pulled shoulder that must of happened when those critters hit us. He just stayed there an' kept an eye on that corral an' handled the gate while the rest of us brought 'em in in little bunches, seeing as they was scattered so. But they was some tired too. They hadn't broke more'n four–five mile around. We combed 'em out here an' there an' brought 'em in. All of 'em, but for one fool mare that must of caught a foot crossing the tracks an' broke a leg an' was hobbling along the other side of the cars. We was back at the ranch here along about midnight. Train was gone when we took 'em some feed next day but you can bet your bankroll, mister, that corral wasn't touched any. Cal here had some cars along there next day and they was shipped out."

Hat Henderson turned slightly to look down at the armchair man, who simply shook his head a little and beckoned with it toward the door. Quietly, accompanied by the soft jingle of rusty old spurs, Hat Henderson went out the open doorway.

The desk man hitched his chair some to escape the sunlight now loosed again directly toward him. He peered at the doorway. There was no one in sight outside. He put his hands on the desk edge and braced himself against them. "Good Lord, man!" he said. "Why were no warrants sworn out? Wrecking a train! Shooting a man!"

"Shucks," said the armchair man. "This is still hoss an' cow country. Not a judge around that'd issue a warrant on a thing like that." He regarded his empty glass and twisted it slowly in his fingers. "No sheriff that'd try an' serve it neither. Specially with Dobe an' that gun of his here, nursin' a bad ankle."

"Good Lord," said the desk man, staring at the other. He rallied. "Maybe that's a good thing. If a trial got started the company might be dragged into it. As things are, I'd say the company is clear enough."

"No," said the armchair man gently. "The company's payin'."

The desk man jerked on his chair. "Nonsense," he snapped. He leaned back and pursed his lips and began rubbing the thumb of his right hand up and down across his fingers. He waited. The armchair man sat still and relaxed, regarding his empty glass.

"Well, yes," the desk man said. "I can see they had provocation. I can sympathize with them, I must say. But being provoked doesn't give them the right to start taking things apart and committing assault and battery. When they cut loose like that, that was their own doing. The company would never have approved. They are personally responsible. They will have to pay."

"On forty a month?" said the armchair man. "Out of the which they got to get clothin' an' gear?"

"That is their problem," said the desk man, accent pronounced. "Things might go smoother out in this country if people thought about such things before they cut loose. Oh, I can sympathize with them again, but it is their problem. Do you realize, man, that the company only received six hundred thirty dollars for that batch of horses? Think of the loss if the company paid."

"A nice little nibble, yes," said the armchair man.

"I'll tell you what I will do," said the desk man. "I'll have the company lawyers help them. You know, whittle it down for them. Counter claims for that horse that broke a leg, for time lost, for injuries to our men. Things like that."

"No," said the armchair man gently. "You don't understand this thing atall. The boys had the best of it. They tromped on that train crew right thorough. That means there's got to be no quibblin'. Payment in full."

The desk man stared at the other, eyes narrowed. "They can be fools about it if they want to," he said. "But I won't. That's what the company pays me for. To look after its interests. It has other interests too, you know, many more. When it sends me out here it trusts me to see that the affairs of this ranch are being handled in businesslike manner. To protect its investment. Well, as I see this, those men had to have their—what you call—fun. Now they'll have to pay for it."

"Oh, they'll pay all right," the armchair man said gently, very gently. "My boys'll pay if I put it to them. They'll get together, them that was in on it an' them that wasn't, an' they'll hock all they've got if they have to, except of course their saddles. An' they'll pay. But that'll be mighty expensive for the company."

"Expensive?" said the desk man. "For the company?"

"Why, sure," said the armchair man. "Come the next day there won't be a rider anywheres on this whole damn spread. The boys'll be gone. Cookie too."

The desk man jerked on his chair. He slapped one hand on the desk top. "Well, then, you'd just have to get busy and hire more men."

"Maybe I could," said the armchair man. "If I scratched around hard enough. But not like these boys. There ain't a one that ain't worth two of the usual run. But, anyways, I wouldn't be doin' it. I'd be gone too."

"Oh, no, you wouldn't," said the desk man quickly. "We have you on a contract."

"Contract?" said the armchair man gently. "What in hell d'you think that contract'd mean to me? If I wasn't tryin' to be polite, I'd tell you what you could do with it."

"Blackmail," said the desk man slowly. "That's what it is. A kind of blackmail."

"Call it anything you've a mind to," said the armchair man. "But you're thinkin' of this thing in terms of laws an' business rules an' the like. An' I'm tellin' you those things don't come into it atall." He regarded the empty glass sadly and reached over the right arm of the chair and set it on the floor. He leaned forward some, his back straightening a bit. "The boys've been talkin' about this, gettin' themselves sort of worked up over it, an' I've been hearin' 'em. They don't go by reasonin'. They go by feelin'. An' they have right good feelin's. They been proud of the company, of this outfit. Proud to be workin' for it. They ain't quite bright enough to understand the reason it's somethin' to be proud of is the work they been doin' for it, what they've made of it. They just been proud. They've made the Slash Y brand an' the boys that carry that iron mean plenty everywheres cowmen still ride hosses an' swing a loop. Not the biggest outfit on the ranges. Maybe not even the best. But a good one. A right good one. Those boys of mine'd stand up an' slug it out or go for their guns against any man or bunch of men that'd say a word against it. They ain't pretty but there ain't a job I tell 'em to do they don't do an' do right. Like that damnfool order. They penned those hosses spite of all the Santy Fee could do. I send 'em eight hundred miles with a herd of cows like last year to Wyomin' an' shorthanded too 'cause you or the company or both won't let me put on more men an' come hell an' highwater an' thievin' Indians an' a bunch of run-off rustlers they deliver. Every last cow except three that died of bloat. Alkali water. An' they bring back the money. Every last dollar of it except what they draw on their regular pay for some spreein' along the way back."

The desk man stared at the other, his lips pursed, pushing in and out. The armchair man leaned forward a bit more, his back straightening more. "An' they don't punch no clocks," he said. "They're workin' for the company twenty-four hours out of every day except when they're raisin' a little fun in town an' if I holler they'll quit that an' come a-foggin' into anything no matter what the clock says. They're ready any time, all the time, night like day, to give the company all the sweat an' muscle an' downright guts an' savvy with hosses an' cows they've got, includin' their necks if that's called for like one of them did on that Wyomin' trip. That's what they're puttin' in. For forty a month an' the feelin' of bein' proud without lettin' that show too much. What's the company puttin' in? Money, that's all. An' this little thing right now is a matter of a little money. They been proud of this outfit. They'd like to keep on feelin' that way an' they'll stick with it long as they do. They feel they done right well by it over at the pens. There was five of them. There was seven of them trainmen, not mentionin' a train. They feel if the company's what they been feelin' it is, it ought to come through for them once in a long while when they're in a tight."

The desk man sat still, very still. He had the look of a man confronting some calamity and powerless to stop it. "And you," he said slowly. "You feel the same way?"

"Yes," said the armchair man. "I got the same feelin's. I growed up with 'em. The rest of the fool world can go to hell in a hand basket but I ain't changin' 'em any." He rose out of the armchair, lean body unfolding to full height. "I've said my say an' I feel some better even if I ain't made a dent in you. Reckon I'll go tell the boys to start gatherin' their gear." He moved toward the doorway.

"Wait a minute," said the desk man. He saw the other stop, turn back some, and stand, quiet, alert, waiting. He sat straight upright on his ladder-back chair and began rubbing his right hand forward and back on his right thigh in the tight-bulged pin-stripe trousers. "You put me in a difficult position," he said. "I might as well tell you that some of the directors think highly of you as manager of this ranch. The men leave and I know what they'd say. What I did. Hire some more. But you leave and they'd be onto me hard. Good Lord, it could cost me my own job. What the devil do you expect me to do? I'm not one of your hell-raising tromping shooting boys. I'm just a city man with a good head for figures. But I have my own pride too. My figures are honest. I can't go slipping in things like wolf poison and repairs to a windmill in my report. Not eighteen hundred dollars worth. I probably couldn't get away with it anyway. Can't we just sit here and figure this out some way?"

"It's all figured," said the armchair man gently. "I don't give a hoot in hell how you put it down. That's your problem. Maybe I can sympathize with you some like you with the boys. But it's your problem. To me an' the others you're the company. You're the one comes out here regular. What you do is what we'll go by. We ain't interested much in how you do it."

"Good Lord," said the desk man. "But I can't see now how I'll do it."

"But you'll do it," said the armchair man gently, affectionately. His voice rose with an edging of urging, almost of command. "Come along, Platt, an' we'll just tell the boys."

Slowly, reluctantly, the desk man pushed together the papers on the desk top and restored them to his inside coat pocket and picked up his small pad and pencil and put them in a side pocket. Slowly, reluctantly, he reached with his left hand and took the derby. Nerving himself to it, he rose to his medium plumpish height and came out around the desk and up alongside the armchair man. A lean arm reached and urged him on ahead, out the doorway, on the short distance to the edge of the veranda.

Along the front edge, to either side, out of range of vision from inside through the doorway, sat nine silent men. About fifteen feet away to the left another lounged easy in saddle on a drooping leggy dun. Still another, with long once-white cloth tied around his waist and dropping down over worn old boots, was coming from the cookhouse.

In the soft luminous dusk, legacy of the sun now below the far ragged edging of mountains, the desk man was painfully aware of eleven men regarding him gravely.

"Platt here," said the armchair man softly, cheerfully, "is going to take care of that little Santy Fee affair."

The desk man was even more painfully aware of eleven men regarding him gravely. He could sense the final, the complete, the absolute necessity of irretrievable speech. "I'll . . . I'll do my best for you boys," he said.

He tried to recoil from the veranda edge but the armchair man was behind him, blocking him. The soft luminous dusk was live and vociferous with leaping shapes and back-slappings and high shrill yells. A higher shriller "Yow-eee!" climbed out of it. A voice emerged: "That's plenty good enough! You savvy those eastern dudes! You can do it!"

He tried to recoil again. A leggy dun seemed to be leaping straight at him, enormous in the dusk. It reared, almost pawing the veranda roof, and dropped down sideways in front of him. He looked up, terrified, into a lean still-battered youngish face. "Put out a hand," said Monte Walsh. "I've a hankering to shake it." Solemnly Monte leaned down and took the limp hand and shook. "I'll drive you to town," he said. "Guarantee to get you there by stage time."

"Good Lord, no!" gasped the desk man, shuddering.

"Move along, Monte," came the voice of Chet Rollins. "It's my turn."

The dun leaped away under spurs and spun, stopping, to stay close to the proceedings. A line had been forming behind its previous position. One by one nine cowboys with the dust of the day's work on them and a ranch cook, redolent of grease and smoke, stepped forward to reach for the desk man's right hand.

He winced. His fingers were being crushed in a big hand. "You're all right, Plug-Hat," said Hat Henderson.

*   *   *

Between the shafts of the buckboard the bony flea-bitten gray jogged forward, betraying its range ancestry by the easy nonchalance with which it ate into the miles of the big land in steady self-chosen unvarying rhythm. Far behind, faint and sinking into distance, were the first evening lights of the range headquarters of the Consolidated Cattle Company.

The desk man held the reins in his left hand. He had no illusion that he was doing much driving. The bay would go where it would go and that would be to town and the livery stable without any assistance from him. He wriggled the fingers of his right hand. They seemed to be all there and intact. He reached with them to fix the derby more firmly on his head. "Plug-Hat," he said softly. "Plug-Hat Platt."

He settled into what seemed to be the least uncomfortable

position possible on the jouncing seat of the buckboard. "Good Lord," he said even more softly. "What a way to do business."

* * *

"Did Monte get took that time? Ye-as, I should up an' say he did. Rolled out flatter'n a blue-corn tortilla. Some of us was in town for this or that which don't matter nohow an' there was this little scrub feller with a fair-looking hoss. Drunk? Was that feller drunk? Ye-as, he was so drunk it sloshed around in him like water in a rain barrel. An' was he talking big. An' aiming most of it at Monte. How that hoss of his could beat most anything else inhabiting hoss-hair. He was such a harmless-looking helpless little hunk of meat that some of us tried to hush him. Seemed a shame for anybody to take advantage of him. But no, he just talked bigger, pestering away at Monte. So, nat'ral-like, Monte took him on. To shut him up much as anything else. Nothing to it. The feller's hoss was fast enough but that dun of Monte's, like always when he starts talking in its ear, just settled to it an' Monte was sitting there waiting at the finish line when the feller got there. Did he pay up? Ye-as, he paid up like a good little feller an' admitted the drinks was on him. An' then be blowed if he didn't start talking worse'n before. Saying he'd been beat fair enough but it was only square he get a chance to make it even. Saying Monte owed that to him. Saying he was disappointed in that hoss of his an' he knew now it couldn't beat Monte's hoss but by gollies he bet he could beat Monte if they was to run a race on their own two legs. Laugh? Was that worth a laugh? Ye-as, I should stand up an' say it was. That scrub little feller wibble-wobbling around alongside Monte with those long legs of his. Did he mean it? Ye-as, he meant it so serious he was wanting to bet his whole roll, what was left of it. Upshot was the feller pestered at Monte so persistent Monte got some peeved an' said if anybody was so blamed anxious to get rid of money he guessed he'd just have to take it.

"Quarter mile it was to be. Monte shed his hat an' his gun an' a vest he was wearing an' he was ready. Surprised? Was he surprised? Ye-as, I should stand here an' say he was. More surprised'n a hen that's hatched a duck. Sudden that feller

wasn't near so drunk an' he started peeling hisself. Peeled off his shirt an' pants an' under 'em he had a rig something like short underwear an' his legs showed up muscle like a strong man's at a circus an' he put on some little shoes with nails sticking out the bottom an' he crouched down like a jackrabbit waiting for a flying start an' when Mac popped the gun he lit out like a small-size express train heading down a grade with a full head of steam on. Why, shucks, Monte wasn't even within hailing distance. Why, shucks again, Monte didn't even run more'n a third the way before he just quit an' came walking back disgusted. Was it a rig? Ye-as, I'm here to say it was. That feller was a crack sprinter from back east somewheres an' Sonny Jacobs'd got hold of him an' put him up to it."

Dobe Chavez
1886

Vᴀsᴛ ʀᴇᴀᴄʜᴇs of rangeland rolled westward, rounded in soft sanded contours under midmorning sun, to lap against a long low ridge running seemingly interminable into the south. Along the flattened crest of the ridge rode two men, Dobe Chavez on a small stocky bay and young Lon Hall on a rangy long-legged pinto, riding line. They rode at a steady jog, scanning the country to the right that dropped in shoulders of humped land down from the ridge. They swerved to the right and down, picking up speed, and gathered a half dozen steers and a cow with yearling calf at her heels into a compact bunch and drove them up and over the ridge and down the eastern slope. They jogged back up to the crest and moved southward along it again.

"Thees hill," said Dobe Chavez. "We follow eet. *Todas las vacas,* all the cows weeth the right brand, we push them over thees hill."

"Sí, señor," said young Lon Hall, eighteen years of lanky enthusiasm, proud to be where he was, with whom he was, doing what he was. "I gotcha, Dobe."

They jogged steadily along, making occasional forays down the western slope and back.

"Let's see something," said young Lon. "What time do you say it is?"

Dobe cocked his head to look from under the wide brim of his sombrero at the sun. "Ees about ten of the clock," he said.

Carefully young Lon undid the button on a pocket of his shirt and took out a somewhat battered gold watch. He pressed on the stem and the face cover flipped open. "Ten, seven and one half."

"Ees what I say," said Dobe. "But ees a good clock."

"It was my granddad's," said young Lon.

They jogged steadily along. Off to the right about a mile, down the western slope and out on the relative level, almost hidden in a small hollow, several small adobe structures came into view. A few haphazard garments hung on a clothesline between two sagging poles. A few chickens scratched at sun-baked ground, tiny specks of busyness at the distance. Two scrawny horses and a burro drooped dejectedly in a rickety corral.

Dobe drew rein. "I theenk," he said, "I theenk I go see my, what you call heem? my couseen José Gonzales who owe me three *dólar*."

"You sure got a lot of *primos*," said young Lon.

"*Sí,*" said Dobe, grinning. "*Muchos primos.* You ride along. Slow. I'll come soon."

"Yep," said young Lon. "And I'll bet you're thinking of his sister. I've heard about her."

"Ees eet wrong," said Dobe, grinning again, "for *un hombre* to smile at *las señoritas?*"

"I ain't saying nothing," said young Lon. "Just wishing you luck." He nudged the pinto forward along the ridge, whistling softly under his breath.

* * *

Lon Hall drew rein and consulted the battered gold watch. He liked the feel of it in his hand. Ten fifty-four. He tucked it carefully back in its pocket. Several hundred yards away, down the right slope, atop one of the humping shoulders of land, were three steers, still, rigid, staring on down beyond. He could make out the Slash Y plain on the flank of one. "Acting kind of funny," he said. He shrugged and slapped spurs to the pinto and swung down, circling. As he topped the humping shoulder just below them to drive them up, he drew rein again, sharp, in surprise. On ahead, in a hollow hidden before, were four horses, two saddled, two carrying pack racks, and two men, one jumping fast for a rifle from the scabbard on one of the saddled horses, the other rising upright, knife in hand, from the half-skinned carcass of a steer.

The rifle bore on Lon Hall's middle and a cold sickness gripped him under his belt.

"Come on down here, sonny," said the man with the rifle. "And easy."

Slowly Lon Hall nudged the pinto forward. Stopped. The muzzle of the rifle was unwavering and enormous.

"You Slash Y?" said the man with the rifle.

Lon Hall nodded. It was difficult to make his neck muscles move.

"Well, then, you can take a complaint back to your boss, Brennan. Your goddamned cows keep wandering over here. Get in the way when we're picking one of our own like today to dress out. You got that?"

The man with the knife was reaching, quiet, furtive, to flip back with one foot the loose hide along the flank where he had been cutting. Lon Hall's eyes flicked to the foot and he saw, just as the hide went back, the brand, sharp and distinct. His eyes flicked back to the man with the rifle and he saw the face hardening more and the certainty showing and he reared the pinto with frantic hand on the reins and whirled it with spurs sinking in streaking away and angling for the ridge top. He heard the rifle roar and a revolver join it and the pinto leaped shuddering and caught footing again and strove upward and shuddered again, rearing high and toppling backward, and he pushed out and away, hard, falling, sprawling, scrambling, and the threshing body of the horse, life ebbing out of it, pitching down the slope, caught him and rolled full on him.

*   *   *

Along the crest of the ridge, trotting smartly on the small neat stocky bay, rode Dobe Chavez, singing softly to himself a little song that fitted him precisely at the moment, something about *un caballero festivo*. He was checking the hoofprints of the long-legged pinto. He saw where they left the ridge top and swerved down to the right. Further on he saw where they returned accompanied by the prints of several cows and went down the slope to the left. "Ees a good keed," he said. "Ees doing the work." He saw where they returned to the ridge top and led on again. He trotted smartly along. He saw where they swerved again down to the right. He trotted on. They did not return. He slowed, then stopped, looking carefully out over the vast empty spaces of broken land. He turned and back-trailed, at a fast lope now, to where they had last swerved aside. He started down the slope to the right, following them. *"Jesú Cristo!"* he said and the bay plunged forward under spurs and down and over in taut-muscled leaps and slid to a stop on its rump beside the body of the pinto. Under it, limp, motionless, blank-faced, eyes closed, pinned by the legs up to the waist, lay young Lon Hall.

No longer *un caballero festivo, un caballero triste* instead, Dobe Chavez swung out of the saddle. He shook out his rope and pushed the loop over the pinto's lifeless head, down around the neck where it thickened. He pulled the rope tight to his saddle on the bay and whipped several coils around the horn, firm and overlapping. He stepped to the bay's head and took hold of the bridle and urged it into motion. It heaved, straining, hoofs digging in, and the body of the pinto pivoted and slid to one side. He knelt by the body of Lon Hall. Gently he turned it, limp and unresisting, so that the head lay up the slope. Gently he felt along the legs and arms, then grasped one wrist with surprisingly delicate fingers. He jumped up. "Ees there!" he said. He started again toward the bay. He stopped, looking down at the body of the pinto. A splotch of darkening blood showed on a shoulder. He knelt down and touched the splotch with a forefinger. The finger pushed on, easily, through the hide.

No longer *un caballero festivo* or *triste,* grim-faced instead, Dobe Chavez searched over the ground. He found the tracings of the pinto's frantic plunge up the slope. He found the half-skinned carcass of the steer, the ears and a patch of the flank hide gone. He stood for a long moment by the tracks of four horses leading off southwestward and his right hand rubbed slowly down and up the old leather of the worn holster at his side.

* * *

The several small adobe structures in their own small hollow seemed to be asleep in midday sun. One of the scrawny horses in the rickety corral raised its head and whinnied. Three or four chickens ran squawking into the nearest rabbit brush. Over the low rise behind the structures came Dobe

Chavez, sweat streaking his face, carrying a saddle and a bridle. He was leading the bay. Two saddle blankets lay over the saddle on its back. And over them, lashed with his own rope, lay the limp body of Lon Hall.

Dobe Chavez dropped the saddle and the reins of the bay, still holding the bridle dragging from one hand. He strode to the door of the larger of the adobe structures and pushed it open. He spoke in Spanish, not asking, not explaining, simply stating. He strode to the rickety corral and in and moved slowly and reached out suddenly and caught one of the scrawny horses by the nose. He stepped in close and threw an arm over its neck and slipped the bridle on. Paying no attention to the two women and one small boy and one smaller girl who had crowded out of the house, he led the scrawny horse out of the corral and slapped the saddle he had been carrying on it. He fastened the cinch. He took the reins of the bay and swung up on the scrawny horse. At a fast walk he led off angling up the long slope toward the ridge top.

*   *   *

On a straw mattress and several blankets stretched on the floor of the bunkhouse lay young Lon Hall, limp, motionless, face boyish and bloodless in the light of afternoon sun through the open doorway. Beside him was Cal Brennan, long lean body hunkered down, gently letting a few drops from a bottle drip between young Lon's slightly parted lips. Five other men stood close by, watching. On the third bunk on the right sat Dobe Chavez, head down, staring at the floor.

Lon Hall's throat muscles moved. He swallowed, involuntary, unknowing. His head rocked a bit and his eyes opened, staring. They focused on the face of Cal Brennan bending over. Tears leaked from the corners of his eyes and a sob shook him and his body stiffened in pain at the movement.

"Easy, boy," said Cal Brennan. "Don't talk more'n you have to. We'll have you to a doc soon. An' we don't need to know much. You recognize any of 'em?"

Lon Hall's head shook slightly. "There . . . was . . . two. And . . . pack . . . hosses."

"You get a good look at 'em?"

The effort of words hurt. "Big man . . . heavy . . . freckles.

Other . . . short . . . dark . . . no hat . . . black hair." He tried to raise up some and pain stiffened him and he fell back, limp again, eyes closing.

Cal Brennan rose upright. "Benton an' Garcia," he said softly. "So that's how they been gettin' that beef they been peddlin' at the fort."

"Goddamn it!" said Monte Walsh. "What got into you, Hat? Letting a kid like that—"

"Jeeeesus!" said Hat Henderson. "How was I to know? He wanted to ride with Dobe."

Over on the third bunk on the right Dobe Chavez shifted weight and started to look up and let his head lower again.

"Jeeesus!" said Hat Henderson again. "So I made a mistake. How was I to know? They been mighty quiet. They been smart up to now."

"They made a mistake," said Chet Rollins. "Not making sure of Lon."

"Hurryin'," said Cal Brennan. "Couldn't know how many of us might be around. Well, I guess the feed wagon'll do, padded enough. Sunfish. You harness the team. Make the best time in you can without bouncin' too much. Tell Mac about it but we'll be way ahead of him. Get back here an' take over when the rest of the boys come in. We might be gone a while. Monte. Pick out good hosses an' saddle 'em. Chet. You dig out some rifles. Dally. You fill some canteens. Powder. Get some grub. An' you Dobe, you listen to me. We got to do any shootin' we ain't shootin' to kill. Not less we have to. Lon's alive. An' Mac's been jawin' about our way of doin' things an' about keepin' things legal. We try an' take 'em in."

Cal Brennan sighed. "An' you, Hat. I ain't as spry as I used to be. I can't keep up, you just forget me. Keep goin'. Get 'em."

*   *   *

They rode, riding hard but not too hard, conserving the deceptive deep-bottomed strength in the tough little cow ponies under the saddles, not for the long low ridge and over to the carcasses of a pinto and a half-skinned steer, but straight southwestward to skirt the far end of the ridge and on to a small jacal and pole corral where two men had squatted for some months claiming to be running a few cows of their own dubious brand. There, in the first dark of night, they found evidences of a quick departure.

Dobe Chavez knelt on the ground, studying the prints of four horses pointed toward the broken badlands to the south. "Ees stupeed," he said. "They take too much."

"Carrying weight, eh?" said Hat Henderson. "Well, we ain't."

They rode, not fast now but steady in the dim shadowing shimmer of a piece of moon, Dobe Chavez in the lead, leaning down often along the shoulder of his horse, dismounting occasionally to lead it through the pooled shadows of the lower levels while he studied the ground.

And the hours passed and in the first flush of light up the eastern sky they found the ashes of a small fire and the stomped ground where four horses had stood and the barely perceptible rounded indentations where two men had rested.

Dobe Chavez bent low by the ashes and tested them with a finger. "Ees warm," he said and swung up into saddle again.

They rode, faster now in the growing light, chewing in saddles on a cold biscuit and a strip of jerked beef each, and dropped into the broken badlands and worked through them in and around the fantastic formations of red rock and hardened purple clay streaked with the dull white of long-ago eroded limestone, and more hours passed and they emerged on the other side and as they topped out on the upper level they saw, far ahead, in the seeming limitless expanse of distance, two horses mounted and two horses packed.

They rode, at a hard lope now, and a half hour passed and they saw that they had been seen and the four horses ahead were lengthening stride and they rode, ramming into it now, forward at full gallop.

They passed the two packhorses, cast adrift and slowing to one side, and they were beginning to string out now in a straggling line across the great bowled expanse as the small secret accumulating differences in horses and men and their riding began to tell. They passed saddle bags ripped loose and thrown aside and the two men ahead swung to the left, racing on fast-tiring horses up a long slope, and disappeared over the top.

They followed, strung out, cutting up the slope at a closer

angle, and pulled in sharp at the top, one after the other, piling into a compact group as horses slid on rumps, braking
hard. On down the other side was a small abandoned adobe
shack. It looked deserted, forlorn, with doorless doorway and
windowless window openings on two other sides, but two
sweat-streaked chest-heaving horses stood close by.

"Holed up," said Hat Henderson. A rifle sounded from
one of the window openings and the whine of a bullet
whipped past him. "Hop it," he said. "Get the hosses down out
of range. An' spread out around."

"You boys . . . listen to me," gasped Cal Brennan, tagging
up, gray-faced and strained and grim. "I don't . . . want . . .
no grandstandin' . . . out of any of you. We got . . . one man
down . . . back in town. That's enough."

Another hour passed and the first angry exchanging of
shots had dwindled to an occasional impatient report from
some vantage point around and a rare warning reply from the
shack and bullets had thudded harmlessly against the outside
of the thick old adobe walls or through the doorway and window openings against the opposite inside walls. The two
horses had shied from the shots and drifted away and been
caught and brought around with the others and Dally Johnson sat on the ground near his own horse holding a mois-
tened handkerchief against his eyes reddened and smarting
from bullet-spurted sand.

Monte Walsh moved along, crouching below the top of the
rise, and dropped to the ground beside Hat Henderson. "This
ain't getting us nowheres," he said. "Me and Chet'll slip
down on that blank side and around the corner. Rest of you
keep 'em busy through the windows and we'll rush the door."

"Shut up, Monte," said Hat wearily. "You heard what Cal
said. An' they got nothing in there. No water. They got to
come out sometime. Maybe when it's dark we'll try something."

It was Dobe Chavez, flat on the ground, peering through a
bit of rabbit brush through which poked the barrel of his
rifle, who caught the snatch of movement at a window corner
and squeezed finger on trigger. And all heard the screaming
yell that came from inside the shack and after a few moments the hoarse shout. There was talk back and forth,
shouted, and a rifle was pitched out the doorless doorway and

two revolvers after it and two men emerged, one big and heavy and freckled with blood staining his shirt at the left shoulder, the other short and dark and hatless and black-haired.

* * *

Day drifted over the big land and in the little town of Harmony two men, one with shoulder bandaged, both guarded by a deputy sworn in by Sheriff MacKnight, waited in the one-room jail for the circuit judge who would be along eventually. Sheriff MacKnight and three others rode out from town, across the vast reaches of rangeland, to the small jacal and searched thoroughly and found nothing. But a quarter of a mile away where the ground was soft and a coyote had been digging they dug too and found the stiffened hides of seven steers and five of them bore the Slash Y and two the Triple 7 of the next outfit to the north. And back in Harmony in a room of the combination hotel and office building young Lon Hall lay on an old brass bed, tended by an ample ageless Spanish-American woman who apparently never slept and watched him around the clock, visited twice daily by Doc Frantz. He was unconscious much of the time at first or asleep in a kind of coma, but color was creeping back into his cheeks and he was awake and aware at times. And every other day, late afternoon, though they were working the wide company range, area by area, tallying and branding, someone from the Slash Y but never Dobe Chavez was there to sit with him a while and take back the day's report.

"If there's any serious trouble," said Doc Frantz, "it's deep inside. Time's the only cure I know. But one thing's fairly certain. He won't ride again."

And young Lon, hearing that, turned his face to the wall. Three different times the woman heard him say, unaware of her presence, apparently to a battered gold watch he liked to keep clenched in one hand: "Well, anyways, I was Slash Y for a while." And once, once only, while he was crying softly to himself, she heard him say: "If only Dobe'd been there."

* * *

Early morning and Cal Brennan and Hat Henderson stood on the veranda of the ranch house. Out in the first corral horses were being saddled. The two men turned to look along the wagon trace leading in from the left. An old man in too-big clothes that seemed to be even older was approaching on an old gray horse. He came steadily on and stopped by the veranda, peering down with watery old eyes from under the limp brim of a shapeless old hat. "Thought you oughta know," he said. "They busted out last night. That Garcia had a gun. Betcha some other goddamned greaser slipped it to 'im. They stole some hosses. Sheriff's chasing them with just about everybody else in town."

"What time?" said Hat Henderson, quick, sharp.

"About dark."

"Which way'd they go?"

"Quit it, Hat," said Cal Brennan. He sighed, looking down at his boot toes. "Mac's after 'em. Well on the way by now. He's a good man. We're pressed for time anyways. An' Lon's makin' it. Seems to be gettin' better." He sighed again. "I don't like it any more'n you do, Hat. But we got work to do."

* * *

More days drifted over the big land and the sun dropped behind the ragged edging of mountains to the west, leaving a vast splendor across the sky, and Sheriff MacKnight, big and tired and dusty on a solid big-muscled roan, rode in along the wagon trace. Men were unsaddling in the first corral and others were scrubbing faces and hands at several basins on the bench along the front of the bunkhouse. Cal Brennan sat at one end of the bench watching the big man approach.

Slowly Sheriff MacKnight rode over and dismounted. He was aware of others gathering around but he looked only at Cal Brennan. "Don't take this too hard, Cal," he said. "I did my damndest. Almost had them twice but Garcia's got too many *primos* scattered south that'd hide them and find them fresh hosses. Lost them over in the Mogollons. Way out of my territory anyway and Jaeger over there had his hands full with his own troubles. You know that country. Nothing to do but quit. For now."

Sheriff MacKnight took off his hat and wiped a dusty hand across his forehead and put the hat on again. "I'll see about getting a reward posted," he said. "And there's something else. Young Hall died today about the time I got back. Kind of sudden. Internal hemorrhage the doc said. He managed to talk some near the finish. Said to tell you he was sorry he flubbed it, he should of rode them down."

Sheriff MacKnight was aware of the tense silence surrounding him. He looked unwaveringly at Cal Brennan. "I got to know how you're taking it, Cal."

Cal Brennan sat still, very still, head down. One hand moved slowly, rubbing over a knee. "I guess we got to leave it as unfinished business," he said. He raised his head. "For now. But if you get wind of 'em, we'll be counting on you to let us know."

"Yes," said Sheriff MacKnight. "I figured that." He sighed heavily. "And one thing more. He said to give Chavez this."

Sheriff MacKnight reached in a pocket and took out a battered gold watch.

* * *

In the lamplit interior of the cookhouse ten men sat on wooden benches along a big plank table. They ate in uneasy silence, uninterested in the food, but intent on it. The only sounds were the small scrapings of forks and spoons and the soft hissing of the big old coffeepot on the stove.

"Goddamn it!" said Monte Walsh. "I could of made a real bronc rider out of that kid!" He looked around, face flushed, angry, and saw that no one was interested in the statement and no one was looking at him. He lowered his head, intent on his own plate.

And outside, on the bench along the front of the bunkhouse, sat Dobe Chavez, staring into the darkening dimness of the big land, a battered old watch clenched in one hand.

* * *

Darkness and the clean breathing silence of night lay soft and serene over the clustered buildings and corrals. Not a light showed anywhere. The small thuddings of footsteps floated from the long low barn and a figure appeared in the doorway carrying something. It moved along the front of the building and to the first corral and in through the gate.

From the doorstep of the bunkhouse rose another figure, big, slope-shouldered, and moved silently on bootless socked feet toward the corral. Another, shorter, square-built, detached itself from the deep shadow beside the doorway and followed. The first figure came back through the gate leading a saddled horse.

"Nobody's pushing you, Dobe," said Hat Henderson.

"Ees my blame," said Dobe Chavez. "He geeve me the lee-tle clock to say eet ees right weeth heem. Eet ees not right weeth me."

"When you know something," said Chet Rollins, "send word. We'll be waiting."

* * *

More days and their nights drifted over the big land and a slim compact swarthy-skinned black-mustached man on a small neat stocky bay rode through the great distances, avoiding the few far scattered towns, stopping at remote dwindled remains of old Spanish villages and even more remote small *ranchos,* squatting by fires at lonely sheep camps where the land rose rugged and forbidding into the Mogollons, and he talked in soft fluent Spanish and some of those with whom he talked remembered carefully what he said and were ready should the occasion come to talk in their turn.

And one evening a sheepherder bedded his flock at a fresh camp up a lonesome box canyon and left his two dogs in charge and walked seven miles in the cloaking starlit darkness before moonrise to a cabin in the lower levels to speak to a man there. And the man there, when the first had left to walk back, mounted bareback on a burro and rode nine miles by a trail twisting through sharply ridged country to a small group of adobe houses and outbuildings where a few families raised a few sparse crops with water from a small stream trickling out of the hills behind and knocked gently on the door of one of the houses and spoke to the man clad only in shirt and ragged underdrawers who opened the door. And in the early light of morning this man harnessed a shaggy heavy-bagged mare to an ancient wagon and drove, with the mare's colt trotting beside her, eleven miles to a small crossroad settlement for a few not much needed supplies and a mile out of the settlement, before going on in, he turned off the little traveled road for a time to follow an old wagon trace and stop for a few moments by an old jacal with the remains of a tiny corral beside it in which stood a small neat stocky bay.

And late the next afternoon, when the sun out of sight below the ragged edging of mountains to the west was framing them in deep glow of color and the men of the Slash Y were jogging in by ones and twos from the day's work, José Gonzales on a scrawny pinto waited in the shadows of an arroyo watching for his man and saw him and moved up out of the arroyo waving his old high-crowned hat and stopped to wait again and Hat Henderson loped to him and talked briefly with him and José dismounted to make marks on the ground and explain them in his broken English and mounted again and dropped into the arroyo moving away and Hat rode on in to the ranch buildings, quiet, thoughtful.

And in the late dark silence of night over the big land three men led three horses out of the first corral, a big rangy bay and a thick-necked black and a deep-chested leggy dun.

"Maybe we ought to send word to Mac," said Chet Rollins.

"The hell with Mac," said Hat Henderson.

"How about Cal?" said Monte Walsh.

"The hell with him too," said Hat. "He's getting old."

*　*　*

Late afternoon again and four men, quiet, saying little, rode up between the sharp hogback ridges where the land rose rugged and forbidding into the Mogollons. They worked up and up into the timbered belt, tiny figures seeming lost in the immensity of rising rock and sudden stretches of high open grassland between vast patches of pine forest. Late dusk and they came to the entrance to a lonesome box canyon and three of them waited while the fourth rode in and after a while returned and the four rode in and on circling past the indistinct blotch of many sheep bedded and two dogs that stood stiff-legged, ruffs rising, but making no sound, watching them pass, and on to the one flicker of flame in the deepening darkness that was the embers of a small fire and the figure of a man hunched beside it. They unsaddled and picketed the horses and sat for a while by the embers, saying little, and they took rolled blankets from behind the cantles of the saddles and spread these on the ground and lay in them looking up at the clean depth of sky and the soft shimmer of the late moon sliding silently over the high rock of the canyon walls.

In the grayness of the suggestion of light before dawn five men moved out of the canyon, on foot, four of them leading horses. The fifth, nondescript in patched odd-assorted clothes, walking in worn heavy shoes tied around his ankles with cord, led the way, twisting up the jagged steep slope of the left rim of the canyon to top out on a level area near its head. He stopped and the others with him and he pointed out and down over the craggy immensity dropping away southeastward and he spoke softly in Spanish. He turned away to start down the steep jagged slope.

"Tell him, Dobe," said Hat Henderson, "thanks. Thanks for the Slash Y. And he hasn't seen us and we haven't seen him."

*   *   *

Early morning sunlight penetrated only in small patches through the tall silent trees and tangled underbrush. The cabin, one-roomed, dirt-floored, set in a cleft of immense tumbled rock, almost back against the cliff wall climbing behind, was well screened. Only a faint trail led from the door winding down a few hundred feet through thick relatively new growth under the great trees that had survived a long-ago fire and to the trickle of a tiny stream angling past. To the left of the cabin in a small corral made of ropes strung between trees were two horses, gaunt scrub mountain ponies. A third of a mile away, to the right along the mountain face and down, hidden in a ravine, were four horses, rein-tied to sturdy brush. Back by the cabin where the faint trail led up from the tiny stream into the cleft of tumbled rock four men moved quietly through the thick growth.

A man appeared in the cabin doorway, big and heavy and

freckled with the edge of some kind of dirtied bandage around his left shoulder and under the armpit showing above his shirt collar, carrying a bucket in his right hand. He looked out all around and yawned and started down the faint trail.

"Benton!" came the voice of Hat Henderson. "We got you covered!"

The man jumped, startled, and turned toward the direction of the voice, dropping the bucket and clawing at the gun in the holster by his side. He fired once, twice, and whirled, running back toward the cabin, and shots sounded out of the brush and he staggered and fell and hitched himself around, up on his left elbow, and fired again and more shots sounded and he dropped the gun and clutched at his body and rolled over on his back, limp and still.

Monte Walsh, long-legged, lean energy driving, was at the doorway of the cabin, gun in hand, peering in, and Dobe Chavez followed, one leap behind.

They turned back. "Empty," said Monte. They moved to where Hat Henderson and Chet Rollins stood looking down at the limp body.

"One," said Hat. "It's still unfinished."

Off to the left several hundred feet, lost in the tangle of growth between, a twig snapped, a small sound distinct in the stillness. They whirled and scattered, tearing leftward through the impeding brush. It was Chet Rollins who called. The others gathered by him. They looked down at the blanket lying in a small hollowed place among the bushes.

"Garcia," said Dobe Chavez, softly, bitterly. "He ees like the wolf."

"He's afoot," said Hat Henderson. "Monte, get the hosses. Chet, find if there's a shovel anywheres around the place. Dobe, let those ponies loose, we can't leave 'em penned here, while I see if there's anything we can chew on."

*   *   *

Noon and four men, leading horses, worked their slow way along and down the great jagged timber-clogged face of the mountain into the foothills, following the boot tracks found in the isolated soft spots. Miles back and up in the cleft of immense tumbled rocks the cabin rested in its own surrounding stillness, a pile of stones marking a lonely new grave.

They came to a half-mile stretch of slide rock and stopped briefly, baffled, and worked below and around it and found where the boot tracks led off again.

"Jeeeesus!" said Hat Henderson. "Hosses ain't much use in this country. But he's moving down. Once in the open an' we'll close in fast."

"I theenk," said Dobe Chavez, softly, bitterly, "Garcia he know what eet ees he do."

Early afternoon and they were mounted, moving faster now, well down, following over spring-greened grassland that rolled gently between strips of treed hollows. The boot tracks led straight, long-spaced as in running, with no attempt at concealment. The general level of the land rose with a seeming emptiness beyond and they topped what had been the horizon and there below, mile into mile like a great dark frozen sea stretched the cinder-black expanse of a long ago lava flow. Hard, brittle, caved and creviced, humped and broken with scant vegetation and that only in the great cracks like carved canyons streaking the surface, it reared in dark menace across the distances ahead.

They sat slumped in saddles staring out over it. "Jeeesus!" said Hat Henderson. "We couldn't trail an elephant out there. Half an hour an' the hosses'd be lame. Dobe, does he know this country?"

"Sí," said Dobe Chavez, softly, bitterly. "Eet ees hees country."

They sat slumped in saddles. "Hopeless," said Hat Henderson. "He can hole there long as he wants. Come out when and where he wants. An' likely this time he won't stop till he's south of the border." Hat sighed. "Well, anyways, we did half of a good job. As Cal said, I guess we got to leave it still unfinished business. Dobe, can you lead us anywheres we can get a real meal before we start back to the ranch?"

* * *

Early morning again and the first light sliding over the long levels shone in soft luminous gold on an open-end shed beside a small sagging corral and behind a small adobe house. The sun edged up, clearing the horizon, and the clean golden light soaked pink-tinged into the side wall of the house and the door of the house opened and a small elderly swarthy man came out, limping on a bent leg, and went to the well a short distance to one side. He lifted the bucket with its limp rope tied to the handle and let it drop with a small splash into the well. He pulled the bucket up and went with it back to the house.

In the open-end shed a man lying on a blanket laid over straw on the ground that was the floor opened his eyes. He pushed to his feet, lean, hard-muscled, stretching like a lazy youngish animal. He looked at the other figures lying asleep on their own blankets on the straw. Two. He frowned and stepped out of the shed and looked over at the corral. Three horses. A big rangy bay and a thick-necked black and a deep-chested leggy dun. He reached into the shed with one foot to nudge the leg of the big slope-shouldered man to the left.

"Hey, Hat," said Monte Walsh. "Where the hell's Dobe?"

*   *   *

And more days drifted over the big land and merged into weeks and three men had returned to the Slash Y, saying little and that straight to the point and going no further than the ranch itself, and men rode off repping at roundups and rode back bringing Slash Y strays and all of them rode out combing the range, selecting thin but fast-fattening four-year-old steers in a big herd to be delivered northeastward at Las Vegas. Late afternoon sun slanted down on busy preparations, gear being checked, horses being shod, the chuck wagon loaded.

One by one the men of the Slash Y stopped what they were doing, standing silent, looking out past the first corral and the other beyond into the far southland.

And out of the seeming limitless distances stretching two hundred and more miles to the border came a small bay, no longer neat and stocky but mud-caked and hollow-flanked, and the man in the saddle was thinned and dirt-stained and his black mustache was ragged fading into the stubble of days on his face and along one cheek was a raw red scabbing furrow that could have been cut by a bullet. Moving stiffly, he swung down and let the tired horse stand.

"Eees feeneesh," said Dobe Chavez and moved on to the bunkhouse and pulled off his worn boots and lay down on the third bunk on the right.

* * *

"Don't ask me to explain anything. I don't understand them. The men around here. Particularly the cowboy variety. I've been waiting on them in this store ever since a doctor sentenced me to time in this high dry country for my health two years ago next month. But I'll never understand them. They'll make it a killing fight over a nickel if they think maybe there's a chance they might be getting cheated and the next thing they'll be throwing away everything they have on something silly that takes their fancy. They'll kill a horse in the line of work and slam-bang cattle around and never even bat an eye. They'll watch a man be thrown sky high and come down to break a leg or worse and they'll laugh themselves sick at him being so clumsy before they bother to pick him up. They'll throw their ropes at anything that moves and almost choke to death just to see if they can run it down and tie it. They think it fun to watch a dogfight or a cockfight or any kind of fight. The bloodier the better. And then, like as not, they'll be all broken up, almost to blubbering like babies, if some little mangy pup or stray cat they have around gets hurt.

"Here's an example of what I mean. Happened earlier this year. Out at the Slash Y. I'm told that's a tough outfit that goes its own way and won't stand for interference from anybody. The way some of them behave in town here doesn't disprove that any. I've heard stories of things when they were first establishing their range I wouldn't dare repeat. Now listen to this. A big wolf out of the mountains was picking off some of their calves. I understand it even got a colt or two. They'd been hunting it and trying to trap it and they couldn't get it. Too smart for them I guess. Finally they brought in a man from up north somewhere, a professional trapper I suppose he was. And he had trouble too but he finally got it. After he tried other things he tried this. He caught a rabbit and kept it alive and tied it up by a hind leg so it could just reach the ground with its front legs. Hid some traps around. Idea was that the wolf would see or scent the rabbit and the

rabbit would jump and thrash around and the wolf would be so busy leaping at it he would stumble into a trap. And it worked. The wolf got the rabbit but a trap got the wolf. You'd think those men would have cheered that trapper. He'd outsmarted that wolf. He'd done what they couldn't do. But as soon as they heard about it they turned on him just like that. Wouldn't speak to him. Just gave him the cold shoulder until he was paid and was gone. I asked one of them why. All he said was and I remember it exactly: 'That wasn't no way to treat a rabbit and it a little old cottontail too.' "

Hattie
1876 – 1886

FOUR TIMES Monte Walsh crossed trails with Harriet Kupper, known to him and all too many other men of the big land as Yellow-Hair Hattie, and anyone can make of those four times anything his own experience and inclination indicate.

*   *   *

The first time was at Miles City. Monte was coming twenty and full of the joy and the juices of youth and he came into Montana territory riding swing with a Cross Bar trail herd. He was paid off with the others on delivery outside Miles City and he promptly adjourned into town to demonstrate to himself and anyone interested he knew how to spend the money in approved style. In the course of a few rather active days and nights he acquired the not very satisfactory cash acquaintance of several women in Madame Rose's entertainment parlor and by way of a short sweet brawl in one of the saloons the quick friendship of a rawhide Texan known as Powder Kent.

"Money's about gone," said Powder one evening. "Let's drift. It'll be getting cold here soon anyways. Start in the morning."

And a little later that same evening Monte, with only some jingly change left in his pocket, wandered for the first time into Thompson's Red Dog Saloon thinking of nothing more than liquid refreshment and saw Hattie.

What caught his attention across the big room and its evening activities was what usually caught attention, her hair. Plenty of it and all of it a soft natural yellow, the true color of the corn tassel. She wore it piled high in a pompadour

with the spangled heads of a few hairpins showing to catch
the lamplight and play this over the soft yellow sheen and it
did what she wanted it to do, kept attention away from the
fact that her face was plain and broad, coaxed into feminine
archness only by the artful use of powder and paint. She was
three or four years older than Monte and looked several more
than that and she was older than he would ever be in certain
knowledges and deep-rooted ways, but her full figure was
trim and definite in tight-waisted dress that took advantage of
every curve and an effortless inviting animal warmth seemed
to emanate from her.

She sat at a table with a prosperous-looking thickset man
in starched white shirt and black string tie who was talking
earnestly to her. She was obviously bored with the man and
his talk and between routine smiles at him to cover the bore-
dom her glance shifted around the room. It reached Monte,
twenty feet away, turning his head in sudden embarrassment
as he saw her looking at him, and it lingered on him, on the
lean young length of him and the clean young sweep of his
jaw and the hungry young vitality somehow singing in him
though relaxed and motionless against the bar.

The thickset man finished his talk, pointing at the clock
above the mirror behind the bar, and rose and took his coat
from the back of his chair and moved through the tables toward the front doorway, past and unaware of Monte, with
the air of a man of importance having important things to do.
The swinging doors swished behind him and over at her table
Hattie turned a bit in her chair, facing full toward Monte
looking now at her again, not looking away, and her head
moved, the movement barely perceptible, beckoning, and he
strode through the tables toward her. He sat on the chair the
man had left and he set his hat on the table and he was
aware of a pulse beating in one temple, strong and insistent,
and as he saw in her broad plain face something more than
the tired and perhaps amused acceptance of the few women
he had known in trail towns here and there he felt what he
had tried hard not to feel for several years now, that he was
young and shy and inadequate, and to cloak that he held his
head high at a jaunty angle and looked straight at her.

"I seen you day before yesterday," she said. "Breaking that
bronc for Jones at the livery stable."

"Shucks," said Monte, trying to be gallant, man of the world. "I been wasting my time. I ain't noticed you before."

"What was you thinking?" she said. "Over by the bar. Looking at me."

Monte hesitated, flushing under the sun- and wind-tan of his lean young face, and she leaned forward a little. "Tell me," she said. "Tell me straight. I want to know."

"Aw, shucks," said Monte. "I was just thinking I'd like to see it down, your hair I mean, and maybe just run my hands through it."

She sat back and a slight smile showed. "That's the nicest thing," she said, "any man ever said to me. Did you really think it?"

"Yes ma'am," said Monte. "And I'm thinking it again right now."

The slight smile held on her face. "Was that all you thought?" she said.

"No," said Monte. "No ma'am. That wasn't all." He could no longer meet her eyes and he squirmed on his chair. "Damn oh damn oh damn," he murmured, reaching for his hat.

"Wait," she said. "What's wrong?"

"Aw, shucks," said Monte. "I ain't got much more'n a dollar. Maybe not that. Chickenfeed." He started to rise.

"Wait," she said again. She leaned forward again, voice low. "Freddie's coming back at eleven, that's nearly two hours. You go out front here and slip around back. Thompson don't need to know. Whatever you have, that'll be enough."

And Monte, around back, feeling that pulse beat in his temple, saw the rear door open and Yellow-Hair Hattie step out, closing the door behind her, and she led along an alley past several small cabins to another of them and opened the door and moved on in. He stood in the doorway and saw a match spurt and a lamp be lit, low, dimly lighting the one front room with its old dresser and glinting brass bed, casting a faint glow on into the small kitchen beyond. He closed the door and fumbled to turn the old key in the lock, feeling again incredibly young and shy and inadequate, and as he swung slowly around from the door what he saw in the broad plain face regarding him gravely from under the piled soft yellow sheen in the lamplight annihilated all else but the immediate moment and he moved toward her, all male and confident in his maleness and ageless and more than adequate.

Later he stood motionless in dark shadow along the alley and watched the thickset man come through the rear doorway of the Red Dog and walk briskly to the cabin and rap softly and the cabin door open and the man enter and the door close. He stood there a few moments, gnawing on a knuckle, and he strode away and found Powder Kent rolled in blanket back of the livery stable and stirred him awake with one foot.

"You was playing poker," said Monte. "You win anything?"

"Twelve dollars," said Powder. "Enough to feed us a while moving south."

"Give me ten," said Monte. "We're staying another day. Me anyway."

"Aw, what the hell," said Powder. "You young ones sure stay itchy. All right, one more day." He was scrounging around under the blanket and one hand emerged, reaching up, holding a crumpled ten-dollar bill with one corner gone.

And the next evening, early, Monte was in the Red Dog and he talked briefly with Hattie, all male and dominant in his maleness, and later he stood by the bar, apparently interested only in the drink in his hand, and watched Hattie talk to the thickset man and send him away disappointed and perhaps angry and only a very little later Monte stood again by the rear door and Hattie came out and together they went to her cabin.

Time passed in the slow swinging hours of night and the first shimmers of dawn were sweeping up the sky when the cabin door opened and Monte Walsh, clad only in pants and socks, stepped out on the little doorstep and stretched, long and lazy, like a lean young animal. Hattie appeared in the doorway behind him, wrapped in an old kimono, broad plain face soft and relaxed and sleepy in frame of long loose hair the color of the corn tassel. Faint and far off a rooster crowed and Monte turned to her with a low chuckle sounding in his throat and he ran his hands through her hair over her shoulders and down her back, pressing her to him, and he stepped back bending some and scooped her up in his arms and eased through the doorway sideways holding her and on in, closing the door with one heel behind him.

And later, with the first direct light of the sun slipping under the curtains of the side window, he stood in the middle of the front room, in pants and socks again, bending to pull on his boots. Hattie, wrapped in the old kimono, handed him his shirt and he put this on and tucked it in. She picked up his gunbelt and stood still, holding it, looking at him.

"Aw, shucks," said Monte. "Ma'am. Hattie. I knew anything to say, I'd say it. But Powder's waiting. We got to be riding."

"I know," she said. "Your kind is always riding on." She handed the gunbelt to him and he buckled it on. She handed him his jacket and he slipped arms into it. She handed him his hat and he set this on his head, pulling the brim down.

Her hand was out again, holding a ten-dollar bill, crumpled and with one corner gone.

"Aw, shucks," said Monte. "That's yours."

"Where'd you get it?" she said. "That friend of yours?"

"That don't make no difference," said Monte.

"You ain't going to be owing anybody because of me," she said and reached and tucked the bill in a pocket of his jacket. She managed a small smile. "It's on the house. You ain't exactly like the rest of them. You're so—you're—oh, I don't know, you're so glad to be alive."

She took his arm and moved him toward the door. "So long, cowboy," she said. "See you again sometime."

* * *

The second time was at Cheyenne. Monte was coming twenty-two, a lean length of trail hand, a match for any man in the workings of his trade, and just about all feelings of shyness and inadequacy in just about any circumstances had long since left him. He came into Wyoming territory riding point with an Eight Bar Eight herd of range cows and was paid off on delivery with the rest of the crew. This was early evening and a few miles out and they all promptly adjourned into town and bellied up to the bar at the Hempstead House as the likeliest emporium for a start on the first-night celebration.

Monte leaned back against the bar, third drink in his hand,

looking lazily about. He started to raise the drink to his lips
and the hand stopped halfway. Across the crowding room he
saw a piled pompadour of soft yellow hair the color of the
late summer corn tassel.

Some of the sheen was gone and the natural color was fading in almost perceptible streaks. The lines of the broad plain
face were beginning to sag a bit and more powder and paint
were in artful use. The full figure was settling toward a suggestion of heaviness. But the same inviting animal warmth,
perhaps no longer quite effortless, seemed to emanate from
her. She sat at a table fingering a half-empty glass, smiling in
routine response at a thin dark-mustached man with checkered shirt and red bow tie across from her. There were other
women in the room, some younger, some more attractive, but
Monte Walsh saw only one.

He became aware of the drink in his hand and gulped it
down and set the small glass on the bar. He moved across the
room, shouldering past people, and he stood near her looking
down. "Hattie," he said. "Hattie."

Her head turned, looked up, and her face whitened under
its mask of makeup and her eyes widened. "Hello cowboy,"
she said and swift, involuntary, a deepening flush started
from the low-cut line of her dress and swept up her throat
and spread glowing over the broad plain face. "Well," she
said. "And if it ain't you."

"You're damn right it's me," said Monte, standing tall,
feeling taller. He jerked his head toward the man in the
checkered shirt. "Let's shake him."

"Now just a minute," said the man, pushing his chair back
and bringing into view the butt of a gun stuck under his belt.
"I been buying—"

"Please Bert," said Hattie, leaning forward. "Please. Take
it easy. He's an old friend of mine I ain't seen in—"

"Too blamed friendly," said the man. "I'm not going to—"

"Quit yapping," said Monte, serene and adequate. "I'm
here and I'm a-howling."

The man said nothing. He was reaching for his gun and
had it. But Monte was leaping to him and Monte's left hand
clamped on the wrist and wrenched and the gun fell clattering
and Monte's right hand had him by the shirt collar yanking
him up to his feet. Monte let go and bored in, fists hammering, careless of the answering blows, and the man went down.

Monte hauled him up and heaved him past the next table toward the bar and Sugar Wyman of the paid-off trail crew coming forward who promptly caught him and wrapped arms around him.

"Well now, Monte," drawled Sugar, holding fast. "Is this thing bothering you?"

"Not any more," said Monte. "Get rid of him somewheres."

"Come on boys," said Sugar to others of the crew gathering around. "Let's have a little fun an' run this thing outa town."

Monte turned back to Hattie sitting still and quiet watching him and he forgot the dwindling clamor in the big room and the other men crowding in boisterous bunch out the front door and he reached with one hand and moved it gently over the soft yellow sheen. "Come along, Hattie," he said. "We're getting out of here."

Quiet, obedient, she rose and he took her arm. "No goddamned back doors," he murmured and led her to the front and out. "Where's your place?" he said.

Quiet, obedient, she took his arm now and led through the dimness of evening around the building and a short way along a lane and to a small frame shack and she opened the door and moved in ahead of him. He stood in the doorway and again he saw a lamp lit, low, faintly lighting the one room and the curtained alcove for a kitchen. He closed the door and stood with back against it, aware of the pulse beating in one temple, strong and insistent, and he was a little ashamed of its strength and insistence, and he stood still, against the door.

"I ain't in such a hurry this time, Hattie," he said. "I got to have it straight." He stepped over to the one dresser and reached into his pants pockets and emptied their contents on the top of the dresser. A roll of bills and several silver dollars and some change. "Hattie," he said. "There ain't a-going to be anyone else, as long as that lasts."

She stood by the lamp, broad plain face smudged some under its single glory of fading gold, and for the first time ever aloud she used his name. "Monte," she said. "Monte. All right, Monte."

That was the way it was as long as the money lasted. They were together most of the time. They went out to breakfast and lunch and supper together until Hattie said that was too expensive and she bought groceries and prepared meals in the tiny curtained alcove. Monte sat across a spindly little table from her and ate whatever she prepared, not much aware of what it was, and he talked, he could always talk to Hattie, perhaps because she listened so well, smiling softly at his young eagerness, not saying much herself, listening and letting him talk. Once Monte rented a gentle horse and a side saddle for her and he swung up on his big rangy black and they rode out with a picnic lunch into low hills where few people went and they found a small valley with cloaking trees and out there in the great spaces of his big land he forgot and she was willing to forget the lunch for an hour and more on the carpet of grass under the trees with tiny patches of sunlight filtering down and glowing on her hair and that was the one thing he would remember longer than anything else. And once he rented a buggy and smart bay team and took her driving through the growing town oblivious of the amused and sometimes indignant or contemptuous stares of people passed and he was proud of the fine-stepping team and of her beside him content to be there. But once only with such things because Hattie said they were too expensive. It was Hattie who worried about the money, counting the days. They had their time together and he never knew what it cost her, slipping away the first morning while he still slept, in promises to the man who owned the Hempstead House and her shack.

Two weeks and a day and the money was almost gone and with it, unknown to him, that she had emptied out of a knotted old stocking from her battered little trunk in the back of the curtained alcove. And in the afternoon, saying nothing to her, leaving her white-faced and wondering in the shack, Monte strode away and to the livery stable and stood with the proprietor by the corral beside it talking with him about the big rangy black munching hay just inside the rails and after a while Monte strode back to the shack carrying his saddle and bridle and blanket roll and laid these in a corner and stepped to the bed and dropped another small batch of bills on the cover. He stood there, tight-lipped, looking at her still and quiet on the chair where he had left her, and what he saw in the broad plain face loosened his lips and drew him

toward her to stroke the soft fading sheen of her hair. "Hattie," he said. "Hattie. What in hell's got into you?"

So more days passed and Monte, all unknowing, was tight-
lipped often now and somtimes, hardly aware of what he was
doing, while Hattie was busy in the tiny alcove, he paced the
small open width of the shack, eleven feet this way and turn,
eleven feet that way and turn, and Hattie remembered a
mountain lion she had seen once in a wooden cage at Miles
City and the same lean vitality and lithe power of movement
and she would be proud that this was here with her, wanting
to be with her, and a warmth would rise in her that there
were times, not often yet times, when she could amost match
its strong insistent drive to her, and then she would think, not
any clear formulation of thought but more a slow seeping of
knowledge, of the cage, of the wooden bars blocking, restrict-
ing, confining.

So more days passed and summer was waning and Monte
took to spending the afternoons over by the stockyards, occasionally lending a hand with the work there, taking the joshing of other men tight-lipped but always with a ready come-
back, and one of these afternoons, late, troubled and unable
to stay away, Hattie went looking for him. He sat on the top
rear rail of the last big pen and when she approached and
spoke softly to him he did not hear. He was staring into distance at the far dust of a trail herd coming and she drew
back, watching, and time crawled along and the herd neared
and several men came riding on ahead and swerved toward
Monte and he leaped down shouting and they all but fell out
of saddles to pummel him in vigorous good humor and their
voices rose in hearty and obscene epithets.

Hattie turned and walked slowly away, feeling the weight
of the years in the slow settling of her once trim figure. She
was almost at the shack when footsteps, hurrying, sounded
behind her and Monte had her by the arm. "What d'you
know," he said, cheerful, incredibly young and alive.
"There's a Cross Bar outfit come along. Old Man Hendricks.
I've rode with that brand."

They were at the doorstep. "What's for supper?" said
Monte. "Damned if I ain't got an appetite."

"It's not fixed yet," she said, sharp and a bit defiant. "I'm
me. I can go traipsing around too."

"Shucks," said Monte, taking her by the shoulders to turn

her facing him. "Sure you can. Come to think about it, I'm hungry all right. But not for food." And again, as once before, he scooped her up in his arms and he kicked the door open and eased through, sideways, holding her, and closed it with one heel behind him.

Supper was late that night, quite late, and they were still sitting by the little spindly table when what Hattie had always known would come came in the form of a rapping on the door and the voice of Old Man Hendricks. "Monte. Monte Walsh. Come on out here a minute."

Hattie sat motionless on her chair. There was no need to move. Monte had not closed the door and after the first exchange their voices rose and she could hear them talking outside.

". . . Like I say, Monte, I sure hate to be botherin' you this way. No, that's a lie. I'm right glad you're around to be bothered. I been short-handed ever since Chalkeye got hisself tromped some in a run a few weeks back. Had to leave him down below Denver. Now Shorty, you know him, always edgy he is, well he has to go mixin' with some damn mule skinner an' get hisself cut up. I can skip sayin' the rest of the boys took care of that skunk of a skinner so he won't be cuttin' any more for quite a spell but Shorty's laid up an' it leaves me in a hole."

"Shucks," said Monte. "Just look around town is all."

"What d'you think I been doin'? Can't find anyone loose around here right now I'd trust far as I can spit into the wind. Not a real rider among 'em. I got two men gone an' that's quite a hole. It'll take a right good man to fill it, meanin' you."

"Aw, shucks," said Monte. "I don't know. I ain't been figuring on anything like this. Not for a while anyways."

"Why not? I hear you're not doin' much of anythin' these days. You tied down?"

"No-o-o," said Monte. "No-o-o. Not exactly."

"Come on then. Tell you what. I saw that black of yours at the stable. Heard you had to sell it. Ill just buy it an' throw it in as a kind of bonus."

Silence. Then Monte's voice with a small wailing note of desperation in it. "Quit it, Hendricks. Why don't you just quit talking."

"Because I got to have you, Monte. I only got five weeks

left to make it on to Boise. Or forfeit the price. I lose this I'm licked. I'm countin' on you, Monte. You never let me down yet."

Silence again. "Goddamn it!" said Monte, desperate. "You ain't the only one I got to worry about letting down."

"Her, Monte? I hear she's regular, a good sport. She knows how things are. Why, doggone it, Monte, I never thought I'd see you hobbled by a skirt."

"Christ a'mighty!" said Monte, almost shouting. "Shut up before I bust you one! Get out of here and leave me alone!"

And inside the shack Hattie's shoulders straightened a bit for a few proud seconds before they sagged again in slow seeping knowledge of the inevitable, if not now the certainty of later and not so much later as soon, and of the rising tensions and bickerings slipping into meanness that could come between, and when Monte came in, tight-lipped, eyes hard, he was surprised to find her the same.

"So I hobble you, do I?" she said, voice tight, brittle. "So I'm something you got to worry about, am I? You got another think coming. I'm me. I can get men better'n you any day I want. You go after him. You tell him you're riding."

Monte stared at her, the line of his jaw stiffening, jutting. "Hattie! I thought you—"

"You been taking too much for granted around here. You said long as it lasted and I agreed. Well, it's about gone. I got to think of myself. I ain't getting anywhere cooped up here with you."

"Goddamn it, Hattie," said Monte. "If that's the way you—"

"That's the way. I ain't saying it ain't been . . . been something to remember. But a woman like me's got to look out for herself. She can't go . . . go getting soft on any of you . . . of you . . . of you come-and-go deadbeats that . . . that never have any real money and think . . . and think . . . just because . . ."

"Quit it, Hattie," said Monte. "I got it. I'm blowing." Moving with swift precision, he took his hat from its nail in the wall and put it on, pulling the brim down, his gunbelt from another nail and buckled it around, his jacket from another and slipped into it.

She sat on her chair, unable to move, rigid in her own resolution, and she watched him move to a corner of the room and take his blanket roll and bridle in one hand, his saddle with the other.

He stopped in the doorway against the darkness of the outside. "So long, Hattie," he said. "You been mighty good to me."

She managed to say it. "So long, cowboy. See you again sometime."

And in the first light of morning she climbed the long rise behind the shack, past the quickie structures of the growing town, and stood still and quiet and saw the long straggling line of cattle stringing out northwestward and watched till it was lost beyond the limits of vision the tiny dwindling shape that was Monte Walsh on a big rangy black, a match for any man in the workings of his trade, where he belonged, moving into distance across the big land.

*   *   *

The third time was at Trinidad. Monte was coming twenty-six and he had been siding Chet Rollins for three years now and the two of them were Slash Y down in New Mexico territory. They came into Colorado with foreman Hat Henderson and two more of the home crew and Sunfish Perkins along to do the cooking, the six of them taking a small herd on consignment up and over Raton Pass and on to a rendezvous with a government agent near Trinidad. They delivered and collected and Hat counted out six small piles of accumulated pay and tucked the rest of the proceeds into a money belt he wore under his shirt and suggested drawing straws but Sunfish said he would take the short one without drawing and stay with the wagon and extra horses and the others jogged away into town for some celebrating, not much because this had been a short drive, but concentrated because they would be leaving in the morning.

They did not think much of Trinidad, it being mostly a mining town and coal mining at that, but as they moved from bar to bar, testing the liquor, they began to feel better and then they hit one that had enough of the right flavor and suggestion of possible things happening.

Monte leaned back against the bar, fifth drink of the evening in his hand, and looked about. Chet started to say something to him and he did not hear it. Across the room he saw a piled pompadour of yellow hair.

Not the soft color of the corn tassel now, yellower, unnatural, and the sheen had the streaky metallic gloss of the artificial. Under it the lines of the broad plain face sagged definitely, almost a grimace behind the calculated layer of powder and paint. The once trim figure had settled into heaviness, bulging against the tight corset under the low-cut dress. She sat alone at a small table in a corner tracing with a finger in spilled liquid on the table in front of her, and only a worn weariness seemed to emanate from her.

Monte stared at her though the warmth of the whisky in him and years dropped away from him and he saw only what he wanted to see and memories meshed in his mind and he moved toward her, unaware of the movement. "Hattie," he said, slipping into the chair across the table from her. "Hattie."

She raised her eyes from the trailing finger and shock showed in them, fading into full awareness. "Hello cowboy," she said. "If I dared do it, I'd say it was you."

"It's me all right," said Monte. "And I ain't forgot. I ain't forgot anything. You was always good to me, Hattie. Good to me. And good for me." He leaned forward, talking, he could always talk to Hattie, and she leaned forward too, listening, not saying much, and it was almost like old times, the two of them across a small table together and she felt the lean vital aliveness of him reaching again to her and the harsh lines of her face under the mask of makeup softened and her eyes brightened and like a slow tide rising in her an echo of the old inviting animal warmth seemed to emanate from her.

Monte leaned back in his chair, aware of a pulse beating in one temple. "Hattie," he said, low, eager. "Have you got a place here?"

Her face paled and she looked down, tracing again with one finger in the spilled liquid. "I've got . . . I've got a room in back."

"Lovely," said Monte, all male and dominant in his maleness. "Just lovely."

She did not raise her head. The broad plain face was dead white behind its mask. Her throat worked and the words came out, dull, tired. "No. Not you, Monte. Not you."

He stared at her and slow seconds ticked past and her

voice came again, harsh, bitter. "Leave me alone. I'm sorry I ever seen you. Leave me alone."

And a little later Monte stood by the bar, morose and sullen, paying scant attention to Chet beside him trying to cheer him some, and he stiffened in sudden flaring anger as he saw Hattie with a dirty coal-dusted miner moving toward the rear door of the room.

Monte too was in motion, hands clenching into fists, and Chet's arms clamped around and held him. Behind the bar the bartender looked at them and then toward the rear of the room. "Poor Hattie," he said. "She has to take what she can get these days. Most everybody knows about her."

The bartender picked up a glass and began polishing it. "Yep," he said. "It don't show much yet. But she's visiting the doc twice a week."

A few minutes later Monte Walsh and Chet Rollins strode down the street and stopped by the little frame house with the cupola the bartender had described. "All you've got," said Monte. "All of it." Chet reached in his pockets as Monte reached in his and Monte went up to the door and knocked and when it opened a short plump goateed elderly man was surprised as a fistful of bills and change was forced into his hands.

"For Hattie," said Monte. "Hattie Kupper. Yellow-Hair Hattie. Do the best you can for her, Doc, the best you can."

*　*　*

The fourth time was at Las Vegas. Monte was coming thirty, losing a little of his hair up from his forehead from always wearing a hat and he was adding some flesh to his leanness but all of it rawhide hard. He and Chet were still Slash Y and Chet and the others were out working somewhere and he was alone at the ranch headquarters except for Skimpy Eagens in the cookhouse and he was busy teaching proper manners to a big-boned young sorrel in the small corral when the word reached him.

It came by jackrabbit telegraph, from rider to rider across the big land, not one of them thinking anything unusual of going twenty to thirty miles out of his way to pass it along. Chalkeye Ferrero, currently with the Triple Seven to the north, brought it the last lap to Monte.

He came fast and his horse was well lathered, but when he swung down he was in no apparent hurry. He perched himself on a top rail and offered remarks on the sorrel and the weather and the general condition of the range. Such amenities out of the way, he pushed his hat up and talked some more.

"Hattie," he said. "Hattie Kupper. You remember her. All that yella hair. She's took bad up at Vegas. Out of her head most of the time. Maybe she won't make it."

Chalkeye took off his hat and put it on again, pushing it up, and he looked off into space. "Yeah," he said. "Out of her head. Damned if I see any sense to it, but she keeps asking for somebody she calls Monte."

Chalkeye thought of a few more things to say but he would have been wasting his time saying them. Monte Walsh, tight-lipped, was dropping off the sorrel, stripping his gear from it, striding away, opening the gate into the big corral and entering. Chalkeye shrugged and jumped down outside and stripped off his own saddle and bridle and turned his horse into the small corral and watched it roll away sweat in the dust. He hoisted his saddle on a rail and hung his bridle on a post. He ambled over to the cookhouse and poked his head in the doorway. "Hi, Skimpy," he said. "I'm figurin' on stayin' for supper." He stepped up into the doorway and turned to see Monte Walsh on a deep-chested leggy dun with a small bag of grain tied to his saddle horn and a blanket roll lashed behind ramming northeastward into the first mile of the one hundred forty across rugged almost trackless terrain to Las Vegas.

That was midafternoon. Early the next evening the dun, gaunted and bone weary but still responding to the urgency along the reins, staggered into Las Vegas and Monte left it in good hands at a livery stable and asked sharp questions here and there to little purpose until he finally found the right doctor at home at the supper table.

"Easy now," said the doctor. "I'll take you to her soon enough. There's no hurry. I've had her moved where I can keep an eye on her. You're a pretty sight, you are. You're going to clean up and unwind a bit and join me for some food or I'll be having you for a patient too."

And after Monte had scrubbed the dust out of the light bristles on his face in the kitchen and gulped some coffee and food, not tasting any of it, the doctor led him down a short hallway and opened the door to a small back room.

"See what I mean," said the doctor gently. "There's no hurry. She doesn't recognize anyone."

In the light of the one lamp on a washstand she lay on an old Spanish bedstead, wasted body shapeless and lumpy under the bedclothes, eyes open and staring, blinking now and again and staring, unseeing, upward, mouth sagging open and breath coming in long slow labored sounds. The broad plain face was gray-toned, shrunken, collapsed. Monte would not have known her except for the hair straggling out on the pillow, all artificiality gone, dull gray with the few lingering still-defiant streaks running through it the color of the harvest corn tassel.

The doctor saw Monte's face. "What did you expect?" he said, a kind of resigned anger in his voice. "The life she's had. Her lungs are all shot. She's rotted inside with what you men gave her. Now I'm not sure but I think it's cancer killing her. She has nothing left to fight it. All I can do is try to keep her resting easy."

"Goddamn it," said Monte Walsh. "And she made a man of me. What there is of me."

The doctor turned away. "You can go now," he said and a small dark Spanish woman who had been sitting silent on a chair in a corner rose and brushed past them by the doorway and was gone.

Monte moved on in and stood by the bed. "Hattie," he said. "Hattie." He stood, staring down, and the doctor brought the chair from the corner and Monte sank onto it, leaning forward. "Hattie," he said. "Hattie. It's me. Monte."

Her mouth closed some and her breathing quickened and her head turned a little toward him and out of a dark drugged somewhere a focus came briefly into her eyes. Her body shook under the bedclothes, struggling to achieve something, and did, and one hand emerged, thin and mottled, and moved clutching along the cover. Monte reached and her fingers closed on his hand, grasping, holding. A long sigh came from her and her eyes closed.

The doctor bent down. "Sleeping," he said. "The first time in days. You're better than anything I can do for her."

And the hours crept along to the rhythm of the slow labored breathing and the doctor left soon, returning now and again from catnaps in his own bedroom and shaking his head and leaving again, and Monte Walsh sat on the chair, bent forward, one hand out on the bed clutched in thin mottled fingers. And the hours crept along and then he was aware, in slow emergence, that the lamp had burned down and out and another dimness filled the room, the first light of day through the one window, and that he had toppled sideways against the edge of the bed and that someone was disentangling the thin fingers from their hold on his hand and laying the thin arm again under the covers and pulling these up over the still set face.

"She's gone," said the doctor.

And a little later Monte gulped coffee again, not tasting it. "Doc," he said. "I came away fast. I ain't got much of anything on me. But I sure—"

"No," said the doctor. "Everything's taken care of. She had some money in an old stocking in her trunk. She's paying her own way to the grave."

Monte wandered out through the old town, aimless, wandering, and he passed a few men he knew who, speaking once or twice and seeing his face, left him alone. Along toward noon he joined the meager procession following the wagon to the old Spanish cemetery and when the earth was heaped in the small mound he wandered away again, aimless, and behind a low picket fence he saw a row of flowers along the front of a house and he stepped over the fence and moved along the row, snapping the stems. A man came around the side of the house, starting to shout, and stopped, seeing the close-triggered deadliness confronting him, and backed away and Monte stepped over the fence again, carrying the flowers, and to the cemetery again and laid them on the small mound of earth.

"Hattie," he said. "Hattie." And suddenly he turned away, moving more rapidly now, aiming, and went into the first saloon along the main street and to the bar.

A half hour and he stood there by the bar, unsteady, swaying, watched in admiring fascination by the bartender, and still the hidden ache in him held out against the whisky and he fumbled in his pockets. Nothing. Movement at the blurred edge of vision turned him, swaying, and a few feet away stood Chet Rollins, worn and dusty and unshaven, holding out a hand and on the hand a few crumpled bills.

"Buy it by the bottle," said Chet.

Monte wandered, swaying, out through the old town, a bottle in his hand, and Chet followed, leading a thick-necked black, tired and gaunted, and Monte stopped well out past the last buildings on a low rise where the ground fell away into the harsh broken beauty of the big land beyond. He sank down, sitting, and raised the bottle and wiped a hand across his mouth and stared into distance and raised the bottle again. It was half empty when he sank back, limp and sodden, and liquid gurgled from the bottle as it slipped to the ground and long heavy snores came from him.

Chet carried him to the shade of a clump of brush oak and took the blanket from behind the saddle of the black and rolled him onto it and folded it over him. Chet stripped the gear from the black and picketed it on fair grass nearby and he walked back into town and came again after a while riding a leggy dun with a small partly-filled flour sack hanging from the saddle horn. He stripped down the dun and picketed it too nearby. He sat by Monte and stared off into distance and the hours crept past and the sun slanted down the sky and dusk dropped gently.

Chet shook himself and went over and picked up the bottle. There was still some liquid in it. He drank this and came back and sat beside Monte still sleeping and after a while he went and got the blanket from behind Monte's saddle and rolled himself in it beside Monte and he too slept.

He woke with the first hint of dawn and built a small fire and took from the flour sack the makings of a small breakfast. Whistling softly to himself, he fussed about the fire and the smell of strong coffee drifted on the morning wind. He walked over and stirred Monte with a boot toe.

"Come and get it," he said. "A little food and you'll be able to travel."

*   *   *

"I reckon Monte holds the record. Seven times I think it is. Yep, this is the seventh time Doc's had to do some repair work on him. You can't go taking on every four-footed powder keg that comes along like he does an' go looking for 'em too without getting bunged up an' stove in an' sat on an' wrung out right often. Seems like he can't hear of a hoss

*somebody's said's only fit for dog meat an' he has to go fuss
with it an' like as not wind up making a good working animal
of it. Why, I got one in my string right now the whole
blamed Triple Seven was shy of, claimed it was too mean to
let live. Monte got hold of it an'—well, it's my roping hoss
these days an' I don't need to go explaining what that means.*

*"No, it ain't bad this time. Collarbone an' one ear in need
of some sewing. Fool hoss tried to roll on 'im. Not bad at all.
Shucks, worst time I ever seen him bunged up it wasn't a
hoss an' it wasn't a cow an' it wasn't anything like that at all.
He did it hisself. All by hisself. With the help of a little old
pair of roller skates.*

*"I an' Chet was with him that time. Over at Albuquerque
for something or other. They had a skating place there, new
thing it was, an' it was mighty pop'lar with the young ones.
Kind of a big barn with a wood floor. Back end of it stuck
out over a gulley an' was up on stilts. There was a gal
Monte'd took a fancy to. Nothing to it but she's got to go
skating. She was good at it too. So we're standing there
watching her an' right soon a young feller's going round an'
round with her an' he's cuddling her right close an' putting
his arm around her. Monte don't take to that an' he bristles
some. Don't look so hard to me, he says. I'll just take a fling
at that myself, he says. Gets a couple skates from the man
that runs the place an' cinches 'em on tight. Starts out.*

*"Laugh? I figured I'd have to hold Chet up he was laugh-
ing so he couldn't stand only I wouldn't of been no help because I was doing the same. Them skates throwed Monte so
fast he looks around to see what hit 'im. Tries to get up an'
they throws him again. Gets mad an' starts working at it for
real an' he's all over the floor like a pinwheel an' it looks like
he's got seventeen legs an' maybe as many arms an' all of 'em
flying at oncet. Everybody else stops waltzing around an' gets
back out of the way. He sure needs the room for the fight
he's giving them two little old skates. He bounces off one wall
an' next thing he's bouncing off another an' his legs're going
so fast trying to stay under where they belong they're just a
blur. He sits down hard an' that stops 'im for a minute. He
sees that gal laughing at 'im. He sees that young feller laughing too an' pointing at 'im for her benefit. I reckon it was
that pointing did it. He helps hisself up an' he heads for that
young feller to try an get his hands on 'im. Don't know*

whether he was getting the knack of it or was plain lucky but he gets to moving an' stays upright. Legs're flying wild but he's making progress. The young feller slips away an' Monte's after 'im, picking up speed. Young feller ducks aside an' Monte goes sailing right on. Can't stop. Can't turn. Don't know how to make them skates behave. Just goes sailing on. Smack into a window in the end of that barn an' right on through an' into that gulley behind.

"*I an' Chet measured it after we gathered 'im up. He went sixteen feet out from that window an' down before he lit.*"

Harmonizing
1887

THE TWO COW PONIES ambled easily along the wagon trace, not hurrying, not loafing, simply reaching in steady rhythm into the miles of the big land. A roadrunner skipped out of bordering rabbit brush and jerked tail jauntily under their noses and skittered on ahead, exactly matching their pace. It spurted forward in challenge, sending tiny splats of dust flicking back, and looked around in stride at them serenely ignoring it and slowed again to their pace. It tried again, sprinting forward with flourishings of tail, and looked back again and in disgust swept off to one side and disappeared in a maze of cactus.

The two cow ponies jogged steadily along. Monte Walsh kneed his leggy dun closer to Chet Rollins's thick-necked black. He looped reins around his saddle horn and reached and took a small leather pouch from Chet's shirt pocket. "I'll bet," he said, taking a small paper from his own shirt pocket and sprinkling tobacco from the pouch along it. "I'll just bet you don't know what's agitating around in my mind along about now."

Chet reached to regain the pouch. He began filling a stubby pipe. "You just feel like talking," he said. "I couldn't miss."

"Too damn smart," said Monte. He extracted a match from a shirt pocket and struck it on blunt fingernail. "Go ahead anyways."

"Simple," said Chet. He extracted his own match and cupped it lit to light the pipe. "You're thinking of coffee instead of whisky."

"Well, what d'you know," said Monte. He watched two

thin streamers of smoke drift from his nose. "How'd you figure that?"

"You never quit trying," said Chet. He blew a small smoke ring and tried to poke a finger through it as it drifted back past him. "Furthermore you brushed your hat. And furthermore again you're wearing that fancy belt."

Monte looked down at the soft deerskin belt that circled his waist through the loops of his faded old levis and under the heavier overriding angled-down leather of his gunbelt. He patted the turquoise-studded silver buckle. "Pretty, ain't it?" he said.

The two cow ponies ambled easily along. A jackrabbit broke from behind a low clump of mesquite, soared in a spy hop, and was away in ten-foot leaps. "It's pretty, yes," said Chet. "But I ain't so sure your wearing it is. You get an Indian girl sweet on you. She gives you that belt. And you wear it to impress somebody else."

"Shucks," said Monte. "All's fair. Ain't that how the saying goes?"

The two cow ponies jogged in tireless unvarying rhythm. On ahead a hawk rose from the remnants of some small creature and soared upward for height. Chet leaned his head back, looking up, stubby pipe poking straight up, and watched the hawk swing in a lazy circle waiting for the disturbance below to pass. "And I'll bet," he said, "you get about as far as before." A bit of ash from the pipe fell in one eye and he dropped his head, blinking, rubbing at the eye. "Which," he said, "is just about precisely nowhere."

The two cow ponies stopped on the crest of a low rise. Below them, down the slope, out of distance on the right, into distance on the left, ran the stage road, becoming for several hundred yards the main street of the unorganized town of Harmony.

Monte Walsh stubbed out the tiny stump of his cigarette on stirrup leather. He fixed his hat more firmly on his head and straightened a bit in the saddle. He turned his head to look at Chet.

Chet Rollins sighed. He knocked ashes and still-glowing bits of tobacco out of the pipe against one boot. He settled his own hat more firmly. "All right," he said. "If that's the way you want to play it."

Monte Walsh slapped spurs to the leggy dun. It leaped into

stride, picking up speed down the slope. Alongside it, sweeping in stout-rumped powerful rush, pounded the thick-necked black.

The two cow ponies hit the stage road and swung along it, racing into town. "Yow-eee!" yelled Monte, pulling his gun and firing into the air. "Harmony, here we come!" Companion shots sounded beside him. The two cow ponies, leaping high at the shots, bucking in midair, raced through town.

An old man in too-big clothes that seemed even older dozing in a rickety chair on the little porch of a general store jerked awake, focused watery old eyes on the racing disturbance, and raised one old hand and slapped it down on a knee. A plumpish man wearing patent-leather button shoes and neatly pressed striped pants with a once-white cloth tied around his neck and the waxed tips of a mustache showing through lather on his face appeared in the doorway of the little frame barbershop. A few leathery faces under assorted wide-brimmed hats moved into view above the swinging doors of the three which were open of Harmony's four saloons. A bony bay between the shafts of an ancient wagon by the blacksmith shop perked, considered the possibility of some action of its own, thought better of it, and gave a plain pretense of hearing nothing.

Swirling dust and hammering hoofs swept on along the street.

Two figures seated on the ground, knees hunched up, leaning back against the wall of an adobe shack, hidden from scrutiny by blankets up around shoulders and huge hats tilted far forward, raised their heads, identified the nuisance, looked at each other, shrugged shoulders, and relapsed into somnolence again. Several whinnies came from the small corral behind the livery stable. On the veranda of the combination hotel and office building two men, one distinguished by a city hat and a gold watch chain, the other by a leather vest bearing a tarnished badge, stopped talking and turned to survey the street. Beside the building a good-sized black bear tethered by a chain to a ragged cottonwood roused from apparent slumber, rose on its hindlegs, batted mechanically at the air with its forepaws, stopped that abruptly, grunted disgustedly, and lay down again.

The two cow ponies reached the other end of town, reared, pivoted neatly, and started back along the street through the dust of their previous passing. A shot sent dirt flying over a mangy yellow dog lying by the veranda of the combination hotel and office building and the dog yelped shrilly and fled around the far side of the building. The watch-chain man on the veranda flinched back toward the open doorway behind him. "What's going on?" he said. A faint smile twitched the lips of the leather vest man. "Slash Y," he said. "In for the mail."

Another shot flicked dust over the shiny patent-leather shoes of the man in the barbershop doorway. He ducked back out of sight.

The old man leaned forward on his rickety chair and watched a leggy dun and a thick-necked black cavort in circles, bucking, crow-hopping, for his particular benefit. He raised both old hands and slapped them down on his knees. "Ride 'em, boys!" he yelled in a high quavery voice. "Ride 'em!"

They lined out again along the street and swung again in circles in front of a small adobe building that defied its general sagging shabbiness with a freshly painted screen door and a calico curtain at the one front window. The black subsided some but the dun surprised itself with its own exuberance, spinning, dancing on hindlegs, exploding in various directions at once. It finished with a high-tail flourish and dropped down by the tie rail, the black beside it, and the two, the immediate job done, looked somewhat sheepishly at each other and promptly drooped, except for mildly heaving sides, into a wise and a patient lethargy.

Monte Walsh and Chet Rollins swung down and loosened cinches. "Think she was watching?" said Monte.

"You're going at this thing wrong," said Chet. "But if it pleases you any, I saw that window curtain move."

Monte pushed his hat up at a jaunty angle, hitched his gunbelt higher on one side to expose more of the deerskin belt and its silver buckle, and led the way to the screen door.

The interior of the little square building, insulated against the outside sun by its adobe walls, was relatively dim and cool. Facing the door, extending almost from wall to wall with narrow passageway around the ends, was a wooden counter with eight stools along it, evenly spaced and fastened to the floor. A few feet behind the counter rose a white-washed partition fronted with shelves on which lay a meager collection of chipped dishes, chiefly plates and bowls and cups, a low wooden box containing worn knives and forks and spoons, a pile of reasonably clean pieces of flour sacking for counter cloths, a dried rattlesnake skin, a stuffed horned toad mounted on a small wooden block, several dog-eared magazines and a flyswatter. A narrow doorway in the partition gave a slice view of the rear room, disclosing several iron pots and a huge frying pan hanging on the back wall and the corner of a big old cookstove. Sounds suggesting some kind of meat-chopping operation came from elsewhere behind the partition. The subtly increasing aroma of simmering chili drifted through both rooms.

Also behind the counter, near the left end by a side window, perched on another stool not fastened down, sat a young woman of pleasing proportions pleasantly accentuated by a tight skirt and a frilly starched shirtwaist whose high currently fashionable collar poked up under a firm chin. The general effect of her face, in the mode portrayed in the magazines on the shelf, was upward, from the chin to neat almost precise mouth, to pert uptilted nose, to eyebrows plucked or trained to rise peaked in perpetual surprise, and to high surmounting upsweep of sleeky brushed brown hair above. A magazine was open on her lap. Something in it had a strong hold on her attention. Not even the squeaking of the screen door swerved her from it.

Monte Walsh stood by the door, hands hooked in the deerskin belt, masculine charm exuding from him. "Howdy Miss Hazel, ma'am," he said, cheerful, hopeful. "Nice day. Outside and inside. Specially inside."

Miss Hazel did not look up. "Go away," she said. "We won't be serving supper for at least an hour."

"Shucks," said Monte. "Anytime's coffee time, ain't it?" He bounced forward, arched a leg over and eased onto a center stool. Chet, following, took one beside him.

Miss Hazel moaned softly. She laid the magazine on a shelf, left her stool, clunked two cups on the counter, swerved with a flounce of skirt to go into the rear room. Monte watched the retreating hip action with approval. "A very nice day," he murmured.

Miss Hazel returned with a big enamelware coffeepot and sloshed a dark fierce-looking liquid into the cups. "Sugar?" she said.

"Shucks, no," said Monte, beaming. "Just dip a finger in and sweeten it."

Miss Hazel sniffed her disdain, set the pot down, retired to her stool and her magazine. Chet Rollins sipped his coffee and studied a calendar on the wall presenting a lurid picture of a resplendent cowboy in buffalo chaps whirling a wide loop from the back of a snorting horse in pursuit of several ferocious longhorns.

"Doggone it," said Monte, plaintive, appealing. "This is five times I've been in here and you ain't even smiled at me once. You better watch out, Miss Hazel, or I'll be getting the notion maybe you don't even like me."

Miss Hazel popped off her stool. The magazine fell on the counter. She put her hands on her hips. "Well," she said. "Well, I just never. I'll have you know, Mister Monte Walsh, that I don't like or dislike you for the simple reason I never think about you enough to do either one. I have better things to do with my mind than to go thinking about any of you deadbeat cowboys that never have much more'n a nickel to spend on anything except whisky and think if you go shooting around and bucking on a horse why then a girl'll just think you're just wonderful."

Miss Hazel warmed to her subject. "And I'll have you know, Mister Monte Walsh, that I know all about you. Maybe you are about the best bronc rider anywheres around and I suppose that means something but you're always in trouble of some kind for being a crazy fool, mostly from chasing after women because anything in skirts looks good to you no matter what and that doesn't make it any kind of a compliment for a girl when you go looking at her."

Miss Hazel paused for breath. A gray-haired pasty-faced man with a sagging paunch under a short dirty apron appeared in the partition doorway. He was minus one leg at the knee and balanced himself on a crutch. "Give 'im hell, Hazel," he said cheerfully. "But not so much he shies away permanent. A customer's a customer." He pivoted on his remaining leg and swung away out of sight again.

"Well, lookathere," said Chet Rollins, pointing at the calendar picture. "See how he's handling that rope. He's a dally man."

"Doggone it," said Monte, rallying, grinning. "You're prettier'n ever, Miss Hazel, when you get riled that way."

"Riled?" snorted Miss Hazel, sniffing again. "Well. I just never. I'm not riled. I'm just plain disgusted. You cowboys are all alike, only you, Mister Monte Walsh, why you're just more so. You think just because a girl has to work for a living, why then you can be free with her and get fresh and just because you buy a cup of coffee she has to be nice to you and listen to your silly talk you don't mean anyway and just use on anything in skirts you think you might get hold of." Miss Hazel retired to her stool, grabbed her magazine, and despite its being upside down became intent upon it.

"Supposing he does get that rope on one of those things," said Chet, still studying the picture. "He'll have himself a time. Look at his cinch. It'll slip first yank."

"Doggone it," said Monte, holding hard to his grin. "What'd I do now? All I said was——"

"Go away," said Miss Hazel. "*Will* you go away."

Chet hunted in a pocket, extracted a quarter, laid it on the counter. "Come along, Monte," he said, swinging on his stool. "I'm thirsty." He led to the door and Monte, reluctant, followed.

They strolled along a stretch of board sidewalk toward the first of Harmony's four saloons. "I ain't exactly rubbing it in," said Chet. "But I told you so. All the same, for a female that don't think of you any she sure knows plenty about you."

"Deadbeat," said Monte. "That's what she said."

"Ain't it the truth?" said Chet, amiable, conversational. "I don't need to ask to know you ain't got much more'n fifteen cents on you. And I've got just about enough for two drinks apiece."

* * *

They stood at the front end of the bar, savoring first drinks, nursing them for mileage. Midway down the bar, behind it, world-weary, having long since seen and heard everything worth seeing and hearing in Harmony, the bartender leaned over a spread-out newspaper. At the other end the man in the patent-leather shoes, freshly barbered, in full regalia of striped suit and gaudy vest and bowler hat, had an appreciative audience of some four of the usual afternoon clientele chuckling at his travel-garnered traveling-salesman tales. His voice carried past the indifferent bartender, on down the bar.

"How come," said Monte, "he always gets the girl in those yarns he's spinning?"

"Because he's telling 'em," said Chet.

The man in the patent-leather shoes finished a fresh tale, paused in verbal stride, took a fat black cigar from his inside coat pocket, expertly bit off the tip, and tucked the cigar between his lips under his trim mustache. He reached with both hands into pockets of his vest and took from one a ten-dollar bill and from the other a match. He struck the match on the bar and lit a corner of the bill. As this flared with a small flame, he held it up, enjoying the sensation around him, and lit the cigar. He blew a fragrant cloud of smoke for the edification of his audience.

"Wow," said Monte at the front end of the bar. "Did you see that?"

"Yep," said Chet. "And did you see him, while they was watching the smoke, shake the thing out and put it back in a pocket? Just a trick."

"Trick?" said Monte.

"Sure," said Chet. "Long as more'n half is left it's still good. Any bank has to take it and give you a new one."

"What d'you know," said Monte. He stood straighter, beginning to rock a bit on his toes. His face began to brighten.

"No," said Chet. "Don't even think of it."

Monte said nothing. He tossed off the remainder of his drink, set the little glass down, and started to move along the bar.

"Wait," said Chet. "You got to—"

"Hush," said Monte. "You keep out of this. I'm doing it."

Chet sighed. He relaxed against the bar and watched the proceedings with solemn interest.

Monte stopped, confronting the bartender. He fished in a pocket and laid a dime on the bar. "Hey, Joe," he said. "A cigar. A ten-center."

The bartender picked up the dime, tested it between his teeth, reached under the bar and laid a fat black cigar where the dime had been.

"And now," said Monte, bright, cheerful. "Now I'm needing a ten-dollar bill."

The bartender straightened, stared at Monte, raised his eyebrows, and leaned down again over his paper.

"Shucks," said Monte. "I only want to borrow it for a bit. Have it back here in half an hour."

The bartender hitched himself and paper a few feet away from the immediate vicinity.

"Tell you what I'll do," said Monte. "If I don't have it back by then I'll give you this belt."

The bartender straightened again, stared at the deerskin belt around Monte's middle, leaned closer, reached to finger the silver buckle. "Don't know what I'd do with the damn thing," he said. "I'm a suspender man. But it's a dull day. Five dollars."

"Ten," said Monte. "You don't watch out I'll make it twenty."

"You'll do what?" said the bartender.

"Make it fifty," said Monte, bright, cheerful. "And dance a jig all over your stingy carcass too."

The bartender rubbed a chin, remembering many things that had happened at many times in the vicinity of his bar with Monte in the middle of many of them. "Well," he said. "In that case . . . But you're only borrowing it, remember. For half an hour."

Cigar in one hand, bill in the other, Monte moved past Chet toward the doorway, bouncing jauntily off his toes.

* * *

Chet Rollins sat on the edge of the little porch of the general store. By turning his head some he had a fine view along the street and of the adobe building with freshly painted screen door. He waited, serenely expectant, letting a small pebble dribble from one hand to the other and back again.

The screen door swung open, wide, all the way to bounce off the adobe wall beside it. Monte Walsh strode out, dismay and disgust plain on his face. Ignoring the two cow ponies drooping patiently by the tie rail, he came along the street, sucking the fingers of his left hand. He saw Chet and slowed. He sank down beside Chet and scuffed at the ground with one boot toe. "You talk too damn much," he said.

"And you," said Chet, amiable, conversational. "You're too damn quick on the trigger."

Monte held up his left hand, examining it carefully. "The blamed thing went with a whoosh," he said. "All of it. Burned my fingers."

"That's what I tried to tell you," said Chet. "You got to hold it so it's burning just at the top. Let the flame be at the bottom and it flares up and gobbles the whole thing."

"Ten dollars," said Monte. "And she just laughed fit to kill a horse. Likely laughing yet."

"What'd you expect?" said Chet. "You're going at it wrong. You ain't noticed how she wears her hair. Stylish." He rose to his feet. "Come along. You got a debt to pay. We got some mail to get."

* * *

Monte Walsh and Chet Rollins emerged from the frame shack that had been the temporary quarters of the Harmony post office for at least fifteen years. Under one arm Chet carried a sheaf of newspapers rolled and tightly tied around a batch of letters. Monte wore a piece of rope around his waist where the deerskin belt had been. They moved along the street, were approaching the combination hotel and office building. The bear tethered to the cottonwood beside the building was sitting on its haunches, scratching itself lazily with one forepaw. Monte stared at the bear, his eyes beginning to brighten.

Chet stopped and looked at Monte. He looked at the bear and back at Monte, who was beginning to rock a bit on worn old boot soles. "No," said Chet. "You ain't that much of a fool."

"Shucks," said Monte. "I feel mean enough right about now for anything."

"Forget it," said Chet. "Hat let us come for the mail today. Today. We don't get back before the day's over he'll have our hides. We better be starting."

"Shucks," said Monte. "A day ain't over till midnight. That's plenty of time. Laugh at me, will she? I'll show her something."

He moved off, bouncing off his toes, up on the veranda, in through the open door. "Hey, Engle," he said to a man wearing a green eyeshade who was writing in a ledger at what passed for the hotel desk. "You still offering to any comer on that critter out there?"

Over by the low front window the man in the leather vest bearing the tarnished badge rose from an ancient armchair. "Lovely," he said. "I was figuring something might develop when you boys hit town. I'll just spread the word."

* * *

Almost the entire population of Harmony, permanent and transient, was gathered near the ragged cottonwood, in a semi-circle out from the building at a respectful distance from the tree itself. Closer in were four figures, the leather vest man with a big nickel-plated watch in one hand, the eye-shade man with a short stick busy drawing a line on the ground in a circle around the tree about ten feet out from the trunk, Monte Walsh stripped of hat and gunbelt and busy tightening the piece of rope around his waist, Chet Rollins standing beside the leather vest man and watching the pro-ceedings with solemn interest. The bear sat on its haunches, body upright, back against the tree, lazily blinking small bright eyes, and yawned in patient resignation.

The eyeshade man completed his circle. "That's it," he said. "You have to stay inside that line. You get knocked out-side you have to go right back in. More than thirty seconds outside and you're disqualified and outside time doesn't count. You mix it with Otto there any way you want, wres-tling, boxing, but you have to keep him busy. You last two minutes inside time, you get ten dollars. Otto won't hurt you too much. He doesn't bite and his claws are clipped. It's only fair I tell you nobody's lasted two minutes yet. Are you sure you want to try?"

Monte was surveying the assembled populace. Out on the edge he saw Miss Hazel, who was clutching a letter in one hand to prove she had just happened to pick this time for a quick trip to the post office. He grinned at the eyeshade man. "Shucks," he said. "Sure I'm sure. Right about now I'm load-ed for bear."

Chet Rollins, unnoticed by anyone, quietly pulled his gun from its holster, checked the cylinder, slipped it back, and moved closer to the leather vest man where he could keep one eye on the bear and the other on the watch in the man's hand.

"All right Monte," said the leather vest man. "I'm clocking this. Say your prayers and step in anytime you feel the urge."

Monte drew a deep breath and moved forward, bouncing off his toes. He stepped over the line. The bear regarded him with only a mild show of interest. He moved forward again, cautious, crouching, and poked an experimental fist into the soft fur of the bear's upright middle. The bear rose a bit off its haunches and as if he had poked a button batted mechanically at him. Monte parried some of the bats and took the others with only slight jars. The bear sank down again on its haunches and yawned its lack of real interest.

"Yowee!" yelled Monte. "This ain't bad!" He plowed forward, rocking the bear's head with a blow alongside its jaw and smashing another into its middle. The bear rose on its hindlegs, suddenly looming much larger, displaying much more interest, and smacked at him with paws flying fast and powerful. It staggered him this way, that way, and with a back-paw flip under the chin sent him flying to one side and down, sprawled across the circle line.

"Yowee!" yelled Monte, scrambling to his feet. "That's what I need! Action!" He plowed in again, head down, fists flailing, and the bear, grunting at the blows, let him come and swept paws out and around and scooped him into a tight hug. Air left Monte's chest with an audible whoosh. He wrapped his own arms around the bear and rocked with it, straining, heaving.

Wild noises were rising from the assembled populace, about evenly matched, for Monte, for the bear. The old man in too big old clothes was close in, jumping up and down in ancient shoes with flapping soles. "Atta boy, Monte!" he shrilled. "Massacree that hunk a fur!"

Monte managed to get some clearance and brought up a knee, hard, into the bear's middle. It grunted, full of interest now, small eyes dancing, and let go of him and as he staggered back a bit followed him on short hindlegs, batting at him with deft powerful jolts. Another back-paw flip sent him rolling, head over heels, outside the circle, to stop close by Chet Rollins's boots.

Chet looked down, solemn, interested. "Forty seconds to go," he said.

Monte pushed up to hands and knees. He reached with one rather limp hand and slapped at Chet's leg. "Shucks," he gasped. "I'll get the son of a bitch this time." He rose to his feet, wobbling, and plunged back into the circle and dove to tackle the bear around its short hindlegs.

The bear, two hundred ninety pounds of it, came down on top of him and again air left Monte's chest with a definite whoosh. Gallantly, as if in respect for a stimulating opponent, the bear rolled off, rose again on its hindlegs, and waited for him to rise. He made it to his knees, weaving, dazed. The bear calmly, as if measuring him for the knockout, cocked its head to one side regarding him intently, leaned forward and smacked one obviously well-calculated blow on the top of his head. Monte collapsed, eyes closing. The bear dropped to all four feet, sniffed him for certainty, and retired to relaxing position against the tree.

* * *

In the dim interior of the livery stable Monte Walsh, limp and motionless, lay stretched along four bales of hay. Scratches and bruises showed on his face, several rips in his faded old shirt, his general appearance considerably lumpy and battered. There were drops of water on his cheeks and the upper part of his shirt was wet. Gunbelt and hat and the roll of mail lay on another nearby bale. On yet another sat Chet Rollins solemnly regarding him.

Chet rose and filled a tin dipper again with water from a pail sitting on the floor. Gently he sloshed water over Monte's face. This time Monte's eyelids flickered, opened, and he stared up at the dim recesses of the timbered ceiling. Suddenly he sat up and looked at Chet.

"You missed by ten seconds," said Chet.

Monte groaned. He moved his head about, testing neck muscles, wincing some. He swung his legs over the side of the bales and stared down at his boot toes.

"Well, anyways," said Chet. "Nobody else ever lasted past a minute and twenty."

"Sure," said Monte, morose. "I'm a goddamned two-legged wildcat. But that don't pay off." He looked at Chet and away. "How about—"

"She laughed again," said Chet. "But if it pleases you any, she didn't seem to be enjoying the laughing much."

"The hell with her," said Monte.

"Like I say," said Chet. "You been going at it wrong. You ain't noticed how she has her nose in those fancy magazines all the time. Hooked full of lady-gentleman kind of stuff."

"The hell with her," said Monte. "I'm through trying. In that direction anyways. Let's get back to the ranch." He picked up his hat, jammed it on his head, took the gunbelt and slapped it around in place, fumbling with the old iron buckle.

"There you go," said Chet. "Always so damn previous. With your bill-burning and playing patty-cake with that bear, now we can't get back in time for a decent meal. And I'm hungry. We eat here. That is, if you ain't afraid to face her."

"Afraid?" said Monte, jerking up straight. "Me? Afraid of that snip-nosed thing? Shucks, as far as I'm concerned, she don't exist any more. Just something to hand out food."

*   *   *

Dusk drifted over Harmony as the last light of the sun, now below the horizon, glowed rose and red up the western sky. The two cow ponies, patient by the tie rail in front of the small adobe building, stood with bridles hanging from saddle horns, limp tie ropes leading from their necks to the rail, and nosed with chomping jaws into two small piles of hay brought from the livery stable. Lamplight shone cheerily out through the freshly-painted screen door and around the edges of the calico curtain at the window.

Inside, on the last two stools at the right, sat Monte Walsh and Chet Rollins busy with soup-sized spoons and nearing the bottoms of two ample bowls that had been filled with chili and beans and stray chunks of chopped beef. Chet was eating in steady rhythm punctuated by occasional breaks for gulps of coffee and big bites of bread, Monte in spasmodic spurts between glowerings into the depths of his bowl. Miss Hazel was deftly removing the debris left along the counter by other now-departed diners, looking anywhere, everywhere, except at Monte Walsh.

The screen door opened and in came the man in the patent-leather shoes, resplendent as ever in full regalia. The sweet scent of shaving lotion emanated from him. His waxed mustache positively glowed in the lamplight. He advanced to the counter, removed his bowler hat with a small flourish and a slight bow toward Miss Hazel. "Good evening, young lady," he said and picked a stool near the left end, sat down upon it and laid the hat on the one beside it.

Miss Hazel gazed at him, fascinated. She looked over at the lean battered disheveled shape of Monte Walsh slumped over his bowl, sniffed, and looked back at the man. One hand rose to test the smoothness of the upsweep of her hair. She beamed her brightest smile.

The man looked about for a menu, saw none, shrugged his plumpish shoulders inside his pin-striped suit. "The dinner," he said. "All the trimmings."

Miss Hazel's smile faded some. "But," she said, "but—but we only have—"

"Oh, come now, young lady," said the man, bowing slightly toward her again. "I'll have the dinner. You know, the specialty of the house. The best."

Miss Hazel backed toward the partition doorway, bumped into the doorjamb, swung hastily around and disappeared. She reappeared almost instantly, having forgotten the usual beginning amenities. Hurrying, she put a cup and two spoons, one regular-sized, one soup-sized, in front of the man, stooped to take the big enamelware coffeepot from under the counter and filled the cup. She disappeared again into the rear room.

The man sat still, very still, surveying the meager array in front of him. Small frown furrows began to appear on his forehead.

Miss Hazel returned, admiring glances at the man interfering with her usual deftness. She set before him a plate bearing two large thick slices of bread and a pat of butter and an ample bowl full of beans and chili with stray chunks of chopped beef.

The man stared down at the bowl, disgust deepening on his face. "No," he said bitterly. "It's too much. I spend all day in this godforsaken hole of a town. I associate with all kinds of unwashed fools. I spend money. I treat the yokels. I jolly the customers. I pull stunts for them. And all I get is forty dollars worth of orders. Forty . . . measly . . . dollars. And now this." His voice climbed in almost a shout. "I won't stand for it."

His voice dropped, contemptuous now. "Look here, my girl. I'm a civilized man. I'll be goddamned if I'll eat any stinking peppered up mess like that. Now you hop to it. Take that swill back and bring me some civilized food."

Over on his far right stool Chet Rollins stirred, shifting weight to rise. A hand on his thigh stopped him. Monte Walsh was uncoiling upward to full lean muscular height. All the defeat and frustration of the afternoon were rising with him, focusing on a convenient and appropriate target. He moved along the counter, a lithe length of dynamite ready to explode. One hand brushed the bowler hat to the floor and the other took his gun from its holster. He eased down on the stool where the hat had been and rested the hand with the gun on the counter.

"Mister," he said, quiet, deadly. "Out here in this godforsaken hole we don't talk to a lady that way. You'll say you're sorry and you'll say it pretty."

Miss Hazel, back against the shelves, face very white, one hand up at her mouth, was staring at the man.

Stiff, rigid on his stool, the man slowly swiveled his head to look at Monte. His eyes flicked down to the worn nicked tarnished deadliness of the gun and back to the bruised battered deadliness of Monte's face. He remembered dirt flicking over his shiny shoes. He remembered a bear becoming interested in a stimulating opponent. With an obvious effort he turned his head toward Miss Hazel. "If . . . if I . . ." he said. "If I offended you, Miss, I'm sorry. I didn't really mean it."

"And now," said Monte, quiet, deadly. "You'll eat that chili."

Miss Hazel, back against the shelves, chewing on the knuckles of one hand, color coming back into her face, was staring at Monte. The man, hurried, quivering a bit, was busy with the soup-sized spoon.

He gulped half a dozen spoonsful, choking on some of them. "It's—it's very good," he said. "But I'm not really hungry." He laid the spoon down, watching Monte out of the corner of one eye, fished a silver dollar from a pocket of the gaudy vest, and laid it by the spoon. Quickly, almost furtively, he swung around and off the stool, scooped up his hat, and made for the screen door.

Monte Walsh uncoiled upward, slipping the gun back in its holster. He watched the man disappear with a soft swish of the screen door. A small wry disgusted grin showed on his lips. "All right, Chet," he said. "Let's get going." He too started for the door.

"Mister Walsh." Miss Hazel's voice caught him, stopped him. It was a soft somewhat shaky appealing voice. "Mister Walsh. Monte. I'll—I'll be through here soon. If you want to, you can . . . well, you can walk me home."

Monte Walsh turned, surprise on his face sliding into slow wide smile. He stepped back to his stool and eased down. "Miss Hazel," he said. "You ain't ever been as pretty as you are this minute. Could I have another cup of coffee while I wait?"

Over on his stool Chet Rollins sighed. He laid a fifty-cent piece on the counter. "Two suppers, a quarter each," he said to no one in particular. He slid around and off the stool, picked the roll of mail from the floor beside it, and ambled along the counter. He slapped Monte on a shoulder. "See?" he said. "I was right. But you better be back by sunup." He ambled to the door.

Outside, slow, unhurried, he approached the thick-necked black, tied the roll of mail by the saddle-whangs behind the cantle, tightened the cinch, untied the lead rope, slipped the bridle over the black's head. Swinging up, he moved off down the street, stopped by the patches of light from over and under the swinging doors of the first of Harmony's four saloons, dismounted and ambled inside. In something less than four minutes he ambled out again, swung up, and moved back along the street, past the small adobe building, on out of town.

*   *   *

Under the clean deep night sky of the big land, a few miles out of town, a lonely moving shape in the soft glow of a half-moon, one cow pony jogged steadily along the wagon trace. Off in the distances a coyote called, mournful, aching, appealing. Another answered, deep-throated, eager. "Well, well," muttered Chet Rollins. "Everybody seems to be doing it."

The black perked ears and cocked its head to one side.

Chet Rollins pulled rein and sat still in saddle. Far back along the wagon trace hoofs sounded. Chet cocked his own head, listening. He caught the beat. "Now that," he muttered, "is downright peculiar. Can't have been much more'n half an hour." He nudged the black forward again, looped reins over the horn, pulled out the stubby pipe and the little pouch and began filling the pipe.

Slow puffs of smoke drifted back as the black jogged along. Out of the long stretches behind, stirring dust faintly luminous in the moonlight, came the leggy dun. It pounded up alongside and slowed to the same easy amble.

"All right," said Chet at last. "I suppose I got to ask questions. What happened?"

"That female," said Monte. "Why, she's downright dangerous."

A nighthawk, swift after some invisible insect, swooped close and the dun, still heated some from the gallop, took the chance to skip sideways and dance a bit. "Quit it," said Monte, clamping down with reins. He moved in close again. "Why, yes," he said. "We hadn't more'n got to her folks' place and sitting on that bench by that scrawny old tree they have and she was cuddling close mighty cozy and right away she begins talking about a cute little cottage with roses growing by the door and chickens scratching around out back."

Off in the distances the first coyote called again and the other answered, much closer now to the first. "Damn racket," said Monte. He slapped one hand on his saddle horn. "Yes," he said. "That female's got marriage on her mind. And I sure ain't."

The two cow ponies jogged along in steady unvarying rhythm. Monte nudged the dun closer to the black and reached to take the pouch from Chet's pocket. His hand stopped moving. He had caught sight of something showing just above the leather of Chet's gunbelt, something silvery and turquoise-studded in the moonlight. He rocked back in his saddle.

"Shucks," said Chet. "While you were milling around getting ready for your show-off stunt with that bear, I found me a sucker."

The two cow ponies jogged along. Monte sat stiff in the saddle, head turned, looking steadily at Chet.

"Yep," said Chet at last. "I figured one fool was enough. I bet on the bear."

Ahead, bunched across the wagon trace, a group of steers blocked the way. The two cow ponies jogged straight ahead, ignoring them, and the steers, waiting till the last second, snorted in annoyance and scattered to let them through. "Aw, shucks," said Monte, nudging the dun closer again and taking the pouch. "I guess you could say in a way that does sort of keep it in the family."

The two cow ponies ambled easily along, two sturdy companionable shapes in the dim vastness of the big land. Smoke from a cigarette and a stubby pipe drifted back behind them, mingling, indistinguishable in the soft night air.

*   *   *

"Yeah, I hear they're doing that over at the X I T. Giving the boys Sundays off. But I reckon they don't if there's any trouble brewing out on the range. Trouble don't pay no attention to Sundays. The way Cal's always let us do is if there ain't much work piled up we loaf around some. Take it a bit easier I mean. Don't start anything, that is. Just finish up anything needs finishing an' loaf around. Don't do any harm, Cal always says, to slow down ev'ry seventh day an' let what souls we got air out some. Good time to catch up on such things as trimming hair crops an' patching gear an' the like.

"Speaking of Sundays reminds me of the time there was a preacher in town holding a revival meeting. Sunfish has leanings that way sometimes an' he talked us all into going. Went there mild as soda pop promising each other not to go messing things up any. Preacher was a long thin drink of water with a face like a prune that looked like he didn't enjoy anything in living. He unlimbers his tonsils an' starts talking. Can he talk? Why, words come out of him so fast you could scarce catch a-holt of 'em. Hell an' damnation man. Sin on his mind mighty heavy. Seems like anything anybody might want to do for a little fun is a sin to him. Takes it for granted we're all so black with sin likely we could never be scrubbed clean. Kind of insulting the way he laid it on to us. But I reckon a preacher thinks he's got a license to waggle his tongue any way he feels like doing. Worst sin of all, he figures, is not going to church reg'lar an' bowing down

mighty low an' hopping to do whatever a preacher like him says. Man who doesn't, he claims while waving his arms around, is going to hell sure an' roast in everlasting damnation till the final trumpet blows. An' after. He's throwing fire an' brimstone around mighty free. Acts like he can give a ticket to the hot place to anyone he feels like any time. Looking at us lost souls like it's meant special for us. Works hisself up a good sweat. When he figures he's got us buffaloed an' backed into a pen an' ready to be branded his brand, he says: Anyone here who still intends to go to hell, stand up and be counted among the damned.

"That's when Monte stands up. If what you been blatting is true, he says, then that's right where I'm a-going an' I'm a-going there at a right good clip. An' Chet stands up alongside him an' Chet says: You ain't gone anywheres yet, Monte, that I ain't been right with you, so I reckon I'll keep you comp'ny. An' Powder stands up along the other side of him an' Powder has his gun out an' he's holding it kind of careless in one hand an' he looks around an' he says: There's plenty more here heading in the same direction an' if they ain't got the nerve to stand up an' say so they'll be getting there a lot sooner'n they been expecting.

"About then most ev'rybody's standing up. But they ain't waiting to be counted. They're stampeding for the way out."

Powder Kent
1888

FIVE TIMES snow fell that winter even out on the lower levels and each time the cold spell held and the snow lingered on the ground, melting in, with little runoff, and in the spring the grasses freshened early and as the season progressed they thickened and topped out strong, keeping well ahead of the stock roaming the Slash Y range. The horses fleshed, developing grass-bellies that would slim down soon with work, and were spunky under saddles. The cattle fattened fast, losing the gaunt-flanked look of winter, and the new calves stood sturdy by their mothers and frolicked in their sudden stiff-legged rocking spurts with the vitality of new life in a good year.

Then the summer sun beat down and no rain fell, not even the usual few but torrential thunderstorms of midsummer, and the grasses turned brown and gold, rippling in the dry winds, curing early on the stem, good feed still but no longer freshening, growing, renewing, and the men of the Slash Y riding the range were careful with matches and sparing with campfires and kicked dirt over even apparently dead ashes before moving on.

It was a good year turning bad. And worse was to come.

* * *

Two strange men came riding in to the ranch head-quarters. They came out of the great distances west and south and their meager worn gear spoke of Arizona, of the hard lonely hiding country beyond the Mogollon rim. They came on two lean wire-tough long-traveling horses and they led two more of the same breed. One of the men was thickset, big-armed, with big features and undershot jaw, and a kind of insolence or a contempt or anger at the world in general showed in his quick nervous actions and his manner of jerking his head as he talked. The other was loose-limbed, slack-jawed, shambling in movement even in the saddle, tagging always a bit behind.

They left their horses by the small corral and walked over by the veranda of the old adobe house where Cal Brennan sat in the mouse-chewed remnants of an ancient leather-covered armchair soaking in afternoon sun, absurdly high-curved-heel boots on the floor beside him, old eyes missing nothing about his visitors and their gear and their horses.

They exchanged the usual amenities with him about the weather and the condition of the country, then the thickset man pushed his point. "Saw some mustangs down in them lower hills," he said. "Understand that's part of your range. Now they ain't much but we ain't partic'lar these days. Mind if we camp there a while an' try runnin' 'em?"

Cal rubbed a hand down one cheek and over around his chin. "Yes," he said. "Yes, I do. I reckon I do mind."

"What for?" said the thickset man, jerking his head. "They ain't doin' you no good."

"They ain't hurtin' me any," said Cal. "An' I happen to know there ain't enough broomtails down that way to be worth your while. You get to chasin' an' find that out an' our own stock might get to lookin' kind of temptin' to you."

"You callin' anybody anythin'?" said the thickset man, jerking his head again.

"Not so as you'd notice," said Cal. "Just thinkin' of what could happen."

"Stingy," said the loose-limbed man.

"You can call it that if you've a mind to," said Cal. "I call it bein' sensible. Lookin' ahead an' avoidin' trouble. For you as well as me. You two're welcome to stick around for supper an' bed down here. In the mornin' whyn't you head for the Domingo reservation. More wild ones over that way an' likely you could make a deal."

"We ain't needin' no advice from the likes of you," said the thickset man. "Nor nothin' else neither." He turned away and the loose-limbed man tagged him.

They rode off into the distances west and south and they

stopped by one of the Slash Y low round water tanks with windmill beside it and watered their horses and filled their canteens and the thickset man scanned the territory around and took a small running iron from the blanket roll behind his saddle and hammered at the side of the tank, low down, until he had punched a hole and the two of them stood for a moment watching water run out to soak into the dry ground.

They mounted and rode on, leading the two extra horses, and dusk took them just over the long ridge fronting the mountains to the west and they made a quick dry camp in a small hollow screened by junipers and picketed their horses and ate sparingly of the meager supply of food in their saddlebags and lay down in blankets with saddles for pillows.

*   *   *

At about the same time, farther to the west, on the far side of the mountains, Powder Kent easy in saddle aboard a rough-built sturdy roan, coming back to the ranch after a three-day jaunt to testify as a witness at a minor nuisance of a trial that had been transferred to Rio Abajo, worked his way up a trail twisting toward a pass through the upper peaks. In the deepening dusk he stopped where a small spring trickled out of rock and let the roan drink and unsaddled and picketed it and built a small fire. He took a can of beans from his saddlebag and with the opener blade of his pocketknife neatly removed the top. Carefully he set the can close in by the fire and pushed it further in with a small stick. Pulling out another blade of the knife, he went to work on the stick, whittling one end flat. Using two other sticks he removed the can from the fire and sat down, ankles crossed out in front with the can between his legs, and dipped the flattened end of the first stick into the can. Slowly, leisurely, he emptied the can. He rose and went to the spring and lay flat and drank. He came back by the fire and carefully pushed what remained of it in toward the center and unrolled his blanket and spread it out. He stood, quiet, listening into the great clean silence all around him broken only by the soft sigh of wind in the tops of the few pines nearby. Out of old habit his right hand moved and his worn gun was in the hand and he spun the cylinder, peering at it. Five shells. He set the cylinder so that the hammer bore on the empty chamber and slipped the gun back into its worn holster at his side. He lay down on one half of the blanket and set his hat on the ground and pulled the other half of the blanket over him.

* * *

Morning like any other morning of the lazy time of year, clear and crisp and warming fast as the sun rose, and the men of the Slash Y were lingering in the cookhouse over a last round of coffee, in no hurry to start the day's work. It was Sugar Wyman who stepped out along the path to the outhouse and came back, longstriding, to stand in the doorway.

"I kind of hate to go breakin' up this little party," he said, "but it might int'rest you-all to have a look out here." His voice was quiet, almost matter of fact, but foreman Hat Henderson was up and striding toward the door before he had finished. Sugar stepped back out, leading past a corner of the cookhouse. He pointed into the great distances west and south.

Far out where rolling grassland set its own horizon against the background of the long ridge fronting the mountains a light gray cloud hugged the ground, sending streamers floating upward. Darker streaks showed in it, twisting, rising, and the whole reached out, stretching, blotting ever more of the low horizon.

Smoke. Smoke rising from a mile-wide front, advancing, and spreading, spreading.

Activity swarmed in and about the long low barn and the corrals and the voice of Hat Henderson boomed through it. "Monte. An' you Chet. Grab a couple butcher knives an' a hatchet an' snap out there an' get a drag ready . . . Dally, harness the team . . . Sunfish, pile some barrels on the wagon an' fill 'em with water an' throw in all the bags an' shovels you can find . . . Dobe, start rigging a string of extra hosses an' take 'em on out . . . Sugar, you an' Joe take the buckboard an' swing around backside of it. Wind's blowing this way so likely it ain't doing too much there . . ."

* * *

Far out on the rolling grassland cattle moved in frightened spurts, gathering in bunches, stopping to look back and moving away again. The small ground-dwelling life of the land scurried through the low growth. The fire crackled on a wider front now, consuming the dry grasses, feeding on its own draft, advancing under the whip of the wind eastward at an eight-mile pace. Smoke rolled ahead of it in gusts and coiled back, twisting, rising, dark and acrid where the flames took patches of small brush.

Well in front and back some from the near end of the lead line of fire Monte Walsh and Chet Rollins, moving silently, swiftly, worked on the carcass of a yearling steer just dropped with a bullet in its brain. Slashing deep with knives and using a hatchet on the neck vertebrae, they cut off the head and heaved this aside. Slashing deep again, they ripped open the carcass, slicing it the long way almost in half, and heaved again to spread-eagle it out, flesh- and gut-side down. Striding to their horses thirty feet away, ground-reined, waiting, nervous but waiting, they grabbed ropes and tied these to saddle horns and paid them out back to the carcass.

"Take the outside," said Monte. "And don't try giving me no argument."

Bending low, they tied the ropes to a forefoot and a hind-foot. Striding again to the horses, they swung up and moved away, dragging the spread-out bloody carcass, heading straight for the lead line of fire.

A quarter mile behind them a big flatbed low-sided wagon swayed and careened forward, husky young draft team digging hoofs deep and lunging into harness, Cal Brennan on the seat with the reins, saddles and empty burlap bags and shovels and three big barrels bouncing on the bed, Hat Henderson and Dally Johnson and Sunfish Perkins scrambling for footing among them and to steady the barrels. A hundred yards farther behind Dobe Chavez plugged grimly along in saddle, cursing softly in Spanish, struggling to keep a dozen skittish cow ponies, neck-roped together in a line, following him at a fair trot.

*　*　*

Westward, mile after mile, over the charred land, on over the long ridge and broken land and small valleys beyond, on

up the slopes of the mountains, Powder Kent on a rough-
built sturdy roan, whistling cheerfully, ambled along the trail
leading down from the pass through the upper peaks. He
rounded a huge shoulder of rock and the whistling stopped
and with it the roan pulled to a sudden halt. Vast and seeming limitless the big land swept away from beneath him, distance merging into distance to be lost at last beyond the
reach of vision toward Texas. Down and out from the lower
ridge, northward some to his left, small across the miles, he
saw a great wedge-shaped scar of charred land where fire had
fanned forward, widening, and smoke rising from the far
front of it. Squinting into the morning sun, he could make
out tiny figures, seen in snatches as the smoke shifted, incredibly small in the vastness, moving along the far front, and
two more well back along the left edge of the wedge where
smoke rose only in thin wisps.

He nudged the roan forward and was moving again down
the trail. Again the roan stopped, pulled to a sudden halt.
Down and to the right, miles away from the blunt-pointed beginning of the wedge-shaped scar, along the outer base of the
long ridge below him, clear and distinct in distance through
the clean air, he saw two men mounted, leading two horses,
moving southward at a steady trot. He saw them stop and
one swing down and bend low to the ground and rise and
swing up and both ride on and where the one had bent a
wisp of smoke rose and increased as wind caught it.

He stared down across the miles and the muscles around
his lean-lipped mouth tightened. Out of old habit, instinctive,
his right hand moved and his worn gun was in the hand and
he spun the cylinder, looking down to check it. He slipped
the gun back into its holster. He slapped spurs to the roan
and turned off the trail, angling southward and down the
rugged slopes in the direction of two men mounted, leading
two horses, moving away at a steady trot.

*   *   *

The first fire raced on, crackling through the low growth,
sending sparks dancing upward in the roiling smoke that
swung and eddied in the wind, obscuring the sun in the immediate area, making a hazy dimness over all, and the men
of the Slash Y, silent mostly, grim-faced, fought for the good

grasses that meant strong flesh to the cattle roaming the range that in turn meant money, a return on investment, to other men two thousand miles away.

Out in front Monte Walsh and Chet Rollins pulled the drag, about thirty feet apart, straddling between them the lead line of fire. Monte on the inside, in past the crackling flames, blood-smeared, smoke-grimed, all but lost in the back-swirls of smoke, erect in saddle with bandanna up over mouth and nose, voice coming muffled through it in constant refrain, aimed at and steadying to the wincing, jumping, side-swinging horse under him: "Hot, boy, ain't it, hot on the feet. But I'm promising you a year's rest to grow out those hoofs again." Chet on the outside, blood- and smoke-smeared the same, pushing steadily through the smoke clouds rolling at him, solid in saddle, holding down his frightened horse, intent on the tricky job of keeping his rope taut against the jerks from Monte's and the drag pulling right, smothering, over the fire line.

Back about seventy-five yards the wagon moved at a matching pace along the edge of the burned-out area, Cal Brennan on the seat with one foot braced and the other on the brake, hands clamped on reins as the draft team snorted and plunged, trying to swing away, and the extra horses, tied in a string to the tailgate, squealed and kicked and, reluctant, followed.

In between Hat Henderson and Dally Johnson and Sunfish Perkins worked on foot with several thicknesses of wet bags in their hands, slapping slapping slapping down on the flickers of flame and the glowing sparks left by the drag, running to vault into the moving wagon and dip the bags in the barrels and pull them out dripping and leap to the ground and back to the slapping slapping slapping. And with them, moving steadily along, Dobe Chavez, shovel in hand, tossed smoldering cow chips back from the line and threw dirt over them.

And several miles away Sugar Wyman and Jumping Joe Joslin, slapping too with bags, stomping with worn blackened boots, kicking cow chips in, worked steadily along the flank of the great wedge-shaped scar where fire showed only in patches, creeping slowly against the wind.

*   *   *

High above the ground wind and the activity moving through it, light gray smoke drifted, floating lazily ever upward, forming fantastic patterns against the deep blue of upper sky, and its message spread out across the big land.

Twenty-four miles to the north three Triple Seven hands, jogging along in saddles, topped a rise and stopped and looked southward into distance and one of them whirled his horse and rode back fast in the direction of the Triple Seven buildings and the other two struck spurs to their horses and rode at a long swinging lope toward the distant signal in the sky.

Eighteen miles to the east where the little town of Harmony drowsed in midmorning sun Sheriff MacKnight rose from his rolltop desk in his little cubicle in the combination hotel and office building known as the Harmony House and stepped out into the hall and on out on the porch to stretch cramped muscles and in the act of stretching stopped, staring westward, and turned to shout in through the doorway behind him and turned again, striding fast, to leave the porch and head along the main street, hammering on doors and shouting again.

Twenty-two miles to the south Sonny Jacobs, wrench in hand atop a small windmill tower, stared north and west and dropped the wrench and climbed down fast and soon men scurried about the buildings of the Diamond Six and another big flatbed wagon carrying barrels and bags and shovels and men careened out onto the open grassland, angling toward the far smoke of the second fire, and Sonny and another man followed in saddles, leading extra horses.

Here and there along a huge arc swinging to the east around the vast stretch of rolling plain, where stood an occasional shack or jacal or adobe house, other men saw and stared into distance and a few of them shrugged shoulders and spat in the general direction of one or another of the big cow outfits but most of them tightened belts and hurried to bring in scrawny horses or mules or burros and slap what they had for saddles on them.

And off to the west Sugar Wyman and Jumping Joe Joslin, working now around the blunted point of the first wedge-shaped scar, looked up to see José Gonzales on a scraggly pinto and his twelve-year-old oldest boy on a burro coming toward them, carrying shovels.

* * *

Farther west and south, well down past the blunted point
of the second wedge-shaped scar that increased eastward, widening under the whip of the wind, a rough-built sturdy roan,
sweat-streaked, moved along the base of the long ridge and
Powder Kent leaned forward and down in the saddle, checking the prints of four horses that had passed there at a steady
trot. The roan stopped and he straightened, scanning the long
stretch of land ahead. He nudged the roan forward again.
The prints swerved, turning to lead up the slope of the ridge,
toe marks deep as if the horses had hurried, and he turned
with them. Near the top of the ridge he dismounted and left
the roan ground-reined and moved on up, bending low, and
lay flat, peering over. Nothing moved anywhere in view in
the broken land dropping down and away to rise again into
the steeper slopes of the mountains. He returned and took
the reins and led the horse, scrambling fast, up and over and
down a short distance. He mounted and headed on into the
broken land, slowly, cautiously, following the prints.

* * *

A little before noon and far out on the rolling plain the
men of the big land fought for the good grasses. Southward
where the second fire raced forward the crew of the Diamond Six, gathering recruits from the lower country, were
leaping into action along its front. Three miles to the north,
about midway now of the long angled front of the first fire,
Monte Walsh on his third horse and Chet Rollins on his second pulled a fresh drag. They moved faster now and behind
them more men slapped with bags and swung with shovels.
Not far away Skimpy Eagens, who had somehow wrangled a
pair of half-broken horses out of the big corral and into harness, bounced forward on the seat of the old Slash Y chuck
wagon, game leg braced against the dashboard, bringing a
supply of jerked beef and a bushel basket of biscuits and a
huge pot of coffee and the makings for plenty more.

* * *

Time passed, fast in movement and action, slow and heavy to the men in the smoke haze, and throats smarted from coughing and muscles ached from the constant slapping slapping slapping. Dobe Chavez and Hat Henderson led now with another drag and two other drags were working down along the jagged narrowing front of the two fires that had spread inward toward each other and merged into the one.

Where Skimpy Eagens had set up a quick camp Monte Walsh, caught ten minutes before in a swirling backlash of flame from a clump of burning brush, lay limp with shoulders and head against a saddle blanket and a wheel of the chuck wagon, hat lost somewhere, face curiously pale under its tan and coating of grime, eyebrows gone and hair singed, breath coming in short quick gasps as the air rasped his scorched lungs. Chet Rollins squatted beside him, holding a cup of coffee to his lips.

"You goddamn fool," muttered Chet. "You ain't fit to be let run loose. Whyn't you pull away? Whyn't you let me take it sometimes?"

Monte raised a limp hand and pushed the cup aside and the hand moved on to slap Chet weakly on the thigh. "Got to . . . keep you . . . looking pretty," he gasped. "Seeing . . . as you ain't . . . got much . . . to start with." He hitched himself up higher against the blanket and the wheel. "Ain't there . . . any whisky . . . around?"

Thirty feet away Cal Brennan sat on the ground, boots off and beside him, rubbing his bent old toes. The big bulk of Sheriff MacKnight hunkered down facing him.

"Plenty of help here now," said Sheriff MacKnight. "If the wind don't get to playing games, the whole thing's about licked." He plucked a grass stem and tucked it in one corner of his mouth and chewed slowly on it. "I'm wondering, Cal. You got any ideas?"

Cal Brennan rubbed a hand down one cheek and over his chin. "One," he said. "An' I'm kickin' myself about it. Should of thought. An' I'm only sayin' maybe. There's nobody livin' over that way but Gonzales an' he ain't tricky nor careless. But a couple hard cases came in yesterday. Wanted to be runnin' broomtails. I said no an' they didn't like it. They didn't like it at all. They rode out that way."

Sheriff MacKnight straightened up. "Reckon I'll be looking

around some," he said. "Your boys must be about bushed."
A few moments later he and two other men drifted quietly
away, westward across the charred land, the hoofs of their
horses sending up spurts of soft fine ash.

* * *

On westward, west and south, up and over the long ridge,
well into the broken land beyond, Powder Kent on a rough-
built sturdy roan pushed along, following the prints of four
horses. He moved slowly, studying the ground carefully
ahead of him.

The roan raised its head higher as if to whinny and
Powder pulled reins and leaned down fast to clamp a hand
over its nose. He waited a moment, listening. Cautiously he
released the nose and nudged the roan forward. The prints
led along a small dry stream bed and between two high
sharply eroded shoulders of hardened clay. He stopped again
and dismounted and tied his bandanna around the roan's
nose and left it ground-reined and moved ahead on foot. The
prints led on, between the high shoulders, and he could see
them swerving to the right, climbing up the slow slope out of
the stream bed, up and up and topping on out of sight.

He stepped back to the roan and mounted and moved forward, slowly, cautiously. He was turning to the right to follow the prints up the slope when small barely perceptible
sounds or the prickling of the hair on the back of his neck
gave warning and he knew in the single poised instant that he
had made a mistake and he reared the roan pivoting on hind
legs back around to the left and saw the two men stepping out
from behind a big rock forty feet away and their guns rising.

He heard the double blast of their guns and the roan shuddered under him leaping and he felt a sudden tearing shock
along his left side and he rocked back in the saddle under the
impact and fell toward the ground and as he fell, instinctive,
out of old habit, his right hand moved and his gun was in the
hand. He hit hard and rolled over with the momentum of the
fall, hitching around toward the two men, and their guns
were blasting again and bullets thudded into the ground
around him and one full into him, smashing a hipbone, and
all of his fast-ebbing vitality was concentrated on the one ter-

rible effort of getting his right arm forward and the gun up, elbow braced on the ground, and the worn old gun roared and bucked in his hand.

*   *   *

Time passed and eastward, out of the broken land, up and over the long ridge, along its outer base, Sheriff MacKnight and two other men moved at a slow lope, following the prints of five horses. "Two of them ain't carrying anybody," muttered Sheriff MacKnight. "But who in hell's the other one?" The prints swung away, leading up the ridge slope, and Sheriff MacKnight and the two other men turned, following them.

And on eastward, mile after mile, over the charred land, on where the good grasses rippled in the lessened wind to far horizon, the smoke haze was lifting and the last drag moved over the last short stretch of fire and was left where it lay and a few men, with no urgency, slapped wearily at the last remaining flickers. Already other men, tired and soot-stained, smoke-grimed, were drifting off into the distances out of which they had come.

Cal Brennan, boots in hand, stood by the seat of the big flatbed wagon. Hat Henderson, big and smoke-blackened, looked down at him from the back of a tired horse.

"Quite a gatherin'," said Cal. "Surprised me, some that showed. We got more'n a few good neighbors. I expect we'll be plenty busy for a while huntin' more range an' shiftin' stock. But when we get straightened out, maybe we ought to be throwin' some kind of a party."

"Yeah," said Hat. A grin broke the darkened mask of his face. "Maybe a barbecue'd be kind of appropriate. Well, anyways, a couple of the Diamond boys'll be staying out a while to watch it down their way. Me an' Dally'll stick around here till dark just in case. You an' the rest go on in."

Twenty feet away the smeared crusted barely recognizable figure that was Monte Walsh stood by a patient bridled horse, breath wheezing some in his throat, and he winced slightly as he breathed. He bent down to take hold of his stained charred saddle and heaved, staggering a bit, to get it up and into place.

"Hey, quit that," said Chet Rollins, moving in. "Get over there in the wagon."

"The hell . . . with you," gasped Monte, reaching under for the cinch. "I ain't . . . dead yet. When I . . . can't ride . . . I will be."

*   *   *

In the cool clean dark of night over the big land the door of the empty Slash Y bunkhouse stood open. Across trodden dust the light from two lamps shone through the front window and the open doorway of the old adobe ranch house. Close by the veranda two horses drooped in tired dejection, dim figures on the edge of the patch of light through the doorway. Inside, in the big front room, the men of the Slash Y, in clothes hurriedly pulled on, stood or sat about, silent, grimfaced. On the floor a blanket covered a still stiffened figure. Beside it, worn and weary and dust-stained, stood Sheriff MacKnight.

"Yes," he said. "We unraveled it all right from the tracks. He spotted them somehow and he took out after them. All by his lonesome. Likely he knew you all were plenty busy. Back down in those badlands below Black Horse Spring they jumped him and knocked him out of the saddle. He didn't move much from where he fell. But he had his gun out. Three shells fired. We found one man right there, done for, drilled neat through the chest and the shoulder. Found the other one wobbling on his horse about three miles away. He couldn't do much traveling. Had lost too much blood. A bullet hole in one leg, up high where he had trouble stopping it."

Sheriff MacKnight took off his hat and rubbed a hand across his forehead where the band had made a red mark. "We patched that one up," he said, "and rounded up the rest of their horses. Were heading here, bringing everything. Then I got to thinking how you boys might get the itch to use a rope on the one that's living. Seeing as I can't let that happen much as I might feel inclined to, I sent the others on into town and come in here myself. Bringing him. I figured you might want that."

"Yes," said Cal Brennan softly. "We do."

Sheriff MacKnight sighed and raised the hand holding his

hat and put the hat on, pulling it down over his forehead. "You want me to leave him here?"

"Yes," said Cal Brennan. "I don't know as he's ever really had any folks, except maybe the rest of us right here. He used to be all Texas. But he ain't talked that way for a long time now. I reckon if he had the sayin' of it, he'd want to stay."

*   *   *

Days passed, slipping into weeks, and the men of the Slash Y spent long hours in the saddle, riding out into the mountains, finding upland valley pockets of good grass and moving cattle in small bunches to them to be left until late November when the snows of winter would come. Monte Walsh sat in the mouse-chewed remnants of armchair on the veranda of the old adobe house, soaking in sun, and watched them go and slowly at first then rapidly the lean rawhide vitality crept back through him, sealing off portions of his lungs with scar tissue, sending down his legs the tingle for the feel of a stout horse under him, and one morning he walked down to the corrals with the others and saddled a deep-chested leggy dun and rode out part way with them and the next day and thereafter rode the full way and all that remained from the scorching was now and again a small spell of coughing and once in a long while a bad spell sending a sudden sharp pain through his chest that hurt more than anyone but himself would ever know.

Over in the little town of Harmony, when the circuit judge came along, a quick trial was held and a lawyer, assigned unwilling to the defense, argued that no one could prove whose bullet did what and that his client had simply been led astray by a companion and the judge agreed that intent and participation were all that were certain and sentenced a looselimbed slack-jawed man who limped some to fifteen years in the territorial penitentiary.

Then the long-delayed rains came, a few sudden swift thunderstorms, and out where the wind had been playing with fine loose ash over charred ground sheets of water swept, soaking the ash into the earth, erasing much of the great jagged scar defacing the land. Moisture seeped down where the roots of the good southwestern grasses waited and a faint flush of new green showed, not much this late in the year, but strong with the promise of the next spring.

And there where the Slash Y buildings seemed to grow out of the ground, a part of the big land, a small rectangular piece of it, incredibly small in the vastness, was enclosed with a sturdy picket fence made and bolted to deep-set posts by Sunfish Perkins and Sugar Wyman. Within the fence a rectangular mound of earth settled slowly, inevitably, under the lash of rain and the warm blessing of sun and the cool clean dark of night. At one end of the mound, set solid into the land, stood a small cross of weathered oak, the legend on it carved by Dobe Chavez from pencil markings laid out by Hat Henderson.

On the upright, above the crosspiece, the Slash Y brand. Below, on the wide crosspiece itself:

WILLIAM (POWDER) KENT
184?-1888
A Good Man With a Gun

*   *   *

"Smartest hoss around is that Monkey of Monte's. Dun it is, which he says is the real hoss color. I kind of favor grays myself an' steeldust's the best of them but I got to admit I never seen a dun yet that wasn't plenty of hoss. Monte sets a lot of store by that old Monkey Face. Was stole once an' he was fit to be tied. He an' Chet did a lot of riding an' Dobe oiled up that gun of his an' went along a few times but no luck. One time they got back here all wore out an' there's that hoss waiting for 'em right by the corral. Feet sore an' plenty thin an' a piece of broke rope dragging from its neck. But here. Scratched like it'd been through plenty fences. But here. Must of come a mighty long ways. But here. Monte he just sat down on the ground and you'd of thought he was going to bawl like a baby. Hoss like that can get to a man.

"Worth more'n a lot of men too. Chet he likes to say that hoss knows more'n Monte hisself. There was the time a comp'ny man was out here an' had a kid with him an' that fool kid took sick an' Doc said he had to have medicine reg'lar in warm milk. Not can milk, fresh milk. Doc was partic'lar on that. Where'd he think we was going to get it? No

milk cows around here. Monte an' Chet they said they'd handle it. Brought in three cows that looked like maybe they could spare some from their calves. Better'n a circus the first times watching Chet rope them things an' Monte wrassle with 'em trying to get some juice. Never too easy but they got used to it a course. But them calves wasn't helpful. Stole all the milk ev'ry chance they got. So Monte took to putting them in the corral days which'd make their mommas hang around grazing in close an' putting the cows in at night an' the calves out which'd keep them hanging around too. Let 'em get together only after he'd got what milk the kid needed. Did that shifting on old Monkey Face 'cause that hoss is always handy an' don't need no catching an' he could just pop onto it any old time bareback without bothering with no bridle or hackamore an' do the job in jig time. Just talk to it with his legs. Nudge that hoss right an' it can spin on a nickel an' give you four cents change. Only a few days an' it knew what the score was good as Monte hisself. Like Chet says, maybe better.

"One morning somebody leaves the gate open or don't fasten it tight an' it blows open before Monte's got his milk. Them calves go scooting out bawling for their mommas an' their breakfast which ain't far away. Monte hears an' goes a-running. But he ain't even needed. That Monkey hoss has everything under control. He's herding them calves right back in that corral an' plunking hisself across the gate hole to keep 'em there an' kicking away any mommas that've got notions of trying to get in."

Hellfire
1881–1893

HE WAS CUT and branded as a yearling.

His father was a big-boned thoroughbred from somewhere in Tennessee that proved to be too all-around mean for track work and was shunted here and there always at a lower price until bought by the Triple Seven in New Mexico Territory for a range stud. His mother was a medium-sized western mare with plenty of mustang in her background, not much to look at, being over heavy as to head and hindquarters, but tough enough to fight four wolves off herself and current colt in a little snow-clogged box canyon in the winter of '81, killing two in the process and carrying scars to prove it for the several years afterward until a mountain lion ran her over a low cliff and she broke her neck in the fall.

She belonged, in a loose sort of way, to Pony Jim Green-wood, who had a small place bordering the Triple Seven range. At least his brand was on her. He claimed he had caught her wild and that was a fair story because he had been a mustanger years back, though there did seem to be traces of other markings under that brand. He tried to ride her some and she would not get over her habit of waiting to catch him unaware and pitch him into cactus, so he let her run loose, figuring she would pay for her keep with the regular increase, what with Triple Seven studs being handy. She came to the Slash Y, heavy-bellied in foal, when something out of the past came close enough to make Pony Jim think it might catch up and he wanted to sell fast and the outfit bought him out, taking over his bit of range and his scattered scraggily stock.

"Homely as sin, ain't she?" said foreman Hat Henderson when they were checking what the outfit had bought and finding it not much. "I'll bet when she drops that load she's carrying, it won't even look like a hoss. I say find some four-eyed fool's mislaid his specs and get rid of her for whatever he'll pay."

"Shucks, no," said Monte Walsh. "Remember those wolves Pony Jim told about? She's the one."

So he was born on Slash Y range out of a Slash Y mare, big-boned like his father, homely as sin like his mother. Deep dun in color with a darker patch along his back shading at the ends into almost-black mane and tail. About eleven months later when Dally Johnson forefooted him and threw him, he fought the rope like his mother fighting wolves and Chet Rollins had to loop his hind legs and the two of them stretch him out and Monte Walsh dismount and sit on his head before Powder Kent could go to work proper with the knife and the iron. Even so, half-sized and spindly as he still was, he tried to fight, thrashing on the ground like a wounded snake, and Powder was sweating by time he was through.

"That thing," said Powder, stepping back, unaware at the time he was bestowing a name, "is sure full of hellfire."

When they let him up he was snapping his baby teeth and kicking in all directions at once and he raced for the herd where his mother was waiting red-eyed and anxious on the outer edge. A while later they were both gone, having slipped past Dobe Chavez and Sunfish Perkins riding herd and headed for the badlands bordering the mountains where there were only simple uncivilized things like wolves and such to worry about. There, though he still had plenty of growing to do to hang enough tough muscle on those big bones, by the time that lion ran his mother over the cliff he was able to take care of himself.

* * *

As a three-year-old he was passed up in the regular break-ing. They combed him out of the badlands all right, along with the few others in there, but when he was in the new holding pasture rimmed with taut barbed wire, he promptly got himself caught in the wire, cut his legs and belly bad, and got himself out again. He was in no condition for any work-ing.

"Jeeeesus!" said Hat Henderson. "I'd swear he done that a

purpose! Let him go an' take his chances. If he dies, it ain't much loss. If he don't, we'll get him next year."

"Shucks, no," said Monte Walsh. "He ain't got no sense at all or else too damn much. Either way we can't let him go a-bleeding like that."

So Chet Rollins and Dally Johnson stretched him out on the ground again and Monte fought him, rubbing axle grease into the cuts, and when they let him up and opened the gate he streaked for the badlands and the simple things like wolves and lions.

"I'll sure be watching, Monte," said Powder Kent, "when you climb aboard that thing next year. That is, if you can even get a saddle on him."

*   *   *

They did not get a saddle on him the next year. They did not even get him down to the holding pasture. They sighted him a few times while they were working the badlands and finding more horses than usual in there but they never were within sniffing distance of him. He knew that rugged terrain the way a coyote knows its own immediate range and he could fade away, simply disappear. Monte Walsh wanted really to take out after him but Hat Henderson said no, they were pushed for time from a late start and to hell with Hellfire anyway.

The next year they never even sighted him though they combed even more horses out of those badlands. It was surprising how many of the Slash Y horses were off the regular range and in that rough country where it took considerable foraging to keep a full belly. They were shy a few too until they caught a glimpse of a horse on up where the big rock climbed in steep canyon-cut mountain slopes and no stock went except in the dryest years when grass was scarce on the lower levels. Two of the men hammered on up and found the missing few. But never a whiff of Hellfire, except maybe some barefoot tracks leading on up in that high-rock region. It was during the next year they caught on to what was happening.

"I spotted old Hellfire today," said Sunfish Perkins. "Out on the flats too. Know what he was doing? He was trying to coax some of the hosses into them hills with him."

"Jeeesus!" said Hat Henderson. "That's his game, is it? I say shoot the bastard, the next one that sights him."

"Shucks, no," said Monte Walsh. "That thing's for me. I ain't a-going to be happy till I've sat a saddle on him."

So they got him that year, though it took considerable doing accompanied by plenty of cussing because he was mighty fast over rough country and they had to go high up and spook him out of half a dozen hiding places and when he was driven down lower he knew how to take them through the thickest thorniest brush. But Chet Rollins was downright peeved by now and Chet when peeved and his thick-necked black and a coil of rope were quite a combination and when Hellfire was pocketed in the same box canyon where his mother took on the wolves the others held the entrance and that combination crashed right after him until Chet had a loop around his neck and choked him into respect for it. Chet kept that rope on him, choking and yanking him until he learned to lead, all the way in.

They took no chances on wire-cutting and put him direct into the high-railed small corral. Monte Walsh got a battered double-rig saddle on him, cinched tight, but had to do that on the ground with Chet and Dally Johnson stretching him out on his side and the solid weight of Sunfish Perkins sitting on his big head. Monte had a fast-dodging time of it putting a stout hackamore on that head, with an oversize knot under the soft part of the lower jaw where it could give punishment when he pulled hard on the reins.

They let him up, blindfolded and with one foreleg doubled up in a pigging rope, and he stood braced on three legs, shuddering in the darkness of not seeing, muscles bunching and twitching under the hide all over him. The others slipped out leaving Monte alone in there with him. All the hands were round about, including cook Skimpy Eagens, outside the rails or on them. Range manager Cal Brennan had come over from the ranch house.

"Monte," said Cal, leaning his long aging frame on the gate. "I kind of like the looks of you all in one piece. You'n Chet've broke every hoss around here needed breakin'. I'm willin' to skip this one."

"Shucks, no," said Monte. "It's a horse, ain't it?"

It was a horse all right. At least it resembled a horse in some ways and it certainly was not anything else. Big-boned and homely as sin with big hammerhead and big-muscled neck that looked thin in proportion to that head and huge humped withers and long slab-sided but deep barrel leading back to heavy hindquarters and all of that looking like crude molded power and set on long thickish legs ending in big splatty hoofs.

Hellfire stood there shuddering and muscle-twitching and Monte moved in, mighty wary, and took the reins and held them in his left hand on the saddle horn and reached with his right hand to loosen the pigging rope and as the rope fell and the foreleg went down he was up in the saddle.

Hellfire stood there shuddering more and Monte leaned forward and flipped off the blindfold and Hellfire went into action.

He was no bucker. That was too usual and tame and civilized for him. He was a high stiff-legged jumper and jolter and twister and wrencher regardless of the pounding and punishment he gave himself. He had the meanness of his father and the concentrated-on-occasion fury of his mother and he put all of both into every jump and jolt and twist and wrench. He piled Monte on the ninth jump and blazed both heels at him as he went rolling.

"Yow-eee!" yelled Monte Walsh, dodging and scrambling to his feet. "I knew that thing'd teach me a few!" With a rush and a flying leap off old boot soles he was back in the saddle.

Eighteen minutes later Monte had been in the dust four times and thirteen jumps was the best he had stayed and he was down now for the fifth time. He staggered up and leaned against rails. Blood dripped from his nose and his head wobbled some and a rip in his old pants down one thigh showed raw flesh where a hoof had scraped. "Well, now," he said between gasps for breath. "That's a start anyhow. I'll get that son of a bitch tomorrow."

Chet Rollins on a top rail looked down at Monte dripping blood and tossed him a bandanna. "He's wore down some now. Guess I'll try him," said Chet and hopped down.

Ten minutes later Chet leaned against rails beside Monte considerably dusty and disheveled and seven jumps had been his best and the rest of the Slash Y hands looked at each other in a self-conscious silence.

"The hell weeth eet," said Dobe Chavez. He opened the gate and eased in.

Fifty minutes later every man in the outfit except Skimpy Eagens and Cal Brennan had been thrown as many times as he would take it and Hellfire stood in the corral a very tired horse, dripping sweat and blowing a bloody froth from nostrils, but more than ready for any further action required.

"Jeeeeeesus!" said Hat Henderson, rubbing a sprained ankle. "He ain't exactly what you might call wear-downable."

* * *

Three days later Chet Rollins sat on a top rail, heels hooked under the next lower, looking with solemn interest at Hellfire out in the corral. Monte Walsh leaned close by against rails, hatless, ripped shirt dark with sweat, wiping away driblets of blood that oozed slowly from his nose down over his upper lip. Cal Brennan stood a few feet away, outside the rails, rocking gently on absurdly high-curved-heel boots.

"My oh my oh my," murmured Monte. "Ain't that a horse."

"It's a jinx, that's what it is," said Cal. "We got other hosses to be broke. You can't spend all your time on this one. Three days you've been workin' him. What do you say?"

"Well-l-l now," said Monte. "I can stay on him. That is, long as I can take it. But I can't ride him. I've learned his ways and I can stay up there but I can't teach him a thing. He don't know nothing but fighting. He plain won't quit." Monte sighed and stared out across trodden dust at Hellfire. "Yes sir," he said. "I always knew some day I'd find a horse I couldn't ride. But I always thought when that happened I'd be mad. Somehow I ain't."

"It's good for you," said Chet Rollins, amiable, conversational. "Keep you from being too all-fired cocky."

"Hopeless?" said Cal. "That it?"

"Oh, there's ways," said Monte. "Fix up a mean rig and beat him into it. Maybe starve him down. But I ain't ever done that yet to a horse. Likewise I ain't ever heard of a good horse being made that way." Monte sighed again and stared across trodden dust at Hellfire, waiting, more than ready for any further action required. "Likewise again I ain't even sure anything'd work with him. Likely he'd make it killing without curing."

"All right," said Cal, crisp, decisive. "Turn him loose. It's comin' winter an' he can't cause trouble. Come spring an' he's up to tricks somebody'll have to shoot him."

* * *

When they turned him loose he did not streak for the badlands. He seemed to know he had won some kind of a victory and stayed with the other horses down on the level and in bad weather close in by the ranch buildings. He could be brought in with the others with no extra trouble at all and when Monte Walsh tried him a few more times he was mighty respectful of a rope around his neck and failed to fight the saddle, seeming to know that was merely a preliminary. But the instant Monte was up he exploded into action and he never quit except to stand stiff-legged, ignoring reins and spurs, gulping in air and gathering strength to explode again.

When spring came and far-riding work was starting, they found a temporary use for him. There were quite a few drifting cowhands, mostly from Texas, roaming through and riding up to the ranch buildings for the good meals they knew they would get and pestering Cal Brennan for jobs to tide them over the season. The Slash Y kept its own men the year round, working with a tight competent crew, not laying off in the fall and taking on in the spring, but it could use another good man now and again if Cal thought he would qualify. When a long-legged Texan would get to blowing about the riding and the roping he could do, Cal would say: "Chet. Bring in old Hellfire." And when Hellfire, respectful of the rope around his neck, was saddled and hackamored and blindfolded and the rope was off, Cal would say to the Texan: "Stick on that hoss six jumps an' you've got a job."

One man did stick. He was big and black and long-armed and he rode in on a sorry swayback horse and he walked in his old boots with a kind of shambling gait and gave his name, smiling, as Nigger Jack Moore. He kept count and after the sixth jump he was either piled or threw himself off and rolled fast to dodge Hellfire's parting heel salute and stood up and said: "Boss, if I gotta have that hoss in my string, I don't want the job." He made a good hand, though stand-offish and not mixing much, and Cal was somewhat disappointed when he drifted away in the fall.

But one day Hellfire threw a man on the third jump, from Colorado he said he was, and the man hit with a leg doubled and broke it and they had to have him around and listen to him for six weeks before he could hobble to his horse and ride on. He was nasty-tempered and took advantage of his condition to display that temper in remarks. If he had stayed longer until the leg was fully healed, he might have left in a real hurry and in somewhat battered shape.

"I see that stunt can backfire," said Cal Brennan. "No more of it. Maybe we can sell him to Stevens when I see him again for meat for that bear-huntin' pack of hounds he has."

"Goddamn it, no!" said Monte Walsh. "That horse ain't a-going to feed no dogs!"

So Hellfire was still around ready any time to throw any man who tried to sit a saddle atop that dark patch along his back and to do any damage possible to that would-be rider in the process and Monte would look off at him a long minute or two if he was in sight before swinging aboard one of the horses he and Chet were gentling and teaching the things good cow ponies need to know before they go on and learn the fine points of doing by doing. And then one day early the next spring Cal Brennan was able to enter in one of the old notebooks he kept for the edification of the company auditor the scrawled notation: *Rec'd for one horse—$75.* And to underline that word *one*.

It was a man in clean new overalls and a straw hat who came along in a buggy and said he was a horse buyer for farms back in the cornbelt. But the man was too casual tossing out the remark that being big-hearted he liked to take off ranchers' hands any odd outlaws they had around eating good grass at a loss. "I can get that kind cheap," said the man, "seein' as how they ain't any other use an' I've got ways of breakin' 'em to plow-pullin'." That sounded plausible but Cal noted that a big-hearted horse trader was something new in his long experience and that when he tried questions the man was mighty vague about the plow-breaking ways. Cal stalled and uncorked a bottle and after a while had this straight. The man was really putting together a string of outlaw buckers for use at rodeos back east some, where the shows were becoming organized and edging into a paying business. "Yes," said the man. "I've heard you've a horse here nobody can ride. No use to you. I'll give fifteen dollars." An hour and a half later and after a look at Hellfire the man reached seventy-five.

"Shucks," said Monte Walsh when he heard. "He's got the disposition of a rattlesnake and the manners of a she-bear with cubs but all the same I'm a-going to miss having that thing around."

Hellfire left the Slash Y tied to the back of the buggy, respectful of the rope around his neck, maybe satisfied some that he had put respect in the man with a forehoof nearly raking the new overalls off him and taking a few patches of skin too. He went holding back until the rope would tighten, then trotting to get some slack and turn that big hammerhead to look into distance at the far mountains where the badlands climbed in rugged many-colored broken ridges to meet them.

* * *

Two years passed the way years do over the range and every now and then during that time word reached the Slash Y by men drifting through or the line-rider grapevine or one of the weekly papers picked up with the mail in town that Hellfire had done it again—had thrown his man or men somewhere along the rodeo circuit. He threw them all and he kept on throwing them and trying to do damage in the process and sometimes doing it and he earned billing above any of the men who tried to ride him and the papers took to using captions like: HELLFIRE AGAIN IN FOUR JUMPS. One time, as a feature stunt at the big show in Denver, not another horse was used in the bronc-riding and he took all entrants and shucked them all, one after another, and one of them was bunged up bad and another was crippled for life by a big splatty hoof that caught him in the hip. And every time word reached the Slash Y a small wry smile flicked on Monte Walsh's lips and he murmured soft to himself: "Ain't that a horse."

Then one day in the next year in the evening Hat Henderson looked up from the paper he was reading by one of the two kerosene lamps in the bunkhouse and said: "Lookahere. Sonny Jacobs won up at Las Vegas."

"That ain't news," said Dally Johnson. "Sonny's got the habit of winning."

"Yeah," said Hat. "But he was riding Hellfire."

Over on his bunk Monte Walsh raised up and started to say something and thought better of it and eased down again. He was troubled in his mind and could not have told just why and he was troubled that way until he and some of the others were in town for a little well-oiled relaxation and ran into Sonny Jacobs passing through.

"Yep," said Sonny, swirling the amber liquid in his glass and watching it swirl. "Yep and yessiree and you can bet your roll on it, I rode him. Old Hellfire himself." Then Sonny looked up, grinning around. "But just among you boys I'm free to say that just means I rode him just past the time limit and right after when I was leaving him that wasn't exactly and precisely all my own idea. He was sure helping me go."

Down the bar a few places Monte Walsh, who had been mighty quiet, raised his own glass and a small wry smile flicked on his lips and he downed his drink and another following and before long he and Sonny were staging a Calamity Jane-style race, rules being each man must stay on his horse, ride up on the platform and in the front door of the first saloon and sink a drink in the saddle and out the back door and around to the front of the next saloon and in and ditto on down the street.

* * *

Two years again and word about Hellfire had been dwindling and then for a stretch there had been none at all. The Slash Y was changing, with Cal Brennan laid up in town with bad feet and creeping age at last, and a new manager was in charge full of modernization methods and fat lazy Herefords were beginning to multiply where longhorns had grazed and the fence lines were slicing once open range into big pastures with more windmills sprouting at strategic spots. But some of the old crew were still there and occasionally talk about Hellfire still floated through the bunkhouse.

"Hey, Monte," said Dally Johnson. "What d'you think happened to him?"

"Aw, hell," said Monte Walsh. "I reckon the bastards ruined him then dumped him. Likely his ankles gave out.

There never was a horse pounded like that. He'd cripple himself to shake a man."

Then one day, a Saturday, with the branding done, they went into town to see a little Wild West show. It was a two-bit affair, mostly fake as most of them usually were, but such things had a kind of fascination for cowmen, even the old-time hands, if only for the fun of picking them to pieces for weeks after in talk.

They rode in early for a good start on the serious business of being properly lubricated for appreciation of the proceedings. By early afternoon they were ranked with the usual crowd on the bleacher-style seats set along one side of a big corral. The show droned along with the usual stunts and a big-voiced presiding barker trying to whip up excitement with words and the one thing that really tickled the audience, particularly a bunch of Apaches from the reservation off southeast, was when an old stagecoach came careening in one end gate to go jouncing across and out another gate with the driver snapping a long whip and two men on top blazing away with blanks followed by half a dozen fake Indians painted scarey and bareback on ponies whooping and yelling and trying to handle bows and arrows and stay on those ponies at the same time and on the way out the coach lost a wheel against a gatepost and tipped with a lovely crash and the driver and two top-blazers went sprawling forward and in among the horses and harness.

Then the barker let out another notch on that voice and whipped up excitement in himself at least and two men came in an end gate leading by a rope around its neck something which seemed to resemble a horse.

Big-boned and homely as sin. Big hammerhead hanging low and just about every one of those big bones showing under shrunken dun-colored hide along slab-sided but deep barrel and hollow flanks and once-heavy hindquarters. A dark patch running from the few remaining wisps of almost-black mane on under the saddle and back to the remnants of almost-black tail. Light splotches showing on the gaunt belly from too-tight cinch scalds where the hair had grown out again white. Ankles swollen to twice normal size. Big splatty hoofs coming down gingerly into the dust and tiny muscle tremors running up the thick legs with every step.

He stood, shuddering and muscle-twitching, big head hang-

ing, respectful of the rope around his neck, and one of the
men loosened the loop and flipped it off and leaped back as
the big head moved, jaws reaching for the arm. He stood, big
head hanging, and as the other man stepped in close, cautious, and took the reins, the big head rose and turned some,
watching out of rolled eye, and as the man swung up, light
and quick, he exploded into action.

Meanness and concentrated fury and utter disregard of the
pain stabbing up the legs from pounding hoofs into starved
weakened body, a good show still, no doubt of that, but slow,
a slow-motion parody to certain men in the stand, the bitter
brutal wrench and the final snap gone.

"Would you look at that," said Sugar Wyman. "Old Hellfire's still willin' to fight!"

Two seats away Monte Walsh sat still and quiet, staring
out across trodden dust at a big unbeaten horse standing stiff-
legged, gulping in air and gathering strength to try again.

He tried and the man rocked and swayed in the saddle and
raked the gaunt slab sides with spurs and waved his hat yipping. He stood again, stiff-legged, and the man swung down
in one swift motion, dodging the heels that blazed at him as
he left, and the other man flipped his loop and Hellfire was
led away.

Up in the stand Monte Walsh stared down at his boot toes.
Slowly one hand moved into a pants pocket and out again.
He stared down at the open palm. Four dollar bills and some
change. He shifted weight to turn toward Chet Rollins beside
him.

"All right, Monte," said Chet. "I got seven dollars. You go
around and start dickering while I see what the rest of the
boys've got."

They bought him for twenty-eight dollars. He returned to
the neighborhood of the Slash Y buildings, slow and easy and
with full escort, the way he had come there once before, with
Chet Rollins's rope around his neck. They did not stop there.
They went right on past and through the open gap in one
fence line and on to the gate in the next. Monte Walsh dismounted and opened the gate and moved in, wary, and
flipped the loop over the big head and away and lost a piece
of sleeve doing it and had to dodge behind the open gate or
he might have lost more.

Old Hellfire faced the open gap as if wondering was there

a trick in this. Then he raised that hammerhead and bugled to all the simple things like wolves and lions that he was coming home. He plunged through the gap and blazed with both heels in passing and hit the gate and knocked it into Monte and sent him sprawling.

"Shucks," said Monte, coming to his feet to watch old Hellfire head for the badlands, not able to streak any more but moving right along at a good trot then into a lumbering lope. "If that thing could talk, he couldn't have said it better."

*   *   *

It was early the next year that Chet Rollins and Monte Walsh, looking for a four-year-old that had jumped and scrambled over the breaking corral rails and made it through fence lines into the badlands with a saddle still on him, came on the bones. There was no mistaking those big ones and the scraps of dun-colored hide clinging to a few. Monte sat still in his saddle, staring down. It was Chet who found the other remains, rib cage smashed in, with bits of a tawny fur showing on the fanged skull.

Monte drew a deep breath. "Must of been two of them jumped him."

"Maybe," said Chet. "Or maybe again only one and they did for each other. The coyotes have sure been working on them both. One thing sure, he put up a real fight."

"Certain he did," said Monte Walsh. "He was always willing."

BELLES OF THE BALL
Rumors Laid to Rest

From a gentleman who came in on the train this morning we have at last learned the identity of the two "ladies" whose charms captivated all present and made festive the occasion of the dance at Holloway's Livery Stable in the town of Harmony last month.

It seems that the masculine attendance at the affair surpassed all expectations. Men of the saddle came in from as far as seventy miles away. All the wives and sisters and daughters of the town did their loyal best but, alas, to put it bluntly, they were in short supply. Complaints on the subject were frequent. Then the two "ladies" about whom so many rumors have circulated put in an appearance. Mr. Monte Walsh and Mr. Chester Rollins, the two inseparables of the Slash Y range whose names should be familiar to readers of this newspaper from previous occasions, had raided a nearby store and arrayed themselves in feminine apparel. About their manly chests were those items which are unmentionable in a family newspaper but are well known to our feminine readers. About their legs swung other items which are normally covered by outer skirts. Our informant states that at least the flowered hats on their heads were properly respectable. He states further that they never lacked for enthusiastic partners the entire evening and that there were several vigorous encounters between jealous suitors anxious for their favors.

The best of these, he solemnly states upon oath, was provided by "Miss" Walsh. When some admirer became too fresh "she" so far forgot "herself" as to pick the offender up and throw him into the hayloft.

All in One Place
1894

SONNY JACOBS, who would have dropped the Sonny if he could have long ago, ambled easy in saddle aboard a sleek grain-fed gray along the road that led to and ended at the range headquarters of the Consolidated Cattle Company. He was plumping around the middle and his broad face had the ruddy full-blown look of good food and soft living, but the squint of the eyes was still there and he sat the saddle with the simple assurance of the old days. Several years on the emerging rodeo circuit and two seasons with Colonel Cody's Wild West Show had given him a traveled sophistication he was rapidly and cheerfully shedding.

He passed a batch of fat lazy white-faced cattle. "Haven't seen a longhorn yet," he murmured. "Makes me feel kind of lonesome." A few of them raised heads to look at him, indifferent and away, through and over the four-strand barbed wire fence that paralleled the road. "Wonder how they feel about that," he murmured. "Kind of like being in jail." He ambled on. The ranch buildings were just ahead. A gate barred the way. He swung down and opened the gate and led the gray through and closed the gate behind him. "Something new all the time," he murmured, swinging up. "Bet the boys don't like that nuisance." He ambled on.

The old adobe ranch house had a fresh coating of soft-toned mud plaster. Curtains, starched and frilly, showed in the front and side windows. The old veranda was painted and along each end small beds of flowers made patches of color. He stared at these, ambling past, finding nothing to murmur.

He stopped by the first small corral and dismounted and led the gray in. Slowly, leisurely, he unsaddled and heaved the saddle up on a top rail and looped the bridle over the horn and watched the gray move toward the inside water trough. He turned to look with knowing eyes at the eight other horses that had crowded to the far side away from him. "Always had good hosses," he murmured. "Monte'd see to that." Suddenly he chuckled. "If that ain't his old dun, Monkey Face. Used to think of trying to steal that thing from him."

He went out through the gate and closed it and turned to look at the other buildings, still and quiet in the serenity of afternoon sun. A new-built chicken house and run stretched out beside the long low plank barn and a mixed flock of hens squatted in dust holes, only a few paying any attention to the self-important scratchings of a flop-combed rooster. "Wonder who rides herd on those things," he murmured.

He wandered over by the cracked surface of the still solid adobe bunkhouse and put one hand on each side of the open doorway and leaned in over the doorstep. Scattered clothing and gear hung from wooden pegs at one end. Old worn straw mattresses and pillows, blanket-covered, lay on six of the bunks along the sides. The other six were bare, empty. "Shrinking," he murmured, pushing back out and looking around again. "Like everything else these days. Put up bobwire and get rid of men."

Smoke floated upward from the tin stovepipe of the adobe cookhouse. He strolled toward this, moving a bit faster. "Hey, Skimpy," he shouted, stepping up into the doorway. He stopped short, holding to the doorjambs.

Beyond the plank table and benches, by the big old cookstove, a short enormously fat woman with gray hair pulled haphazard up on her head and partly covered by a torn dustcap was turning, big spoon in hand, to glare at him. "You stop that noise," she said. "Mrs. Morris'll raise hell. You'll wake the baby."

Sonny's lower jaw dropped some. "Baby?" he said.

"Up at the house," said the woman, contemptuous of his ignorance. "The boss-man's wife."

"I'll make like a mouse," said Sonny. He took off his hat and tried a smile. "Morris? Only Morris I remember's old Jake used to hang around at the Triple Seven."

"Him?" said the woman, relenting some. "That one? With a baby? It's a young one, nephew or something."

"Running the Slash Y?" said Sonny.

"He's been to school," said the woman. "Back east some-wheres. He knows everything. Or thinks he does. You ever work here?"

"No ma'am," said Sonny. "I was Diamond Six to the south. But I was around often. Whatever happened to Skimpy? Skimpy Eagens, did the cooking."

"How should I know?" said the woman. "Nobody tells me much. But I hear them say he fell down one day right by the stove here. Dead when they found him. I suppose you'll be staying the night and I'll have to be feeding you too."

"I was kind of counting on that," said Sonny, backing out. He wandered over by the bunkhouse again and sat on the bench along the front of it. He laid his hat beside him and leaned back against the adobes. "Skimpy too," he murmured. "There was nobody could make doughnuts like old Skimpy." He slumped further on the bench, feeling the warmth of the sun-soaked adobes against his back. The familiar remembered quiet and there's time-for-all-things of the big land began to seep into him.

He turned his head slightly. The woman was in the door-way of the cookhouse, stepping down, carrying a thick-sided big cup of hot coffee. She came over and set the cup on the bench beside his hat. "If you're like the rest of them," she said, "you never get enough of it. I keep a pot on the stove."

"Thank you, ma'am," said Sonny. "I sure like to think I'm still like the rest of 'em. Where is everybody? I mean the menfolks."

"Over in the southeast pasture," said the woman, turning away to return to the cookhouse. "Dipping sheep."

Sonny slumped further on the bench. "Sheep," he mur-mured. "Oh . . . my . . . God."

* * *

Far down the road and off to the right seven small figures moved, seven men mounted, jogging across the big land. They came to the fence paralleling the road and hesitated briefly while one dismounted and opened a wire gap and they rode through and the gap was closed and they jogged for-ward along the road.

Sonny Jacobs, relaxed and lazy in angled shadow now on

the bench along the front of the bunkhouse, watched them come.

They approached the gate that barred the way and one of them, a lean length of rawhide thickening some at last with the slow subtle sag of the beginnings of middle age, struck spurs to his horse and it leaped ahead and reared, wheeling on hind legs, and dropped down alongside the gate and the man leaned down from the saddle unfastening the latch and the horse danced, backing and pivoting with short springy steps as he pulled the gate wide open. The others rode through and again the horse danced, enjoying the game, and the man leaned out from the saddle, pulling the gate shut, swinging low to reach through and fasten the latch.

Sonny Jacobs sat motionless in his shadow. "That's Monte," he murmured. "Yessiree, that's him all right. I've seen 'em all on the bigtime and there never was a man like Monte on a hoss." He watched them jog to the small corral and dismount and one of them stride off toward the ranch house and the others lead the horses inside. He turned his head slightly to see the one man jump on the veranda of the house, hurrying, and open the door and disappear inside. "Must be Morris," he murmured. He turned his head slightly again to watch the others. "Why, there's Sugar, though he sure has been putting on weight . . . And Dally hiding behind a mustache . . . And Old Red Hawkins that use to be Box 4 . . . And who'd of thought it, Short-Hair Hale that was barbering in town when I left . . . Damned if that young one don't look like Gonzales's boy Juan making out to be a man."

Sonny sat motionless in his shadow and listened to voices from the corral. "Where'd that hoss drop from?" "Fatter'n a barrel, what's the brand?" "T Bar J." "G'wan, never heard of it." "Hey look at that saddle." "Fool stunt, weightin' down a hoss with all that silver." "Must be a dude loose somewheres."

Sonny grinned lazily to himself and watched them leave the corral and head in his direction. A voice lifted among them. "Oh, no! Look at 'im sittin' there! It ain't nothin' but a homely fat hunk of wolf bait!" They converged on him and he was yanked up from the bench and batted about and insults, raucous and ribald, assailed his ears.

"Whew-w-w-w," said Sonny, pulling loose, holding his

nose. "I should of stayed away. What's that stink? I can't stand it. Don't tell me. It can't be. It ain't—"

"Yeah," said Dally Johnson, dry, disgusted. "The company's tryin' some this year."

"Bat his brains out," suggested Old Red Hawkins. "We scrubbed good out at the tank."

"Ba-a-a-a-a," chortled Sonny, slapping his sides, watching the muscles tighten along Monte Walsh's jaw, a speculative glint rise in Monte's eyes.

"Know why?" said Sugar Wyman. "Because there's money in 'em. That's the one thing seems to count nowadays. You tell 'im, Juan. You been to school too."

"The sheep are a two-crop stock," said young Juan Gonzales. "The lambs . . . and the wool."

"Ba-a-a-a-a," chortled Sonny.

"Quit it," said Sugar, a flush climbing up his face. "What the hell difference? Things ain't what they used to be."

"Ba-a-a-a-a," chortled Sonny. "Ain't that a lamb I hear blatting? You better be hopping, Monte, and playing nurse-maid."

"Asking, plain asking," said Monte Walsh. He hurtled into Sonny and carried him over and down. Dust rose as they rolled, hammering, grunting and heaving, now one on top, now the other. The dust settled some and Sonny lay on his belly and Monte sat astride him, rubbing his face in the dirt.

Monte stopped, holding Sonny's head up with hand fixed in his hair. "You hear any blatting?" he said.

"Only . . . my own," spluttered Sonny, cheerfully, happily, spitting out dust. "I see . . . some things . . . ain't changed."

* * *

Shadow lay over the big land. To the west the sun dropped below the rim of the mountains. There would be light for an hour and more but the golden glow was gone. Only the last brief legacy remained, deepening like memory into distance.

Seven men sat or lay about the old bunkhouse in the slow semi-somnolent state of a good start on the digestion of a good meal.

Sonny Jacobs moved on his chair, quietly letting his belt out another notch. "Morris don't eat with you," he said.

"Would you?" said Dally Johnson, looking up from a bridle he was fitting with a new chin strap. "Would you with a wife an' kid right handy?"

"That problem's missed me," said Sonny.

"Morris is all right," said Old Red Hawkins from his bunk. "Talks like a goddamn book an' carries his nose way up there somewheres but something has to be done an' he'll climb down an' get his hands dirty like most anybody."

"I got no complaint," said Short-Hair Hale from the old table where he was playing solitaire with a dog-eared deck of cards. "He gave me a job when I went on the wagon and with the shakes I had wasn't worth much."

"Maybe you're thinkin' you're worth somethin' now," said Dally.

"Morris'll do," said Sugar Wyman from his chair. "For the way things are now. He gets by. With us pushin' him. He's learnin'. But he sure ain't no Cal Brennan."

"Who in hell would be?" said Dally.

Silence in the old bunkhouse.

"How is Cal?" said Sonny gently.

"So blinkin' old it hurts to see it," said Dally. "But still Cal. On the talkin' an' bitin' end of him anyways. Feet gave out on him a few years back. He's sittin' around in town not able even to hobble any. Reckon it was them damn boots he used to wear. Uses a wheelchair now."

"He's still got all his own teeth," said Sugar. "Which you sure ain't."

"Yeah," said Dally. "His teeth. Sunfish's there too, takin' care of him. You remember Sunfish. Hell, nobody'd ever forget him. They got a saddle'n harness shop for somethin' to be doin'. Cal does the thinkin' an' Sunfish does the clerkin' an' they play checkers like it was a regular war atween 'em when there ain't anythin' else doin'."

Silence in the old bunkhouse except for the soft swish of cards.

"Hey, Juan," said Dally. "Trot over to the barn an' rout out one of them other mattresses. Sonny here'll be needin' it."

"Might make it two," said Old Red. "He looks kind of soft to me."

"Check them fool chickens while you're out," said Sugar.

"Stay away from that corral," came the voice of Monte Walsh from his bunk. "I'll tend to the horses later."

Young Juan Gonzales rose from his chair and disappeared out the doorway.

"I saw Hat up in Denver last week," said Sonny. "Same old Hat. Near broke my hand. Made me promise to tell what's doing down here if I go back through. He was all fancied up like for a wedding or a funeral but he claimed that's his regular wear these days."

"How's he doin'?" said Sugar.

"Fine. Just fine. Commission buyer at the stockyards. Told me he was thinking of putting money into a restaurant."

"Sounds like him," said Sugar. "He was always keepin' busy. A workin' fool. An' expected the rest of us to keep right up with him."

"Which I'm free to remark we did," said Dally. "Which I kind of admit it took some doin' now an' again. I miss them days."

Silence in the old bunkhouse except for the soft tread of young Juan returning with a rolled mattress in his arms and a pillow over one shoulder. He laid these on one of the empty bunks and took a blanket from a high shelf over the wooden pegs at one end of the room and spread this over them. He sat again on his chair, silent, respectful, content to be there and to listen.

"I kind of thought," said Sonny, "Hat'd be taking over here when Cal left."

"So did he," said Sugar. "An' the same for the rest of us."

"Yeah," said Dally. "The same. But the comp'ny thought diff'rent. Cal made the wires hot but it wasn't no use. They sent in this Morris fresh out of some cow college an' a year or two in the comp'ny offices an' it was plumb bad for a while. But I reckon Hat he was beginnin' to age some an' he—"

"Like the rest of us," said Sugar.

"Yeah. The rest of us. I reckon you know, Sonny, how when Hat got real mad which lucky wasn't more'n every other year or so everybody able to move within about ten mile went into hidin'. Sure you do, seein' as how oncet you wasn't out of the way fast enough an' he threw you clean over a corral fence. Well, along this time things kept happenin' an' we expected Hat to blow an' maybe kick this Morris clean back to Chicago an' all he did was chew on his mouth till it was raw most of the time. I reckon maybe Cal'd been askin' him to hold on an' see it through. You know how it was, he'd do about anythin' for Cal. Then one day it was some little thing like it always was, little things addin' up an' addin' up, an' Hat he picked up a shovel, near a new one too, an' he snapped that hick'ry handle over his knee an' threw the pieces away an' he picked up this Morris an' tucked him under one arm all shoutin' an' thrashing aroun' an' carted him up to the house there an' plunked him in the chair by Cal's old desk an' he said: 'Figure my time an' figure it fast.' "

"Wasn't twenty minutes," said Sugar, "before Hat was headin' out of here."

"Yeah. Headin' out. Rest of us, soon as we knew, was packin' to leave too, those of us still aroun', when I guess Hat he'd stopped in town because Cal he come larrupin' out here in a buggy. He talked an' he talked an' he said he couldn't blame Hat too much but he wasn't goin' to have the rest of us runnin' out on his old brand just because the goin' was rough."

"So we stayed," said Sugar.

"Yeah. We stayed. Cal saw this Morris standin' on the porch over there chewin' his fingers an' he swung the buggy over there an' he said: 'Git in.' They drove off an' I expect Cal talked plenty more because when this Morris come back on a hoss he borrowed in town he looked like he'd been wrung out some. He moped aroun' the house a day or two an' one mornin' he come out here talkin' almost like a man and it's been some better since."

Silence in the old bunkhouse. Old Red pushed up from his bunk and slid a chair in by the table and bent to it. "Whittle that deck down," he said to Short-Hair Hale, "an' start dealin' euchre."

"Did Dobe stay?" said Sonny.

"Certain he stayed," said Sugar. "You ever know Dobe to pull out of anythin' rough? He stayed till things was better. But he had other fish to fry."

"Yeah," said Dally. "Other fish. You tell him, Juan. He's your kin."

"El Señor Chavez," said young Juan grinning, "he is married to my father's sister. He is living in Carrizozo. He is deputy sheriff. He is—"

"You ought to see 'im, Sonny," said Sugar. "He's fatted till that old gunbelt won't even go around him any more. Sticks the gun in his pants when he thinks he might need it. Waxes his mustache an' dresses pretty. Damn politician, that's what he is. You ought to see 'im, jollyin' the men, pattin' the women, kissin' the babies. He's running for sheriff hisself this year. Old one's retirin'.''

"He'll win too," came the voice of Monte Walsh from his bunk. "And make the best goddamned sheriff they ever had over that way."

Silence in the old bunkhouse, broken only by the soft swish of cards and Old Red's low rumble: "Pick it up, you short-haired jackass. This'll be my point."

Sonny Jacobs moved on his chair, rolling a cigarette and scratching a match to light it. He looked at the bunk where Monte Walsh lay flat, staring up at the ceiling.

Sonny looked away. "Chet," he said. "Chet Rollins. I thought sure he'd be here."

"Ain't you heard?" said Dally. "Thought you came through town."

"No," said Sonny. "I come down by Vegas and Anton Chico. I'm heading for the old Diamond to see what's been happening there."

"You won't find much," said Sugar. "It's broke up. Half a dozen small ranches now. It's broke up."

"Yeah," said Dally. "Broke up. Like we're doin'."

Silence in the old bunkhouse. "Made it," said Old Red softly. "Now if I just euchre you oncet, I'm out."

"In town," said Sonny.

"Why, yes," said Sugar. "If you'd been there an' looked sharp, you'd of seen it. Holloway's livery stable."

"If I wasn't blind," said Sonny. "It's been there long as I can remember."

"Sure it has," said Sugar. "But it's wearin' a new sign. Holloway an' Rollins."

"Yeah," said Dally. "An' Rollins. Chet's bought into it. Did some fancy hoss-tradin' an' worked a deal. Holloway's retirin' an' Chet's part owner an' manager."

"Two months ago," said Sugar. "An' for quite a time before that he was almighty poor comp'ny aroun' here. Savin' his money. Nursin' every goddamned nickel. Always figurin' an' figurin' an' moonin' aroun' like a silly kid that ain't never saw a skirt . . ."

"Ha!" said Sonny. "So that's it."

"Yeah," said Dally. "That's it. He's gettin' married. Next week. You know her. Old Man Engle's daughter, that has the hotel in town."

"No," said Sonny. "Not Mary Engle? Chet? And Mary Engle? Why, the last I knew she was shooing the rest of us aside like flies and Monte had the inside track."

"That was when she was young an' giddy," said Dally. "You might say didn't know no better. She's growed up now. Oh my lordy yes, she's growed up now. Had a couple years back east with relatives somewheres and come home with notions. Quite a lady. Why, a man wouldn't dare spit anywheres near her. Come back an' she knew what she wanted. Looked around 'n picked Chet. He didn't have a chance. You know how it is, them that ain't chased women much, when they go, they go. Chet sure went. You know Monte, he can't stay away from anythin' in skirts an' he was sniffin' around again an' she—"

"Shucks," said Sugar. "Monte ain't the marryin' kind."

"Yeah," said Dally. "He ain't. But you know Chet, about the steadiest man ever did a real day's work. Put his mind to it an' quit foolin' with us no-good cowhands that're gettin' to be out of date anyways, he could be anythin'. I reckon she knows that. Women got a nose for things like that. The way I hear it she plain outright told Monte to go sniff somewheres else, that Chet's the better man."

"I'll be frizzled and fried," said Sonny. "Monte. Tell me it ain't true. I didn't know you ever let—"

"She is a silly woman," said young Juan, sitting up straight on his chair, indignant. "Monte is always the better man. Than anybody."

"Shut up, Juan," said Monte Walsh, swinging his feet to the floor and rising from his bunk. "You're so goddamned young." He moved toward the doorway and stopped, looking down at Sonny. "What could I do?" he said. "She's right, ain't she?" He moved on and out.

Sonny started to rise, to follow. "Sit down," said Dally. "Let him be. He's almighty touchy these days. If it ain't that I've rode with him so long, he'd of took me apart for talkin' like that. But he's got to get it rubbed in somehow . . . I reckon we've covered most ev'rybody yappin' here like old maids at a sewin' circle. Except Joe. Joe Joslin. It don't seem right to be callin' him Jumpin' Joe any more. He's buried out back there alongside Powder. It happened two years back. We was bringin' cattle out of the hills an' a early storm hit. Snow an' sleet an' the wind makin' a racket an' dark comin' fast. We was separated, hurryin' to clean 'em out. His hoss must of slipped an' he went over a bank. Broke a leg an' was mashed some. Froze when we found him by first light. I reckon he was knocked out when he hit an' never come out of it. Like to think that anyways. He was a good man, Joe was, even if his notion of jokes was sometimes kind of sour."

"He was the best," said Sugar. "One of the best. There never was another just like Joe. Why, when we was kids an' ridin' up the trail with Cal, Joe he used to—"

"Yeah," said Dally. "A good man. I reckon most of us are when we're dead. Or married. Which in some ways is about the same. But these ain't cheerful topics to keep worryin'. Your turn, Sonny. You tell us how you been gallivantin' through all them big towns givin' people all the wrong notions how it used to be out here . . ."

*   *   *

And outside, in the gathering dusk, while slow talk drifted on in the bunkhouse, Monte Walsh emerged from the barn carrying a new bridle made of soft hand-worked leather with a light snaffle bit. He moved past the first corral and in through a gate to the larger corral. His lips rounded in a low whistle. By the far side a neat, compact, clean-legged roan raised its head and looked toward the sound. He whistled again, moving forward, and the horse trotted to meet him and pushed at him with its head and nibbled along one of his arms. He reached out, scratching around its ears, rubbing along its neck.

Slowly, deliberately clumsy, he put the bridle on and the horse stood with head firm, jaws opening for the bit. He let the reins drop to the ground and the horse stood, a clean solid compact shape in the dusk. He moved around it, deliberately awkward, bumping it, and lifted each foot in turn. He bent low and crawled under it, scraping against the belly, knocking against the legs, and the horse stood, firm, turning its head to watch him.

"Shucks," murmured Monte. "I know you think I'm seventeen different kinds of a fool, but you got to be ready for anything."

He took the reins and led the horse out of the corral and in one swift motion was astride the bare back. Together, one being, a part of each other, the man and the horse moved out and away. They stopped where the ground dropped toward a wide arroyo, well out of any possible sight from the ranch buildings. Monte swung a leg over and slid down and the horse stood, watching him, and he stepped to a clumped juniper and pulled from under the low branches a bulky package. An old sidesaddle wrapped in burlap bags.

He yanked the saddle along the ground and bumped the roan with it getting it up in place and he heaved, pulling the cinch tight, and the horse stood, head turned, watching him. He took the bags and tucked them into his belt so that they hung down around his legs. He moved by the horse's head, flapping the bags with his hands, and the horse stood, watching him.

Awkward, not deliberately now, he put his left foot into the left stirrup. Holding to the saddle and the horse's mane, he pulled himself up, struggling to get his right leg and foot through between his left leg and the horse and into position over with knee hooked around the humped rest on the saddle, and the horse stood, firm, braced against his maneuverings.

"Silly goddamned thing," he murmured. "They got forked legs just like us. But this is how they do it."

Monte Walsh, in a burlap skirt, rawhide length of him draped on a sidesaddle, went riding in the deepening dusk.

II

Doc Frantz, who himself had almost forgotten he had been christened Frederick Walter, sat in his favorite chair with his slippered feet up on a table he used for a desk and looked out the front window of the old adobe storeroom which with slow alterations through the years served him as home and office. This was his favorite position. With chair and table thus precisely placed he could see neatly framed by the window most of the major points of occasional sudden interest in the little town of Harmony.

Doc had come into the Territory fifteen years before, no youngster even then, tired of an east coast practice inherited from his father that consisted chiefly of prescribing unnecessary but soothing pills for elderly ladies. He had been aiming at Albuquerque and a possible post at a sanatorium there and along in the night at a stage relay station on the way several lank grim horsemen appeared out of the dark demanding that the driver take a hurry call for a doctor on to the next town and the driver spat out his tobacco quid and remarked he could do better than that and before Doc was quite sure what was happening he and his little bag were hustled out of the coach and onto a horse and he was being led at a pace that jolted his back teeth through clean starlit distances to the few scattered squat shapes of the buildings of a tiny village lost somewhere in the immensity of the big land and then in the light of two smoky lamps in a small smelly saloon he was probing for a bullet deep in the chest of a young cowpuncher he would have said should still be in school and instead had just had a pint of whisky poured down his throat and was muttering as the overdose of alcohol took him: "Don't take no mind of my hollerin' an' thrashin', Doc, just yank the son of a bitch out."

The bullet had cracked a rib and grazed the heart besides doing damage to a lung and it was three days before Doc could tell himself with any certainty that his patient would live very likely to stop other bullets at other times in other places. During those days, unable to avoid such things, pinned to them by proximity, he sewed up several wicked knife slashes in two swarthy-skinned men who seemed proud of needing such attention and forgot their quarrel in the common enterprise of insisting upon paying for the stitches and pooled their resources to present him with a goat and he lanced a big abscess on the rump of a mule belonging to a man named Holloway who had recently started a livery stable and he was told he now had credit coming to him there and he treated for snakebite a mangy yellow dog and acquired a worshipping shadow in the form of the black-haired eight-year-old owner of the dog and he set and splinted with pieces of barrel stave the broken arm of another young cowpuncher who came riding in with the arm hanging limp and pressed a pair of spurs on him in payment and he found himself looking often into the distances of the harsh bitter beautiful land

and speculating on the powers of the hot chili, inescapably mixed into the only food available at the one little café, to clear the phlegm from a clogged throat and loosen congestion in the sinuses. Somewhere along the line, probably that first night when he was all but kidnapped from the coach, he must have complained that his trunk was still in the boot. The clothes in it were unimportant, but the books and instruments were not. He was inquiring about ways and means of getting on to Albuquerque after it when a man he vaguely recognized as one of the kidnappers came into town driving a wagon and in the wagon was his trunk and tied to the tailgate by a lead rope was a tough little cow pony. "Yours, ain't it?" said the man, reaching back to pat the trunk. "I an' the boys been chasin' it an' roped it off up by Tijeras. We're a mite low on cash these days, Doc, but we figger mebbe you can use that there hoss." Doc was confronting that situation of increasing livestock supposed to be his now when one of the men whose slashes he had sewed hobbled up grinning apologetically and talked fast in mixed Spanish and English which the wagon man translated as meaning that this here greaser's woman was down with her sixth and she had dropped the other five with no trouble at all but this one this time was bad very bad and perhaps *el señor medico* would find it in his great goodness to do something.

Doc Frantz had sighed—and picked up his little bag. Across the way was an abandoned adobe storeroom, doorway and windows blank but walls and roof still sound. "Put the trunk in there," he had said . . .

Doc sat in his favorite chair and looked out through the glass that had been freighted in long ago by a grateful but otherwise penniless patient and set into a new frame in the blank window space by another. After fifteen years he had long since stopped fooling himself by thinking he would get on to Albuquerque someday or would even want to do anything that foolish. He had $213 in the town's new and only small bank and would have difficulty making anyone accept any of those dollars in exchange for anything he might want in town and the high dry dusty climate of this incomprehensible country had given him the apparent wrung-out constitution of a desert burro and he had recently graduated with honors of appetite from red chili to the fiery green and wondered how anyone could enjoy a meal without it.

He sat on his favorite chair that had been repaired with hand-carved spindles by another patient and looked out at the major points of occasional sudden interest in the little town of Harmony that was no longer quite so little, organized now, beginning to take on some shape with a few new buildings beginning to outline a central plaza and a few new streets beginning to straggle out a few blocks. Not much of a place, an unwary visitor from elsewhere might have said. Just a sleepy little town drowsing in late morning sunlight. But to one of his intimate acquaintance with it, the omens were unmistakable. Angled across the plaza from his window the windows of Old Man Engle's Harmony House wore the highly unusual sheen of a recent washing and the wide porch and two-story front had their first fresh coat of paint since the original of forty-three years before. This was mid-week and yet several wagons were drawn up by the two general stores, having brought families that usually showed only on Saturdays. A surprising number of cow ponies for this time of day drooped along tie rails and every now and then another rider or two drifted in and dismounted and looped reins and disappeared through swinging doors.

Doc Frantz sat by his window and several hundred feet away, in the relatively dim interior of Thornburg's nameless little saloon around a corner from the two slightly more respectable emporiums of liquid refreshment on the plaza, Chalkeye Ferrero hoisted a drink. "Whoosh an' hello an' crack the whip," he remarked to sundry of his fellows. "Maybe us horny hoptoads're out of place at doings like today. I seen three plug hats an' a topper an' a pair of spats over at the hotel. Not to mention a frilly female what looked two holes through me without even seein' me. But I reckon we got to be on hand when ol' Chet gets hisself hitched."

A stagecoach crawled out of distance to the northeast, marked by its plume of dust, and grew larger and seemed to pick up speed as it approached and it rolled to a creaking stop at the station a half block off the plaza along what had been and still qualified as the main street. Two more obvious aliens from the mysterious fashionable regions far to the east, a man and a woman, climbed carefully out, glancing apprehensively about at the half dozen swarthy-skinned onlookers who had silently materialized out of nowhere to see the sight. A wrinkled whisky-mottled old face with scraggly chin whiskers and topped by a few tufts of scraggly gray hair appeared in the coach window. "Snakes an' tarant'las an' centeepedes," it said. The woman shook her skirt vigorously, ignoring the remark, and opened and raised a dainty parasol over her flowered hat and veil while the man tried vainly to slap the dust out of his clothes and they moved along the street, stepping cautiously around holes in the board sidewalk, to the Harmony House and were greeted on the porch by Clark Aloysius Engle himself in frock coat and checkered vest and high starched collar.

Sugar Wyman and Dally Johnson, ambling past somewhat slicked and scrubbed with packages containing new shirts under arms, stopped to watch Old Man Engle escort his latest visitors inside the old hotel.

"If you was to ask me," said Sugar, "I'd ante Chet'll sure have to be halter-broke if he's goin' to travel much with that kind of comp'ny."

Back across the plaza behind his window Doc Frantz turned his head and grunted something resembling a greeting as Sheriff MacKnight came in through the front doorway and closed the door after him to shut out the glare and shoved his own favorite chair into secondary position by the table and eased his big bulk into it. Together in habitual companionable silence they looked out the window.

"Interesting," murmured Doc. "An interesting social mixture. Relatives and guests of the bride one distinct variety. Friends of the groom another. Quite another."

Into view along the other side of the plaza came a small neat stocky bay, tired and dusty, and stopped by the tie rail of a low adobe building with the simple sign Harness Shop and the man in the saddle in plain dark dusty suit and widebrimmed wide-banded sombrero was stout and swarthyskinned and black-mustached and he swung down with easy grace despite his weight and went into the shop.

"Chavez," said Sheriff MacKnight. "You owe me a dollar, Doc. You still don't know 'em like I do. Better'n a hundred twenty miles but he's here. A gathering of the clan."

"What there is left of it," said Doc Frantz.

Across the plaza, inside the little shop, Dobe Chavez leaned back against the one small counter and reached to slap the thick thigh of Sunfish Perkins perched on it and looked over and down steadily at old Cal Brennan in his wheelchair. "Ees good," he said, "to see you. Ees thees woman all right for Chet?"

"He thinks so," said Cal. "An' that's all that matters."

Back across the plaza again, behind their window, Doc Frantz and Sheriff MacKnight turned heads and grunted greetings as Justice Coleman closed the front door behind him and shifted the one remaining chair to his regular position. He took cigars from a pocket and passed them. "Secrets," he said, settling into the chair. "Just revealed. I made out the license a while ago. Mary's middle name is Witherspoon. Rollins's is Arthur."

From one of the straggling side streets came an old deep-chested leggy dun and the man in the saddle was a lean length of rawhide beginning to thicken a little at last around the middle and his worn old boots were newly polished and his fresh-washed pants had the press of a night under a mattress and his shirt was new and colorful and a gay silk handkerchief was knotted loosely around his throat and his old wide-brimmed hat had a new beaded band. The dun trotted briskly, spring in each step despite its age, and the man sat flat to the saddle, a part of the horse beneath him, and they angled directly across the plaza and stopped by a tie rail near the big barnlike structure of the livery stable and the man swung down in one smooth easy motion and looped reins and opened one of the big doors of the stable and disappeared inside.

"Walsh," said Justice Coleman. "He gave me some business the first day I ever hit this town. He has rarely disappointed me ever since."

"Right," said Sheriff MacKnight. "I'll lay you another dollar, Doc, the lid blows off something this afternoon. It don't fail often when Monte's in town."

* * *

A mangy yellow dog, great-grandson of one once treated for snakebite, wary of the wagons by the stores and of the cow ponies along rails, wandered across the plaza, seeking some shade for siesta. There was none in the relentless glare of the sun almost directly overhead. That provided by the scrawny little trees planted a few weeks before by a committee headed by Chester Arthur Rollins at the urging of his fiancée Mary Witherspoon Engle was thin and speckly and not worthy of the word.

The dog sniffed the base of the flagpole recently erected in the center of the plaza, displayed mild interest, raised a leg in lazy routine, and wandered on. It shuffled along the front of the livery stable and near one and between the wall and several recently planted lilac bushes found the closest approximation to shade immediately available. It turned around twice and lay down, head on paws. Its eyes closed. They opened and the head rose.

A sleek grain-fed gray had appeared out of somewhere and was trotting around the plaza. It stopped in front of the livery stable and Sonny Jacobs leaned back in silver-studded saddle to look up at the sign. He pushed his big hat further up his forehead. "And Rollins," he said. The gray trotted on and stopped by Bennie Martinez's Twenty-Four Hour Café. Sonny swung down and strolled in.

The dog's head dropped on its paws. Its eyes closed. The little town of Harmony drowsed in the sun, deceptive, apparently empty of humanity. The dog's eyes opened and it rose to its feet and slunk away around the building in disgust. The two big doors of the stable were creaking open.

Monte Walsh emerged between them and pushed each in turn all the way back and hooked it to the wall. He disappeared inside. He emerged again on the driving seat of a light wagon drawn by a heavy-set old mule with a scar on its rump. He pulled reins to stop and looked around. "Now where'd that fat-faced baboon go and get to now," he murmured.

The small door that led into the corner of the building partitioned off inside for an office opened and Chester Arthur Rollins emerged. His square-built solid body was encased in a new brown business suit. His suntanned throat was encircled by an already limp collar on a striped shirt and by a black string tie. His serious round face whose cheeks were beginning to jowl just a bit was topped by a new brown hat with very modest brim.

"My oh my," said Monte. "You got the look already. What for'd you put on that fool coat?"

"Just trying to get used to it," said Chet, stepping up to the seat. "She says a man ought to be wearing one when out in public." He pulled up his neatly pressed pants at the knees and settled back on the seat. "A businessman, anyways," he said.

Monte looked sideways at him and away and clucked to the mule. It waggled one ear, recognized authority along the reins, and leaned lazily into the harness. The wagon moved up the street and around a corner of the plaza.

"It's not so bad," said Chet. "Keeps out as much heat as it keeps in. Same principle as an Indian and his blanket."

"You'll be coming down with sunstroke," said Monte. "Mistaking that puny little thing for a hat."

"Maybe so," said Chet. "But I'll be doing it stylish." He took off the brown hat, turned it over in his hands, grinned, and put it back on. "I don't mind," he said. "It was kind of fun letting her pick it out."

The wagon turned another corner and was moving along the other side of the plaza, past a onetime adobe storeroom. Chet waved cheerfully at three figures seen dimly through the one wide front window.

"Walsh and Rollins," said Doc Frantz behind the glass. "You never see one without the other being somewhere handy. A man and his shadow—though I'll be blistered if I've ever figured out which is the man and which the shadow."

"Two men," said Sheriff MacKnight. "Two good men at anytime in anything whenever the chips are down."

"With a woman being added," said Justice Coleman.

The wagon moved on, the mule plodding lazily, expending no more energy than the absolute minimum for movement.

"Yep," said Chet, amiable, conversational. "I don't mind. Wait'll you see me in the outfit I got for the ceremony."

"My tongue ain't hanging out," said Monte. He stared straight ahead. "And I'm standing up just like I am now. This is me. Just like now. I ain't climbing into any goddamned monkey suit even if Old Engle's got one might fit."

The wagon moved on and turned another corner, away from the plaza, along the main street and past the stage station.

"Have I asked you to?" said Chet gently.

"No," said Monte. "But she did."

The wagon stopped in front of the low adobe structure beyond the station, by the open doorway with the sign Freight Office. Chet stared off into distance. "You ever start being anything but just what you are," he said gently, "and

I'll kick your teeth in." He jumped down. "Come on. This one's from Hat up in Denver. I got a wire from him saying he can't come himself but he wants you to kiss the bride for him." Chet led in through the doorway. "Howdy, Pablo," he said to a short thickset man lying on several bales of hay. "You got another package for me?"

The man raised himself on one elbow, pointed at a heavy wooden crate, and relaxed again.

Chet started forward. Stopped. Stared at the legend stenciled on the top of the crate. "No," he said. He sat down on a bale of hay and took off the brown hat and rubbed his forehead. "No," he said. "Not another one of them. We got three already."

Monte cocked his head, looking. The legend was neat and specific: Empire Stove Company. "What d'you know," he said. "Shucks, you can always put her to work and set up for a bakery. That is, if she can bake anything worth eating. Let's get it out of here. That is, if town life ain't making you soft."

Together they hoisted the crate and took it out and heaved it into the wagon. "Motto of this country," said Chet. "When in doubt, send a stove." He settled himself on the driving seat, pulled up his pants, and took the reins. He clucked to the mule and the wagon turned and rolled alongside the warehouse to the alley behind it. The mule plodded at its own pace and they moved toward the center of town again, past the backs of the staggered buildings along the main street.

"Yep," said Chet. "Dobe sent one and Doc had one brought in and one of her relatives sent another. We'll have to draw straws which to use."

"Hold an auction," suggested Monte.

The wagon moved slowly on.

"That little house Cal owns on Oak Street," said Chet. "He's having it fixed up. Says Mary and me we're to move in soon as we get back. Says he ain't—he hasn't made any money out of it yet and he isn't ready to break the habit. Says if I try paying him rent for the first year he'll have Mac throw me in jail."

The wagon moved slowly on.

"You know," said Chet. "He'd do it too."

The wagon stopped at the rear of the Harmony House

which jutted all the way back to the alley. "Come on," said Chet, jumping down. "You ain't—you haven't seen this." He led up the three steps and through the rear door into what had been the dining room until a larger and more respectable replacement had been extended out the other side of the building. The old room had been emptied of the old things stored in it and the walls repainted and it contained now a rather startling array of items. Three new stoves were side by side along one wall, six Mexican leather-and-cane chairs along the opposite wall. A slick shiny leather-covered davenport claimed one end of the room and on it were piled framed pictures and beside it stood an oval-mirrored combination umbrella stand and hat rack. A long table in the middle of the room, made of two smaller tables pushed together, seemed about to stagger under its load of two full sets of flowered dishes and stacks of linen and towels and a variety of fruit bowls and gilt-edged water pitchers and basins and soap dishes and a silver punch bowl.

"Wedding presents," said Chet. "Ain't it amazing what people will do? I mean isn't it. This was her idea, all of them in one place."

"My oh my," murmured Monte. 'Geeting married has some angles I never figured."

Chet stepped over and patted a tooled sidesaddle resting on one of the Mexican chairs. "Sunfish," he said. "Made it himself."

"Yeah," said Monte. "I know."

Chet pointed at two soft colorful Indian saddle blankets on another of the chairs. "Sugar and Dally," he said.

"Yeah," said Monte. "I was along when they got them over at Domingo. How did that thing get in here?" He pointed at a low board-bottomed wire cage in a corner containing one temporarily disheartened rooster and six discouraged hens.

"José," said Chet. "Brought them in yesterday. Mary kind of thought they should stay outside but I put them in here this morning. I ain't—hell—I'm not going to shortchange old José. All in one place means all in one place."

"Yeah," said Monte. "Eggs for breakfast. If she knows enough how to cook 'em. I suppose you want that fourth one in here."

Ten minutes later the fourth stove had been uncrated and

brought in and was being maneuvered into position beside the other three. The inner door from the hall that ran back through the building opened and the lady of the parasol, minus it and veil but still wearing the flowered hat, came a few steps in, saw the two of them, heard Monte cursing as he pinched a finger setting the stove down, and retreated hastily.

"Haven't seen her before," said Chet. "Must be Aunt Effie. Hard to believe Old Engle branched off that kind of a family tree. I got to go in there now and meet all of them. Some kind of lunch doings. You coming?"

"Hell, no," said Monte. "If I got to face the whole herd this afternoon, that once'll do me plenty."

"Three o'clock," said Chet.

"Yeah," said Monte. "Three o'clock. Go on in there now and behave pretty and watch your language. "I'll take the wagon back."

"You got the rings safe?" said Chet.

"Yeah," said Monte, patting a pocket. "All but the one that's going in your nose." He went out the rear door and stepped up to the seat and took the reins. The wagon backed in an arc then started forward, along the side of the building toward the plaza. "Stammering like a goddamned school kid," he muttered and slapped hard with the reins, stirring the mule into a slight show of energy. He heard a window opening.

"Monte."

He pulled reins and looked to the right and up. The firm fine-featured face of Mary Witherspoon Engle with soft brown hair piled in elaborate curls above it, flushed and lovely and utterly feminine on her wedding day, regarded him gravely from a second-story window.

"Please, Monte. It's only a little while. Don't do any drinking until it's over."

"There you go," said Monte. "Always so damn sure what I'm going to do."

"Not just for me, Monte. For Chet. He wouldn't like it either."

"Chet," said Monte, bitter. "So you're working on him already."

"Working on him? What do you mean?"

"Drunk or sober," said Monte. "It never made no difference to Chet."

"Oh, for heaven's sake, why must you be so difficult? We want this to be quiet and dignified, that's all. Just a nice quiet wedding. I want Chet to make a good impression. Uncle John's come. Maybe you don't know, but he's Haley Feeds. If he likes Chet maybe he'll back him for an agency here. All Chet needs is a start. He can get to be a big man in this territory."

"He ain't ever been anything else," said Monte. He slapped savagely with the reins, driving on.

Five minutes later he emerged from the livery stable, leaving the big doors to be closed by the gangling loose-jointed boy who slept in the back stall and was paid half the wages of a handyman and liked to call himself, when alone, the assistant manager. He walked the forty feet to the dun, swung up to ride the 160 feet to the rail in front of the Twenty-Four Hour Café, swung down, looped reins, and went inside. Ignoring remarks from along the bar he strode over and joined Sonny Jacobs at a small table.

"Knew you'd be here sooner or later," said Sonny. "Likely sooner. So I made preparations." He waved a hand at a bottle and two glasses, one already in use. He tipped the bottle and poured and shoved the second glass toward Monte. "Look like you need it," he said.

Monte picked up the glass, held it up, looked at the clear golden color against the light coming in over the swinging doors. He set the glass down. He pushed his old hat with the new beaded band higher up his forehead. "Telling me what to do," he said. "She was always almighty good at that." He picked up the glass again.

*   *   *

The yellow dog came from behind the livery stable and forward along the side. There was shade now, the slim-edged shadow of the building, but the dog was intent on other things. It trotted with its own peculiar sidelong gait out into the plaza, remembered the flagpole and swerved to investigate this again, found nothing new, and trotted away in the direction of the Twenty-Four Hour Café. It stopped, sitting in the dust, and scratched vigorously with a hind foot at one ear. An empty bottle soared out of the café, over the doors and sidewalk and the cow ponies along the rail, and landed ten feet away. The dog jumped and looked quickly around, located the bottle, approached warily, sniffed it, and trotted on in disgust. It slipped furtively past the cow ponies, dodging a sudden sideway kick from one that had apparently been asleep, and moved along the side of the café toward the rear. Sometimes at this time of day the lid of the garbage can there was put back on by an unsteady and inefficient hand.

The plaza drowsed in the sun of early afternoon. Old Man Engle, uncomfortable in his fine clothes which still smelled slightly of moth flakes, appeared on the porch of the Harmony House. Two men came around the side, the old Negro cook and the stringy half-cured consumptive ordinarily a clerk in one of the stores hired now for the day as a special waiter. Each carried a wooden sawhorse. They set these across the street in a corner of the plaza as directed from the porch. They went back around the building and came again, each carrying two planks. They laid these on the sawhorses, forming a long table, as directed from the porch. They went back around the building.

Old Man Engle stood on the wide porch with its spindled railing and wiped a finger around inside his high starched collar. He was more than willing to be released for these few minutes from the stringent gentility and active preparations currently inhabiting the old hotel he had bought from the original owner, sight unseen and price so low he had not even haggled, twenty-two years before. After more than two decades of slow settling into the easy relaxing low-standard living of this still incomprehensible country, a process facilitated by the loss of his wife midway, and an equal period of rather consistent detachment from both family trees rooted in Ohio, he was having difficulty behaving as his daughter thought proper for the occasion.

He looked about the somnolent sun-soaked plaza. There was no sign of activity anywhere unless the buzz of flies and the swish of a tail or stomp of a hoof could be called activity. The little town of Harmony held its own deceptive harmony in the heart of the big land. Old Man Engle was not quite deceived. He too had lived with it long enough to know its sudden possibilities. He might almost welcome one before this access of gentility was over. He went back into the hotel.

On down the main street behind the cloaking facade of the Twenty-Four Hour Café proprietor Bennie Martinez and his bartender were no longer quite so busy. They were into the inevitable early afternoon slump. A few men leaned lazily against the bar as if they had become fixtures there. Others sat at tables twisted into contorted positions which seemed to defy comfort yet did not and a few of them snored softly. Conversation was at low ebb. A general atmosphere of waiting, not for anything in particular but simply for anything, pervaded the old café.

Sonny Jacobs and Monte Walsh still sat at their table and Sugar Wyman and Dally Johnson sat with them and the table was littered with scraped dishes that had carried cargoes of enchiladas and tortillas. There were four glasses on the table now and Sonny's first bottle was empty and another, half empty, kept it company.

"Best thing about chili," said Sugar, somber, serious, with the air of a man imparting profound truth, "it encourages drinkin'." He reached for the half-empty bottle.

"Ex-clu-sive," said Sonny, paying no attention to him. "That is pre-cisely and exact-ly how I hear it is. Very ex-clu-sive."

"Aw, shucks," said Monte. "There ain't much room in that front parlor and she's got a flock of relatives."

"You can have 'em," said Dally. "Matter of fact, you got to have 'em. You got to be there. Best man."

"Ex-clu-sive," said Sonny. "And by the which and the wherefore, why then are we here? Us and the others here and around."

"Can't let ol' Chet hang hisself an' not be on hand," said Dally.

"An' for the doin's after," said Sugar. "See Chet in his fancy harness an' wish 'im the luck he likely ain't goin' to have. A sort of kind of a—a—"

"Re-cep-tion," said Sonny.

"I reckon so," said Sugar.

"They got that old piano tuned," said Monte. "Going to haul it out on the porch and a cousin or somebody's going to do some singing."

"Fe-male?" said Sonny, staring at him.

"Chet says it wears a skirt," said Monte, squirming some on his chair.

"Sing-ing," said Sonny. "By a fee-male relation. Oh . . . my God!"

Monte sat very still, gnawing on a knuckle.

"Engle's payin' for a barrel of beer," said Dally. "Goin' to set it up outside there."

"Beer," said Sugar. "Might as well be water. An' you know what I bet what for? Somebody's smart little ol' idea for tryin' to keep us animals out there an' from crowdin' in an' steppin' on toes." He reached and poured a round, emptying the second bottle.

"Quiet and dignified," muttered Monte. He picked up his glass, drained it, set it down. "A funeral," he said to no one in particular. "That's what they're doing to it. Chet's getting the woman he wants to bed down with him permanent and they're treating it like it was a funeral." He rose from his chair and walked swaying to the doors and looked out over them. The Slash Y buckboard was moving past, drawn by one of the smart-looking trotters he had trained to harness, and Herbert Y. Morris very proper in sober Sunday clothes was on the seat, bound for the Harmony House. Across the way he saw Doc Frantz emerge from his doorway in sober dark suit and starched collar and be joined by Justice Coleman from his doorway around the corner in full regalia, striped pants and frock coat and high collar, and the two of them walk with slow dignity toward the Harmony House.

"Goddamned funeral," muttered Monte. "You'd think they was burying him." He stood looking out and slowly his shoulders stiffened and his head rose higher and he reached up and pulled his hat down on his forehead and then he suddenly turned and strode swaying toward the table and he bounced off his boot toes as he strode. He leaned both hands on the table edge and talked fast and Sonny's broad face widened in a grin and Dally sat up on his chair, eyes brightening, and Sugar hugged himself crooning softly, "Got you, Monte, got you" and Monte turned again and strode swaying out the doorway, sending the doors flapping wide, and threw a leg over the dun and rode angling across the plaza to the harness shop and behind in the café Sonny was up and moving from man to man along the bar and at the other tables and Sugar and Dally came out the doorway and separated, staggering some, and Sugar went around the corner toward Thornburg's nameless saloon and Dally went two doors along the street to Nordyke and Perea's Jinglebob Emporium.

Over in the little shop Monte talked fast again and Dobe Chavez grinned behind his black mustache that had flecks of

gray in it and strode out and swung up on his bay and loped
off toward the older part of town with its ancient weathered
small adobe houses wandering here and there and Sunfish
Perkins rubbed a hand over his thinning crop of grizzled hair
and said, "I'll go you better'n that, I'm on the Fourth committee" and picked up his hat and went out through the little
back room.

Old Cal Brennan sat in his wheelchair and looked at the
one of his onetime boys who would always have been his favorite son of the wild jackass if he had been forced to a
choice though he never would have said so. "Monte boy," he
said. "Don't ever grow old. If only I could still straddle a
hoss. But I'll think of something."

"Horse!" said Monte. "I been forgetting!" He was outside
again and on the dun and scudding across the plaza and
down one of the straggling side streets. The dun slid on its
rump by a small corral beside one of the last houses and he
was leaping to the ground before it had stopped moving and
he vaulted over the fence, taking a bridle made of soft hand-
worked leather from a post as he landed inside. A neat,
compact, clean-legged roan that had perked ears and shied
away some when he came over the fence whiffled at him now
and stood for him and opened its mouth for the bit. He unhooked the gate and led it out and was on the dun again,
leading the roan. At a fast pace they threaded through a cluster of adobe shacks and tumbledown sheds, scattering several
dogs and a batch of near-naked children, and were across the
main street where it swept west out of town and loping along
the alley behind the buildings.

They approached the rear of the Harmony House and
Monte pulled to a stop and swung down and looped the reins
of the dun around the handle of a rusty abandoned pump by
one corner. He held the reins of the roan and looked about,
swaying some again, feeling the warmth of the recent action
and of the whisky in him. "Got to surprise Chet," he murmured. "He ain't said a thing, but he's wondering what I
got." A sudden grin touched his lips. "All in one place," he
said. He led the roan to the three steps and the door above
them and reached up and opened the door. He stepped up
and in and turned, facing out, and pulled gently on the reins.
The roan whiffled softly at him, questioning, reluctant, and
stood by the steps with head stretching out as he pulled. It

put one forefoot on the first step, testing, and as he spoke to it, low, reassuring, its muscles gathered and with a scramble of hoofs it was up and in. He led it the few feet to the first of the four stoves and tied the reins to the oven handle. "Ought to be solid enough," he murmured. He pulled from a pocket a small square of cardboard with a string through a hole in it and tied this to the cheek strap of the bridle. He stood by the horse, patting its neck, rubbing its ears. "You sure can't be called a stove," he murmured. Faintly from the front regions of the building he heard a piano and a feminine voice singing "Oh Promise Me." "Hey," he said, "I better hurry." He strode to the back door and out and the horse stood, quiet, turning its head to watch him go, whiffling softly as he closed the door. He went around and forward along the building, conscious of the swaying in his stride and tightening muscles against it, and he hurried up the front steps to the porch and Chet was waiting in the doorway for him, Chester Arthur Rollins surprisingly mature and dignified in shiny black shoes and striped trousers and black cutaway coat and gray vest and high winged collar and white bow tie, and the light leaping in Chet's eyes seeing him come was something he would never forget.

*　*　*

Quiet and dignified. A little southwestern territorial town could turn the trick, in a small way, and the bride had no reason to be ashamed of the selected townspeople rubbing elbows with the relatives from the States. The big land and the brand it laid on its own were outside, temporarily removed, shut off by the four walls of the front parlor, and all inside was sober and genteel and respectable, except perhaps for the one apparent incongruous touch, not so much actually out of place as symbolic of what was happening, of the old being submerged in the new, the lean rawhide length of the best man in his simple range clothes made reasonably clean and neat for the occasion. The bride even smiled at him, recognizing perhaps out of her own early pre-traveled years that there was a rightness to his being there, understanding too perhaps that to the groom, dazed now and overwhelmed by what he was doing, the one touch of reality in the whole seeming unreal procedure was that same man standing by him in worn old newly polished boots with gay silk handkerchief knotted loosely around suntanned throat, fighting as hard as ever he had on a bucking horse to hold himself flat to the saddle of this kind of affair, producing the right ring at the right time and even a wry little reassuring grin when that too was needed.

Quiet and dignified. The bride had the wedding she wanted. The minister from Albuquerque pronounced the words "man and wife" and there was the usual hovering hushed hesitation and then people in their sober respectable finery were coming forward to congratulate and shake the groom's hand and implant genteel restrained kisses on the bride's cheek and Monte Walsh, swaying a bit in the release of tension in tightened muscles, moved against the current and to the doorway into the other front room that was the lobby and to the outer doorway onto the porch and raised his hands high, waving, and threw back his head.

"Yow-eeeee!" he yelled. "They've done it!" And on and about and around the plaza the little town of Harmony erupted into an impromptu version of a fine violent frenzy.

The air rocked with racket, loud and clamorous and increasing, reaching into the old hotel. Wedding guests gasped and stared about in confusion and babbled silly questions and some crowded by the front window of the front parlor to peer out and the more daring pushed into the lobby with its big window and a few even out onto the porch.

From the corner by the Twenty-Four Hour Café and Thornburg's nameless little saloon, led by Sonny Jacobs and Sugar Wyman, riders were boiling forth into the plaza, scattering dust on skittering cow ponies, racing into the circuit around, yipping and pulling guns and shooting holes in the sky. Out in the center Dally Johnson was running a flag up the pole. Grouped about it a haphazard Spanish band, hastily recruited by Dobe Chavez—three guitars and a banjo and a snare drum and a trumpet and one brass horn—was striving hard to make itself heard. Forty feet away Sunfish Perkins and Old Red Hawkins were busy with fireworks purloined from the stock imported for the Fourth of July celebration next week, setting off firecrackers a pack at a time, while Short-Hair Hale waved an exploding Roman candle in each hand. And over in front of the harness shop, serene in his wheelchair, old Cal Brennan with a rifle in his hands was apparently bombarding the Harmony House itself, methodically knocking off one by one the cracked wooden knobs of the onetime fancy scrollwork jutting up from the roof.

Monte Walsh eased rump down on the top step of the porch and contemplated his handiwork with solemn satisfaction. Shiny black shoes stepped down beside his old boots and striped trousers bent at the knees as Chet Rollins eased down beside him. Together they looked out at the still increasing clamor. The circuit of riders was complete now, strung out all the way around, racing in fine noisy fettle. The yellow dog and three others, unable to resist the contagion, dashed about, erratic, aimless, dodging hoofs, barking their best. Dobe Chavez had joined Sunfish Perkins and the two of them with the aid of a grooved board were launching skyrockets. A wagon, commandeered from beside one of the stores, loaded with yelling black-headed youngsters, streamers of toilet paper trailing behind, Chalkeye Ferrero on the driving seat, careened out and into the racing circuit.

"Well, well," murmured Chet Rollins. "The boys are sure doing themselves proud."

Inside in the lobby his bride stood by the window trying to decide whether to cheer as she might have a few years before or to be shocked into tears as somehow seemed called for now. Near the front doorway Aunt Effie had dashed daringly forward to take Justice Coleman by the arm, impeding his progress to the porch for a better view.

"Stop them," she demanded. "Stop them before they kill somebody!"

"Madam," said Justice Coleman, "I would not think of trying that even if I had a regiment of cavalry behind me. Have you ever tried to stop an avalanche?"

"The sheriff then," she wailed. "I know there's one. I met him."

"Madam," said Doc Frantz, trying to get past to the porch, "if you will bother to look you will see that he has left us to go help with the fireworks."

The gunfire dropped away, guns emptied, and the yipping of the racing circuit had a less terrifying sound. More people were pushing out on the porch. A sleek grain-fed gray, veteran of the show world, frisky and full of the juice of the grain, cavorting in superb gyrations out in the plaza, suddenly turned and drove straight for the Harmony House. It wove through the riders dashing past and clattered up the steps to the porch and Sonny Jacobs swayed in the saddle, waving his hat, shouting something about kissing the bride. There was a general frantic retreat into the lobby, on back into the rear regions of the building. A shrill scream sounded, echoing along the hall and to the front, followed by what could have been the crash of a heavily loaded table going over and a wild barrage of thuds and bumps and bangings.

"Good God a'mighty!" yelled Monte Walsh. He was up and leaping past the gray into the lobby, on down the hall, past several frantic people hurrying forward, one of them still emitting dwindling screams. The head and shoulders of a neat compact roan, broken reins dangling, wild-eyed in a kind of frightened indignation, appeared in the open doorway to the back room.

Monte threw up his arms, shouting, and the horse backed away inside and three desperate squawking chickens flapped out and past him as he leaped into the doorway and paused an instant, shuddering at what he saw. The roan was very busy, apparently intent on completing the work already begun, hoofs crunching on crockery, legs tangling with the remains of the overturned table, bucking and whirling and kicking in what seemed several directions at once at everything brought within range. Towels and wash cloths sailed about. Sheets and pillow cases were being trampled. A hoof connected with an arm of the davenport and with a fine new crash the pile of framed pictures went to the floor.

Monte groaned and plunged forward, dodging around, and had hold of the bridle. The horse jerked its head and threw him and he landed among the Mexican chairs with a crunch of canes snapping. He plunged again and had hold of the ears and he hung his weight on the head, holding it down. The horse quieted some and he talked, slow and steady, and it stood, still, muscles quivering under its hide. He eased up on the head, talking slow and steady, and it stood, quiet, and when he let go of the ears to take hold of the bridle it seemed to be almost ashamed of itself and tried to nuzzle against him. He drew a long breath and looked around, wincing at the wreckage. In the inner doorway he saw Chet Rollins, round face rigid, eyes wide, and peering from behind the shocked startled disgusted furious face of the bride. He turned away. "Luck and me," he muttered. "How'd I know a damn silly woman'd go screaming in its ear?" He led the roan to the rear door and opened this. He stepped out and down and pulled gently on the reins and with a scramble of hoofs the horse was out and down too. He led it a few feet and dropped the reins and it stood, ground-tied as he had taught it, and he went to the rusty abandoned pump and un-looped the reins of the dun and swung up and moved away along the alley.

Chester Arthur Rollins stood in the rear doorway of the wrecked room and watched him go. The clamor from the plaza still sounded, dwindling, but he did not hear it. Mrs. Rollins was saying something in a sharp tone behind him but he did not hear her. He closed the door behind him and stepped down and went to the roan and reached to the small square piece of cardboard tied to the bridle and turned this to read the one sentence printed in pencil on it: *You will want her to be riding with you and not get hurt.*

The door opened again and Mrs. Rollins was in the door-way and other people were gathering behind her and perhaps she and they were speaking but he did not hear. He was watching a lean hunched figure riding slowly away on an old deep-chested leggy dun. Suddenly he moved, disregarding his fine striped trousers and cutaway coat, and he was on the roan bareback, leaning down for the broken reins, and it wheeled neatly for him and was off in clean smooth stride after the dun. It pulled up alongside and at a touch on the reins slowed to match the other's slow jog.

Together an old dun and a young roan jogged along the alley that had become little more than a trail out of town now and the rider of the dun stared straight ahead.

"It's the best horse I ever had under me," said Chet.

"Yeah," said Monte, staring ahead. "It's all right. It'll take care of her."

They jogged on.

"Goddamn it!" said Monte. "Go on back there. Leave me alone. I messed things plenty. I let you down a time like this. I ain't fit to be——"

"You overgrown infant," said Chet gently. "You ain't— you haven't ever let me down. It was just another fool wed-ding like they have by the dozen everywhere. You've fixed that. You've put your mark on it. You've made it something to remember."

They jogged on.

Monte's head rose and he looked sideways at Chet and a small wry grin twisted his lips. "All in one place," he said.

"They sure were," said Chet. "She sure can't say they weren't. Now maybe you're ready to come back and help wind it up. There's no ring in my nose yet. Come on, I'll beat you back. I'll bet this thing can run the legs off that old crowbait of yours. If it does what I think it'll do, it'll take me right up on the porch and into the lobby. Give Aunt Effie another thrill."

*   *   *

Shadows of late afternoon lengthened around the deserted plaza littered with considerable debris that would remain there until the junior partner of the firm of Holloway and Rollins would return from his honeymoon in Kansas City and at the urging of his wife revive the clean-up and beautifying committee. The sawhorses and planks would be removed the day after tomorrow but the bits of broken glass and pieces of beer mugs around them would stay until the committee would fill two buckets with them. The nails in the flagpole and the scorchings where Sunfish Perkins and Dobe Chavez and Sheriff MacKnight had experimented with pinwheels were unsightly and would require particular attention. The three of the scrawny trees trampled flat would have to be replaced. So would the tie rail snapped in two when Chalkeye Ferrero tried to drive and stand up and shout and look about all at the same time and toppled to the ground and the wagon with its load of yelling youngsters careened into the rail, and the damage might have been worse if Monte Walsh, coming in along main street on an old leggy dun at full gallop with a young roan two jumps behind, had not swerved and raced alongside and dived off the dun to take the off horse of the team around the neck and bring the wagon to a halt in a cloud of dust. The outline of the Harmony House against the sky would never be the same again with every one of the little wooden knobs of onetime fancy scrollwork gone. The dents on the front steps and porch made by the hoofs of a grain-fed gray and that same young roan and those on into the lobby made by the roan would be covered with paint that would not quite hide them and in time Old Man Engle would tell a tale about them with a postscript about some other marks in a back room growing taller with each telling. And across the way the glass in the front window of Doc Frantz's office, cracked where an errant skyrocket had hit, would remain until replaced after a few months by a workman paid by Justice Coleman. The crack did not interrupt Doc's daily view. Or Sheriff MacKnight's. But it did Justice Coleman's.

The plaza was deserted now for the inclusive sufficient reason that virtually the entire immediate movable population of Harmony was assembled a half block from the northeast corner by the stage station where the driver of the five-thirty stage sat on the box, already thirty-five minutes late, and waited patiently while more rounds of farewells drew out the delay.

A nervous drummer in notions and drygoods poked his head out a window of the coach and spoke upward. "This is ridiculous," he said. "I have to make a train tonight."

"Quit bellyachin'," said the driver. "Rollins don't get married every day." He spat a stream of tobacco juice down by the near wheel. "Come to think of it," he said, "they won't want you knockin' aroun' in theah with 'em. You climb out an' up heah with me."

Tallied overall it had been a surprisingly successful afternoon, perhaps because most of the imported guests had been startled and stampeded into accepting almost anything and the friends of the groom had blown off any grouch or grudge with the steam of their own stampede. Doc Frantz's social mixture had managed to mix medium well. Old Man Engle, relieved that the ceremony itself had not been interrupted, had shooed everyone out of the wrecked back room and closed and locked the doors and surprised himself and daughter by taking a firm stand. "Forget it for now," he said. "What's done can't be undone and it isn't as bad as it looks. I'll assess the damage tomorrow and write it off as operating expenses. Not many people ever get a plate-eating horse for a present." And while the women remained on the porch, an audience not overly enthusiastic but still an audience, the men had drifted down to mingle with the doings on the plaza. Sonny Jacobs, mildly apologetic for his previous performance, had made amends by demonstrating how his gray could waltz to music. Young Juan Gonzales, rigged in a fiesta costume hastily borrowed, had jumped up on the planks beside the beer barrel and beat out a Spanish dance with tapping toes and slapping heels. There had been a brief explosive interlude when Sugar Wyman and Dally Johnson found an empty keg and a piece of board and rubbed resin on them and began to saw the board over the keg and that could have stopped everything with everyone running for cover to protect tortured eardrums but Monte Walsh had got to them in time to block that particular performance with a flying tackle performance of his own. Cousin Eunice in sober respectable floor-length gown, all unaware her once careful hairdo was in rather fetching disarray from scrambles back and forth in the hotel, had been flutteringly impressed by the flavorous encouragement of a stout black-mustached onetime outlaw with a bullet scar along one cheek and enticed out on the steps to discover that singing to three guitars in the hands of racial masters of them was much more invigorating than singing to a decrepit old piano. Two of the native residents, known variously as Tío Pedro and Primo Leyba, had come forward offering their own attraction and in a pit hastily formed with a tarpaulin held against legs by willing hands Pedro's bright-colored gamecock had finished off Leyba's more deadly-looking dark one in one minute and twenty-seven seconds. To the bride's surprise it was Uncle John Haley himself who refereed the bout and who, after leading several dozen horny horsemen, now minus their horses, in a toast to her in warm beer, recognized the inadequacy of the beverage for the occasion and the company and conferred with Bennie Martinez about a special price for a half case of whisky. Which was not as dangerous as it might have been because the time was short. There had been only one brawl and that brief and almost cheerful, no killing animosity in it, more a mere release of energy and a playing to the gallery than anything else.

"Well," sniffed Aunt Effie to the bride. "Things do seem to have got out of hand. Not what we planned at all. But my heavens, I must say, I have never seen anything quite like it."

And now Mary Engle Rollins was receiving the last tearful goodbyes and solicitous admonitions from the women and Chester Arthur Rollins was in brown business suit again and his back was sore from slappings and his right arm limp from shakings and the other men had stepped back some in instinctive courtesy and he stood by the coach door facing Monte Walsh.

"You got all the bags?" he said.

"Yeah," said Monte. "They're all aboard."

Thirty feet away old Cal Brennan sat in his wheelchair and Sunfish Perkins was beside him. "I sure hate to see that," said Cal softly. "What's left of the Slash Y is goin' fast now. The heart of the old outfit's splittin' right there while we watch."

The two men stood by the coach, looking at one another, in the midst of the crowded space removed and tight in their own pocket of simple elemental isolation.

Chet's lips moved as if he would speak but no sound came.

"There ain't no way to say it," said Monte. "So don't try."

Chet nodded. Suddenly he reached and grasped Monte's arm and his fingers tightened in a grip that would leave a bruise for days to come and he turned away quickly to fumble with the handle of the coach door and at last get it open for his wife coming to him.

The driver pushed the even more nervous drummer over on the box to have elbow room and snaked out his whip snapping and the four horses heaved into the harness and the coach moved, rolling into the long road leading northeastward. A few men ran to swing into saddles and ride out with it, yipping and yelling. Not Monte Walsh. He sat on a corner of the platform in front of the station, gently rubbing one arm, and while the crowd slowly dispersed, drifting away in the letdown of the departure, he sat there, still and quiet, watching the far dust of the coach dwindle into the nothingness of empty space.

*   *   *

Lights showed now in some of the buildings around the plaza. Not many. Most of Harmony retired regularly with the sun. Over at the Harmony House only glimmers could be seen around the edges of windows. Old Man Engle, with all of his guests who would not be leaving until tomorrow safely inside, had locked the doors and pulled down shades. Much might yet happen in the neighborhood of the Twenty-Four Hour Café and the Jinglebob and Thornburg's nameless saloon before the last of the riders would have wandered away into the early hours of the morning.

The doors of the Jinglebob flipped open and Monte Walsh emerged, swaying some, and looked vaguely about at nothing and sat down on the outer edge of the board sidewalk. Voices rose inside, touching off a burst of raucous laughter. "What've they got to be so goddamned cheerful about?" he said to the mangy yellow dog as it slipped past to go back along the building.

He pushed up and looked vaguely about again, trying to remember where he had left the dun. After a brief search he found it waiting patiently around the corner by Thornburg's and he rode back and angling across the plaza to the little harness shop and tried the front door. Fastened. No light showed inside. He walked around to the door into the rear room and rattled the handle.

"It ain't locked," came the voice of Cal Brennan.

He pushed in and saw a match spurt and in the glow old Cal sitting up in his bed and reaching to light the lamp on a stand beside it.

"I don't sleep much," said Cal. "But I sleep often. Age is sure mighty aggravatin'."

Monte might not have heard him. He stepped over and reached in a pocket and pulled out a small roll of bills and dropped these on the bed. "Morris paid yesterday," he said. "I got that left. Maybe you and Sunfish'll take it and find out from Engle what's broke and replace what you can before they—before Chet gets back."

"Glad to," said Cal. "An' I just might make up any diff'rence myself."

"No," said Monte. "I did it."

"You sure did," said Cal. "There ain't nobody else with the same holes in his head could of done it just like that. You always was kind of thorough . . . Hey. You goin' already? Blow that thing out for me."

Monte bent over the lamp and blew it out and moved toward the door.

"An' another thing," came Cal's voice from the sudden darkness. "I ain't felt so good in weeks. I been lookin' at those silly damn blobbles on that buildin' for at least two years thinkin' what good targets they'd make."

Monte closed the door and moved around the shop and

swung up on the dun. At a slow jog he headed out of town. Time passed over him as slow distance dropped away under the hoofs of the dun and the sound of them, single and lone in the darkness, was strange and lonesome to him. Then he was at the gate to the ranch enclosure and he passed through without dismounting, instinctive in habit, unaware of what he was doing, and then the dun was unsaddled and in the small corral with feed and water for it and he was in the weathered old bunkhouse lighting the lamp and looking around. The untidy disorder of the morning's slicking and polishing was there but he saw none of this. He was staring at an empty stripped bunk. He stepped to the doorway and looked out at the dark shapes of the other buildings still and serene in the dim starlit darkness. "It ain't the same," he said. "It ain't ever going to be the same again."

He reached his right hand into his right pants pocket and pulled the pocket inside out. Empty. "Nothing and nobody," he said. "Just like before." And something stubborn in him said no, not quite. He had a horse and bedded deep in mind and muscles were the skills and the rawhide hard endurance of a trade, of a way of life, that was slipping fast from him and his kind but that still lingered in some of the far rugged stretches of the big land.

"Over by Pietown," he said. "And the Datils. I wonder what's doing there." He turned back into the bunkhouse and made up his meager blanket roll and blew out the lamp and strode out into the night. He moved over by the silent cookhouse and laid the saddle roll down on the doorstep and went inside and in the familiar dimness gathered a few things and put them in an empty flour sack and went out and picked up the saddle roll. Five minutes later he and the old dun were jogging westward toward the mountains and the river beyond them and the range country on beyond.

*   *   *

"A good man? That's one over there by the bar. As good an all-around hand as I ever came across. Not many like him any more. Pulled me out of a spot last spring when I was late with the branding. Of course you can't get him right now. He's got some money in his pocket. Wait a few days and it'll be a different story. Of course by then you may have to bail

*him out of hock to the sheriff but it'll be worth it. He'll feel
he owes you something and you'll get all you paid for and
more. Of course you won't be able to hold him more than a
season. He's got some kind of an itch that keeps him moving
around. But he'll see you through whatever he says he will
and you'll be almighty sorry to lose him when he leaves. But
he'll leave. You can't hold him when he gets that itch. You
can't change that kind. Maybe it's a good thing you can't.
They're part of the old days that are sort of fading away.
Something's going to be missing from this country when the
last of them's gone.*

*"Oh, yes, another thing. If you have any horses around
that've been giving you trouble, just mention that to him.
They won't after he's worked them over some."*

Drifters
1894–1901

DRIFT with the years, here and there and wherever the south-western rangeland still stretches uncluttered from fence line to slow creeping fence line . . . from job to job and none of them meaning much because nothing is ever the same again and they are more and more just jobs and not a way and a sharing of life that sings grim or rollicking as occasion calls in the lean swift summons on mind and muscle . . . drinking too much and too often because only in the heat of the alcohol haze do remnants of the past seem near and almost attainable again. But these remain, unalterable while change in the name of progress claims the big land, the hard clean core of individuality in the man, the echo of the past sounding in him in the instant instinctive attitude toward existence . . .

* * *

They had worked through the huge leased foothills pasture and gathered the cattle, a motley mixed three hundred, and would be shoving these on down the miles to the big holding corral. Four men. Two of them young, part-time cowboys seasonally hired out of the nearest town, on two thin horses that, from the scant sweat streaks showing, had shirked their share of the work. Another the owner, stout, fleshy, full-faced, uncomfortable in sweat-sodden clothes ill-suited to the occasion, racked with a slow-burning irritation that with the price of beef what it was and his note at the bank coming due he had no margin to hire more men and was forced to ride out himself in the heat and the dust like a mere hired hand. He sat heavy in saddle on a sweat-soaked big-muscled nervous bay that dripped bloody froth from the bit in its mouth.

And the fourth a thickening length of rawhide with many little wrinkles fanning out around the eyes and two lines deepening by the nose down past the mouth in the lean weathered face, sitting easy and erect in saddle on an old evenly-sweated deep-chested leggy dun that had never shirked to the last ounce of effort and had done more than half of this particular job without regarding that as anything more than part of a routine day's work.

The cattle were well bunched now and the four men sat quiet for a moment to give the horses a breather and gasping shouts from behind turned them to look at an elderly scrubby-bearded man in overalls, minus a hat lost somewhere along the way, a piece of rope in one hand, running toward them. He stopped, red-faced and pop-eyed from exertion, old chest heaving, fighting for breath. "Hey," he said. "Hey . . . you got . . . my cow . . . in there."

"That's too bad," said the stout man. "That's just almighty God too bad. I'm fenced tight. If your goddamn cow gets in with my stuff, that's your lookout." He sat up a bit straighter on the bay. "I'll bet it ain't even branded," he said.

"Branded?" said the elderly man. "It's a milk cow."

"That's too bad," said the stout man. "They all look alike to me."

"You don't understand," said the elderly man. "It's our only one. We got to have that milk."

"That's too bad," said the stout man. He seemed to derive some secret satisfaction from repetition of the words. He sat up even straighter in the saddle. "All right, I'll give you a chance." He waved a hand at the bunched herd. "Just go out there and get it."

The elderly man turned toward the herd. He started forward. Stopped, staring at the mass of cattle shifting restlessly in the hot sun. He started forward again.

"But there's one thing," said the stout man, voice suddenly hard. "If you get to scattering my stuff, I'll throw a rope on you and drag you good."

The elderly man hesitated without looking back. He started forward again and was close to the edge of the herd. He stared out over the shifting cattle. He pushed ahead and was a short way in among them. He slapped gently with the rope in his hand, trying to clear a way. A two-year-old Hereford steer, annoyed, hooked at him and he jumped back and bumped into another steer which kicked out and sent him sprawling. He got to his feet quickly and backed away more, limping, and stood still, staring at the herd.

The two young men looked at the stout man and looked away and sat very still on their thin horses, looking away, and the stout man watched the elderly man and a sardonic excuse for a smile twisted his lips and the elderly man stood alone staring at the herd, and his scrubby beard quivered as his old mouth shook in a kind of frustrated helpless hopeless fury and what could have been tears from his watery old eyes mingled with the sweat streaking his face.

"Take it easy, Pop," said Monte Walsh. "I'll get her for you." The leggy dun moved toward the herd.

"Walsh!" shouted the stout man, sudden anger plain in his voice. "You keep out of this!"

The dun wheeled, pivoting on hind legs, and faced the big nervous bay. "What d'you know," said Monte. "Were you thinking of trying to stop me?" He pushed his worn hat with its frayed beaded band higher up his forehead and looked straight at the stout man. "I kind of wish you would," he said. He waited. The dun wheeled again and moved toward the herd and stopped by the elderly man.

"Brindle, ain't she?" said Monte. "With a crooked horn."

The elderly man looked up and wiped a hand across his face. His throat worked but no sound came. He nodded.

"Yeah," said Monte. "And scratched where she went through the fence. Better put a yoke on her after this." The dun moved on, weaving into the herd, quiet and confident, shouldering the way. The ripple of its passage died away behind it, leaving no extra disturbance. It moved in an arc and was coming back, nudging ahead of it a young brindle cow with a crooked horn. The cow was out in the open and dodged fast to get with the others again and the dun leaped, blocking, and Monte dropped sideways down from the saddle, grasping a horn in each hand as he dropped, and stood firm, holding. "Get that rope on her," he said.

The elderly man hurried to flip an end of his piece of rope around the cow's neck and fumbled to tie it. He stepped back, pulling to test the knot, and looked up at Monte in saddle again. His old throat worked. "I was kind of good too oncet," he said. "But that's a long time now." He turned away, yanking on the rope, and the cow followed.

The dun moved again and stopped facing the big bay.

"Walsh," said the stout man, voice tight, grim. "As soon as we get this herd penned, you're through."

"You don't say," murmured Monte. He reached up and pulled his worn hat down more firmly on his head. "Ain't it too bad," he said, "you can't just do that. I happen to of quit about ten minutes ago."

*   *   *

They came around the base of a high steep mesa, seventeen wild desert broomtails, scrub stock thin and stunted, tired but with considerable endurance still in their thin wiry bodies. This was the third day of the running and they were into the fifth swing around the vaguely defined sixty-mile circuit of the barren forgotten range that had been theirs undisturbed before and they would not leave even now. They came strung out in little bunches, stopping to look back and moving on, no longer quite so afraid of the dusty unshaven thick-shouldered big-nosed man on a tired buckskin loping along several hundred yards behind them.

The man closed in, shouting, and they spurted on past the mesa into the open of desert plain and the man swung away to the left in by the mesa base and out of narrow noontime shadow there rode Monte Walsh on a fresh rested gray.

"They ain't breakin' much now," said the big-nosed man. "See you." He and the tired buckskin kept on, at a steady jog now, to skirt the mesa and strike straight across the middle of the wide circuit toward the other side eleven miles away where two horses waited, picketed in a shadowed arroyo, and Monte and the gray swept out after the broomtails, closing in on them to keep them moving in their constant wearying spurts . . .

Hours passed and shadows of the far-scattered lonely steep mesas were long across the land and the seventeen broomtails were being forced away from their wide circuit, stumbling at a lagging pace, driven hard by the big-nosed man on a mottled roan and Monte Walsh on an old deep-chested leggy dun. Ahead spread two stretches of hasty improvised fence, angled in, funnel-like, to a small opening into a stout renovated corral. The broomtails saw and broke in final desperation, scattering, and the mottled roan and the leggy dun raced, heading them, and they thudded forward along the stretches of fence and saw the opening and scrambled through, jostling one another. The dun slid to a stop on its rump and Monte leaped down and closed the improvised gate and leaned against it. He took off his old hat and wiped a hand across his forehead and down over the three-days stubble on his face.

The big-nosed man was beside him. He took a dirty bandanna from a pocket and wiped sweat from his face and neck. "You ever run 'em before?" he said.

"Not since I was a kid," said Monte.

"You was born to it," said the big-nosed man. "Wisht I'd of known you a few years back."

The broomtails were quieting now, slowing in their search .for another opening, long tails dragging on the ground. One by one they stopped, standing dejected, heads dropping low. They seemed smaller, thinner, more misshapen, in the absence of motion.

"Cripes," said the big-nosed man. "Look at 'em. They ain't what they used to be at all. Nothin' but runts left these days. I'll be lucky if I make expenses. Reckon I'll go back to black-smithin'."

"Yeah," said Monte. "There ain't more'n five even worth topping." He straightened and put on his hat at a jaunty angle and a wry grin touched his lips. "Shucks," he said. "Well, anyways, maybe I'll get enough out of it for one good drunk."

* * *

They came out of distance, going into distance, Monte Walsh and an old leggy dun. Afternoon sun slanted down on them, a man and a horse, complete in themselves, all that they owned together on them and in the blanket roll behind the saddle, moving together across the immensity of the big land.

Monte felt the falter in the old dun's stride and he pulled reins and swung down. He stood by the old head with its grayed muzzle, stroking along the bowed neck, and he noted the slight quivering in the old legs. "Goddamn it," he muttered. "If I could carry you a while, I'd sure do it." He moved out, walking, holding the reins, and the old dun followed.

Monte staggered forward several steps. The dun had nudged into him from behind. "G'wan," he said, walking on. "Forgotten your manners? I taught you to lead right fifteen years ago." He walked on. "No," he said. "Must be closer to twenty." He walked on.

He staggered forward again and caught his balance and half turned. "Quit that," he said. "Want me to give you a leathering? Personal?" He walked on.

He staggered forward again. This time he stopped and turned around. The man and the horse looked at each other.

"All right," said Monte. "Have it your way. Maybe you're right. Just keep on like always. Take things as they come." He swung into the saddle.

They moved on and time passed and the falter came often now and ahead in a hollow of the rising rangeland showed the squat buildings of a small ranch. They moved down the slope and stopped by a small poled corral that was empty except for a single nondescript middle-aged draft horse. Two men appeared in the doorway of the log house thirty feet away.

"I hear you got a few horses you need rode," said Monte.

"Could be," said the older of the two men. "That is, depending. We don't want them spoiled. They're good stuff. I suppose you've got a name."

"Walsh," said Monte.

"I suppose maybe what goes with it sounds something like Monte."

"Yeah."

"That's ticket enough. Five dollars apiece to get them so they handle right regardless. Light down and join us, food's on the table."

The two men turned back into the house. Monte led the old dun into the corral and stripped it, heaving his saddle up on the fence and hanging the bridle on the horn. He checked the small trough. Plenty of water. He undid the latch and opened the door of a stout shed in one corner and looked in and entered. He came out with an armload of baled hay sections and dropped these by the trough. He slapped the dun on the rump and went over and latched the shed door and as he headed back for the gate he detoured a bit to slap the draft horse too. "Howdy bub," he said. "You'll never win no prizes." He left the corral and strode over and into the house.

Twenty minutes later he came out and strolled toward the corral. He leaned against the gate looking over. His hands tightened on the gate top till the knuckles were white. Inside, the old dun lay on its side where it had crumpled down, limp legs sprawled, neck and head stretched out, the lifeless eyes staring into nothingness.

The two men had followed Monte out. "Hey," said one of them. "Look. Just like that. What did it?"

Monte swallowed, slow and with difficulty. He had trouble holding his voice steady. "Old age," he said. "And hard work."

"Too bad," said the other man. "He looked like he was all horse in his time."

"Yeah," said Monte. "He was all right. Whatever it was, any time, he did it."

The two men saw Monte's face, the flat forsaken rigidity of it, and they turned away and moved toward the house. One of them stopped in the doorway. "Hey, Walsh," he called. "Those horses are in the pasture down by the creek. We'll bring them up in the morning."

Monte might not have heard. He stood leaning against the gate, hands tight on the top. Slowly he opened the gate and went in and closed the gate behind him. Slowly he went to the shed and opened the door and reached in and took out an empty wooden box and closed and latched the door and carried the box and set it on the ground by the rails of the side fence. He sat on the box, still and quiet, and looked at the limp body of the old horse lying in the dust. He sat on the box, still and quiet, and the dusk of this high foothill country dropped swiftly out of the mountains beyond and twice before full darkness came one of the men in the house appeared in the doorway and peered over at the corral and saw him sitting there and turned back inside and once he stirred a little on the box and said to the draft horse munching hay by the water trough: "This time too. Do you understand that? He hung on till he got me here." The cool clean dark of night took the big land and he sat on the box, still and quiet, and the draft horse moved in close by him and stretched its head to sniff him and he reached to pat it along the jaw unaware of the movement and the light in the log house winked out and he rose from the box shivering some in the night chill and went to his saddle on the fence and untied the saddle roll and took his jacket from it and put this on and turned up the collar and went again to the box carrying the blanket and pulled this around his shoulders and sank down again on the box. He leaned against the rails behind him and his head dropped forward some and from under the brim of his old worn hat he looked through cool clean dark at the dim blurred shape of the limp body lying in trodden dust and on back into the miles and the years of a long long trail with a good horse under him . . .

In the first flush of dawn he was up and moving. He opened the door of the shed and set the box inside and took the gear from an inside wall and went out and harnessed the draft horse. He opened the gate and led around to the far side of the corral where a rough log-runnered low stoneboat lay among weeds and hooked the traces to the front eyebolts in it. He drove the draft horse hauling the stoneboat around and in through the gate and maneuvered until the stoneboat was close along the backbone of the stiffened body of the old dun. He took hold of the stoneboat, first one end then the other, and heaved it tight against the body. He looked up. The two men were standing by the open gate, each with a coiled rope and a hackamore in a hand.

"Need any help?" said the younger man.

"Want it," said the older man. "Do you want it?"

"No."

"All right. We're going to get them. There's coffee on the stove."

The two men started away. One of them half turned back. "Down by those cottonwoods," he said, pointing, "we had a root cellar. Just a nuisance, found we didn't need it. Caved in now but a nice hole." They moved on, toward the distant line of trees and brush that marked the creek.

Quietly, steadily, alone with the draft horse, Monte took his rope from his saddle and shook out a loop and dropped this over the four stiff legs of the dun, lifting them to slide it under, and pulled on the rope to tighten the loop. He unhooked the traces and led the draft horse around, facing away from the side of the stoneboat, and tied the rope to the traces hooked together. He took the long driving reins and clucked to the draft horse and it pushed ahead, heaving as the strain came, and the body of the dun tilted up and over and down on the stoneboat.

Quietly, steadily, Monte untied the rope and coiled it in close to the loop around the stiff legs and laid the coil on the old dun's body. He went to the shed again and took a shovel and laid this on the stoneboat, wedging it under one stiffened leg. He led the draft horse around again and hooked the traces to the eyebolts.

In the first full sweep of color from the rising sun over the big land Monte Walsh and a nondescript willing draft horse and the body of the old dun moved downslope toward a clump of cottonwoods three hundred yards away. The hole there, onetime sod roof caved in and onetime supporting poles pulled out long since for firewood, still showed well-defined sides a few feet down and was perhaps five feet deep in the middle. The stoneboat stopped along one side. Once again the traces were unhooked and the coiled rope paid out, across the hole to the other side, and tied again to the traces. The draft horse heaved again into the harness and the body of the dun tilted up and over and down into the hole. Monte climbed down in to unloop the rope and toss it out. He climbed out and took the shovel and began to cover the body with dirt from the sides. He worked his way around, beveling down the sides, and had the body well covered. He stood looking at the now rounded hollow with its leveled center and shook his head and dropped the shovel and hooked the traces to the eyebolts again and drove the draft horse down to the creek several hundred yards farther away and hunted along this for good-sized stones. Two loads hauled to the hollow and the leveled center was covered.

Back at the buildings, he left the stoneboat where it had been, the harness and shovel in the shed, and closed the gate on the draft horse and went into the house. The coffee in the pot had almost boiled away though the fire was dying out. What was left was thick and strong. He managed to pour a cup without too many grounds and stood in the doorway sipping the hot liquid and watching the two men, mounted now on two lean cow ponies, coming back driving seven horses ahead of them. He watched the seven horses approaching, four dark bays and two sorrels and a roan, young and full of the eager alertness of youth, stepping easy and brisk and still unaware of saddles and what they meant. He shook his head slightly. Good animals. They would shape up well for the bridle path and one or two perhaps even for the show-ring. But not one of these. He finished the coffee and reached back to set the cup down and moved toward the corral to open the gate and begin the day's work . . .

Three weeks here and on to the next place, riding a borrowed horse, and on to other places, riding borrowed horses between, and looking, always looking. And one day he stood by the main corral of a big outfit talking to the owner-manager, a tall thin Englishman in riding breeches and polished eastern boots. A dozen sleek horses, most of them big halfbreds, were in the corral.

"There they are," said the Englishman. "They are not finished. Not by a long sight. Some not even started. Our regular man is in the hospital. We will pay you the same wages as long as you are here. That is, if you—" He stopped. Monte was not listening. He was looking at another horse in a small pen beside the corral.

Dun in color with a slight extra darkening along the back and showing in the short mane and full tail. Young with the pent energy of youth leaping in the stout muscles under the dun-colored hide as it shifted restlessly in the narrow pen. Broad between the eyes that shone with resentment and indignation at the close cramping quarters. Deep-chested with clean legs tapering down to rock-hard range hoofs. Deceptive in seeming smallness compared to the others in the corral because of the compact solidity of the whole tight-knit body.

"What d'you know," murmured Monte. He jerked his head toward the pen. "What about that one?"

"That one," said the Englishman, dry, clipped. "That one sent our man to the hospital. I have not decided what to do with it except not to waste another man on it. Not much breeding anyway. If you are worried—" He stopped again. Monte was not listening. He was looking at the young horse in the pen and his shoulders were rising a little as he stood taller in his old boots.

"Look here," said the Englishman. "I assure you that riding that beast is not included in the pay."

"Pay?" said Monte, turning to him. "Forget that. I'll top off the whole bunch for you if you'll just give me that one."

The Englishman stared at him, startled. "It will be your funeral," he said. "I would not think of asking any man—"

"Shucks," said Monte, grinning. "It's a horse, ain't it."

*　　*　　*

They came along a rutted road that led out of seeming nowhere and on into the same, Monte Walsh and a young deep-chested leggy dun at the easy fast jog he had taught it along with many and many other things. Clouds rolled along the horizon and wind whipped past them, a man and a horse, complete in themselves, all that they owned or needed to own on them and in the blanket roll behind the saddle with the recent addition of a new slicker rolled and tied to it.

They jogged along and the wind skittered a tumbleweed past directly in front and the dun, deliberately, for the simple fun of it, shied in mock terror and leaped sideways. "Quit that," said Monte, serene in saddle, not particularly meaning it. "Act your age." He patted the dun's neck. "Maybe that's just what you're doing," he said.

They jogged on. The clouds climbed, arching closer, and rain came with the wind, the first spattering of big drops. Monte flipped the rein-ends together in a loose knot and dropped them over the saddle horn. He reached back, fumbling to untie the slicker. "Knew I'd be needing this," he murmured, intent on the operation. He had the slicker around and unrolled, flapping in the wind. He fought with it and had his left arm through the left sleeve. The dun, jogging steadily along, turned its head and rolled an eye, watching him. He had the slicker across his back and struggled to get his right arm into the right sleeve. It slipped partway in and the dun exploded upward, rising in a high buck, spine arched. Monte rocked in the saddle, arms caught up and behind him in the slicker, and the dun lit, hard, and rose again, twisting, and Monte sailed off and landed with a thump ten feet away.

He sat up, legs stretched out, leaning back on arms still caught in the slicker. The dun had stopped and stood, head turned, ears forward, watching him. In the pelting rain, indifferent to it, the man and the horse looked at each other. Monte worked his right arm on through the right sleeve. He stood up, pulling the slicker around him, and walked over and faced the horse head-on. "So you had to do it at least just once," he said. "You been waiting. Watching your chance." He reached up and rubbed around the ears wet now from the rain. "Well, now," he said. "You've done it. You've done it good. You try it again and I'll rip your hide off and stake it out to dry. Personal." He hitched the slicker higher around his neck. "Of course," he said, "I don't mean warming up of a morning." He swung into the saddle and pulled the slicker from under his rump so it lay back over the saddle roll and buttoned the three top buttons over his chest and tucked the lower flaps over his knees. They jogged on.

The rain passed, as swift as it had come, leaving a freshness over the land and small puddles in the road ruts. Monte dropped the reins again over the saddle horn and took off the slicker flapping in what was left of the wind and rolled it and twisted around in the saddle, hooking one leg to hold, and tied it in place and there was no explosion during this operation, only a contented jogging.

The sun came out and went to work on the dampness in Monte's clothes and on the soaked old felt of his hat and wisps of vapor rose from the warm hide of the dun as the stout young muscles moved beneath it and the road topped a rise and dipped down to cross a stream and a railroad track and was suddenly the brief main street of a small railside settlement.

They stopped by the tie rail in front of a shaky peaked-roof store. Monte dismounted and looped reins and stepped up on the sagging porch and went in through the open doorway. He emerged and sat on one of the two warped chairs on the porch, a can of peaches in one hand, top removed, a tin spoon in the other. He reached with the hand holding the spoon to push his hat up his forehead, dipped the spoon into the can, began to enjoy the peaches.

The storekeeper shuffled out, a wispy ineffectual-looking man with a drooping sandy mustache, and sat on the other chair.

"The Box D," said Monte around a mouthful of peaches. "Where's it at?"

"Up the road about twenty mile," said the storekeeper. "You come to three big pines on the right and you turn there. You'll see the wheel tracks. About five mile back in by the mountain." He wiped a hand over his mustache, brushing away a few crumbs. "So they say. I ain't ever been in there."

Monte finished the peaches, tilted the can for the last of the juice. He flipped the empty can toward a pile of rubbish beside the porch, wiped the spoon on a shirt sleeve and held it out to the storekeeper. "Good as new," he said. "Use it on the next one." He took out the makings, saw they were dry enough, and rolled a cigarette.

Across the roadway, widened here, was a neat square building whose front window proclaimed in gold letters:

Lawyer
Abogado
Attorney at Law

This was rather a remarkable building in that it defied the general character of the settlement by being freshly painted. White. The front door, paneled, was a solid bright red.

Out in the roadway two small boys, barefoot, in too-large cut-down jeans and ragged shirts, launched a chip of wood with a twig mast and a leaf sail on one of the shrinking puddles. The tiny boat toppled over and the two small boys shouted at each other, tossing the blame back and forth. One of them picked up a handful of mud and threw it at the other, who promptly replied in kind. Mud flew fast. The first boy fled, running toward the remarkable building to duck around the side and the other boy unleashed a final barrage after him and a fat fistful of mud smacked against the bright red door. Suddenly speechless, stricken, the second boy dashed away.

The red door opened inward and a man stepped out, plump, red-faced, bushy-eyebrowed, wearing striped trousers held up by fancy braided suspenders and a pink shirt and a spotless celluloid collar with a flowing black tie. He regarded the outside of the door in indignant disgust. He disappeared inside and emerged with a damp cloth and rubbed vigorously. He regarded the door again. The bright red was smudged and less bright where he had rubbed. He disappeared inside again and emerged again with a small can of paint and a brush. With quick angry strokes he repainted the outside of the door.

"My oh my," murmured Monte. "He sure is proud of that hunk of wood."

The storekeeper grunted. "Paints it every month," he said.

"Regular. Last time was just last week." He rubbed a hand over his mustache. "Proud of a lot of things," he said.

Monte rolled another cigarette, struck a match, sent two streamers of smoke upward from his nose.

The two small boys were back again, friends again, retrieving their boat, making adjustments of its rigging. The red door opened and the plump man dashed out, surprisingly fast on his feet, aiming straight for them. He grabbed one boy by the arm while the other streaked away. He held the squirming boy and cuffed him smartly on the side of the head. He let go and kicked out with excellent aim as the boy fled. He turned back, triumphant, and the red door closed behind him.

Monte flipped his cigarette stub away and stirred on his chair.

"Nice day," said the storekeeper. "After the rain and all." He rubbed a hand over his mustache. "I'd keep it that way. He'd have a lawsuit slapped on you before you hit him more'n once."

"You don't say," murmured Monte. He took out his pocketknife and began cleaning dirt from under his blunt battered fingernails.

A train tootled and came puffing along, disdaining to stop, merely slowing in mild recognition of the settlement. A big burly man in patched cinder-stained clothes and limp straw hat with the marks of long knockabout travel on them and him sat on the floor of a baggage car in its open doorway, legs dangling out. As the train slowed, he pushed out and landed in the roadway and rolled over and came to his feet with the agility of considerable practice at this kind of maneuver. While the train moved on, tootling again and picking up speed, he reclaimed his hat and wandered over by the store front. He looked at the storekeeper, then at Monte, then at somewhere in between them. "Maybe," he said, "maybe you'd know of a job." He thought that over. "A temporary job," he said.

"Job?" said the storekeeper. "Last job here was three years ago and there was seven men wanted it."

The man reached inside his patched shirt, scratching. He looked in the direction of the departing train. "I should of stayed with it," he said. "When's the next one?"

"Four hours," said the storekeeper. "Going the other way."

The man sighed and turned around and sat down on the edge of the porch.

A few flies buzzed and the sun went on with its own indifferent work, drying the puddles, and the young dun stomped a hoof occasionally out by the tie rail and slowly Monte Walsh straightened on his chair. He snapped the knife shut and rose from his chair and stretched and he stepped past the storekeeper and went into the store and he bounced off his toes as he went. He came back out and in one hand he held a new paint brush and a small can of paint whose label asserted in brave letters: *Canary Yellow.* "How much?" he said.

The storekeeper stared at him, then at the things in his hand. "Thirty-nine," he said, "and fifteen. Call it fifty cents."

Monte fished with his other hand in a pants pocket and pulled out a fifty-cent piece and handed this to the storekeeper. He sat again on his chair and shook the small can vigorously and took out his knife and pried up the top of the can. He set the can and the brush and the can top carefully down on the porch floor beside his chair, put the knife in his pocket and took out the remaining coins that had been in there with it. Three silver dollars, a quarter, a dime, two pennies. He put the smaller coins back in his pocket and held the three silver dollars in his hand. He reached with a boot toe to nudge the burly man sitting on the edge of the porch. "How'd you like to make three dollars?" he said.

"Quit it," said the man without turning around. "There ain't that much money in this whole place." He heard the chink of the coins in Monte's hands and turned to look.

"That building over there you been staring at," said Monte, jingling the coins.

"Yeah," said the man, staring at the coins. "What about it?"

"Well, now," said Monte. "It happens to be mine. Belongs to me. I been thinking—"

"Hey," said the storekeeper. "Where'd you get the notion you—" He stopped. Monte was looking at him.

"Yeah," said Monte to the burly man. "It's mine. I been thinking it don't look right. That door. Too damn red. Sticks out like a sore thumb. Hurts the eyes. Ought to tone it down some. You just take this can here and paint it for me. I'd do it myself but I'm feeling plumb lazy."

"You mean," said the burly man, "all I got to do is paint that door and you pay me three dollars?"

"Why sure," said Monte. "Only there's one thing. Man in there who rents the place is mighty peculiar. Off in the head. Ought to be locked up but we feel kind of sorry for him and let him roam loose. He might get to bothering you, claiming the place is his. Just don't pay him no mind."

The burly man was scratching again. "Three dollars," he said.

"Why sure," said Monte. "Those three. To show you my heart's in the right spot I'll give them to you right now."

The burly man held the coins. He bit each in turn and tucked them away somewhere in his patched clothes. He leaned on his stomach along the porch floor and took the can of paint and the brush. He rose to his feet and headed across the roadway.

"I ain't heard a word of this," said the storekeeper, rising and heading in through the store doorway. "I been inside all the time." He perched on a stool behind the counter where he could see out the front window.

Monte Walsh pushed his hat further up his forehead and leaned back comfortably on his chair.

Across the way the burly man set the can of paint down by the right side of the red door, dipped the brush in, went to work. His strokes were large and expansive and the brilliant yellow paint smeared with the fresh red paint to produce a superb conglomerate of color.

The door opened and the plump man appeared. He stared in shocked disbelief at the yellow streakings. He reached a finger and touched one and stared at the fingertip. He focused on the burly man, brush in hand, and his voice climbed in shrill indignation.

The burly man turned his head and winked at Monte on the store porch and turned his head back and put his left hand on the plump man's chest and shoved him staggering inside the building. The burly man closed the door and went on with his work.

The door opened again and the plump man stepped out, voice shrilling, and shoved the burly man backward. The burly man laid down his brush, grabbed the plump man in both arms and heaved him ten feet away to stagger and sit down in drying mud. The burly man picked up the brush, closed the door again, and went on with his work.

The plump man pushed to his feet, shaking with fury. He lowered his head and ran straight into the burly man with fists flailing. The burly man, somewhat heated now himself, took hold of the flowing black tie and the front of the pink shirt with his left hand and held the plump man at arm's length. Deliberately he wiped the wet brush in his right hand across the plump man's face. He dropped the brush and bent, still holding, to pick up the can of paint and lifted this high and emptied it over the plump man's head.

Across the way Monte Walsh rose to his feet. "I reckon I better be moving on," he said. He stepped down from the porch and unlooped reins and in one swift motion was in the saddle. He struck spurs to the dun and it reared, pivoting, and leveled out into the road. "Yoweee!" yelled Monte in one of its ears and it stretched out, racing away.

* * *

They had brought a small herd down out of the hills, six days of hard riding, and checked it in at the railside pens, Monte Walsh and the gaunt old hook-nosed oldtime ranchman who had taken Monte on for the season and quickly got over his worry that he could afford to hire only one hand this year. They had shaved at the water trough by the pens and stripped to the raw behind a screen of bushes and scrubbed themselves in the creek that ran past the sleepy little town and beaten much of the dust out of their clothes with branches and they made a fairly respectable pair, in a rugged way, when they sampled the liquid refreshment at the first of the town's two saloons.

They were in the second now, which called itself a restaurant to attract the family trade and justified this by serving food as a strictly minor sideline to those foolish enough to order it. They sat at a table discovering that even with appetites honed by six days of short hurried rations they were among the foolish. But the liquor was good.

"Smart," suggested Monte. "They get you in here for food then you got to fill up on drink." He studied the leathery slice of beef on his plate. "Why, shucks," he said. "I bet they use this stuff over and over. It don't look like it'd ever wear out."

At another table fifteen feet away, facing Monte, two swarthy men under high-crowned wide-brimmed black hats seemed to be arguing violently in Spanish and were really indulging in an amiable and, to them, interesting conversation. With them but sitting back out of the direct line of verbal gunfire was a dark-eyed dusky-skinned woman in a flowing many-pleated skirt and a tight tempting bodice. There was a bright flower tucked into her dark hair and two dainty turquoise circlets dangled from her ears. She no longer paid any attention to the conversation bouncing past her. It was ridiculous that two presumably robust men should be so interested in the respective supposed speeds of various horses and not in her. And on her one night out for the month. Ridiculous, even if one was a husband of eight years' familiarity. She was well aware that about fifteen feet away a rugged length of Anglo rawhide had been looking at her while pretending not to for the past ten minutes. She permitted her head to turn a bit more toward him and her soft dark glance to focus briefly on him and the trace of a smile to show on her face.

The hook-nosed man saw Monte's eyes brighten, his whole body tense some. The hook-nosed man pretended to reach for something in a pants pocket and while executing this maneuver had to shift sideways on his chair and this gave ample chance for a casual glance backwards. He faced Monte again. "Watch it," he said, low-voiced. "These monkeys around here are mighty touchy about their women. You'll get a knife in the ribs."

"People," said Monte, expansive. "Just people."

The hook-nosed man executed his maneuver again, lingering at it. He faced Monte again. "Ripe," he said. "Can't say I blame you. Don't mind me. You get to be my age you talk discouragin'."

At the other table the woman spoke rather sharply and the two men stopped talking and looked at her. She spoke again and they shrugged shoulders and rose from their chairs. The woman rose too and they moved toward the front door. The woman paused briefly in the doorway, reaching up to fuss with the flower in her hair, and her glance flicked to Monte and again the trace of a smile showed on her face.

The hook-nosed man tried a piece of something from his

plate and chewed methodically, watching Monte. "Take it easy," he said. "An' remember we're leavin' first thing in the mornin'."

Monte said nothing. He sat still, tapping with one finger on the table. He counted out a full minute. He stood up, stretching. "Kind of close in here," he said. "I need a little fresh air." He strolled to the doorway and out into the dusk. He rolled a cigarette and lit it. On down the street he could see the three figures moving slowly, the two men again immersed in their conversation. They stopped by a small frame house and one of them, unmistakable in flowing skirt, went into the house and the other two continued on, at a faster pace, arm motions indicating still more talk.

Monte waited, finishing the cigarette. The two men had turned a corner, around a building, out of sight. Darkness was taking the town. He strolled down the street. He stopped by the small frame house and started to roll another cigarette. He was not certain at first that he caught the soft whisper from the window. It came again: "Around back."

Monte looked up and down the street. He dropped the unlit cigarette and stepped into the darker shadow along the house side wall and moved to the rear. He stood close against the back wall. A door opened with a tiny squeak and the woman stepped out, vague in the darkness but unmistakable again in flowing skirt. The door closed with another tiny squeak.

"Over here," whispered Monte.

She moved toward him and looked up at him in the darkness, peering at the lean weathered reckless ruggedness of his face under the brim of his own hat.

"You are a cowboy, yes? I like cowboys."

"We have our points," said Monte.

"But you are not always thinking only of the cows and the horses, no?"

"Shucks," said Monte. "Right now there ain't a cow or a horse anywheres on my mind."

"And you think I am pretty, yes?"

"Shucks," said Monte, reaching to touch one of the turquoise circlets. "Right now at this particular moment I think everything pretty there ever was is put together right here in you."

"You tell the lie," she said, pushing away his hand. She hesitated, peering at him. "But maybe—maybe not for just right now." She moved in closer, tossing her head a little. "You will tell me more of the lies, yes?"

"Shucks, ma'am," said Monte, taking her arm. "As many as you want." He led her back, away from the house, toward a small arbor with thick cloaking of grapevines . . .

In the second saloon which called itself a restaurant the hook-nosed man, defeated, abandoned his attack on the substances on his plate. He pushed the plate across the table beside Monte's. He beckoned to the bartender and obtained liquid substitution. He looked up at the clock on the wall. He took an old pack of cards bound by a piece of string from a shirt pocket and untied the string and began playing solitaire . . .

In the small arbor behind the small frame house Monte Walsh was temporarily through telling what might or might not be lies at this particular moment to the woman in the flowing skirt. She was in his arms and his head was bent as his lips moved through her hair down past a turquoise circlet to nuzzle her neck and she quivered in gratifying response and his right hand moved down the small of her back, pressing her closer to him. He stopped, hearing, and felt her stiffening in his arms, hearing too. A small sound, seeming to float in the still air back to them. The click of the front door of the small frame house closing.

He stepped to the entrance to the arbor and stood, still, listening. The silence from the house was somehow alive, ominous. Then another sound. The tiny squeak of the back door opening.

He flicked a glance into the darkness of the arbor behind him. The woman had stepped out of her shoes and slipped through the back entrance and away, into, or around behind, clumped bushes to one side. He stared into the baffling black of the darker shadow along the rear of the house. Nothing. Apparently nothing. Only the slight tingling of the sensing of something there and perhaps elsewhere too.

"Luck and me," he murmured. He stepped out into the open of the yard and moved, cautious, alert, range-trained muscles tensed, poised, aiming toward the rear of the next building. Out of the corner of vision, from the left, he saw the one man rushing, knife in hand, and he whirled and stepped to meet the onrush and his left hand leaped to take

the man's wrist and wrenched and his right knee surged up
into the man's groin and in the instant of action he was
aware of the other man, from the right and behind now, and
he felt the tearing shock of the other knife slicing in and
grating on a rib and he flung back around with his right
arm flailed like a club and the weight of his body turning
with it and the arm struck the other man across the neck and
knocked him away and down.

He felt the blood running beneath his clothes, down around
his belt, and he staggered ahead and around the corner of the
building and leaned against the wall and only then did he
think of his gun and he pulled it, waiting, and no one came.
He backed along, holding to the wall, aware of the weakness
taking him, and he was at the front by the open of the street.
He dropped the gun in its holster and moved up the street,
staggering, weaving from side to side. "Like a goddamned
drunk," he muttered. He made it to the corner of the second
saloon building and inched along, clutching at the front wall,
and fell forward in through the doorway and as he fell he
saw the hook-nosed man rising and the table going over and
cards spilling to the floor. "You sure called it," he said and in
the saying blacked out . . .

*　*　*

Sunlight through a neat clean window with neat clean
fluffy side-curtains filled the small room with a warm morning glow. Monte Walsh was gradually aware that he was
awake and likely had been for a while and that he lay on a
soft bed with a neat clean sheet over him and was staring at
that remarkable window. Such as clean and curtained were
somewhat outside his usual experience. He rolled his head a
bit to look around the room. A framed lithograph of some
flowers on one wall, another of a mountain scene on another
wall. A hanging mirror with a dresser under and a scarf laid
over this. Two straight-back chairs and a small table with
pitcher and basin. A thunder mug on the floor between the
table legs. His boots standing in a corner. His gunbelt hanging on a hook above them.

He started to sit up and understood immediately that was
not a good notion. With cautious fingers he explored what he
could of the bandage encircling his upper body under the

armpits. A tight and thorough job. He lay still. He rolled his head a bit to look out the window. A short stretch of bare dirt yard ending abruptly in what seemed to be part of a barn. Two posts with a rope strung between them.

From somewhere outside the window frame a woman appeared. A plump well-rounded brisk-moving woman who carried her weight with a swish of hips as she walked. She held a basket in one hand. She set the basket down and began to hang damp clothes on the line between the posts. A man's shirt with a rip showing in it. A pair of pants. Short-length underwear with another rip showing. A pair of socks. With a slight feeling of indignation Monte recognized his shirt and pants and underwear and socks.

The woman picked up her basket and came straight to the window and peered in. Suddenly aware that Monte was awake and looking at her, she jumped back and swept out of sight beyond the window frame again.

Monte lay still. "What d'you know," he murmured.

He rolled his head. The door to the room was opening inward, being pushed all the way back, and the woman was in the doorway. "Wonderful," she said. "Doctors are just wonderful. He said you'd be waking up this morning and be weak and all that but you might even be chipper and certainly hungry. He said you're about the toughest piece of masculine meat he ever worked on. He talks like that and all, the doctor. Masculine meat and all that. Like he was a butcher and not a doctor. But he doesn't mean it. He's really a doctor you know." She was moving briskly about the room, straightening the scarf on the dresser, pulling the curtains back to let in more sunlight.

"Please, ma'am," said Monte, "who—"

"Your things out there," said the woman. "I just washed them out. Goodness but they were bloody. You have to wash blood out right away or it stains. Let it dry in hard and it stains. But your socks! Goodness, don't you men ever think to change them?"

"Please, ma'am," said Monte, "who—"

"And those rips in them," said the woman. "Just you set your mind at rest about those. Soon as they're dry I'll be mending them soon as I get the chance. Goodness knows there should be time enough. He said, that's the doctor, you'll likely be trying to get up before you should and I'd better keep your things out of reach for a few days."

"Please, ma'am," said Monte. "Who took my clothes off me?"

The woman looked at him, startled, and a strong flush spread up her full good-natured face. She looked away. "Why your friend did. Of course I had to help him and all. We had to do something before the doctor got here. You would keep bleeding. We'd think we had it stopped and you'd start again." She looked at Monte, a trifle defiant. "And if you're worrying about anything like that I want you to know I'm a married woman. Married women know things. I have a very good husband even if he is older than me. He doesn't go getting himself cut up with knives and likely over a woman too."

She started toward the door. "You men. Gabbling so you keep a woman talking so she can't get things done. I'm forgetting what's on the stove." She disappeared.

Monte lay still. She reappeared with a bowl of hot soup on a plate in one hand, a pillow in the other. She set the soup on the dresser and came over and slipped an arm under Monte's neck and raised his head and shoulders and put the pillow under, on the one already there. She brought one of the chairs and put it by the bed. She brought the soup and began to spoon it into his mouth.

"I don't usually give meals," she said. "Just rooms. This is a rooming house. But I want you to know I don't have to do that. Just for something to do. My husband makes good money. He's with the railroad. He's a fireman. But what's a woman to do with no children? Just sit around all day? I'm not the kind to sit around. I have to have things to do. Well, you certainly took that soup like you liked it. If I do say so, I make good soup and all. How do you feel?"

"Hungry," said Monte.

"You men," she said, rising and starting toward the door. "But I know you. Oh, how I know you. You can't run a rooming house without getting to know. I've got some stew warming on the stove. From yesterday. Stew's always better and easier to chew when warmed over." She disappeared.

Monte lay still. He could feel the warmth from the soup beginning to spread through him.

She reappeared with another bowl on another plate and sat

down again on the chair by the bed. "Do I have to keep feeding you?"

"Shucks, ma'am," said Monte. "I kind of like it."

"All right," she said. "Open your mouth. I don't mind. It's something to do. I cleaned the whole house yesterday and put out clean sheets you'd think just as if I knew something would happen so I haven't much to do today. You're the first cowboy I've had. But I think that's a silly word because you certainly aren't a boy. It was old Mr. Wentworth who had this room. He's railroad too. Only retired. I made him move upstairs last night. Oh, he grumbled and he grumbled about all those trips up and down taking his things and all but I thought you'd be best in here. Downstairs. Close to the kitchen . . ."

She talked on and Monte realized there was no need to pay particular attention and he chewed slowly on the stew which was a fine far jump from the food at the second saloon and he noticed that she was not as heavy as she had first seemed out the window and that the arm reaching out to him was soft and round with smooth tempting skin.

The bowl was empty and the woman rose and set it on the dresser and put the chair back in its place by the wall. She stooped over the bed again and slid one of the soft round arms under Monte's shoulders and raised him to fluff the pillows higher. For an instant her full bosom brushed against his cheek and looking up he saw a curl from the brown hair held up on her head with celluloid hairpins drop down over her forehead. He pursed his lips and blew softly and the curl bounced and the woman straightened up quickly and looked down at him, surprisingly, for the moment, silent.

She turned away, brisk, and took the bowl on its plate and moved to the doorway. "Rest," she said. "That's what you need now. This house isn't so big so that if you need anything you can't just call. My husband has the day run west from here. One day going then he stays over and comes back the next day. I don't know why I'm telling you that except because maybe you'd be wondering why sometimes he isn't here. Well, that's why." She disappeared.

Monte lay still. He lay still thinking of the jaunty swish of well-rounded hips. He lay still thinking and was asleep . . .

He was aware again that he was awake, staring this time at

the doorway. The hook-nosed man stood there, regarding him gravely.

"I've got to be going," said the hook-nosed man. "Got to get back to the place. But I've took care of everything. Your hoss is at the stable. Paid up for a month. Same for this room and board. It took a little more'n what you had coming but what the hell. You been doin' two-three men's work. Paid up for a month. You'll be up and around by then."

"A month," said Monte. "Lovely. Just lovely."

The hook-nosed man stared at him. "Cracked," he said. "You get carved up an' talk like that. Well, anyways, I've found me another man. Got to have him. Wish it was you but it's take what's available. Maybe you'll come around next year."

"Maybe," said Monte. "I get around."

"Hate to leave you like this but you know how it is. Not so bad. A clean room and good food."

"Why sure," said Monte. He looked out the window into the yard where with jaunty swish of hips the woman was taking down his shirt and pants and underwear and socks. "Don't you worry none about me," he said. "It ain't going to be bad at all."

*   *   *

They had swept one of the last stretches of open range rising toward the Mogollons, the men of three outfits, some of them regulars, some of them seasonal, most of them young. They had the cattle bunched, nine hundred head and more, and four men rode circle while the others were gathered by the two chuck wagons absorbing a midday meal. They would be cutting the herd by brands soon and driving these to their respective ranges and in a few days fence crews would be at work putting in permanent divisions.

A deep-chested leggy dun ambled into view out of somewhere and the man in the saddle looked out over the scene and his face brightened and he rode toward the wagons. He dismounted and dropped reins and the dun stood, patient, ground-reined, and he walked to the first wagon.

The younger men studied him in silence. "How ya, Monte," said one of the older men. "Ain't seen you in a long while."

"I been moving around," said Monte Walsh. "Found out something. Scenery doesn't change much from here to there." He reached out. The cook by the fire had heaped a plate and was handing it to him.

"Fill up," said this one. "You're just in time. I was about ready to clear away."

"Thanks," said Monte. He waited for the cup of coffee. He moved off a brief distance and hunkered down on his heels and started on his first meal in a day and a half.

Over by the other wagon a thin man with sharp eyes and a small trimmed mustache, new owner of one of the outfits and boss of the day's operations, watched Monte gulping coffee and attacking the plate of food. "Look at him eat," he said to another man beside him. "You can always spot them first sight. Those oldtimers think they can ride in, pick up a meal anytime anywhere."

"Why not?" said the other man. "It's been going on a long time."

"Not that I grudge it to them," said the thin man. "But it gripes me how they drift around expecting a handout. I've learned to stay clear of them. Too set in their ways. Too damn independent. Why just last month I had one quit me just because I sold a horse out of his string. Too good a price to miss. 'If I'd asked you,' I says, 'you'd of said go ahead, wouldn't you?' 'Sure,' he says, 'but you didn't ask me.' And he quits me just like that."

The men were mounting and riding out. Monte handed his plate and cup to the cook and hunkered down again to watch the work in progress. The main herd began to dwindle and two smaller herds to develop, held short distances away.

One of the men, young and energetic on a horse the same, was well into the main herd driving a lean long rangy cow toward the outer edge. He had her out and headed for one of the smaller herds and she dodged to one side and he jumped to head her and she doubled to the other side and around him and back into the main herd, boring in toward the center. "Damn!" he said, loud and distinct, and started after her again.

"Hold up!" shouted another young man. "I'll show you how it's done!" He drove in, scattering cattle as he went, and had the cow moving toward the outer edge. She snorted and ducked under the nose of a big steer and was boring into the middle again. A third young one, shouting derisively at the first two, was pushing in, scattering the cattle more. Work was stopping all around as all the other men watched.

"Quit that!" yelled the thin mustached man from his post by the wagons. "Let that one go for now! You'll bust up everything! Close them up!"

"My oh my," said Monte to the cook. "Letting one old cow act up like that. Downright scandalous. Ain't there one good horse in the whole bunch?"

The thin man, twenty feet away, heard. He turned toward Monte. "I suppose," he said, sarcasm edging his voice. "I suppose you think you could do better."

"Why sure," said Monte. "Nothing to it."

"You talk big," said the thin man.

"Big?" said Monte. "Just normal size. Any good horse'd have her out of there in no time at all."

"I suppose," said the thin man, heavily sarcastic. "I suppose a stove-up drifter like you would be having a good horse? Like nothing." He turned away.

"Mister," said Monte and his voice snapped the thin man back around and caught the attention of other men further on. "Maybe I will talk big. I'm just going to show you something. If those school kids you got trying to act like men'll stay out of the way, that horse of mine is going to cut that cow out of there and do it all by himself." He strode to the dun, ignoring the voices as the word spread, and swung up and the dun, alert to the mood along the reins, head high and with springy steps, trotted toward the main herd.

The other men were silent now, watching.

The dun eased in, not springy now, quiet and flowing, moving through the herd with scarcely a ripple, and Monte guided it to the old cow and the cow dodged away, slipping between other animals in full knowledge of the game, and he held the reins in command until he knew the dun had her singled and her direction fixed. He looped the reins in a loose knot and dropped them over the saddle horn and he raised his arms and folded them across his chest. The dun moved on, intent after the cow. Dodge and twist as she would always the dun was there, intercepting her, crowding her, shouldering her, driving her toward the outer edge, and Monte swayed and swung, knees gripping, rump flat to the saddle, arms folded, a grim little smile on his face."

"See that son of a bitch ride," said one of the younger men. "Sittin' there no arms."

The cow was forced to the edge, forced on out. She was being driven toward the smaller herd of her brand. She had room to maneuver now. Angry, desperate, determined, she dashed to one side and to the other. Always the dun was there, an instant or two ahead of her, blocking, forcing her on. The dun leaped and whirled and leaped, spinning within its own length, a dedicated flash of stout-muscled movement, and Monte whipped about, arms folded, and grinned as his hat went off.

The cow made a frantic spurt and was behind a clumped juniper, racing around. The dun was there to meet her. She doubled back around and again the dun was there. She was blocked—but so was the dun. It could not get around either side after her without her dashing around the other. The two of them stopped, the cow panting behind the juniper, the dun in front of it, facing each other through the branches.

"Why doggone," said Monte. "You going to let a mangy old cow buffalo you?"

The dun waggled an ear. Suddenly it plunged straight forward, leaping right through the juniper with thrashing of branches, and rammed into the startled cow. Its jaws, open, smacked on the cow's shoulder and closed with a wicked snap on a fold of hide and muscle. The cow bellowed in surprise and pain and sudden fear—and pulled loose and dropped her head and shuffled in weary resignation toward the smaller herd.

Monte paid no attention to the shouts of the other men. "Well, well," he murmured, patting the dun's neck. "You keep right on and someday maybe you'll be almost as good as old Monkey Face himself." He turned the dun and headed for the wagons and leaned down from the saddle to scoop up his hat as he went.

"That was quite a stunt," admitted the thin man, grudging, as if the admission was not wholly pleasant. "Now was there any particular reason why you came by here?"

"I could use a job," said Monte.

"Too bad," said the thin man. This seemed to please him a bit more. "We have all the men we need. But I'll give you a hundred dollars for that horse."

Monte's face hardened. "No," he said.

"Two hundred."

"No."

"Two hundred fifty and something to ride away on and that's final."

"Mister," said Monte. "You can push it up till the number's so goddamn big you can't even say it and this horse he ain't for sale." A wry grin showed on his lips as he swung the dun to ride on. "We drifters," he said, "we got to be drifting. See you. I hope never."

* * *

Drift with the years, here and there and wherever the big land still finds a need for a man and a horse and the old simple unthinking acceptance of danger and duty and trust as part of a day's work and the stern hard-won skills that are less and less important as open range becomes fenced pastures and ranching becomes more and more merely another form of farming . . . working hard and playing hard and standing up to the consequences of any act because that is the way it was and the pattern set by the past . . . and now and again, maybe every other year, never when broke, always with some money in a pocket, wander back to a little town that is no longer quite so little, growing, growing . . . once for the christening of a baby boy whose parents, after long argument, have compromised on a name, Clark Montelius Rollins . . . again to help lower into the ground the body of a lean old man who was imprisoned all the last years in a wheelchair yet who once summed in himself the full strong flavor of the old days . . . or perhaps simply to sit on the porch of a fine new house with the ever more dignified and ever more prosperous proprietor of a combination livery stable and feed store whose dignity and prosperity fade into meaningless additions to the man himself in talk in the slow leisurely southwestern manner with long friendly gaps between of things that have been and never will be again . . .

* * *

They came around the side of the house, Monte Walsh and a round-faced six-year-old boy who held Monte's hand and looked up from under a wide-brimmed jauntily creased little hat bought the day before by Monte.

"Look at me," said the boy. "I'm as big as your belt already."

"Growing like a weed," said Monte. "Have to tie a brick on your head one of these days."

The boy thought about this and gave it up with a little shrug of shoulders. They reached the street and started along the middle of it toward the plaza.

"Where's your gun?" said the boy.

"Shucks," said Monte. "Those things are out of style around here."

"But you've got your spurs," said the boy.

"Why sure," said Monte. "Without them I'd feel plumb naked. Think you can keep a secret?"

"Course I can," said the boy.

"I like to hear 'em jingle," said Monte.

The boy saw a small stone in the street and kicked it on ahead. They moved up to it and Monte gave it a kick. They moved to it again, swerving so the boy could have his turn. "Monte," said the boy, looking up. "My dad says you're the best man that ever—that ever—had a leg on a horse."

"Plumb impossible," said Monte, taking his turn. "I couldn't be that."

They moved on. "Why not?" said the boy, taking his turn.

"Because he is," said Monte.

They moved on, swerving all over the street to keep the stone ahead of them. They reached the plaza, promptly forgot the stone, and turned right.

"Why can't I go with you?" said the boy. "Yesterday you said I could."

"Shucks," said Monte. "It ain't going to be much. I'm just going to try out a couple horses old Mac picked up somewheres cheap."

"I want to go," said the boy.

"Quit that," said Monte. "I heard your mother say you wasn't to go into the stockyards."

"She doesn't want me to do anything," said the boy.

"Women," said Monte. "Peculiar things, women. Tell you what. We'll ask your dad."

They turned in through the big open doorway of the livery stable. Monte stepped to the little door into the inside office, opened it. "Hey," he said to a gangling loose-jointed man who was shuffling papers at an old desk. "Where's the boss?"

"Gone out a while," said the man. "Trying to collect a bill."

"Goddamned businessman," murmured Monte, closing the door. He moved back along the stalls and entered one, ignoring the boy, who stood near the wide doorway watching him. He led out a deep-chested leggy dun, stripped off the halter, slipped on his bridle, heaved his old saddle into position.

"I want to go," said the boy.

"Sure you do," said Monte without looking around. "That don't mean you're going." He pulled the cinch tight, swung into the saddle.

"I want to go," said the boy, rubbing hard at one eye.

"Tell you what," said Monte. "Suppose I was to fix it so you wasn't exactly *in* the stockyards but you could see all right." He held a hand out and down.

The boy ran to him and grasped the hand and Monte pulled up and the boy was on the dun with him. Monte sat well back on the cantle and settled the boy in front of him behind the horn. "Here," he said, putting the reins in the boy's hands, "you take those."

The dun turned its head, inspected the arrangement on its back, saw the reins in the boy's hands, decided to pay no attention to them, responded to the nudge of Monte's spurs and the message of his legs down its sides. They ambled out the doorway, Monte ducking a bit, and around one end of the plaza and jogged seven blocks down a dwindling street and came to the array of low jerry-built buildings and pens which passed for the town's relatively new stockyards. As they approached Monte looked ahead and saw by the gate in the back side of the first and largest pen half a dozen men and among them the big gray-mustached figure of Sheriff MacKnight. Inside the pen two horses, a medium-sized solid bay and a long-barreled rawboned buckskin, were neck-roped to rails in a corner. Along the street side of the pen ran a long shed, flat roof sloped streetward.

"Made for us," said Monte, taking the reins. "Regular grandstand."

The dun moved in close along the shed and stopped midway. Monte stood in the stirrups and took hold of the boy under the armpits and hoisted so the boy could scramble onto the roof. "Go on," he said, "and sit down where you can see over. Don't go too near the edge. Got that?"

"Course I have," said the boy.

By stretching Monte could peer over the near edge and he watched the boy go up the gradual slope and sit cross-legged about a foot from the other edge and look back at him.

"Now stay there," said Monte, "and don't go trying any tricks or I'll paddle you good. Personal." He sank down into the saddle and sent the dun at a fast lope back around the shed and the pen to the group by the gate. He swung down and looped reins around a rail and began to unsaddle.

"I see you brought an audience," said Sheriff MacKnight. "Does his mother know he's here?"

"Shucks," said Monte. "She don't want him in the yards. Well, I got you for a witness that maybe he's somewheres hereabouts but you can take an oath he ain't *in* the yards."

"That's right," said one of the men. "He ain't."

"He's *on* a roof," said another. "An' he's *at* the yards. But by jingo he aint *in* a one of 'em."

"Same old Monte," said another. "He don't never change."

"All right," said Monte. "What's with those two things in there?"

"They come into the territory from somewheres," said Sheriff MacKnight. "Nobody knows about 'em. Brands blotched so they don't mean anything. Somebody picked 'em up over by Chico and brought 'em to the auction here last week. Feeling foolish I bought 'em and now don't know what to do with 'em. They'll lead, after a fashion. But they shy away from saddles. Scared out a couple of the boys here. Maybe you'll tell me if they're worth trying to work."

"I get a leg over," said Monte, "I'll know."

"Better take the bay first," said Sheriff MacKnight. "We've had a time with that other one."

Five minutes later the bay stood, bridled and saddled, and two men held it by the cheek straps. Monte took the reins, winked at the boy on the roof, and in the single flowing motion was aboard. The two men jumped back and the bay soared upward, coming down hard, thrusting for head-play, and felt the iron grip on the reins and grunted in exasperation and plowed forward, bucking and crow-hopping.

"Shucks," said Monte, serene in saddle. "You're not much more'n a small-scale firecracker." He waved at the boy and

pulled the bay around and it bucked back toward the gate-
side and he swung down and away, holding to one of the
reins, and the horse stood, snorting but obedient to the taut
rein. "Broke," said Monte. "Likely at about four and been
running wild a few years. Take that out of him and you've got
a good horse. Moves nice. If Chalkeye's still around he'll
smooth him out for you."

Twelve minutes later the buckskin stood, bridled and saddled, blindfolded, legs braced, one man hanging his weight
from its ears, two men holding the cheek straps.

"Mean," said Sheriff MacKnight from outside the gate.
"Too damn mean. Forget 'im, Monte. You ain't as young as
you used to be. I got one good one out of the deal."

"Shucks," said Monte. "It's a horse, ain't it." He waved at
the boy, pulled his hat down tighter, and was in the saddle.
The men jumped away, making for the fence, and he flipped
off the blindfold and the buckskin shot forward, high-rolling,
twisting and wrenching in concentrated fury. Fast action,
wild and whirling, seemed to fill the pen. Minutes passed and
it seemed even to gain in momentum. Suddenly the horse
stopped, shuddering, gulping for air, and Monte was erect in
saddle, gasping, hat gone, a few drops of blood dribbling
from one nostril.

"Leave him!" shouted Sheriff MacKnight.

"Leave him . . . hell," gasped Monte. "I'll show . . . the son
of a bitch." He raked the horse with his spurs and it squealed
and shot forward again and whirled, around and around, diz-
zying, and snapped into a series of frenzied buckings, blind
with rage, straight for the shed.

Monte caught a glimpse of the boy, almost due ahead, forward on the very edge of the roof, legs hanging over, staring
in frightened fascination. "Get back!" he yelled and the horse
crashed into the shed wall, shaking it, and he saw the boy, in
the act of trying to get legs up and crawl back, be shaken
loose and falling, falling, down almost under the plunging
hoofs, and he pulled back on the reins with all his strength
and the horse rose, up, up, tottering on hind legs, and he
pulled heaving with his whole weight and the horse toppled
backwards and he tried to push out and away and the shed
wall cramped him and he went down between the dropping
horse's body and the wall. He struggled up, battered and
limping, as the horse scrambled to its feet and he leaped at

the horse's head, waving his arms, an animal snarl sounding in his throat, and he drove the horse back and away from the small limp fallen body and he turned and picked this up and as he did he saw the one small arm dangling at an odd angle . . .

He sat on the steps of the back porch of the fine new house and stared at a bumblebee busy at a lilac bush and all unaware of the movement he rubbed gently along his left leg that was scraped and discolored from hip to knee under the worn cloth of his old pants.

"Quit sniffling, Mary," came the aging voice of Doc Frantz through an open second-story window. "It's nothing but a broken arm. A nice clean break that'll heal in a matter of weeks. Good for him. Kind of like a badge. Shows he isn't a baby any more. He's a boy."

He sat still and quiet and stared at the bee and faintly he could hear the sound of Doc Frantz going downstairs to the front door.

"I did it to a leg," came the voice of Chester A. Rollins through the window. "At about the same age. I was kind of proud of it. And do you know, I don't think there's a piece of Monte that hasn't been cracked up one time or another."

"Monte," came a woman's voice close to tearful anger. "All the time it's Monte, Monte, Monte. He doesn't talk about anything else and neither do you when he's here. It's all his fault."

"The hell it is. Mac says he damn near got killed saving the kid."

"Yes. After he took him there and caused it all. It's his fault and you needn't swear at me. For the life of me I can't see why you keep encouraging him to come back here. Oh, you were friends once but now you've gone way past him and it just doesn't—"

"Past him!" The voice was flat, hard, uncompromising. "I'm not even up alongside him and I never have been."

"Oh-h-h, you know what I mean. You're getting to be a real successful man and I'm proud of you, you know I am, and just last week they made you a director of the bank and . . . and . . . and you know how it is, he comes here and everything's all upset while he's here and you don't get much of anything done and after he's gone you're restless for weeks and can't really settle down to your business. And what is he anyway? He's just getting to be an old saddle bum who looks older than he is and smells of liquor half the time and . . . and . . . and there you stand right by an open window with air blowing on poor Clark in the bed. I should think you'd have sense enough—"

The window closed with a sharp snap.

He sat on the step, still and quiet, and watched the bee moving from spray to spray. It rose for altitude and flew away around the corner of the house.

"Go on, drift," he said. "That's the best thing us drifters can do." He stretched up and walked around the same corner of the house, limping some, and out into the street and along it toward the plaza. At the corner he saw a small stone where a small boy's shoe and a man's boot had left it. A wry grin showed on his lips and he stepped forward and swung his right foot and sent the stone skipping on out into the plaza. He turned right and moved along and turned right again, in through the big open doorway of the livery stable. He opened the door to the inside office where the loose-jointed man still sat, feet up on the desk. He stepped in and took his gunbelt from a nail in a wall and buckled it around his waist. He picked up his saddle roll and opened the door again.

"You leaving?" said the man.

He said nothing, indifferent to or not even aware of the question. He went along the stalls and led out the leggy dun and bridled and saddled it and tied the roll behind the cantle. He swung up and the dun moved forward and he ducked his head a bit and they went out the wide doorway.

Together the man and the horse, complete in themselves, all that they owned and all that they needed on them and in the saddle roll, jogged steadily along the road out of town, westward, toward the mountains and the river beyond them and the remnants of range land on beyond.

* * *

The legend of the Lost Burro Mine very nearly claimed two more victims last week. James Mills and Charles Baxter of this city had obtained what they thought was an authentic old Spanish map and gone into the mountains west of here to search for the alleged mine. On the fourth night something—

they believe it was a mountain lion—stampeded their horses. They were unable to find them the next day. They packed what they could carry on their backs, intending to walk out. But by the second day of walking they had lost their way. Four more days they wandered with their food gone and by this time Baxter was very ill from exhaustion and exposure. Mills was preparing, as a last resort, to strike out alone to try and find help when a man came riding up—leading their horses.

A cowboy hunting stray cattle for La Cumbre Cattle Company in that territory had come on their original camp, figured from what was left there what must have happened, searched for and found their horses, and trailed them to their present position.

"It was a terrifying experience," Mills said yesterday from his home on Third Street where he and Baxter are recovering from their ordeal. "The Lost Burro Mine," he said, "can remain lost as far as we are concerned."

A Middle-Aged Man
1906

HOT WINDS, dry and dispiriting, blew dust along the streets and sent small dust devils whirling to seek out cracks around closed windows and doors to the constant annoyance of harassed housewives. The plaza, that pride of the citizens of Harmony, was no longer a source of proud comment. The flowers in the bed encircling the flagpole had long since shriveled to prickly brown corpses. The clumped bushes in the corners were dejected wilted skeletons. Only the trees, of considerable size now, held to some of their green, but their leaves seemed to rattle in the winds and their thin shade offered little relief from the glare and heat of the sun. There was no water available for such a luxury as public greenery. Even homes had their water rationed by the town water company. The few scant oases of relative freshness on the outskirts marked the holdings of old-fashioned folk who had not yet joined the march of progress and still used deep wells of their own. Drought, that periodic specialty of the southwest, lay prolonged and heavy over the big land.

The front door of the small sturdy bank building on the southeast corner of the plaza opened and the Honorable Chester A. Rollins stepped out, blinking a bit into the sunlight. The coat of his neat business suit was folded over his left arm and he held his hat in his left hand and his shirt, sleeves rolled up, was open at the neck with his tie ends, untied, hanging limp. The furrows developing in his forehead and the lines around his mouth were deeper than usual and gave his round jowled face a grim discouraged look.

He raised his right hand and wiped sweat from his forehead under its receding hairline and walked angling across the plaza to the barnlike building of the Rollins Livery Stable. He opened the small door to the musty inside corner office and looked in. "Anything doing?" he said to the gangling loose-jointed man who sat at an old desk with a magazine spread open in front of him.

"A salesman's got the buggy," said the loose-jointed man. "I gave him old Dolly, figuring she'd take the heat best. He says he won't put her out of a walk." The man pointed at a picture in the magazine. "I been reading here about these Haynes automobiles. You really going to get one?"

"No," said Chet Rollins. "Not this year. The way things are going right now I couldn't even buy a bicycle."

"So you didn't do so well over at the bank," said the loose-jointed man.

"No," said Chet. "I didn't."

"And you a director," said the man.

"That's just it," said Chet. A grim little smile flicked on his face. "When we checked all the figures, how deep I'm in already, I voted against myself." He started to close the door.

"Hey," said the loose-jointed man. "If you ever do get one of the things, what'll you run it with?"

"What it takes," said Chet. "Gasoline."

"I mean where'll you get the stuff?"

"Stock it right here," said Chet. "Add that as another line. More people'll be getting the things." He wiped his right hand across his forehead again. "That is, if we don't all go bankrupt in the meantime." He closed the door and walked to the much newer two-story building next door to the Rollins Feed Store and in through the wide open doorway. The dim interior of the first floor, a dirt roadway straight through to another wide open doorway at the back with low wooden platforms running along the two sides, seemed almost empty. A few scant piles of baled hay on the left side, a few piles of bags of grain and milled and mixed feed on the right side. Near the back end of the inside roadway stood an empty flatbed wagon with a patient drooping team in the harness. On the right side platform a short heavyset man in overalls was sacking grain from a bin, weighing the bags on a balancing scale.

Chet walked past the front stairs on the left which led up to the front offices rented to a land development company, a surveyor, and Harmony's latest young lawyer. He pulled himself by a post up on the right side platform, waited till the heavyset man tied the bag on the scales and lifted it off, then stepped onto the scales himself. He reached to lay his hat and coat on a pile of bags, then juggled the weights until the lever arm fluttered in balance. He emitted a small groan and loosened his belt a notch. "I'll be running out of belt soon," he said to no one in particular. He stepped off the scales, picked up his hat and coat, turned to the heavyset man. "Hey, Sam," he said. "Is that Harvey Kneale's rig?"

"Yeah. He's upstairs waiting for you."

Chet started to jump down from the platform, thought better of that, walked to the three steps down, crossed the roadway, went up the three steps to the left side platform and on up the back stairs and opened the door at the top into his private business quarters. A single large office, neat and clean and businesslike. A calendar and a few framed pictures of Harmony worthies with appropriate inscriptions and a chart of the town and immediate environs on the walls. Four reasonably comfortable side-armed chairs for visitors, two on each side of a table on which was a neat stack of newspapers and several magazines. A hat tree in a corner. Two wooden filing cabinets. A small bookcase containing an assortment of catalogues. A still-new flattop desk with a padded swivel chair behind it. An office obviously dedicated to businesslike business. Except perhaps for two possibly distracting touches. The window near the desk was big, the biggest yet installed in town, and the desk was so placed that anyone sitting at it, with a slight swing of the swivel chair, could look out over the roof of the house across the alleyway behind the building, on over the roofs of other houses beyond, on past the last marring patch of the growing town into the great open indifferent spaces of the big land. And in the corner opposite the hat tree four incongruous objects hung in a row from wooden pegs: a limp coil of old hemp rope, a pair of battered old spurs, a worn gunbelt with the nicked handgrip of an old .45 showing from the holster, a rusting Slash Y branding iron.

Chet nodded to a hunch-shouldered long-jawed man in dusty range clothes who sat on one of the chairs by the table, big hat off and on the table. He walked to the hat tree and hung his own hat and coat on it and pulled off his tie with a savage little jerk and hung it too. He walked around behind the desk and eased down into the swivel chair and opened the middle drawer and took out an old stubby pipe and began to fill it from a small leather pouch.

The long-jawed man rose, picked up his chair, carried it over by the desk, set it down, hunched into it. The two men looked at each other.

"I reckon you know why I'm here," said the long-jawed man.

"I can guess," said Chet, striking a match, lighting the pipe.

"I been everywhere," said the long-jawed man. "I've wore out my backside traipsing around. There ain't any grass anywheres. Not that I can get. I got to keep on feeding."

Chet sighed. He rose and went around the desk to the filing cabinets, pulled out a drawer, hunted a bit, took out a folder. He came back to his desk, eased down, started to open the folder.

"Don't bother," said the long-jawed man. "I know the figures well as you do. Maybe better. I stay awake nights thinking of 'em. I know you been giving me a discount too. Don't think I ever thanked you proper on that."

Chet sighed again. He struck another match and was busy with the pipe.

"I got to keep on feeding," said the long-jawed man. "Or sell for what I can get. An' you know what that means the way things are. Wiped out." He looked down at the floor. "Back where I was five years ago." He looked up. "No sense beating around the bush. This dry spell's got to break sometime. Maybe you could keep me going for one more month." He looked down at the floor again, interest apparently focused on the toe of one boot. "Two weeks anyway," he said.

Chet raised his right hand and wiped sweat from his forehead. He stared at the folder on the desk, unable to look at the other man. The lines of his face hardened. "No," he said, flat, tired. "I can't do it. I can't get any more credit either." He frowned at the folder and poked a finger at it and his voice tightened, bitter. "I'm carrying half the whole goddamned county as it is. The bank's been carrying me. One in Albuquerque's been carrying our bank. There's an end to it. Everything's stretched to the limit."

Silence in the neat office dedicated to businesslike business.

"That final?" said the long-jawed man.

"You think I like it?" said Chet, sharp. "You think I get

anything out of turning you down? Headaches, that's what I get, saying no all the time. That's it."

"Don't fret yourself," said the long-jawed man gently. "I knew before I come it'd likely be that way. Felt I owed myself one last try." He stood up and stretched a bit. "I been busted before," he said. "You think I don't know you been carrying me longer'n you had any right to?" He hunched down into the chair again, unwilling to leave without some gesture of understanding, of friendship enduring past defeat. He looked around the room and saw the four odd items hanging from their wooden pegs. "Never noticed them things before," he said. "Never thought of it but maybe you've worked cows too."

"Yes," said Chet, easing some. "I rode my share once."

"Sure you did. I should of known." The long-jawed man leaned back in his chair. "Reminds me of something I saw last week. Some reason it sticks with me. Maybe you'd of liked seeing it. I was way over past Magdalena looking for grass an' I come on an outfit that was cutting back on its hosses to only what they could get by with. Save what grass they had for the cows. They'd rounded up all the hosses they had extra, including some that'd been running loose for quite a time. Was planning to work 'em over in the morning an' see what was worth saving. There was— But maybe you're busy. Got things to do."

"No," said Chet, settling back in the swivel chair. "I haven't a thing to do except sit here trying not to think how much I owe the bank."

"Yeah. An' how much the rest of us owe you. But quit that. It won't do no good. Well, like I was saying they had them hosses gathered an' some mean ones in there too an' there was this man that'd come drifting in sometime along the afternoon an' hung around for a meal an' he'd seen what was doing an' he'd said if they didn't mind why he'd just stick around a while an' maybe help out some with the riding. The men there they was young mostly an' they thought they was good the way young ones get to thinking nowadays an' they liked to fancy themselves up with fancy-priced gear, like I say, the way young ones're apt to these days, an' they didn't know just how to take him, being as he was older an' didn't look like too much to them. They wasn't mean, just young an' full of good opinions of themselves, an' they figured to take him as a kind of a joke an' they joshed him plenty an' he didn't pay them much mind at all, just went about his business of bedding down with a patched old bedroll the kind I ain't seen in years back of the bunkhouse. They kept on batting it among themselves, calling him dad an' even grand-dad an' old round legs an' things like that an' saying likely he couldn't last even two minutes on any old plug that really kicked up its heels a few times an' you know, I was getting a mite peeved myself 'cause I ain't so young too any more but I can still straddle a hoss or two like I bet maybe you can too. I stayed on the night 'cause I figured it might be interest-ing. I'd had a look at him an' them young ones was right, he wasn't much to look at, not casual-like an' quick an' not ex-pecting much. He could of been just a saddle tramp drifting around an' he had a bad cough now an' again. But I'd seen him move, quiet an' easy an' putting each foot down like it knew right where it was going, an' if you looked close he wasn't so old as he looked, maybe not much more'n you there yourself, only beat-up and hammered around by hard living. Minded me somehow of some of them oldtime trail hands I knew back when I had my own first boots. He did look kind of worn-out in oldtime gear about gone through in places. But I had me the feeling there was still plenty man left inside them old things. Like I say, I stayed the night an' then come morning . . ."

The sun rose strong and clear over the burnt brown grasses of the parched land. All of the men of the outfit were there and with them some from other ranches, drawn by word of the day's doings. Breakfast and the first-rising horseplay and joshing were over, out of the way. Most of the men sat on top rails of the smaller of the two adjoining corrals, ready for turns in the saddle. The foreman sat leaning against the tall post from which hung the outer gate, closed now, and a tally book and a pencil showed jutting from his shirt pocket. Twenty feet away by a corner post, shoulders slumped and feet hooked behind the second rail down, sat a middle-aged man, worn and nondescript from battered hat to scarred old boots.

Beyond, in the larger corral, thirty-three horses moved restlessly, aware of the annoyance coming, and among them, proud and powerful, seeming to tower above most of the others, moved a raw rough long-legged hammerheaded big bay. Two men, mounted, rode through them, cutting out the first batch of four.

Someone opened the gate between the two corrals and the first four were driven through and the gate closed. Ropes swirled and men moved warily and two of the four were bridled and saddled.

"Now take it easy," said the foreman. "We're not aiming at exhibitions, just to see how they behave. They've all been broke at one time or another."

"Hey there, Dad!" called one of the men. "You going to show us on one of these?"

The middle-aged man shook his head. He shifted a quid of tobacco from one cheek to the other. "Kid horses," he said.

Laughter rose around the rails. "Ain't he a wise one," said a young voice. "Bet he'll find an excuse every time."

The middle-aged man might not have heard. He sat, still and quiet, watching the proceedings from under the pulled-down brim of his battered hat.

The two horses were ridden, nothing much past snortings and a few mild crow-hops, and the foreman wrote in his tally book and the two were led away through the outer gate and the other two prepared. The sun arched higher, warming toward the heat of the day, and the work moved along, four horses driven into the smaller corral at a time, and there were some flurries of real action, brief but fast, and the men, intent on the work, forgot the middle-aged man on the top rail by the corner post and he sat there, still and quiet, occasionally spitting tobacco juice into the dust below him, and watched the proceedings from under the brim of his hat.

A small nervous roan was being saddled. It sidled away, flinching, uneasy. The middle-aged man straightened a bit on his rail. "Stay off that one," he said, voice striking out into the corral. "You want to ruin him? Split hoof."

"Keep your nose out of this, Granddad," said the man, trying to fasten the cinch.

"Wait a minute," said the foreman. "Take a look."

The roan was held, firm, and one man warily inspected its feet. The right forehoof was broken in front, cracked under up to the frog.

"You sure got sharp eyes, Dad," this one called out cheerfully.

"I ain't blind," said the middle-aged man. "When I look at a horse, I see all of him."

"That's for sure," said someone. "You see so goddamned much it scares you out of getting on any of 'em."

He might not have heard. He sat, slumped down again, and watched the proceedings with lean weathered jaws moving in slow rhythm, spitting occasionally, and again the men forgot he was there and the work moved along with the rougher ones coming now and the last batch was driven in, five to round out the thirty-three, saved for the finish, all of them tough and full of fight and among them the big hammerheaded bay.

One by one the other four were taken and there was considerable action getting them under saddles and one man was thrown to hop away with a sprained ankle and another was kicked in the stomach and was violently sick for a few minutes and a kind of grimness settled over the corral and the men around it, a feeling of response to challenge, and then the four had been ridden and the big bay was alone in the corral. It stood in a corner, aware, muscles tensed, and no one made a move toward it.

"Ain't that the one you called Bullet?" said someone.

"Yeah," said the foreman. "We broke him about three years ago, partway anyway, and he messed up two men while we were doing it. Got away and been running with the mares ever since. We haven't been exactly interested in trying to do anything with him. I guess we'll just shuck him, get rid of him."

Over by the corner post the middle-aged man straightened on his rail. He spat his tobacco quid into the dust, slipped down from the rail, hitched up his old pants. "Hell," he said. "Get a rope on him. I'll ride him."

A ripple of ironic cheers and sarcastic comments ran around the corral. These dwindled into silence as the middle-aged man seemed not to hear and stooped down to tighten the worn old-fashioned spurs on his scarred boots. They rose again, drowning out the objections of the foreman.

"Call his bluff!"

"Let 'im kill hisself!"

"Think he's made his will?"

"Ask him how he wants to be buried!"

Men had jumped down inside the corral, trailing ropes.

They forefooted the big bay and threw it with a jar that shook the fence and jumped in and hobbled its feet, fore and hind, and tied a blindfold over its eyes. They let it up and it stood hobbled, breathing hard, nostrils red-socketed. Two men slapped on a saddle and two more worked to get a bridle over the big head.

The middle-aged man stepped in close, took hold of the bridle, pulled it away, looked at the wicked bit, and threw the bridle over his shoulder. "Hackamore," he said.

"Anything you say, Dad. It's your funeral."

A stout hackamore was brought, adjusted over the big head. The saddle was cinched tight. Two men held by the hackamore and another, cautious, loosened the hobbles and dodged lashing hoofs. The horse stood, quivering, waiting in the darkness of the blindfold. The middle-aged man moved in closer, reaching for the reins.

"Hold it!" A young man, a lean young length of whipcord, jumped down from a rail and strode out. "Don't do it," he said. "Just because you been ragged, don't go breaking your neck. I'm willing to believe you been a ripsnorter in your time. You think he ought to be rode, let me take him."

The middle-aged man turned to look at the young man. He reached out and patted the young man on the arm. He turned back to the horse.

"Don't do it. That thing's a keg of dynamite."

The middle-aged man turned to look at the young man again. He said something, clear and distinct in the dust-moted air of the corral, and he turned back and had the reins and in one smooth motion was up and in the saddle. The other men jumped away and he reached, fumbling with the knot on the blindfold, and flipped the cloth away.

The big bay rocked upward, swallowing its head, spine arched, whirling in midair, and came down hard. Again and again it rose, whirling, jolting down stiff-legged. It stopped. The middle-aged man, erect in the saddle, settled himself more firmly into it.

The big bay screamed and launched into a circuit of the corral, bucking and pitching. Around and around it went, seeming tireless, and minute after minute passed and cheers and shouts struck through them and the horse and the man were oblivious to these, intent on their own deadly desperate game, and the horse stopped, shuddering, heaving for breath, and the man sat erect, rump flat to the saddle, a part of the animal beneath him.

He reached up and took off his hat, tugging to loosen it, and slapped the horse alongside the head with it and raked with his old-fashioned spurs. The big bay screamed again and was off into another circuit, pitching wildly. Minute after minute passed and throats were hoarse around the rails and the horse stopped again, shuddering.

"Open the gate!"

"Let 'em out!"

"Give 'em room!"

The outer gate opened and the big bay plunged through and leveled into full gallop. Men with saddled horses near raced to them and vaulted into saddles to follow. The big bay plowed to a stop and swallowed its head again, exploding into action more furious than before. Men rode in a circle around it, yipping and shouting encouragement, and the middle-aged man swung with every twist and wrench and waved his hat, answering yip for yip. Suddenly he swayed, dropping down to the right side. The cinch had loosened under the pounding and the saddle was slipping around.

"Grab the hoss!"

"Grab a cyclone you mean!"

"He's a goner now!"

"Not a chance! He'll be killed sure!"

No. He was around and under the big bay's neck, hands clamped to the noseband of the hackamore on each side of the big jaws, feet up and around and old spurs hooked in the cinch now pulled up over the back. He clung there while the horse reared, trying to paw him off with its forefeet, and one hand worked on the noseband, twisting this to clamp it tight and choke off the big bay's breath.

The foreman, running up, gun in hand, responsibility hard on him, stepped in close to the plunging horse, dodging, watching his chance, and shot it in the head just behind an ear. It crumpled down and the middle-aged man crawled out from under as it went down.

He pushed up to his feet, slow, and stood looking at the lifeless body of the big bay. "Goddamn it," he said to the foreman. "Why'd you go and shoot him? He'd of made a right good horse."

Sunlight from the wide window that faced west lay across the still-new flattop desk and a stubby pipe on it in the neat office that was dedicated most of the time to businesslike business.

The long-jawed man shifted on his chair.

"Yes," he said. "I think maybe you'd of liked seeing that. That man can ride. There ain't any better word for it. He can ride. That hoss wasn't anytime anywheres near shaking him. He'd of rode it to a frazzle if it took all day. Even with that saddle gone I'll bet he'd of wore it down. Like I say, it sticks in my mind. Coming back I kept thinking about it an' there's two things I keep remembering. One's the way he looked the moment he was up there on that hoss. He was bigger, taller. He wasn't any drifting saddle tramp. He was a whole man an' he'd be one wherever he was and whatever he might be doing an' right then he was doing what he was born to do. He was taking a beating the like of which I never hope to have and he had a little old smile on his face like he was enjoying every bit of it."

The long-jawed man shifted again on his chair, remembering. "An' the other thing," he said. "It's what he said when that young one tried to stop him like I told you. He just looked at him an' he—"

"I know," said Chet Rollins. "He said 'Shucks, it's a horse, ain't it.' "

The long-jawed man sat up straight on his chair. "Well, I'll be," he said. "How did you—" He stopped. Chet had risen and was moving around the desk and past, toward the open doorway.

"Sam!" he called down the stairway. "Hey, Sam! Kneale'll be down in a minute! Scrape together what he needs and load the wagon!"

The long-jawed man was up, surprised. "Hey. You said you was in a hole. What d'you think you're—"

"I'm doing some more carrying," said Chet. "Somehow. I'll make out. Somehow. I been forgetting a lot of things. That's what this country teaches you. To hang on. Somehow." He had picked the man's hat off the table. He held it out. "Get on down there before I change my mind."

The long-jawed man clumped down the stairs, bumbling thanks as he went. The Honorable Chester A. Rollins, businessman, bank director, current chairman of the town council, was alone in his neat office. He closed the door and moved to the wide window and looked out, over the roof of the house across the alleyway, over the roofs of other houses, on past the last patch of the growing town into the great open spaces of the big land. Seen thus, in the far long perspective, the fence lines and the telegraph poles and the other marks of man and his changes in the name of progress were lost, dwindled, absorbed into the overall immensity and drought was a mere passing blemish with its own burnt brown beauty and the land stretched away, serene and indifferent, to the distant lonely magnificence of the mountains.

"Yes," he said softly. "Yes. He's still out there. Somewhere. Where he belongs."

*   *   *

"And I suppose you intend to be a fireman too."

"No, ma'am. When I get bigger I'm going to be a cowboy. Like Monte Walsh."

An Ending
1913

A MAN and a horse.

A tall squint-eyed aging man, outside any conceivable exact calculation, any age at all past the half-century mark, lean and weathered like a wind-whittled mountain pine, and an aging compact cow pony, dun in color, wide between the eyes, stout-muscled, deep-chested.

They jogged along a road that climbed in slow gradual slope, dipping to cross dry arroyos that dropped away to the right, then climbing again. Spring crept through these lower levels, soft in the sun-warmth of the afternoon air, freshening in the faint new green in the scant clumped grasses and along the whiplike branches of the few scrub willows in the arroyos. Winter still held the heights on ahead, entrenched in the high canyons and up the forested steeps of the mountains where the snowpack clung, settled and hardened through the months past, to a depth of ten feet or more. Yet even there, unseen, beneath the white mantle, the old recurrent promise stirred in tiny rivulets seeping down, the beginnings of the thaw.

The man and the horse jogged along, quiet in the mutual respect and shared confidence of the years, climbing slowly, steadily, toward the distant heights. They stopped where another road came in from the left and a low store building and several squat houses and a few outlying sheds marked the start of a junction settlement. The man swung down and the horse stood, patient, ground-reined, and the man stepped up on the low porch of the store building and opened the door.

The storekeeper, in overalls with once-white cloth tied around his waist, was behind his counter weighing out beans from a barrel into paper bags. He stopped, scoop in hand,

and looked up. "Monte Walsh!" he said. "Now I know spring's on the way. You headed on up to the valley?"

"Yep," said Monte. He closed the door behind him and pushed his battered old wide-brimmed hat up his forehead. "Got to get the place in shape. Be taking some stock up there in a couple weeks. You got any of that molasses plug left?"

"Sure, Monte, sure. I been saving it for you." The storekeeper turned to his shelves.

"Say, Monte," said a round-shouldered round-bellied man sitting on a kitchen chair by the stove. "What's this I been hearing about you throwing young Mike Morrell through a plate glass window?"

"Shucks," said Monte. "It wasn't no plate glass window. Just a plain ordinary everyday kind of a little old window. He asked me that same fool question one time too many."

"What question?"

"Why, when was I going to turn my horse in on a goddamned autymobile."

The round-shouldered man rocked on his chair, slapped his knees. "Wish I'd of been there," he said. "Wish I could of seen it." He turned toward a thin man in overalls and sweater on another chair on the other side of the stove. "I'd of give a dollar to see that," he said.

"Knew I had some," said the storekeeper, setting four small flat oblongs wrapped in tinfoil on the counter.

"They ain't got any anywheres in town," said Monte, taking the oblongs, stowing them in pockets. "What'll it be? I reckon they've gone up like everything else these days."

"Well, now," said the storekeeper, scratching behind one ear. "If you've got the nerve to chew that stuff, I ain't got the nerve to charge you for it. But maybe you'll keep an eye out for a good log. Something I can use for a ridgepole. I'm thinking of putting me up a barn."

"Sure," said Monte. "Sure thing. I'll haul one down for you first chance I get."

The door burst open, flapping wide, and a boy, maybe all of fourteen, gangling, knobby-limbed, stumbled over his own big feet hurrying in. "Monte!" he said. "I knew it was your horse! I just knew it!"

"Why sure," said Monte. "He ain't changed none. Not like a goddamned machine that goes to changing models all the time."

"Remember what you said? You said I could come up and be with you some this summer! You'd teach me to rope! You did now, you said it!"

"Why sure," said Monte. "Soon's school's out and the weather's decent, you come up for a week or two." He reached out and slapped the boy on a shoulder. "I got a ways to go before dark. See you." He moved to the doorway and out, closing the door behind him.

"You heard him," said the boy to the storekeeper. "You heard him say it. If my folks still won't believe me, you can tell them. You heard him."

"I always feel better when he's been around," said the round-shouldered man. "More like maybe life's worth worrying along with. Now can anybody tell me why that is?"

"Who is he?" said the thin man from the other side of the stove.

"Who is he? Why—why—why he's Monte. Monte Walsh."

"You're new here," said the storekeeper. "You'll be knowing him like the rest of us. Works for old Judge Hartley down in town who owns most of that big valley on up past the river. What the mining company doesn't own, that is. Runs cattle up there for the judge and keeps the place open for fishing and such when the judge can be up there. Spring and summer, that is. Spends the winter in town knocking around, part of it in jail usually when the judge can't get him off for some devilment or other. Fusses around with a few horses. You get one from him and you got something."

"Best damn man with a horse I ever knew," said the round-shouldered man. "They'll just about sit up and talk for him. Wonder why he never went in for rodeoing and things like that."

"Monte?" said the storekeeper. "He ain't that kind. He's real."

"I'd give a dollar," said the round-shouldered man, "to of seen him when he was a young one. I'll bet he was something to keep book on."

"To be straight about it," said the storekeeper, "I expect you'd have to say only the judge pays him but he works for half the whole county. All of us up in here. Just about anything needs doing, you holler for Monte. You lose some stock that wanders off and you can't find it, you holler for

Monte. If he ain't already come on it, and's bringing it in.
You got a horse needs gentling, you holler for Monte. You
get a sick animal and no vet'll come up in here, you holler
for Monte. You can't get your deer or your elk for some
winter meat, you just mention it to Monte and he'll take you
where they are. You get yourself into any kind of trouble in
the back country and more like than not it'll be Monte comes
riding along and gets you out of it. You got a branding job
on your hands, you don't even need to holler, likely he's
already there ready to help. One thing he won't do. That's
help string a fence."

"He don't like 'em," said the round-shouldered man. "He
don't like 'em at all."

"Fences?" said the thin man.

"Fences," said the storekeeper. "And automobiles."

*　*　*

The man and the horse jogged along the road that climbed
in more perceptible slope now. It dipped through cut banks
to cross an arroyo. Damp spots showed along the arroyo bottom, moisture seeping underneath, through the sand.

They jogged on. The dun pricked up its ears. The faint
popping sound of a straining motor came from somewhere
behind. Monte pulled rein and turned in the saddle. A shiny
new automobile, a touring car with top down, its shininess
already becoming overlaid with dust and a few mud streaks,
was coming up the road.

"Good God a'mighty," muttered Monte. "Even up here."

The car approached, straining up the grade in second gear,
and he recognized at the steering wheel, in goggles and visored cap, the field superintendent of the mining company.
The car stopped alongside the dun. The motor died with a
gurgling gasp.

"Well, well," said the superintendent, pushing up his goggles. "You see me bringing progress even to the back country. I figured I'd pass you about here. This thing is really
something." He patted the steering wheel. "Saw you leave
town three hours ahead of me. Now I'll be on up in the valley way ahead of you. If we could get that decrepit old nag
of yours in here, I'd give you a lift."

"Thanks," said Monte, dry, disgusted. "I reckon we'll make it on our own."

"Sure," said the superintendent. "But slow. Damned slow. Old-fashioned." He patted the steering wheel again.

"Mighty early, ain't you?" said Monte.

"Early?" said the superintendent. "Why, I've got a crew up there already getting the mine in shape. I'm aiming at a record this season. Start taking out ore in a few days. Next week I'll have a crew checking the track up from town and clearing any drifts left. We'll be rolling three weeks ahead of last year."

"You'll bust your buttons," said Monte. "Being so goddamned modern and in a hurry."

"Why not?" said the superintendent, cheerful. "It's no skin off your nose. Only mine." He pulled down his goggles, began to adjust the gas and spark levers under the steering wheel.

"From here," said Monte, hopeful, "it looks like that thing up and died."

"Watch," said the superintendent. He climbed out, took the crank from the floor of the car, went around to the front, inserted the crank, heaved grunting with it. The motor exploded into life with a roar and a cloud of exhaust and the dun, startled, leaped sideways and stopped, ashamed of itself, and looked off into distance. The superintendent dashed back around, jiggled his levers, and the motor quieted. He climbed into the driving seat, waved cheerily, and was off up the road.

"Stinks worse'n goats," muttered Monte, sniffing. He nudged the dun with old tarnished spurs.

The man and the horse jogged on up the road. The air was becoming chill now. Clouds hugged the tips of the heights ahead. Monte buttoned his jacket and pulled up the collar.

They jogged on. The road dipped through cut banks to cross another arroyo. Damp spots were plentiful here and a trickle of water ran and out in the middle of the arroyo sat the once-shiny new automobile, hub-deep in wet sand, motor dead, wisps of steam rising from the brass-bound radiator. The superintendent, goggles gone, a shovel in his hands, dug vigorously by the front wheels.

"Well, well," said Monte, pulling rein. "So you'll be up there way ahead of me."

"Shut up," said the superintendent, traces of cheerfulness still in him. "You will notice I brought a shovel. I'm learning. Tried to creep through slow. Should have come with a rush." He moved around by the rear wheels.

Monte, serene in saddle, watched. "Hell," he said. "I ought to leave you here." He took out one of the small oblongs wrapped in tinfoil, unwrapped a corner, bit off a chunk. He chewed in solemn satisfaction, watching.

The superintendent put the shovel in the back seat of the car, adjusted his levers, picked up the crank and went to work with it. The motor exploded into life again. He dashed around, jiggled his levers, climbed in. The motor roared again with splatting of cylinder reports and the car inched forward and sank back as the rear wheels churned deeper than before.

The motor idled, out of gear. The superintendent had hold of the steering wheel with both hands and bent his head down over them.

"My oh my," said Monte. "You won't get nowheres that way. Back as far as you can, then stuff some branches under."

The superintendent raised his head and looked at Monte. "Out of the mouths of something or other," he said. The motor roared and the car inched backward about two feet and stopped, rear wheels churning down. He shut off the motor, climbed out, began breaking branches off the few willows along one bank and stuffing them under in front of the rear wheels. He cranked again, grunting, no trace of cheerfulness left in him, and was back behind the steering wheel. The motor roared and the car lurched forward a few feet, slid back, lurched forward, slid back.

"Keep that up," said Monte, "and you'll need reshoeing mighty fast."

The superintendent shut off the motor, climbed out, walked around the car, bent low to inspect the rear wheels, kicked at one of them. He looked at Monte. "You start laughing," he said, "and I'll start chunking stones at you. You got any more bright ideas?"

"No," said Monte. A wry grin showed on his lips. "But I got a decrepit old horse." He nudged the dun forward and around in front of the car. He shook out his rope and tossed the loop end onto the hood of the car. "Tie that to something that won't pull off," he said, "and get that silly contraption to percolating again."

The motor roared, straining in low gear, and the rope taut from the front axle to Monte's saddle horn tightened under the tension as the aging dun, muscles bunching, heaved forward, hoofs digging deep, and the car moved ahead, slowly, slowly, then faster, crunching through sand, and was out on the firm ground where the road led on through the cut in the bank.

"What da'you know," said Monte. "It come out of there just like a bogged cow."

"That makes us even," said the superintendent, untying the rope and regaining some cheerfulness in the process. "I talked down your horse and now you've called my machine a stupid cow. You need help on anything at the ranch, just let me know and I'll send a man over. Anytime." He was back behind the steering wheel, feeling fine again. "Hell of a road," he said, putting on his goggles. "When it's fixed the way it should be, will be, I'll bet I average twenty miles an hour coming up." With a wave of one hand he drove cheerily on.

"Fix the road," murmured Monte, coiling in his rope. "It's a goddamned highway already. That's another angle on the fool things. Got to fix roads for 'em or they ain't worth a hoot. Supposing you want to go where there ain't no fixed up roads?" He patted the dun on the neck and it waggled an ear back at him and he nudged it with his spurs.

The man and the horse jogged on. The sound of the car faded on forward into distance. The road topped out on a high level that stretched for miles toward the swift uprise of the first ridges jutting out like gigantic knees from the mountains. Far ahead Monte could see the car following a wide sweep of the road toward the broad cleft that led between two ridges into the valley.

There was a new sound now, that of running water. They left the road, turning to the right, and jogged several hundred yards and stepped on the brink of a steep-walled gorge. Two hundred feet below the river roiled over rocks, racing toward the lower levels.

"Doing right well," murmured Monte. "The runoff's really starting."

They jogged back to the road and followed it again, roughly paralleling the deep slice of the gorge angling across the
high plain. The shadow of the mountains grew longer,
stretching out over the level, and they jogged into this and
the chill in the air increased and the winds of late afternoon
began to move down from the cold heights and Monte fastened the collar of his jacket and shook briefly in the saddle,
caught in a fit of coughing. The dun stopped, aware, patient,
waiting, and when he was through moved forward again.

Snow lingered in the hollows of the plain now, soft, dribbling away at the edges, and the road was damp with the
wheel tracks of the car showing distinct. The ground rough-
ened, rocky, more broken, and the snow was deeper in the
hollows. Ahead was the broad cleft between the two ridges
and the sound of rushing water became steadily louder. Here
the river, running between relatively low banks, swept down
and around the blunted end of the ridge to the left, across the
broad opening into the valley, past the cliff-front of the ridge
on the right, and raced on in great curve to work down ever
deeper into its gorge. The road led straight to it and crossed
on a low wooden bridge, log-piled, plank-surfaced.

They jogged to the bridge and stopped. Monte tilted his
head back a bit to look out over the wide stretch of high
upland valley, miles of it receding far back into the mountains, steep-sided, ending at last in sudden upsweep of forest.
Snow, spreading out from the blanketed slopes, still held
most of the floor, varying in depth, but patches of new green
showed in the last shadowed light of the afternoon. The
brush-lined stream, shallow, that swung in slow curves down
through the middle, was no longer frozen, ran clear and cold
to join the river to the right below the bridge. Off from it,
close under the right-hand ridge, he could see the log buildings of the ranch, deserted, smokeless, dead, waiting for him
to quicken them with life again. Off to the left, across and
further up the valley, partway up the left-hand ridge, was the
cluster of odd-shaped buildings that marked the mine, the
squat hoist building with covered runway leading to the main
shaft, tool and dynamite sheds, ore dumps. Smoke floated upward from the stovepipe in the roof of the hoist building and
several figures, tiny across the distance, moved about alongside. Clearly discernible, like a gashed pencil mark, even

under the snow, the railroad embankment led down-valley from the ore dumps along the side of the ridge to a high stilt-timbered trestle over the river about four hundred yards up-stream from the wooden bridge and picked up again on the other side to disappear into the broken country downslope.

Directly across the bridge, to the left of the road leading on, was another cluster of buildings, one of them large, combination store and year-round home, many-chimneyed from big fireplaces, smoke drifting from several of them, with a big barn behind, the others small, snugly-fitted cabins for the miners' families who would be there through the summer.

He nudged the dun forward and its hoofbeats sounded hollow on the bridge and they stopped in front of the large building. A long-legged black dog dashed out from somewhere and circled the dun, barking in mock menace, wagging tail apologizing for the duty of announcement. A lank long-faced man in heavy pants and flannel shirt appeared in the doorway and stepped out, followed by a faded gray-haired woman with a wool shawl around her shoulders.

"Monte Walsh!" said the lank man. "We been talking for two days that you'd be showing soon! Why, it's been since Christmas when you made it up here with our mail."

"I got another batch," said Monte, turning in saddle to untie a package fastened to his bedroll behind the cantle. "And I got a little something special in it for Sairy there."

"I knew you wouldn't forget," said the woman. "What I was talking about last time. A bracelet."

"Shucks," said Monte. "How'd you ever guess? It's turquoise. Real Indian stuff."

"Hogan said you'd be coming along," said the lank man. "We been waiting supper. You see them clouds building up above Old Baldy? Might be nasty after a while. You ain't going another step. Put your hoss in the barn and give him a good bait of feed. You're staying the night right here."

*   *   *

Night over the high upland valley and far on up where the crest of Old Baldy reared like a ragged knife edge snow swirled in the wind gusts and on down the steep slopes and spreading through the whole range this was mixed with sleet and rain falling on the snowpack, working down, running in tiny rivulets under the great soggy blanket of dirtied gray-white.

Monte Walsh stirred on the narrow cot in the little side room directly off the big storeroom. He lay still, listening. In the background, over all, permeating the air everywhere, the rumble of the river two hundred feet away outside the building. Overhead, on the roof, the light patter of rain. Beyond the closed door, the soft slapping tread of footsteps passing.

He sat up, throwing off the old quilt, swinging feet to the floor. He reached and pulled on his socks and reached again, rising, and pulled on his pants. He stepped to the door and opened it.

Across the dimness of the big cluttered room the front door was open. A shapeless figure in old slippers and night-shirt with a blanket wrapped around stood in the doorway, looking out.

Monte moved across the room.

"Listen to it," said the lank man. "I been living here so long I can tell just by the sound. It's rising. Rising fast."

*   *   *

Morning and the clouds had parted and the sun shone in snatches through. Mists drifted along the ridges and clouds clung masking the mountains, but there was a cheerful brightness in the valley. Monte Walsh and the lank man sat on two old chairs on the roofless platform that served as a porch. The black dog lay at the lank man's feet. Two hundred feet away the river raced, flood-strong, turbulent, not quite a foot under the planking of the bridge.

The black dog raised its head, identified an approaching arrival, dropped its head. Around the corner of the building, striding brisk, efficient, came the mine superintendent in riding breeches, lumber jacket, peaked cap, and mud-splashed puttees over heavy shoes. "Morning," he said, full of cheer. "Morning." To Monte: "I see you got here. That horse of yours isn't so decrepit after all. I should know, shouldn't I?" To the lank man: "My crew's grumbling about cooking for themselves this weather. Think you could feed them for a few days? Fifty cents per man per meal."

"Sixty," said the lank man.

"Robber," said the superintendent cheerfully. "Skinflint. Miser. Greedy folk don't get to heaven. But it's a deal."

"Wait a minute," said the lank man. He turned his head. "Sairy!"

The gray-haired woman appeared in the doorway.

"Hogan here wants us to feed his men rest of the week. We'll soak him plenty. Get me that new fishing pole I want. Get you that new dress. You want to take it on?"

"And a hat," said the woman, turning back into the building.

"Well, maybe," said the lank man. "You got two hats."

"You got three," came the woman's voice, fading away. "If you can call those things hats."

"Settled," said the superintendent. "A big business deal put through just like that. If they were all that simple this would be a wonderful world." He took a cigar from a pocket, bit off the end, lit it, looking toward the river. "Say," he said. "I never saw the water that high before."

"It's been higher," said the lank man.

"Looks like it might make a meal of that bridge," said Monte. "Without paying sixty cents."

"Don't you worry yourself any about that bridge," said the superintendent. "It's sound. I ought to know. I put it in. Well, I'll have the men down here about one for the first of those meals. Have to work them hard in between to make up for that fancy price." He strode away, back around the corner of the building.

Monte Walsh and the lank man sat on the two chairs, looking at the river.

"Think it's still rising?" said Monte.

"Four inches since before breakfast," said the lank man. "If it keeps going depends whether there's been a freeze back up there to slow it down."

The gray-haired woman appeared in the doorway again and came out, carrying a big bowl of raw potatoes and a paring knife.

"You peel," she said to the lank man. "And help with the dishes. Or no new fishing pole."

The lank man sighed. "Henpecked," he said. "First I'm a miser. Now I'm a mouse." He took the bowl and set it down between his feet. He took the paring knife and picked up a potato.

"Shucks," said Monte. "I got a list of things I'll be needing from your store. But that can wait." He pulled out his pocketknife, opened a blade, reached for a potato.

*   *   *

The clouds had closed, a solid dark grayness overhead. Stringy mists drifted through the valley, hugging the ground. Rain fell in a steady drizzle, eating into the snowbanks, spreading in a sheet of multiplying streams over the ground. The river raced in heaving flood, lapping at the plank surfacing of the bridge, sending spray over it. The debris of winter, carried by the current, piled against the side stringers.

Monte Walsh and the lank man sat on the two chairs inside the big storeroom by the one front window.

"I ain't told you," said the lank man. "I was over to your place last week. That tree by the house's down. Hit a corner. Knocked a hole in the roof. It'll be dripping water inside. You'd be a fool to think of going over weather like this."

"Miser," said Monte. "Skinflint. You ain't going to heaven. You're thinking of some more sixty centses."

The lank man looked steadily at him. "Want me to bat your ears off?" he said.

Outside, two hundred feet away, little creakings, lost in the tumult of the water, ran along the bridge and twenty feet below the current sucked at the footing of the piles and with a cracking and wrenching of timbers the middle section gave way and ripped loose and raced in pieces downstream. Relentless in rising onrush, the river tore at the jagged sides remaining.

Monte Walsh and the lank man leaned forward, looking out the window.

"Don't you worry none about that bridge," said Monte. "It's sound. I put it in myself."

"No sense being too hard on him," said the man. "It's gone out before. Once back in '97 before I came here, but I heard about it. Again six years back before you first was up here. Some day they'll boost it high enough, like that railroad thing on up. Nothing bothers it."

"What d'you know," said Monte. "Looks like we're plugged in here for a while."

"So what?" said the lank man. "None of us're going anywheres."

* * *

The rain had slackened some, only a fine scattered spray soaking the air, but there was no sign of a break in the grayness overhead.

Monte Walsh and the lank man sat on the two old chairs by the front window of the big room, facing each other. A checkerboard lay on a small keg between them. In the room directly behind the gray-haired woman moved about, passing and repassing the open inner doorway, setting eleven places at a long table.

"Jump me," said the lank man.

"G'wan," said Monte. "I do that and you take two."

"You got to. It's a rule."

"Maybe," said Monte. "But somehow your rules always go your way. I bet you spend all winter practicing this fool game."

"I can beat him," came the woman's voice through the open inner doorway. "Two out of three games, every time."

Faint, far, up the valley, a low rumble sounded, rising in pitch and sustaining this then fading, dwindling into silence. Small tremors shook the building. Dishes on shelves in the back room rattled slightly.

"Up at the mine," said the lank man. "What in hell d'you think they're doing? Using dynamite? They can't be ready for blasting yet."

"That fool Hogan," said Monte. "He's apt to be doing anything."

* * *

The rain had increased again, a steady downpour flooding the hollows, beating into the snowbanks. From far upstream, ripped loose by the current along the sides, blobs of dirty white slush and ice bobbed on the surface of the river. Water sluiced off the slant roof of the store-building, making its own small gulley downslope to the river.

Monte Walsh and the lank man and the gray-haired woman sat at one end of the long table in the back room finishing a hearty meal.

"Going to be a dry summer," said Monte. "Always works that way. A wet spring, a dry summer."

"Yeah," said the lank man. "Like there's just so much can come down. We're getting it all at once." He produced a plump silver watch from somewhere about his clothes, consulted it. "Where're those men of Hogan's? Trying to do us out of our sixty centses. It's one forty-five already."

"Hat or no hat," said the woman. "If they can't be somewheres near on time, I'm not cooking."

"Shucks," said Monte to the lank man. "One thing. You won't have so many dishes to do. Now me, I don't have to worry about that. Nothing like being a guest. Non-paying too." He rose, looking at the woman. "I sure enjoyed my food, Sairy. Specially the potatoes. They was peeled so proper." He strolled into the front room.

"Oh, you'll pay," the lank man's voice followed him. "I got half a dozen little jobs figured out for you already."

"Why sure," said Monte, sinking into his chair by the checkerboard. "You just tell me and I'll get after them. That is, after you help me fix that roof over at the place." He leaned back in the chair, listening to the small clatter of dishes and pans from the kitchen opening off the back room, looking out the window at the river. "My oh my," he murmured. "Regular Noah's flood. Winter's sure on the way out. It'll be wildflower time soon."

A blurred figure dashed past outside, splatting mud at every step. The front door flapped open and the mine superintendent staggered in. Water dripped from his peaked earflapped cap and from the raincoat over his lumber jacket and his heavy shoes and puttees were gooey with mud. He closed the door and leaned against it, chest heaving.

"Too late," said Monte. "Meal's over. Likely double the price now."

"Don't be . . . funny!" gasped the superintendent, fighting for breath.

The lank man was in the inner doorway, a plate in one hand, a cloth in the other. "What's going on in here?" he said.

"We had . . . a slide," gasped the superintendent. "Big one . . . busted up . . . three men . . . bad."

Monte was up, striding forward, helping him to the other chair by the checkerboard. "Easy," said Monte. "Easy now. Tell it slow."

The superintendent gulped in air. "No warning," he said. "It just came . . . all at once. Right above us. Buried some of the sheds. And the shaft. Lucky no one was in there. But it caught three of us. Took them on down. Must have slammed them against trees on the way. They're alive, but they're in bad shape."

"Where?" said Monte.

"In the hoist building. There's a fire going and it's dry. But they're in bad shape. You hear me? Bad shape. Bones broken. Maybe hurt inside."

Monte turned away, slumped into his chair, stared out the window. The lank man, unaware of his own movement, wiped at the plate with the cloth.

"Don't just stand there!" said the superintendent. "Get busy. Harness your team. Get out your hay wagon."

"I notice," said Monte, bitter, "you ain't mentioning your goddamned autymobile."

"Shut up," said the superintendent, turning to him. "If you have to know, it's stuck in about ten feet of mud." He turned back to the lank man. "Look. We can lay mattresses on the wagon. Rig a tarpaulin over. Take them down to the hospital in town."

"Town?" said the lank man. "Take them? You crazy? The bridge's out."

The superintendent whirled to the window, leaned forward on his chair, staring. "Oh good God!" he said. He whirled back. "You don't understand! I've got to get them to a hospital! Or get a doctor with what he'll need up here!"

"You think I knocked down your bridge?" said the lank man. "You think I got another one in my pocket I can slap out there? Supposing I did, it wouldn't help any. That road's nothing but a mess of mud now. A wagon wouldn't get half a mile. I'm telling you there's no way out or in till this flood goes down."

"How long will that be?"

"Four–five days," said the lank man. "A week. Hard to say this time of year. But we'll just bring them down here to my place and do the best we can till then."

"Stupid!" said the superintendent. He pulled off his soaked

cap and clutched at his damp hair. "Don't you understand? They need a doctor, medicine, expert attention! As soon as possible!"

"You think I got those things in my pocket too?" said the lank man, exasperated, angry at the whole situation.

Monte Walsh stirred on his chair. "The railroad trestle," he said. "Could a train get up in here?"

"That's it!" The superintendent jumped to his feet. "At least one man's got some sense. Rig a snowplow in front and plenty of men with shovels just in case, a train could get in. That's it. All we have to do is get a message down to the company."

The gray-haired woman was in the inner doorway beside the lank man. "Get a message down?" she said.

"Yeah," said the lank man. "How you going to do that? There's no way out."

Monte Walsh stirred on his chair again. "The trestle," he said.

"Sure," said the lank man. "Oh sure. Any one of us might scramble over. You get on the other side, then what? A man wouldn't have a chance. Rough country for three–four miles, still choked with snow. Turning into slush up to your neck. Try to follow the tracks and every cut'll be plugged with drifts packed in. Try to follow the road and you'll be wading in mud. Give out in no time. So you're a goddamned buffalo bull and you make it across that flat out there. Then you got fifteen miles with them damn gulleys all along. Every one'll be running, trying to act like the river out there. How you going to cross them? So you ain't drownded or knocked on the head or washed away. Who knows what'll it be like down below? Nothing but mud flats and more gulleys. It's forty-seven miles to town and that's if you go direct. It can't be done. There was a man tried it first year I was here, weather something like this, only not near so bad. You know what happened to him? We found him six weeks later, what was left of him, wedged atween rocks in the gorge. It can't be done. Not till things slow down and dry out some."

"You through yapping?" said Monte Walsh.

"Yeah. Why?"

Monte rose to his feet. "Because you're all wrong. Maybe a man couldn't do it. But a good horse could. Mine's going to."

"Good God, man! How'll you get him across?"

"Shucks," said Monte. "That horse'll go anywheres I can and plenty places I can't. Sairy, fix me a couple sandwiches. I'll be needing them even if this ain't going to be no picnic. Hogan, get your goddamn message written down so's I'll have it straight." He strode to the small side room and in.

"Is he joking?" said the superintendent. "I never know just how to take him."

"No," said the lank man slowly. "He ain't joking."

"No," echoed the gray-haired woman. "He's not joking. He's just doing what he can't help doing."

"And what's that?" said the superintendent.

"Being what he is," said the woman and turned back to go into the kitchen.

*   *   *

He stood by the cot looking down. Spread out on it was his bedroll, opened earlier for his morning shaving. He moved, swift and sure, and sat down on the edge of the cot and pulled off his battered boots and took his extra pair of socks and put these on over those already on his feet. He stood up, tugging hard to get the boots back over the double thickness. He picked up his worn old gunbelt and hefted this in one hand then poked out all the cartridges from their tiny loops to fall on the spread-out bedroll. He took the gun from its holster and loaded five of the cylinders and let the rest of the cartridges lie on the bedroll and put the gun into its holster and strapped the belt around his waist. He took one of the two big bandannas and folded it over and wrapped this around his neck, loose, and pulled his shirt collar up over it and buttoned the top button. He shrugged into his worn winter-lined jacket and checked the side pockets for his old leather gloves. He settled his big wide-brimmed old hat on his head and struggled, grunting some, to get his streaked old slicker on over the jacket. He looked down at the meager array of items remaining on the cot. "Be back for those later," he murmured. Suddenly he picked up a small packet of frayed old papers that could have been letters out of some long-ago time and he fingered through these and pulled out a small stiff old photograph. Faded, browned, blurred. The tiny figures barely distinguishable. A group of assorted squint-

eyed rawhide-hard men in old-fashioned range clothes standing in front of the sagging veranda of a weathered adobe
ranch house. He looked at this for a moment and tucked it
carefully away, inside the slicker, inside the jacket, in a pocket of his shirt. He strode out into the big room.

Sounds of the gray-haired woman's activity came from the
kitchen, faint against the permeating rumble of the river outside. The superintendent was bent over the store counter
writing rapidly on a piece of heavy paper. The lank man
stood by the window, staring out.

The lank man turned and moved to confront him. "Don't
do it. Those three are maybe done for anyway. Don't make it
another one."

"Quit fretting about me," he said. "I've rode with men taking cattle through weather like this who'd think it was only a
breeze."

"Maybe. Maybe. But you ain't so young any more."

"Shucks," he said. "I'll make it down to Macready's store,
that's only twenty-some miles, and telephone the rest of the
way." He moved on, around the lank man, out the door, and
around to the barn.

Seven minutes later, with a brown paper parcel in his one
saddle bag and a flat packet wrapped in oilcloth with a string
tied around it in a jacket pocket, slicker fastened against the
rain, dripping hat brim pulled low, he rode through splashing
mud toward the upslope of the left-hand ridge and the gray-
haired woman, shawl wrapped around and open umbrella in
hand, and the lank man hunched down under the umbrella
beside her and the superintendent standing oblivious to the
driving rain a few feet away watched him go.

They reached the upslope, the man and the horse, and the
dun slowed, slugging into the climb on uncertain footing,
slipping back, scrambling forward, working up, working up,
and they were on the long pencil-gash of the railroad embankment. They moved along it and were at the blunted
ridge end with the trestle just ahead and the rushing river beneath.

He swung down and stood by the head of the horse, talking to it, stroking it along the neck. He stepped out, holding
the reins, onto the first few ties with the open spaces between
and the rushing river below and he turned around, facing the
horse. He pulled on the reins, gently, then harder with steady

pressure, and the horse stretched out its neck, legs braced, immovable. He pulled steadily, talking slow, reassuring, and the dun's sides heaved in a long sigh creaking the wet saddle leather, and its weight eased forward and one forefoot reached out, testing the first tie. The hoof settled, firm, and the other forefoot reached to the next tie.

He backed, feeling backward with each foot in turn, and slowly, one tie and one hoof testing at a time, the horse moved out after him.

Slowly, slowly, then a shade faster as they had the slow rhythm of it, the man and the horse moved out on the trestle.

His left foot, reaching back, slipped on the wet wood and he tottered sideways and the horse stood, braced, head firm, and he caught himself, hauling on the reins for leverage, and was back in balance.

Slowly, slowly, plain above the stark tracery of the trestle against the blank grayness of sky beyond, the man and the horse moved above the rushing river.

He was at the far edge. He stepped back to solid ground, the rock of the remnant of ridge beyond the river, and aside, and with a leaping scramble the horse was there with him. He took off his hat and waved it and jammed it back on his head and was in the saddle again and the dun moved, striking into a lope along the solid remnant of ridge and then was over and dropping into the broken country beyond. The man's head bobbed for a moment, sharp against the skyline, and then was lost from sight.

"I'll never open my big mouth again," said the superintendent. "I talked down that horse."

* * *

A long ride and a wet ride and a cold ride . . . A man and a horse, aging both, still rugged in the simple unthinking endurance of the life they shared, moving together across the great brute spaces of the big land that had shaped them to its own . . .

Broken country here, rough and ragged with rock spines thrusting up and pools of slush between and scattered still-crusted drifts of old soggy snow. Slow going. They held to the high spots as much as possible, slugging grimly through the low spots, slipping sideways into pools and scrambling out, smashing through drifts when there was no way else, working down, working down.

Time passed and the rain slackened some and the thin drizzle was worse than the pelting rain had been, seeming to seep through the slicker and soak into the clothes beneath, and they were out on the high plain that stretched its miles to the renewed arroyo-cut downgrades beyond. The dun, warmed to the work, impatient at the mud clutching its hoofs, struck into a fast lope. "Easy," he said, slowing it. "Easy. We got a long ways to go."

Time passed and there was no sound anywhere but the whisperings of rain on the drenched ground and the small creakings of wet saddle leather and the suckings of hoofs pulling out of fetlock-deep mud and splatting in again and they had angled over to reach the road, itself a shallow flowing stream, and they discarded it and followed along, paralleling it, to take advantage of its bank-cuts into and out of the arroyos ahead.

Time passed and the dun plowed on, hoofs sinking deep with every step, and he could feel the steady wearing strain in the stout muscles moving under him and they were working down again and came to the first real arroyo. The water rolled, strong and turbulent, dirty brown, heavy with silt. He let the dun stand, relaxing, gathering strength, and while it stood he estimated the flow against the height of the banks. He nudged the dun forward. It moved out, unhesitating but slow, into the water, feeling for the bottom ahead. The water roiled up around his boots and they were across, on the other side.

Another arroyo. And another. Always another. To work off to the right and try to head them would be to wander into broken twisted all but impassable country. To work down to the left would be to run into the river itself. They held to the fairly straight line of what had been the road.

Ahead now was a wide arroyo where a shiny new automobile had been bogged in moist sand only twenty-four hours before. They stopped, looking out over forty feet of rushing silt-heavy water that flowed from bank to bank. He leaned forward and patted the dun's neck. "I reckon we got to swim it," he said. He studied the main current. It swept around a curve from upstream to strike the near-side bank about fifty

feet to the right and swung across to meet the far-side bank
about a hundred feet on down below the road-crossing.

Obedient to the reins, the dun turned right and moved
along the bank. Where the current hit, slicing in, they
stopped again. He pulled off his gloves and tucked them in a
pocket of the slicker. He unbuttoned and peeled off the slicker itself and rolled this and turned in saddle to tie it by the
dangling whangs behind the cantle. He took his rope and tied
one end tight to the saddle horn and the other end about his
chest, under the armpits, and held the remaining coils in his
left hand. He took the reins in his right hand and nudged the
dun forward. It moved with short steps, reluctant, and
stopped at the very edge of the bank. "We can't get any wet-
ter," he said. "You've done it before. Maybe not as bad but
you've done it. You're doing it now." He struck with his
spurs and the dun, knowing, unhesitating now, hunched hind
legs in close and leaped out into the rushing current. They
dropped down and water rose almost to his shoulders and
they bobbed up and he could feel the dun under him, swimming strong, strong and steady, and they swept downstream,
angling across, and the far-side bank seemed to leap to meet
them and the dun heaved, finding some footing, and had
forehoofs on the bank, pulling up and out, and the bank
crumbled under and it fell back, floundering, off balance, tilted
by the current, and he was sucked out of the saddle. He tried
to strike out, swimming, and could make no headway, hampered by the dragging weight of clothes and jacket, and he
swept on downstream, bobbing under, out, under, out, gulping air as he could, and suddenly the rope tightened around
his chest and he hung in the water with the current rushing
past him. The dun had battled to the bank again, further
down, and was up and out, standing solid, braced. Hand over
hand he went along the rope, choking, strength ebbing, and
with a final effort was partway out on the bank. He lay there,
legs still dragging in the water, hands clenched on the rope.
The dun whiffled softly at him and he hitched himself forward and was all the way out and he lay there in the clinging
mud by the strong patient hoofs and the coughing took him,
hard and long, and this passed and he lay there and gradually
he became aware of the icy chill soaking into him and the
shivering shaking his body. He reached up and took hold of a
stirrup and pulled himself to his feet and leaned forward over

the saddle and slowly the heaving of his chest subsided. He straightened and one hand reached to stroke along the neck of the dun. "All the mean things I ever called you," he said. "Forget 'em." He pushed away from the horse a few feet and flapped his arms and twisted his body, slowly then with increasing vigor and he could feel the lean hard energy still bedded deep in his aging muscles creep through them again. He rubbed a hand over his dripping head, hatless now, and fumbled around his neck to pull out the soaked bandanna. He opened this and put it over his head and tied it under his chin. He untied the rope and coiled it in. He reached for the slicker. Gone. He opened the saddle bag and took out a soaked mud-streaked mess that had been a brown paper parcel. He let this fall to the ground. He shrugged. "We're wasting three men's time," he said and swung up into the saddle.

*   *   *

The storm, spreading out over the lowlands most of the day, had passed there now, retreating into the mountains again, leaving streams searching through the bottoms and morasses of soft sticky mire between. Yesterday's promise of spring was faint and forgotten now as the sharp chill of early dusk, moist and penetrating with a hint of a possible freeze, tainted the air.

Macready's store and the several squat houses and the few outlying sheds that marked the start of a junction settlement were wet and forlorn in the deepening grayness, seemed lost and deserted in the immensity of the sodden land. The only movement discernible anywhere was that of a mud-streaked man, arms crossed with hands under his armpits, hunched in saddle with reins looped around the horn, on a tired mud-soaked dun-colored cow pony jogging forward along the side of the remnants of the main road.

They stopped in front of the store building. He swung down, moving stiffly, and stepped to the door. Padlocked. He grunted and kicked at the door. He looked around. There was no sign of life anywhere. He pulled his old mud-streaked jacket up on the right side and took his worn old gun and aimed down at the padlock. The gun roared, a sudden shattering sound in the stillness. Once. Twice. He put the gun back in its holster and twisted the smashed lock from the hasp and opened the door. Dim and deserted inside. He stepped to the one counter and lifted the chimney off the oil lamp there and took a match from the box beside it and lit the wick. He set the chimney in place and stepped to the crank phone on the wall by the end of the counter, fumbling for the oilcloth packet in his jacket pocket. He held this in his teeth while one hand took the receiver off its hook and the other hand cranked. He held the receiver to his ear. No sounds. Dead. He cranked again, vigorously. The same.

"Goddamned modern contraptions," he muttered.

He let the receiver fall, dangling. He pulled the dirtied bandanna off his head and let that fall too. He stepped along by the shelves past the counter and picked up a hat, tried it, let it fall, took another and jammed this on his head. He shrugged out of the old soaked mud-streaked jacket and let that fall and took a new one from a shelf and shrugged into it. He was putting the oilcloth packet into a pocket when he heard sounds by the door. The storekeeper, in rubber boots and raincoat with a shotgun in his hands, stepped in.

"Hey! It's Monte!"

"That goddamned telephone," he said. "What's wrong with it?"

"Line's down. Been down since about noon. What's the—"

"Trouble up at the mine," he said. "You got a fresh horse anywheres around?"

"Hell, Monte. Nobody's brought any in. Not in weather like this. They're all out—"

"Pay you for these things sometime," he said, striding forward. He pushed past the storekeeper, out through the doorway.

"Hey! Wait a minute! What kind of trouble? You had any supper?"

There was no reply. The man and the horse were moving away, into the dusk, slugging steadily into the stiffening mud along the side of the road.

* * *

Night over the big land, the cold clean starlit night of the quiet following the storm. Far back in the mountains rain still fell, mixed with sleet, and the river raced, out of the heights, down through the broken country past the upland valley to drop into its deepening gorge. A week, ten days, two weeks would tame it to fordable dimensions and during the summer, except in brief flurries following the few thunderstorms, it would be lazy and shallow, fed only by the remote year-round springs, wandering between sand and gravel beds along the bottom of its course. Now it raced, strong with the strength of the melting winter-hoarded snows.

Across the high gorge-cut plain, down again over the arroyo-slashed slopes, across the miles of mud-strewn levels, forty-some miles overall as a raven might fly, what had been the road and would be again led to the edge of a long escarpment, a sheer slant dropping ninety feet, almost vertical, to the lower level beneath. Here the road turned sharp right, over the edge, leading down, a narrow rock-ballasted slice little more than one-wagon width cut into the face of the steep slope angling down to the renewal of plain beneath.

A mile and a half beyond, out on the lower plain, tiny beacons in the bigness that stretched to dark horizon all around, glowed the last few lights of the sleeping town.

Out of the dim distances receding back to the great bulk of the mountains jogged a weary mud-caked cow pony. The man in the saddle sat hunched forward, head down, and now and again coughing shook him and the horse stopped and when he was through moved forward again.

They halted at the edge of the escarpment where the road led down. Running water had ripped away most of the road fill, leaving the rock ballast, rough and ragged underfoot. Here and there thin streams still seeped out of the face of the slope, trickling down.

He patted the horse on the neck. "Almost there," he said. "You've pulled through enough mud to yank the hoofs off a steer. But it ain't far now."

They started down, slow, careful of footing in the cloaking dimness of night, holding to the inside. They were a fourth of the way down with the darker menace of the slope rising sharp to the right above them and the emptiness of space dropping away to the left. Ahead now the roadway suddenly narrowed. In the hours past water pouring over the lip above had cascaded down to wash a gash in it, leaving only a slim passage. Water still dripped from above, falling with tiny splattings on the stones beneath.

The horse hesitated, doubtful, and the thought flickered in

his mind that he ought to dismount and lead on foot and the chilled weariness in him checked that and the horse moved forward, cautious, testing for each step. He heard the first soft sucking sound above and other sounds following and he looked up and saw the small slide of stones and wet earth starting, increasing, acquiring momentum downward. The horse heard too and he felt the tired muscles bunch under him and it leaped forward for the wider way beyond and swung its hindquarters outward to avoid the slide sweeping past.

A stone grazed his right boot and the slide was past and he thought that they had made it and then he was aware of the saddle sinking back under him. The will and the skill and the experience of the years were there in the old dun, but the instant snap and surge in the muscles were gone, left along the miles behind. The rear hoofs had hit on the edge of the gash and the support there had crumpled before the horse could gather itself for another leap. He threw his weight forward in the saddle and the hind legs of the horse beat in desperate scramble and it sank back, back, and it clung with straining forehoofs as if waiting for him to climb over it to the safety beyond and he was out of the saddle, boots shaken loose from stirrups, up along the neck, when the forehoofs ripped away and they were falling. They hit on the steep slope ten feet down, the horse under, and bounced out and hit again and the heavier weight of the horse fell away from him and the reins were jerked from his hand and the horse dropped somersaulting on down and he slid, spread-eagled along the face of the slope. One hand caught a small bush and this slowed his downward rush and the roots pulled free and he rolled over and over, hitting against stones, and jolted to a stop in a shallow puddle at the bottom.

He lay still, dazed and battered. Slowly he turned over and crawled out of the puddle. He remained on his hands and knees, head hanging, for several minutes. He was sweating under his damp clothes, yet he shook as if with a strong chill. Slowly he pushed to his feet and went to the body of the horse where it lay, limp and still, head doubled under, neck snapped. He heaved and strained, straightening out the limp head. The lifeless eyes stared unseeing into the night. He stood and looked down for a long moment and the lines of his lean aging face were rock-hard. His own voice seemed to come from far away to him.

"I never told you," he said. "I never thought to. But you was the best. You was the best of them all."

He turned and moved away, limping, swaying, toward the last few lights of the town a mile and a half away.

* * *

On the edge of town, in the front room of a two-room house, by the light of an oil lamp, four men sat around a table playing poker, lazily, without much interest in it.

"Ain't it about time to quit?" said one, yawning.

Something bumped against the front door and the handle turned and the door opened and Monte Walsh staggered in. His eyes burned unnaturally bright in deep-sunk sockets and his face showed a high flush under its tan and dried slpash-ings of mud. He staggered to the table and leaned with one hand on a corner. The other hand fumbled in a pocket of his ripped mud-stained jacket and took out a small oilcloth pack-et. He dropped this on the table. "Get it . . . to Scofield . . . of the mine company . . . fast," he said. A fit of coughing shook him and he wiped a hand across his mouth and it came away with flecks of blood on it.

The four men had jumped to their feet. One of them pushed a chair toward him.

Monte sank into it. "I reckon . . . I'm kind of . . . played out," he said. Slowly, like an old pine falling, he toppled side-ways out of the chair to the floor.

* * *

In the cold clean dark of the small hours of the night mov-ing toward morning a rail engine and two cars and another engine behind worked upward through the high broken coun-try, smashing into soggy drifts with pointed plank plow in front, puffing to a stop in choked cuts and blowing steam in impatience while men with shovels swarmed forward.

Back down across the miles, in the back room of the two-room house on the edge of town, Monte Walsh lay under blankets on an old brass bed, eyes closed, breath coming in short ragged gasps.

One of the poker players, dark-haired with dark drooping mustache, stood by the foot of the bed, going through the pockets of Monte's worn damp clothes, putting what he found on the top of a small dresser. A young man, pants and suit coat pulled on over pajamas, sat on a chair by the head of the bed with a small black bag at his feet.

"I've done all I can right now," said the young man. "I suppose we could take him to the hospital in the morning, but I don't think moving him any is advisable. He can stay right here. That is, if you don't mind."

"Mind?" said the black-mustached man. "Hell, man, that's Monte."

"Who is he anyway?" said the young man.

"I just told you. That's Monte. Monte Walsh."

"I know that," said the young man. "I patched him a few months ago after that big brawl at the Wild Goose. I mean has he got any family? Any relatives? They ought to know."

"Never heard of any," said the black-mustached man.

The young man rose, picking up his bag, and started for the other room. "I'll be back after I get a little sleep," he said.

"Wait a minute," said the older man. "Here's something." He held up an old photograph, limp, water-smeared. "Yeah. On the back. A name and address. Maybe you can make it out."

"I'll just take that," said the young man. "I'll stop at the telegraph office and see what I can do."

*   *   *

Spring crept through the lower levels again, regaining its hold. The sun shone warm and reassuring, into its second day of erasing the effects of the storm. Wagons and an occasional automobile rolled along the main streets. Here and there clerks swept sidewalks or washed away the last of the mud splashes and dirt stains from storefronts. A few people were already out walking to the post office, the courthouse, the several two-story office buildings. Life, normal everyday living, moved in the slow leisurely southwestern manner throughout the town.

On the outskirts, in the back room of the two-room house, Monte Walsh lay on the brass bed, motionless, eyes closed, face drained of color under its weathered tan to an ashy leathery look. Drops of sweat glistened on his forehead. His chest, under the light cover, rose and fell, rose and fell, in short gasping breaths.

In one corner of the room lay an old worn saddle, horn bent and broken, and an old worn bridle.

On a chair by the back door, coatless, sleeves rolled up, collar of his wrinkled shirt open, sat the young man, his small black bag open by his feet. He stared down at his clasped hands and frowned at them.

On a chair by the head of the bed sat a solid square-built man. His simple plain obviously expensive clothes were rumpled and wrinkled. His eyes, deep-creased at the corners from long-ago wind and sun, were red-rimmed now in his round jowl-cheeked face from most of a day and a night of sleepless travel. The quiet authority of his presence seemed to fill the small room. He was barely aware of the young man ten feet away. His whole attention was concentrated on the still figure on the bed. He reached down to a basin of water at his feet and dipped a handkerchief in and wrung it out and leaned over the bed to wipe Monte's forehead.

The young man rose to his feet and stepped to the foot of the bed and leaned on the brass rail between the corner posts, looking at the square-built man. "I hope you realize," he said, voice low, urgent, "that I've done everything I possibly could. If there was anything more, I'd be doing it. I've been right here most of the time. But I don't understand it. The fever's burning him up. I can't check it. He's been like that ever since I first got here. In a coma. He kicks up sometimes like he was trying to come out of it. But he never does."

The square-built man might not have heard. He was wiping Monte's forehead again.

"You hear me?" said the young man. "I can't understand it. Exposure, yes. Bruised and banged, yes. And pneumonia. Yes. All that's understandable. But a man like that ought to be able to fight it. He's made of gristle and rawhide. It's inside. His lungs. He's been spitting blood. It's as if they were damaged bad before and this things broken them loose inside him."

The square-built man looked up, focusing briefly on the young man. "I know," he said. "He scorched them bad once." A twinge of bitter remembrance crossed the square-built man's face. "It should have been me," he said.

The front door of the house opened and someone entered. The mine superintendent stood in the inner doorway. "Any change?"

"No," said the young man.

"One of them died last night," said the superintendent. "But the other two will make it all right. I think he ought to know."

Silence in the small room.

The superintendent shifted weight from one foot to the other, uneasy, embarrassed. "You know," he said. "Of course you know that the company is paying all costs. For anything you can do for him."

Silence in the small room. "Well," said the superintendent. "I'll be looking in later." He turned and was gone.

The young man sighed. "Does that damn fool think I'm worrying about my bill?" he said. He went again to the chair by the back door and sank onto it, tired, legs sprawled out.

Over on the bed Monte Walsh stirred, body twitching under the cover. His eyes opened, staring upward.

The square-built man leaned toward him, quick, eager. "Monte," he said. "Monte. It's me. It's me."

Monte's head turned slightly toward the sound and his eyes, vacant, unaware, seemed to be looking at the square-built man and his glance moved on, vacant, glazing, and his eyes closed again.

The square-built man stood up, hands at his sides clenching into fists, arms shaking with the tension in them. His voice was a hoarse bitter sound in his throat. "He doesn't . . . he doesn't even remember me."

The square-built man moved aimlessly about the room. He stared out the one window, unaware of what he saw. He stopped by the back door and opened it, staring out into the clear clean brilliance of sunlight over the renewing land.

"That's all right," said the young man. "Leave it open. It's as warm out as in."

The square-built man might not have heard. He stepped out and bent down to sit on the doorsill, staring off into distance. Mechanically, out of old habit, he took a short stubby pipe and a small leather pouch from a pocket and began to fill the pipe. He stopped. His fingers tightened on the pouch, spilling tobacco from it. Again a twinge of remembrance crossed his face. He put the pipe and pouch back in the pocket. He sat still, staring into distance. He seemed to feel the helplessness of sitting still, a need to be doing something. He reached out, barely aware of what he was doing, and picked up a stick from the ground beside him and took out a small pocketknife and whittled slowly at the stick with long slow strokes.

Time passed and a small pile of thin shavings grew between the dusty expensive shoes of the square-built man and five times the front door of the two-room house opened and people walked softly to the inner doorway, men and women and once a thin knobby-jointed boy, and they asked their question and the young man answered and they looked at the still figure on the bed and walked softly away, closing the front door gently behind them.

Time passed, slow and inevitable, and the small pile of shavings increased and the young man was on the chair by the head of the bed. He held Monte's wrist in his right hand and looked at his watch in his left hand.

Monte's arm jerked away from him. Monte's eyes opened again and his body thrashed under the covers as if he were fighting, feeble but fighting, fighting, to break through, to break out of the weakness that held him. His head rose a few inches. His voice came, gasping, but the words clear and distinct. "Find him . . . find him . . . tell him . . . tell him . . . no goddamned . . . autymobile . . . could of . . . done it." His head dropped back.

"Who?" said the young man, bending over. "Who? Tell who?"

A last flicker of fading vitality. A small dwindling sound. "Rollins . . . Chet Rollins . . . in . . . in . . ."

The young man bent lower, feeling for the pulse that was no longer there. He jerked a bit at a sharp sound behind him, the snapping of a half-whittled stick in two hard-gripping hands.

*   *   *

Night over the big land and another day.

The simple service was over. The wagon, drawn by two

stout willing draft horses, had rolled out the road to the escarpment a mile and a half away and up the newly filled road past the crew working on it and on across the flats, leaving the road, mile after mile, and up some into the broken country beyond. At the base of a high rock headland the simple coffin had been lowered into the ground, the simple pine box containing the still body in old worn range clothes and with it the old tarnished gunbelt and spurs. The battered old saddle with smashed horn and bridle had been lowered to rest on the wood. The grave was filled now and the mound of fresh-turned earth warmed under the afternoon sun. Everyone had left now, everyone but the square-built man sitting on a large stone, waiting, and another man in overalls and wool shirt who worked, as he had since midmorning, with hammer and chisel on the granite rock wall rising behind the head of the grave.

"Cut it deep," said the square-built man. "I want it to last. I want it to outlast any of us. And our kids. And our kid's kids."

Time passed and the tiny chips flew from the rock and the square-built man sat as still and quiet as the stone beneath him and looked into the great distances that fell away from the massive bulk of the mountains, down and away, seeming limitless, serene and indifferent, with the town a mere small meaningless smudge lost in the immensity.

The overalled man finished his work. "You want anything more?" he said. "A verse or something like that? I wouldn't charge a cent extra."

"No," said the square-built man. "That says it all."

The overalled man moved toward the two saddle horses waiting patiently fifty feet away. He put his tools in a bag tied to the horn of his saddle. He mounted and rode away, down the slopes toward the lower levels. He and the horse grew small, receding out of sight below a ridge.

The Honorable Chester A. Rollins, successful merchant, banker, three-term mayor of his town, new representative from his county to the new legislature of the new state of New Mexico, rose from the stone and stood at the foot of the grave, looking at the legend graved deep into the rock of the rising cliff.

The Slash Y Brand. And below this:

MONTE WALSH
1856-1913
A Good Man With a Horse

"Yes," he said softly. "Yes. It's a lonesome lonesome world."